HAD I A HUNDRED
≡ MOUTHS ≡
New & Selected Stories 1947-1983

HAD I A HUNDRED MOUTHS

New & Selected Stories 1947-1983

WILLIAM GOYEN

Introduction by Joyce Carol Oates

Clarkson N. Potter, Inc./Publishers

DISTRIBUTED BY CROWN PUBLISHERS, INC., NEW YORK

WORKS BY WILLIAM GOYEN

NOVELS

The House of Breath
In a Farther Country
The Fair Sister
Come, The Restorer
Arcadio

STORIES

Ghost and Flesh
The Faces of Blood Kindred
The Collected Stories
Had I a Hundred Mouths:
New and Selected Stories

PLAYS

The House of Breath, a ballad
for the theatre
The Bite of the Diamond Rattler
Christy
Aimée, a play with music
The Fair Sister, a play with music

OTHER WORKS

A Book of Jesus
Wonderful Plant
Nine Poems

All of the stories included in this edition have been previously published
individually, some of which have appeared in *TriQuarterly, The Missouri Review,* and
The Southwest Review.

"An Interview with William Goyen" first appeared in *TriQuarterly,* a publication of
Northwestern University, and was reprinted in *The Texas Humanist.* © 1983 by
TriQuarterly, reprinted by permission.

Published by Clarkson N. Potter, Inc., One Park Avenue, New York, New York
10016 and simultaneously in Canada by General Publishing Company Limited
CLARKSON N. POTTER, POTTER and colophon are trademarks of Clarkson N.
Potter, Inc.
Manufactured in the United States of America

This edition was prepared by Reginald Gibbons.

Library of Congress Cataloging in Publication Data
Goyen, William.
    Had I a hundred mouths.
    "This edition was prepared by Reginald Gibbons"—T.p. verso.
    I. Gibbons, Reginald. II. Title.
PS3513.O97H3   1984   813'.52   85-493
ISBN 0-517-55764-9

10 9 8 7 6 5 4 3 2 1

First Edition

CONTENTS

◻◼◼◻

INTRODUCTION BY JOYCE CAROL OATES ... vii

LAST STORIES, 1976–1982

HAD I A HUNDRED MOUTHS 3

THE TEXAS PRINCIPESSA........................... 20

ARTHUR BOND.. 29

WHERE'S ESTHER?..................................... 34

PRECIOUS DOOR 40

IN THE ICEBOUND HOTHOUSE 48

TONGUES OF MEN AND OF ANGELS............. 61

GHOST AND FLESH, 1947–1952

THE WHITE ROOSTER................................. 81

THE LETTER IN THE CEDARCHEST............. 96

PORE PERRIE 120

GHOST AND FLESH, WATER AND DIRT........ 134

THE GRASSHOPPER'S BURDEN 145

CHILDREN OF OLD SOMEBODY................... 161

BLOOD KINDRED, 1952–1975

THE FACES OF BLOOD KINDRED................. 175

OLD WILDWOOD... 183

RHODY'S PATH... 196

ZAMOUR, OR A TALE OF INHERITANCE....... 206

BRIDGE OF MUSIC, RIVER OF SAND............ 230

FIGURE OVER THE TOWN 236

INTERVIEW, 1982

AN INTERVIEW WITH WILLIAM GOYEN........ 251

INTRODUCTION

William Goyen has always been the most mysterious of writers.
He is poet, singer, musician as well as storyteller; he is a seer; a
troubled visionary; a spiritual presence in a national literature
largely deprived of the spiritual. Yet there is something driven
and demonic—"accursed" Goyen would say—about his art. The
extraordinary cadences of the language exert a hypnotic power
that the events of the fiction roughly dispel; the reader is confronted by beauty, and ugliness; then again beauty and ugliness
in the same instant, housed in the same image. Arthur Bond's
curse is a worm buried in "the sweetest part of the thigh" but we
also understand that Arthur Bond *is* his curse; the worm is his
soul, his very being. The fantastic diver of "Bridge of Music,
River of Sand" is both a suicide and a redeemer. In "Figure Over
the Town" Flagpole Moody absorbs all the projections of the
town yet remains a symbol of the artist—stubborn, isolated, pre-
carious, triumphant. The hermaphrodite hero of the novel *Arcadio* is probably Goyen's most powerful symbol of this inexplicable
doubleness—the physical expression of a paradox that is primar-
ily spiritual. All serious art celebrates mystery, perhaps, but Goy-
en's comes close to embodying it.

A story by William Goyen is always immediately recognizable as a story by William Goyen. He is not boasting when he
says in the interview with Reginald Gibbons included at the end

of this collection that people in his life (his family and relatives in East Texas) had the speech, and he inherited the voice. Speech and voice are distinctive—the one natural, the other refined, calibrated. So seemingly fluid and artless are the stories they give the impression of being "merely" narratives of memory. The voice of the unconscious, the surreal, is most seductive when its cadences are colloquial, as in these masterful openings: "I started out to tell about what became of two cousins and their uncle who loved them, according to what the older cousin told me. But some of their kinfolks' lives would have to be told if . . ." ("Tongues of Men and of Angels"); "Now this is about the lives of Old Mrs. Woman, Sister Sammye, and Little Pigeon, and how they formed a household; but first . . ." ("The Letter in the Cedarchest"); and my own favorite, "Do you remember the bridge that we crossed over the river to get to Riverside? And if you looked over yonder you saw the railroad trestle? High and narrow? Well that's what he jumped off of. Into a nothing river. 'River'! I could laugh. I can spit more than runs in that dry bed. . . ." ("Bridge of Music, River of Sand"). So fluid is the voice the stories seem to tell themselves, each story distinctive yet part of a large communal narrative, like a broad river fed by numberless tributaries. And Goyen's characters too, when one comes to know them, are frequently kin—"blood kin"—whose stories and lives reflect and help to define one another. All are caught up in the fundamental mystery of life, all are compelled to speak of the "trouble" that occasions their tales. ("It starts with trouble," Goyen says in his interview. "You don't think it starts with peace, do you?")

These are tales of vanishings and hauntings, love-making and rape, mutilation, murder, abandonment, rediscovery. In "The Faces of Blood Kindred," a story that seems more autobiographical than most, the young protagonist has left his home and has become distinguished (as a writer, perhaps?) yet his most powerful revelation has to do not with his own individuality or uniqueness but with his kinship with a cousin to whom he does not speak when they happen to meet—years after an unfortunate incident of betrayal. The young man is alone, estranged from his kinsman, yet a single glance confirms their blood tie: "struck like a blow against ancestral countenance . . . leaving a scar of resemblance, ancient and unchanging through the generations, on the faces of the grandmother, of the aunts, the cousins, his own father and his father's father; and would mark his own face longer than the stamp of any stranger's honor. . . ." The doubleness that is both curse and blessing in Goyen's imagination is resolved in such moments of dramatic epiphany.

Though Goyen's art is carefully revised and refined, its impetus is unconscious, intuitive, "passional" as D. H. Lawrence would say, springing from blood- rather than mind-consciousness. Hence the mesmerizing quality of such stories as "In the Icebound Hothouse" and "Old Wildwood" and the dream-like incantatory "Children of Old Somebody" in which language itself is active; a character, or a focus of vision, by way of words. Goyen has said that when he is deeply immersed in his writing ". . . I have the feeling it's coming from outside of me, through me. An absolute submission, absolute surrender. It's being *had*, possessed. I'm being used." The storyteller uncle of "Had I a Hundred Mouths" is a nurturing, even a maternal presence; his is the power of seduction—"the surrender of listener to teller, almost in a kind of love-making, of sensual possession, yet within innocence and purity." Thus, even when we read Goyen's stories silently we *hear* them: they are, as Goyen rightly says, ballads, serenades, anthems, even hymns of universal loneliness and salvation, the same powerful themes struck again and again in different keys, by way of different characters. Language *is* character here, but it too is always changing.

Reginald Gibbons shrewdly points out that Goyen is interested in more than "the shape of a man"—he is interested in "the significance of the shape of a man"—hence the emblematic nature of the fiction which is symbolic rather than allegorical, haunting and provocative rather than didactic. An early story like "The White Rooster" suggests the D. H. Lawrence of "The Escaped Cock" and has an ending that is dramatically logical, emotionally inevitable, yet it differs from Goyen's more mature—and typically Goyenesque—work in that it *has* so emphatic an ending. Elsewhere, Goyen's stories are not resolved in any conventional way; nor do they simply trail off into silence. Image-centered, as our dreams are image-centered, each story is a unique cluster of (often contradictory) occasions—a field of contending forces, one might say—like the numerous medallions Goyen recalls his mother sewing, one by one, before quilting them together into a whole. The wholeness is present in the imagination (or in the unconscious) but it must be *quilted* into being by way of the artist's craft. It must be discovered or, better yet, uncovered. Hence the visionary writer trusts to his yet-unarticulated vision to guide him and to provide him with the necessary voice. When I say that a story by William Goyen is always recognizable as a story by William Goyen this is not to say that the voice is always the same voice—far from it. The canny, funny narrators of "The Texas Principessa" and "Where's Esther?" bear no kinship what-soever to the distraught narrator of "In the Icebound Hothouse." Yet the cluster of occasions of "The Texas Principessa" includes a nightmare image—the deadly spider at the heart of a peach innocently eaten—and the exiles of Horty Solomon (heiress to a Texas Jewish fortune in drygoods!) and Esther Haverton ("How could we know *that* was what it was? That we were losing a whole person?") are not so radically different from the exile of the speechless narrator of the icebound hothouse, the poet compelled to write to assuage the violence of his interior vision.

Goyen has said that he felt at times he was "the receiver of a cursedness": the carrier or bearer of images denied by his kinsfolk and neighbors in East Texas. The Ku Klux Klan, for instance, appears frequently in his stories, even in so relatively benign a story as "Figure Over the Town" where no one is terrorized or lynched. (Goyen was born in Trinity, Texas, in 1915, and spent his childhood in a house very like the large crowded disorderly house of the grandmother central to some of the stories in the "Blood Kindred" section of this book.) Images of physical muti-lation and malformation recur in Goyen's fiction as the outward expression, I would suggest, of the unacknowledged evil of his world, which the artist is accursed (and blessed) to acknowledge. Like many another writer Goyen chose exile of a sort while passionately retaining his childhood's experiences. He could not remain in Texas, "couldn't live among my own," he knew himself estranged, alienated, yet his destiny was to focus his creative powers upon the very world he'd left—hence the doubleness of many of his emblematic heroes. His case, Goyen said, seemed "a very personal thing, almost demonic—a curse: dark. Therefore the meditational quality, a prayer-like quality, almost 'Help me, Save me, Deliver me.'" If there was an evangelical minister preaching the salvation of the soul in Goyen's childhood there was also the Ku Klux Klan tarring and feathering Negroes, setting them ablaze to run in the streets. ("I saw them running like that, twice.") How ironic it is, that the artist/writer/poet who *sees* and *feels* the horror of such events is so frequently denounced by his kinsmen and his fellow citizens as mad, or wicked, or spuriously "muckraking"—as if the measure of sanity were the capacity to assimilate horrors without comment. Goyen's bouts with madness—of which he briefly speaks—are the very emblems of the fissures of consciousness accommodated by his kinsmen and neighbors back home.

But the stories are not finally stories of alienation, violence, or madness. The most startling images—the naked diver of "Bridge of Music, River of Sand," for instance—give way to a narrative meditation that roots the stories in the familiar human framework of exile and return, loss and rediscovery, death and redemption. The image of two brothers—one dead—on a door floating in a Texas flood gives way to a curious sort of harmony. The split tongue is an angel's tongue—perhaps! It has been said of Goyen's fiction that its spiritual significance resides in the very telling itself, in the voice given body and form by way of the writer's vision: and it might be said that the reader, in reading, in *hearing* this unique voice, completes the spiritual event. My suggestion is that William Goyen's stories be read slowly, no more than one at a sitting, perhaps, and that the reader suspend his expectations of what the "normal" should be no less than the "conventional" in terms of the short story. Simply allow the words to sound, and to resound. Words too are physical—rhythms and cadences spring from the body. This is an art of healing and the process cannot be forced.

JOYCE CAROL OATES

LAST STORIES

1976–1982

HAD I A
HUNDRED
MOUTHS

For June Arnold

On Good Friday, in the warm afternoon, the two cousins lay huddled against their uncle's bony body, each nestled in the crook of an arm. Often the cousins would be left in their uncle's care, and their habit was to take off their clothes because of the Gulf humidity and lie cool on the bed together and listen to his stories, which were generally about the joys and despairs of desire. It was a murmur they heard, a gruff whisper, a telling voice that the older cousin would hear all his life. The uncle smelled of whiskey, which he drank from time to time from a bottle under the bed. "When you boys going to get you some?" he suddenly asked at each meeting, as though anything had changed since they had met before. "I don't know," the younger cousin would answer, eight. But the older cousin, eleven, was already bound and not free enough to give any answer to such a question.

The uncle nestled his two nephews against his frail breast (it was said that he had TB). He seemed lonesome, not a part of anything. He had stayed home in the little town all these years, while big cities bloomed up nearby and "offered opportunities," living on, after his mother and father had died, one after the other, of pneumonia, in the epidemic, and after Louetta had gone, and his brothers and sisters had left, moved to somewhere else or died somewhere else, stayed under the roof and shelter of the old house his father had built, and never saying much, except when his sister and sister-in-law would come from Houston on holidays and bring their sons, his favorites. Then he would come alive and open his mouth and out would come stories. On this Good Friday afternoon it seemed like he might be getting ready to tell another story about a woman and a man. The younger nephew lay like a blank-eyed doll nested in the uncle's embrace; he might even have been dozing; he seemed to be in some peace under his uncle's arm, in some kind of a haven, unthreatened. After all, he was a fatherless child. His mother, the uncle's sister, had run his father off, so all his kinfolks said, because he was lazy and couldn't make a living. She worked in a sewing room at a factory. Did his mother think she was making a living? They had no clothes. He wanted to go find his father in Shreveport. He'd heard them say he was there. When he got old enough he would, too. He told this to his cousin.

But the older nephew was feeling another thing. He was beckoned by some new feeling and he felt powerless before it; and, most of all, he didn't care. He felt that he would go all the way with some feeling, when it would soon come, and not hinder it because it was wrong, and not be afraid of it, not care what happened, overwhelmed. His storyteller uncle had something to do with this feeling, he was not sure what; but surely it was a feeling that had first come to him from his uncle; it seemed to be in the command of the man, it seemed called up in him by the man's very nurturing presence, something like what motherliness had been for him not so long ago but now pushed away forever; and by the seduction of storyteller, the surrender of listener to teller, almost in a kind of love-making, of sensual possession, yet within innocence and purity. A dark new life had started under the command of his uncle and the hot spell of the stories that boiled like steam, tolled like a bell, sang like a solemn singer's song out of his mouth. But he already knew the feelings of lust. And why wouldn't he? Later, in the wrestling with it, he figured

that he had already come in lust long ago, born in it, that he had
already inherited it in his flesh long before he laid his head on
the naked breast of his uncle and heard his tales of barns and gins
and woods and under bridges, already had it in his blood, had
been waiting only to be brought to it when the time came. Then
that would change everything, that coming of something. It had
already come, in a dark way, to some men and women of his
family: some ran far away in its seizure and never came back,
leaving everything; Aunt Blanch, Louetta's mother, did, the
uncle had told, with a man, ran away with him from everybody
—mama, papa, husband, child—and he was a young good Mexican that had worked on the place, named Juan Melendrez, the
uncle had told, from the Rio Grande Valley, and Blanch's husband, Joe Parrish, then disappeared and never returned, either,
leaving Louetta an orphan of fourteen in her grandparents'
house; sometimes people just suddenly ran away from everything
and never came back. Life seemed dark, and sad beyond any way
to tell it: there seemed no mouth that could utter the pain, only
eyes to shed tears of it or heartache of it. Where was there any
comfort? Where was God? In Sunday School the nephew had
been shown the picture of a sweet man gathering under his arms
a crowd of little children and the words under the picture said
COME UNTO ME. Where in this family, thought the nephew, was
this comforter? And lying in the cradle of his uncle's naked arm,
he felt as close to that man as to his uncle, and as in need of him,
on that Good Friday afternoon.

But did the younger nephew need anybody? Who knew? He
did not seem to hear. Or did he hear and just not care? Who
knew? All the older nephew knew was that the stories fell upon
the ripe ground of his brain, as in the Bible, and were ripening
there and one day might come, bountiful fruit, from his own
mouth. Then, in that rich time it would seem that he had not
enough mouths to tell—or to retell—the stories of his uncle, and
his own, now, there would be so many and they would come so
richly and so fast. But the younger nephew seemed deaf. Wasn't
that peculiar? Why was that, the older nephew asked himself,

asked God, others, for all his life. Some heard and some did not, though the same news fell on the ears of each. And he also asked himself which one had peace, the teller-on—the mouthed—or the silent one in whom the story stopped. But did telling-on make any difference, help anything? The older nephew already had little peace. At home, more was expected of him than he could fulfill. But he would never let them know of his inade-quacy. He carried the world, boy Atlas. His father, his uncle's brother, could not make enough money from his job to give his family what they "deserved," whatever that was; but that was his father's cry, and especially when he was drinking, "I can't give you all what you deserve. I'm not good enough for you." The older nephew's mother reminded him of his mission, charged him to be the one who would give them their deserving. That was what he would have to look for, those apples of gold such as Hercules sought—as in the story in school—and temporarily took the world upon his shoulders so that Atlas, who knew where the golden treasures were, could go get them and bring them back. Who would relieve the older nephew of his weight so that he could go? Well it would surely be his uncle who would bring him this ease. It was with these feelings that he heard the uncle's suddenly solemn voice. What was this voice, this tone? What story?

It was in the dark afternoon on a November day of sleet, told the uncle. We waited and we waited for Louetta to get home from her trip into town. The darker it got the scareder we got. More sleet fell and sleet was all in the frozen grass and in the trees. At four o'clock it was getting like night, it was so dark. Ben, they said, you better go on to the woods and look for her, Louetta's bound to be lost. I'll take the big lantern, I said. And so I started out alone. It was freezing cold, and dark fallen, just about. The sleet cut at me. I got to the haunted woods of the old sawmill. They was so lonesome and you couldn't hear nothing but the dropping of the stinging rain, sleeting. Nobody ever went back there in the ruined sawmill woods, back in there where the ruined kiln was, and the old log pond. Black people said it was haunted and that bad spirits lived there in the deep pineland because of a terrible thing that happened once, back in the days when the sawmill was flourishing. A white foreman and his strawboss caught three niggers fucking a Cushata Indian squaw back in there and they cut off their nuts and roasted them in the kiln and made the Cushata woman eat em. But the white men had been fucking the Cushata squaws as long as there'd been a sawmill. Squaws come over from the reservation at Moscow to give the white men some pussy for some salt pork from the Commissary, or for some coffee. Cushata's supposed to have put a bad spell over the sawmill, one day a man'd fall under the logs in the log pond and his head'd be crushed between the logs; next a man would lose a whole hand in the planing saw; and there was some bad fires. Course the Cushatas was thieves and come in and stole at the Commissary and from people's houses, couldn't trust one of em, black niggers hated red Indians, red Indians despised the black niggers, the white man didn't trust either one of em, black *or* red, so—the best thing to do was drink a little whiskey and stay away from all of em; 's what your gran-daddy did and what I did. When the sawmill finally died out, some folks said that was why, that the Cushata curse had finally got its vengeance. I don't know much about those days and glad they're gone, by the time I was old enough to sneak out to the old sawmill was a wild grown-over thicket man or boy could hardly stand up in, said was snakes in there big as a man, and the mill fallen down and the Cushatas just about all died out, starved to death mostly, or had TB.

Anyway, I was walking over the frozen leaves on the old sawmill road and calling for Louetta. It scared me to hear my call in the woods. Louetta! No Louetta. I went towards the old kiln where there was a cave made under the fallen trees that were hit a long time ago by the tornado come on us out of Oklahoma and made a cave out of brambling together the great clumps of tree roots; time had made walls and the living trees, living on with leaves and vines, made a sheltering cave, dark and cool—the kind of a thing you will sometimes see nature make better than any man could, twas something of nature, a beaver could have made it, or wind of a big storm could've, and natural roots and earth wrapped over and bound together, could last a hundred years of time. I started towards that, when I heard a soft wailing, and on top of that a man's low voice, agrowling. I went quiet as I could towards the cave and I heard more and more the growling and the wailing. And then I heard the words of the man growling low how good it was, and the soft wailing. I laid in the bush until it was over and quiet and then I saw the man, a big red nigger, seemed aglow with redness all around him—ever seen that in a nigger? I don't know why it tis—I saw him come out of the cave and go on off. I was so scared. I waited until his footsteps was gone and then I shone my light onto . . . Louetta, lying in the cave. I thought she was dead. Louetta! I said. When she saw my face in the lantern light she wailed and whispered, Ben, Ben, please don't look! Please go away, please don't tell anybody, just let me alone. What happened? I said. The Nigra ran out at me in the woods, Louetta whispered, and I couldn't stop him. In the dark cave was the warm smell of woman, and I knew what the nigger had done. Well I'm not going to leave you, Louetta, like this, I said. Then help me to the river, she said. In Trinity River I put her down and she told me to go away a little, and I stood in the bushes and saw her wash and I was seventeen and felt what it was, of a man and a woman, the growling and wailing, that the red nigger knew, and what Louetta, my cousin, knew now, what he'd showed her in the cave, even though she was softly awailing in the riverwater, as she washed herself. This all come on me. Even in my hate of the nigger I felt a wanting for the woman washing herself of him, and the smell of the cave was all in my nose and all over me, on my hands that had helped Louetta up and to the river, a smell of the nigger stuff and the woman. I didn't want to wash that off, life, but then I didn't want them to smell it on me when we got home so I bent down into the river and washed my hands; and then it seemed like I'd made love to Louetta and that we was both awashing ourselves of it. When Louetta come out of the river, I wanted her. And I grabbed her. And took what the nigger took. I was just like him. She was hot, and still crazy, and ready, and took me, wailing Oh no, Oh no, please don't; said not you, not you. Just like the Nigra. But I was naked in the river—who took off my clothes? —and I was all over her. I said you've already done it now, the nigger made you ready, give to me what you gave to him. I was just like the nigger. And then in the midst of her wailing I took her, soft and made good by the red nigger. And I heard my growling, too, but I couldn't stop and Louetta couldn't stop taking me. We was both seventeen. There's a wildness, once it starts, you can't stop. That's what happens with it, you get crazy with it, once you've had it, once you've started. You boys will see, one day; and you'll remember what you uncle told you of it. The uncle growled, and the nephews were afraid. But the uncle went on. Now he seemed different than he had ever been in the older nephew's memory. We washed together, the uncle went on, me and Louetta, cousins, and when we washed each other, we both felt damnation on us; the Cushatas had put damnation on us through the nigger. And that was the beginning. From then on, Louetta just couldn't stop wanting it and whispering of it, was a crazy woman; and I wasn't any different. We did it in the cave, day and night, wild. We was lost.

When the black baby was borned in the cave and I helped Louetta with it, black, and said Oh my God Louetta black, it's black, I took it to the Orphanage up at Longview. But they would not take it, black. All day I was wandering with the little black baby boy, through the woods and hiding in the deep groves, wondering what to do. It was a warm little thing with big white eyes and I hated to give it up cause I felt that it was part mine, you understand. Towards dark I took the baby to Aunt Kansas Tate, our washerwoman way back in the woods in Niggertown, and begged her to take it, and she looked, black, at me, the way they do when they're stern like that, a kind of look of God, and I knew she thought the baby was mine. Who is its Mama? asked Kansas Tate. And I told her that I found the baby in the woods. Must be God's child, she said. And then she held the warm child and I saw her love, and she took the baby boy. She named him Leander . . .

Louetta and I watched the boy grow. When Kansas Tate came to our place to wash and iron, the little boy Leander played near the washpot, under the Chinaberry tree. And I saw Louetta watching him from the window. Leander was different, twas in his eyes. After all, he was borned in a cave of tree roots that the tornado from Oklahoma had made in 1918, tore up half of the county. He was as light-complected as a light Mescan boy, and real different. Something of Louetta was on him, and sometimes I'd catch her standing at the back door peeking and staring out at the little boy playing in the woodpile. Leander grew on. A look of Louetta was strong over him. But I never saw her talk to him. Sometimes I'd play with Leander, and as he grew up I taught him marbles and we'd shoot em; and I showed a lot of things a father would have shown him—how to aim and shoot a beebee gun, how to whittle a slingshot; and we hunted rabbit once, back of the old road. Until the Klu Klux boys caught us and warned me not to do it again. This hurt me before the boy, because what could I say to the boy, that we couldn't be friends or that we would have to hide to be friends. And so we slipped out to the cave in the sawmill woods where nobody ever came and we hid in the cave and played jack-knife and I told him stories and answered some of the questions that he was beginning to ask. And Leander grew. Louetta and I had made love oh I guess a million times by that time. We'd never got enough since the first time. We did it back in the woodshed at night and sometimes in the barn in pure daylight. But the hiding was terrible and our feeling of sin was terrible. How could we stop? I guess nobody in the world has ever stopped something like that, once it's started. But Louetta said she felt doom, said something terrible was going to happen to us, and I worried for fear she would do something to herself, sometimes she was ahurting so. But then we'd want each other again and no suffering God made, I hate to say it, could keep us from that wanting. One day you boys might know that, hope to God you won't, but one day you might, and guess you will; because nobody's perfect and we all got flesh on us.

When Leander was twelve Louetta came one day to where he was, working and helping out on the place, and gave him a red ring for his twelfth birthday that he put on his finger. He loved that ring and kept it there. I don't know why but I felt Leander was part my boy, that I'd helped make him, I'd held him first of anybody in the world and carried him when he was just borned, so he was that much mine. But the boy had two fathers, one run away, black, and one keeping a secret, white. I loved Leander. The town was afraid of him, though, because he was so light-complected and carried something unusual over him, not like any others. Sometimes I would see Leander watching Louetta when she was in the yard and I saw him gazing at her with such a look, almost as if he knew.

And now I'm going to tell you something. One night Louetta was sitting in the hot dark on the gallery; a darkest night, black as ink, was over us, the way it is back here when the moon's away, black as ink. The rest of us had gone up the road to see about old Uncle Ned that was sick. And Louetta saw a shape coming in the dark and she could not see who it was; and before she could call out anybody's name the figure was on her and tore at her and she could see that it was black and she begged and she fought. This's what she told me, because when I came home I found Louetta torn and wild and I smelled the smell again and saw that she'd been taken again. And I said was it the red nigger come back and she said black black. I run in the dark to get my shotgun that I kept in the hall in the corner, but then I heard a terrible sound, one I'll never forget, one of broken well-water, the groan of the deep porch well, and Louetta had thrown herself in the well. And right then the others came back, Mama and you boy's mothers, Holly and Eva, and I run for the boys to come and help bring up the body of Louetta from the well. When I held the cold body of Louetta how could I show all the feelings I felt before the others, just for a cousin? I tried not to pull that frozen body to my flesh like I had done so many times, my secret to my own damnation, and then I saw that Louetta's blue hand was clutched as though it held something it would never give up; and when nobody saw me, I broke open Louetta's hand and there, what she clutched and held on to, to her very death, in all her feelings of shamefulness and her, I'll bet you, tenderness, and would not even now give up until I broke the very bones of her hand, was the red ring of Leander. Fighting his wild hands, Louetta must have clawed it off Leander's finger. My howling was so loud that they ran to see if a snake had bit me or a blue hornet stung me, and before they knew it or anybody ever saw, I swallowed the red ring. It burned down my gullet like a coal of fire. I didn't know how I was going to live with my feelings. I wanted to jump into the well, but I couldn't show my hurting; and I couldn't show my shamefulness for all these secrets; and I couldn't show my despisement of Leander for killing my own secret Louetta—too many feelings for one person ever to stand and I don't know how I did it. But so much was happening. The boys wanted to run to Niggertown and round up the man, and I don't know what kept them from it, God himself did, I guess, if He could be in such an infernal place; because we all begged them to wait until Louetta was buried and they agreed if we would bury her the next day. The whole town was roiling and bonfires were burning all night and the boys put on their sheets and burnt a cross on the hill; was like the end of the world. All the pore niggers in Niggertown hid in their houses.

At the funeral suddenly come from out of nowhere Leander and Kansas Tate and stood by me. Leander was dirty and wild and looked like he had been hiding in the thicket all night long and Kansas Tate was in her black strongness and with a face that dared everybody. And suddenly Leander broke from us and ran and fell in the dirt of the open grave of Louetta and wailed and wailed, and oh the sight of that boy in the dirt of his mother's grave made me cry like a baby. People thought it was all for Louetta, but some was for Leander. Leander's hurting was terrible to see. They couldn't get him off the grave, he clung in the dirt, but the pallbearers in their white hoods seized him and dragged him away. Kansas Tate cried out that the Lord would strike them dead for blaming an innocent Negro boy and making him pay for somebody else's evil deed and they had to hold her in her wildness and daring of everybody. But the Klu Kluxes shouted burn him, make him pay for the one that raped and killed a white woman, a nigger in the hand is worth five in the bushes; and Clarence McKay, an old friend of Kansases but a leader of the Klu Klux, said Kansas I can't stop them, they'll have to have them a scapegoat. And Kansas Tate cried out, scapegoat? scapegoat? Leander's not a scapegoat! He's a Christian boy that loved Miss Louetta. But they dragged Leander on off into the woods. Back in the woods, no matter what I knew about it or what I felt, I couldn't lay a hand on Leander. The red ring laid in my gut and cut it like a claw. Most of the Klu Kluxes sympathized with my hurting for my cousin Louetta, but when they tore off his clothes from his brown young man's body they had to hold me to keep me from running to stop them and protect Leander; but then I rushed with them when they cut him clean as a woman and hung his young manhood on a tree branch. And I stood there crazy with the red ring of Leander and Louetta in me and saw them tar and feather Leander's brown young body, now neither man nor woman, and I vomited on my knees in the night. And there on the ground in the flare of the Klu Klux torches I saw the gleaming of the red ring, my damnation to curse me. I wanted to stomp it into my own vomit and crush it into the ground, but I took it and put it in my pocket.

And then they brought Leander into town and run him howling down Main Street on that funeral night and then they let him go, hollering to him to get out of town. That night Kansas Tate in her misery fell in a stroke and died, and I run far into the woods and drank my whiskey in the dark of the deep woods and laid like a log in the leaves. And then I crawled and hid in the dark of the cave.

The uncle took a long swallow of whiskey. And then he said, very low, I've never told a soul this story until now. Had I a hundred mouths I could not have told the story; it was too much of a story to tell. I've kept the tale of Leander and Louetta a secret all these years and have drank a ton of whiskey on it. And now I've told it to you boys, my brother's son and my sister's son, one just becoming a man and the other still adozing in his little boyhood. And the uncle reached again under the bed and brought up the bottle to his mouth. The golden fumes of whiskey spread over the nephews, and the carnality of that moment, the despairs of the flesh and the sorrows of the story of Leander brought life down upon the older nephew so heavily that it seemed unbearable; and he wondered how he would ever bear his feelings that his heart and his body were just beginning to give to him. He understood then his uncle's feelings and the ton of whiskey used to deaden them, but he vowed he would never deaden life, that he would feel his feelings full and that he would not fall under their burden as his uncle had, in hiding and numbness. He would feel and he would tell, even as his uncle had, finally, this afternoon.

But the uncle had more to tell. His voice went on, graver than the nephew had ever heard it. That day as I laid in the cave and wanting to die, I heard a sound, and it was Leander rolling on the ground in the leaves and grunting like an animal dying. He'd torn his flesh from the bone trying to get off the tar that had clung to him like another skin. He had skinned himself. And then I laid and watched him go to the river where his unbeknownst mother had washed herself of what had made him, and there I had washed myself, too. And there by the river I saw Leander, rising up out of the river, a scary figure, and I saw him tear at himself and I heard his wailings of pain. I'll drown him, I said to myself. But I heard myself call, Leander! Leander! I called. When he saw me, who I was, he howled at me like Satan the devil, white eyes flashing, and came out of the water, steaming and red like a young Satan, and spit at me like a fiend. I saw his burnt face and I saw his clawed bleeding body and I saw him limp from a foot that had been bad hurt. Leander! I cried. I ought to kill you for what you done. But I can't help it I am your friend and I ask you to remember all our life together; sometime

I'll tell you how I held you when you was just a little baby. I will help to heal you if you will let me. And then I held out the red ring and Leander fell passed out and I picked him up from the water like a raw piece of meat and took him to the cave and tied him to a root. Poor lonesome lost nigger boy, there's not any more can be done to you for what you did and I can't kill you, like somebody'd tell me to.

I kept Leander hid back in the cave, tied to the tree root, and nursed him, every day I'd come and feed and doctor and nurse him, right there in the deep cave of trees where he was borned and where he was made on the night I heard his maker crying out, sixteen years ago. He never asked one question never said one word. I set and drank my whiskey. In the secret woods, in the cave, Leander was healing from the Klu Klux. He never told his feelings, never said a word. He hid his hate, and what love could he have? The foxes and the deer came to the cave and put their noses to his face, and the birds knew Leander. Summer and winter and spring Leander saw come over the woods; and Leander was seventeen. Every night I'd come and walk him out of the cave and in the light of the moon, I saw the terrible scars and patches of white on him. His beauty was ruined and all over his face was white scars and his torn mouth was healed crooked and his lips looked like they were burnt away. The healed skin on his face and on his arms and all over his body had turned white. In the moonlight I saw that Leander was striped and spotted like an animal. He limped because of his hurt leg some way, but he would never let me see what was the matter with it. His big eyes glared pure white, his hair was all coming back wild and long like a white man's and twas of a reddish color like his bedeviled father's. Who was this boy? Who could live like that, who would want to, you answer me that. And he never showed his feelings; no matter how many times I asked the question why would you do something like that, he would look at me with that terrible look as if he was asking, do what? When I finally held him up against the wall of the cave and said tell me, tell me why you would do something like that, and I almost told him about the red nigger his father and that he had done it to his own mother, but I couldn't, I couldn't do that, I guess I just loved Leander too much to kill his heart like that, if he had any of it left, and if any of his heart was left he was probably saving it for his mother and his father if ever he would find them. Anyway, when he didn't say a word I finally realized that he couldn't, that his voice must have been burnt out of his throat. Because when I finally held him by the throat he groaned a sound of ah-ah-ah and his breath smelled of old smoke of the Klu Klux Klan. Leander was burnt inside too. Poor lost nigger boy. So I just came and sat in the cave with him and drank my whiskey in the dark, as quiet as he was. This was when I give him back the red ring and he put it on his burnt finger.

I begun some days to let Leander loose. He strayed from the cave more and more. I warned him not to, but he'd wander in the woods. I saw him begin to leap and to run, the way a cripple does—or a crippled animal. Because that's what he would have looked like to any hunter if any had come out there, and they would have shot him dead. Once when I came and could not find him and I was afraid to call out his name, I looked and looked and finally found him by the log pond where the old kiln was and heavy trees that vines crawled up to the top of and then fell down, all blooming, morning glory and honeysuckle and muscadine vines, and trumpets; this was where I found Leander. I saw him sitting on the old walls of the kiln, looking into the pond. It was just at twilight. An owl begun to make its hurting sound. And I thought, who is this creature of the woods, borned in the woods and burnt in the woods and healed, and hiding in the woods from his persecutors and from all humanity? And at that time I was afraid for Leander and for myself, wondering what we would ever do. There was a road going to be built soon across the woods—that's the Highway now, I-17—and I heard talk of some kind of a plant going to be started—which is now of course the Dye Works that turned the river yellow—and I was scared. And I said to Leander, you muss not ever do that again, run off from the cave that far. But Leander didn't want to go on living hiding, I saw that, he wanted free, I could see that. And I knew that he had seen himself in the pond.

But he went on. Leander went on living, continued the uncle. Why? You'd have thought he'd just hang himself from a tree or drown hisself in the log pond—many times I expected to come and find that he had done that, killed himself by his own hand. Like his mother did. But Leander stayed alive and kept living, don't know why. And then one day when I came to the cave he was gone. I looked everywhere. I couldn't call because I didn't know who'd hear me. At first I run this way and then I run that way and then I was going around in circles. If even a branch of a tree cracked, I thought it was Leander. Then I got my bearings from the black piece of smokestack of the old saw-mill that stuck up like a knife and I ran to the kiln and whispered Leander! I saw some birds that must have been his friends and I asked the birds, where's Leander? And I saw a doe and her fawn and they perked up and looked right at me and I said, please tell me where has Leander gone. Because he'll never make it all alone. And then when I shone a light into Leander's old dark corner of the cave, something gleamed. And there, on a tree root, dangling on a string, was the red ring, the sad red ring. The uncle reached under the bed, drew up the bottle of whiskey to his mouth and took a deep swallow from it, the deepest of all. Then he was quiet for a long time. Finally the older nephew asked, "What happened to Leander?" and the uncle answered softly, "I never saw Leander again. I went away and never came back again to the cave in the sawmill woods. Wasn't too long before bulldozers leveled the place and men came in and built the state highway through there: I-17. Underneath the highway lays forever the red ring."

And then they lay silent together for a long time, the uncle, the older nephew and the young one. And in a while the nephews heard their uncle sleeping. But the older nephew did not sleep. He lay fiercely awake and felt the flesh of his uncle against his side, the beat of his heart and the breeze of his breath, whiskey-laden, upon his cheek.

· · ·

Some years later, the older nephew, who had long ago left the place, came back home to his uncle's funeral. He had died, they called and told him, alone in a drifter's Mission, drunk on a cot, in Houston, where he'd gone to seek his brother and sister (who had renounced him) but had gone to the Methodist mission, Harbor Lights, near the Ship Channel on Navigation Boulevard. And as he stood at the grave, a group of hooded white figures came out from the trees and gathered around the coffin; and he saw, when one of them lifted for a moment his mask, the face of his young cousin. Did he want to speak, to tell something to him? The older cousin felt a chill of terror and rage; but he held still until the preacher, who had stepped forward and was reading Galatians 6:8, "For he that soweth to his flesh shall of the flesh reap corruption," had finished. And then he turned his back to the place and left it forever—or so he vowed.

And then more years passed and the older nephew had drunk his uncle's whiskey, had looked here and there, had lost love and speech, had been living hidden for nights and days away from life in a dark world of fear and dumbness, Leander's brother, bound back to the land of his uncle. And returning home late one night on a darkened street in a cold city, the older cousin heard a ghostly sound of breaking glass, and he saw coming towards him out of the darkness a startling shape of beauty and oddness. As if drawn together, the figure and the cousin moved toward each other; and when they confronted each other it was as though they had come together out of the ages, face to face. The nephew looked upon a phantom face, as if what face had been there had been burned away and this was the painted mask of it. The creature's head was covered with a rich mane of hair, and in the streetlight there appeared to be a red glow over it. The being was clothed in a glimmering garment of scales of glass; and colored feathers were reflected in their mirrors. And the nephew saw that gaudy rings glistened on scarred brown hands. Leander! he whispered. Why did he think that this was the burnt boy, the orphan child of lust, that on a long-ago Good

Friday afternoon signaled the end of his boyhood? Leander! he called. But there was no sign of feeling in the shadowed ancient eyes which, for a searing moment, locked upon him. And then the phantom being moved around the nephew and went on, swathed in the delicate tinkling of glass.

Leander! he softly called, once more, Leander! And he was calling to his uncle and his uncle's sorrow and to all storytelling, all redemption: Leander, Leander. But the figure steadily moved away, as if it were made of glass and falling delicately to pieces in its ruined march, into the gloom of the night, farther and farther away from any recognition, any redemption, any forgiveness.

And all that night the nephew put this down and told again the story that his uncle told him, a story that he could not have told before had he had a hundred mouths to tell it with. In the morning, in the silver light of dawn over the old city of his miracles, miraculously refreshed he saw in the mirror his naked body, its skin, its haunch, its breast: the ancient sower's flesh, the reaper's.

THE TEXAS
PRINCIPESSA

Who would've dreamed that I would get the Palazzo? Well let me try and stay on what you asked me about before we were so rudely interrupted—by me. That ever happen to you? Start out to tell one thing and get off onto another? Well let me try and stay on what you asked me about. Welcome to the Palazzo.

The Texas Principessa had married a Naples Prince of an old line. Hortense Solomon (we called her Horty) was herself of an old line—of dry goods families. Texas Jews that had intermarried and built up large stores in Texas cities over the generations. Solomon's Everybody's Store was an everyday word in the mouths of Texas people and an emporium—which was their word—where Texas people were provided with everything from hosiery to clocks. The Solomons, along with the Linkowitzes, the Dinzlers and the Myrons, were old pioneers of Texas. They were kept to their faith by traveling Rabbis in early days, and later they built Synagogues and contributed Rabbis and Cantors from their generations—except those who married Texas Mexicans or Texas Frenchmen. These, after a while, melted into the general mixture of the Texas population and ate cornbread instead of bagels and preferred barbeque pork and tamales to lox and herring. That ever happen to you? Let's see where was I?

Oh. The Naples Prince, Renzi da Filippo, did not bring much money to the marriage because the old line of da Filippos

20

had used up most of it or lost it; or had it taken from them in one way or another—which was O.K. because they had taken it from somebody else earlier on: sometimes there is a little justice. That ever happen to you? Renzi was the end of the line. Someone who was the end of a line would look it, wouldn't you think so? You could not tell it in Renzi da Filippo, he looked spunky enough to *start* something; he was real fresh and handsome in that burnt blond coloring that they have, sort of toasted—toast-colored hair and bluewater eyes and skin of a wheaty color. He was a beauty everyone said and was sought after in Rome and London and New York. Those Italianos! About all he had in worldly goods was the beautiful Palazzo da Filippo in Venice, a seventeenth-century hunk of marble and gold that finally came into his hands. Had Hortense Solomon not given her vows to Renzi in wedlock, Palazzo da Filippo might have gone down the drain. It needed repair in the worst kind of way—all those centuries on it—and those repairs needed a small fortune—which Horty had a lot of. As soon as the marriage was decided upon, there was a big party. The Prince was brought to Texas and an announcement party was thrown, and I mean *thrown,* on the cold ranch river that flowed through the acres and acres of hot cattle-land owned by the Solomons. The gala stirred up socialites as far as Porto Ercole and Cannes, from which many of the rich, famous and titled flew in on family planes. Horty Solomon—which was very hard for Italians to say so they called her La Principessa di Texas—started right in with her plans for fixing up the Palazzo. The plans were presented in the form of a little replica of the Palazzo used as a centerpiece for the sumptuous table. Two interior decorators called The Boys, favorites of Horty's from Dallas, exhibited their color schemes—a lot of Fuchsia for Horty loved this favorite color of hers. "You're certainly not going to redecorate that Palazzo" (they said Palazzo the way she did, so that it sounded like "Plotso"), "you're certainly not going to furnish it out of Solomon's Everybody's Store!" The Boys declared to Horty as soon as they heard of her plans to redo the Plotso da Filippo. "Nor," said they, "are you going to make it look like a West Texas ranch house. We're using Florentine silk and Venetian gold, with rosy Fuchsia appointments!"

When Palazzo da Filippo was in shape, the Texas relatives poured in. The Palazzo was crawling with them, young and old. The Palazzo could have been a big Texas house. Black cooks and maids from East Texas mingled with Italian servants. The Venetians loved it. "Viva la Principessa di Texas!" they cried. Those Italianos!

Here I must inform you something of which you were asking about, that on his very wedding night in a villa in Monaco (the beautiful Prince gambled on his wedding night) the beautiful Prince Renzi burst a blood vessel in his inner ear and succumbed (the newspapers' word for it). He just plain died in his wedding bed is what it was. You were asking about how he died. Vicious talk had it that the only stain on the nuptial (newspapers' word)—only stain on the nuptial sheets came from the Prince's ear. Crude. The poor bride, who had been married before—a big textile man from Birmingham, Alabama—was stunned. Poor Horty. Tragedy dogged her, as you well can see. I myself have never experienced the death of a husband but I have experienced two divorces and let me tell you they are simular, they are like a death. They are no fun. My last divorce was particularly nasty. Thank God there was no issue, as the Wills said. Both my husbands were without issue. Issue indeed. That's a joke for the last one, who issued it to *Old Granddad* instead of me—mind as well say it; and excuse the profanity—that one had little issue except through his mouth . . . when he threw up his Bourbon. Crude, I know. But that's mainly the kind of issue *he* had. That ever happen to you? Let's see where was I. Oh. Anyway, this left me in London, quite penniless; tell you why I was in London some other time. Don't have time for that garden path now—it's a memory lane I choose at the moment to take a detour from. But the thing of it is, this is how Horty Solomon got the Palazzo da Filippo, which is what you were asking me about: under the auspices of a sad circumstance—a broken blood vessel leading to death; but a tragedy leading to a new life for her. And for me, as you will soon hear the story (that you were asking about). Anyway, Horty went on with her plans for the Palazzo, now all hers.

As I said somewhere—I can't tell a story straight to save my life, my mind races off onto a hundred things that I remember and want to tell right then, don't want to wait. That ever happen to you? *Anyway,* as I said somewhere, Texans flooded into the canals of Venice because of the Principessa: *Venezia* was half Texas some days—and loved it. And if you've ever heard a Texan speaking Italian, you won't believe the sound of it. Big oilmen came to the Palazzo and Texas college football players—Horty had given them a stadium in Lampasas (they called her Cousin Horty)—Junior League ladies, student concert pianists (Horty was a patron of the Arts, as you will see more about), and once a Rock group—they had that Grand Canal jumping, and some seventeenth-century tiles *fell,* I can tell you. And maybe something from even earlier, a Fresco or two from the Middle Ages. And talented young people who wanted to paint or write came over to the Palazzo. See what Horty did? Some of them were offered rooms in the Palazzo, to write in or paint in, or practice a musical instrument in; and they accepted. See what she did? Palazzo da Filippo jived, that was the word then; it was in the nineteen fifties. That joint jumped, as they said.

I said back there that I was going to tell you why I was in London. Or did I? Can't remember. Just try to remember something with all this noise around here. Italians are noisy, sweet as they are—singing and calling on the Canals. Now where was I? Oh. London. Well, forget London for the time being—*if* I haven't already told it to you. Just keep London in the back of your mind. Now where was I? Oh. Well, you have asked me to tell you what you are hearing—the story of the Texas Principessa, my old schoolmate and life-long pal, that you asked about. After the Prince's death, Horty pulled herself together and got the Palazzo together—a reproduction of Palazzo da Filippo was engraved on Renzi's tombstone *with* Horty's changes incorporated (which, of course, I thought was rather nifty, wouldn't you?)—and Horty pleaded with me in April by phone and cable to come stay. "Come and stay as long as you want to, stay forever if you're happy in the Palazzo; just come on," Horty said, long distance, to me in London. Horty loved to have people in the house. This doesn't mean that she always loved being with them. Sometimes I've seen it happen that a motorboat would arrive and disburse a dozen guests and a week later depart with the same guests and not one of them had ever *seen* the Principessa. Horty would've confined herself off in her own apartment in the far right top wing and there remain in privacy. Simply did not want to have anything to do with them, with her guests. "That's Horty," everyone said. They'd had a grand time, gone in the Principessa's private motorboats to Torcello, to lunch at the Cipriano, to cocktails at other palazzos, been served divine dinners with famous Italians at the da Filippo. But no Horty. She usually —she was so generous—gave expensive presents to her guests to get them to forgive her. Once she gave everybody an egg—a sixth-century—B.C.!—egg of Chinese jade. Amounted to about a dozen eggs. Somebody said the retail value on those eggs was about $150 apiece. Where was I? Oh.

Well this was in April and in May I came. Horty at once announced to me that there was no room for me at the Palazzo! She was getting crazy over painters. She'd become more and more interested in painting, Horty did, but that's no surprise because she always seemed to possess a natural eye and feeling for painting, not so curious for an heiress to generations of garment salesmen, even though you might so comment. For Hortense Solomon inherited good taste and a tendency for her eye to catch fine things when she saw them. Though there were Brahma bulls leering through the windows of the Solomon ranch in West Texas, what those bulls saw inside was fine china and Chippendale, silver and crystal and satin and silk. Those bulls saw the handiwork of a chic decorator and an elegant collector; not every bull sees *that*. So a seventeenth-century palazzo in Venice was not so far a cry for Horty to fix up.

Well here was I living over at the Cipriano where Horty, who couldn't do without me till I got there and then banished me—to a terrific suite, I must say, and footed by her—and here was I coming across the Canal every day to observe the goings on at the Palazzo. Frankly I was glad to have me a little distance from the commotion. Well-known artists came to live in the Palazzo da Filippo and to set up studios there and in the environs. Horty patronized them. Gave them scholarships as she called them. A few were very attractive, I must say, and some very young—Horty's eye again. The Venetians adored La Principessa di Texas. They appreciated her for unscrewing the horse's outfit from the horse sculpture in her garden on the Grand Canal when the Archbishop passed in his barge on days of Holy Procession. The Principessa had commissioned the sculpture of a beautiful horse possessed of some wild spirit, with a head uplifted and long mouth open in an outcry. On it sat a naked man, again possessed of some wild spirit, seemed like, and his mad-looking head was also raised up in some crying out. You did not see the rider's outfit but the horse's was very apparent, and the Principessa commissioned the sculptor—a then unknown but handsome sculptor—to sculpt one that was removable. Which seems to apply to a lot of men that I have known—where was it? A lot of them seem to have removed it. Put it in a drawer someplace. Or mind as well have. Where was I? Oh yes. The horse's outfit. On high holy procession days the Texas Principessa could be seen on her knees under the belly of the horse with grasping hands, making wrenching movements. The Italians coined a phrase for it. When they saw her going at the horse as if she were twisting a light globe, they said to each other that La Principessa di Texas was "honoring the Archbishop." The community generally appreciated her decency for doing this; some felt that the Archbishop should give her a citation. And a few called her a castrator —in Italian of course—*castratazionera,* oh I can't say it right but you know what I mean; and of course a few from home in Texas said she was a dicktwister—had to put their nasty mouths into it. Crude. Where was I. Oh. An American painter came to visit Horty one afternoon. He was showing in the Biennale, which is what they call the show of paintings that they have every year.

Horty and the painter drank and talked about his painting. When the Principessa turned around from making *another* double martini for the American painter—she hardly gave it to him when she had to whirl around and make another one—*pirouette* is what you had to do when you made drinks for that man. Unless you just made a whole jug and gave it to him. Anyway, she whirled to find him urinating in the fireplace. The Principessa was so impressed with the American painter—imagine the audacity!—that famous summer afternoon that she asked him to stay. He stayed—over a year, it turned out—and you can see some of his paintings in the palazzo gallery, they have become very sought after and the painter very famous—though dead from alcoholism not so many years after that. More proof of the ability of discovery that the Principessa had, which is what an article about her recently said. And of the tragic cloud that kept lurking over her life. Even with all her money and the good that she did people, that cloud lurked. And of course it got her, as you well know.

Because Horty's dead. As you well know. Which is what I started out to tell you the details about when you asked me. Well, it was when we were lunching on the terrazzo of the Palazzo. One of those gold June days that Venice has. I'll go right into it and not dwell on it: Horty was bitten by something, some kind of terrible spider, and blood poisoning killed her before we knew it. Guess where the spider was? In a peach. Living at the core of a great big beautiful Italian peach from the sea orchards of the Mediterranean. Horty cried out and fainted. We'd all had a lot of champagne. By the time we got her to the hospital she was dead. Doctor said it was rank poison and that Horty was wildly allergic to it. When she broke the peach open out sprung the horrible black spider. I saw it in a flash. And before she knew it, it had stung her into the bloodstream of her thigh, right through pure silk Italian brocade. I'll never eat a peach again, I'll tell *you*. All Venice was upset. The Archbishop conducted the funeral himself. Horty'd left quite a few *lire* to the Church. We forgot to unscrew the horse's outfit, but when the funeral procession passed by, all the gondoliers took off their hats. Those Italianos!

And I am the new Principessa—except of course I am not a Principessa. But the Italians insist on calling me the new Principessa. The Palazzo is mine. Who ever dreamed that *I* would get the Palazzo? When the will was opened back in Texas they read where Horty had given the place to me! I almost had a heart attack. The will said "to my best friend." But what in the world will I do with a Palazzo, I said. I have not the vast fortune that Horty had. But you have all the paintings of the famous dead American, they said. Sure the family have all fought me for the paintings of the dead American painter. Just let somebody find something good and everybody else tries to get it. Like a bunch of ants. That ever happen to you? They couldn't care less about the Palazzo. But the paintings are something else. The Museum has offered half a million dollars for one. I will not sell yet. And that man that peed in the fire died drunk and broke. Ever hear of such a thing? But they say the pollution is just eating up the paintings. *And* the Palazzo. So far *I'm* safe, but I wonder for how long? And the very town is sinking. Venice is a little lopsided. I don't know where to go. I hardly know how I got here. Sometimes I think who am I where am I? That ever happen to you? But the Texas Principessa is a saint in Venezia. Better not say anything in this town against Horty, I'm telling you. Those Italianos speak her name with reverence and the Archbishop says her name a lot in church. I have offered the horse to the Church, without outfit, but the Archbishop suggested—he's so cute, with a twinkle in his eyes, those *Italianos!*—the Archbishop suggested that *il cavallo* stay where it is. Because it is an affectionate monument for the townspeople, particularly the gondoliers. They point it out to tourists. I hear they're selling little replicas near the Vatican. The sculptor is very upset. He's made many more sculptures (not of horses) but nobody ever paid much attention to any of his other work. Isn't everything crazy? Aren't our lives all crazy? Some days I can't believe any of it. Sometimes I want to go home but I hear Texas is just as crazy. Anyway, that's the story of Horty Solomon da Filippo, the Texas Principessa. Which is what you asked me about, isn't it?

But one more thing. Next morning after the funeral I saw below the terrazzo something sparkling in the dew, something pure silver with diamonds and rubies and emeralds—like something Horty would've worn—and I saw that it was a gorgeous web. And there in the center, all alone, was the horrible black insect that I am sure was the one that had lived at the heart of the peach that killed the Texas Principessa and brought the Palazzo to me. How could something so ugly and of death make something like that . . . so *beautiful*? I had the oddest feeling, can't describe it. That ever happen to *you*?

Well, that's the story, what you asked me. What happened.

ARTHUR BOND

Remember man named Arthur Bond had a worm in his thigh. Had it for years, got it in the swampland of Louisiana when he was a young man working in the swampland. Carried that worm for all his life in his right thigh. Sometimes for quite a spell Arthur Bond said it stayed peaceful, other times twas angry in him and raised hell in him, twas mean then and on some kind of a rampage Arthur Bond said, stung him and bit him and burnt him, Arthur Bond said, and itched and tickled and tormented him. Arthur Bond himself told us that he was a crazy man then.

He was sick a lot from the worm. Nest was in the sweetest part of the thigh, if you will look there on yourself and feel of it, there where the leg gets the softest and holds the warmth of the loin, halfway between the knee and the crouch, where it's mellow and full and so soft, like a woman's breast if you catch hold of it. (I have noticed that the parts of a man and a woman are a lot alike and feel the same, and why not? One God made them both, settled that in the Garden, *Man and Woman created He them,* though God knows it still don't seem to be settled in some, but don't want to get into that.)

One time worm begun to try to come out his knee, Arthur Bond said, said saw its head in a hole that had opened up in his knee. Doctors tried to pull the worm out but it broke off and drew itself back into Arthur Bond's thigh and lived on—without a head, Arthur Bond said. Jesus Christ a headless worm. Doctors saved the head, put it in a bottle of fluid and the face was pretty, face of the worm when you looked in and saw it looking at you lolling in its fluid was like a little doll's. Nobody, no doctor anywhere could kill out that infernal worm from the swampland of Louisiana living without a head in Arthur Bond's pale thigh, he died with the worm, old and vile and aflourishin, in his thigh. Poor Arthur Bond, how that worm of the swampland tormented him all his life since he was eighteen and went into the ground with Arthur Bond when he was sixty-six. But the head of the worm with its pretty doll's face still bobbles in a bottle where Arthur Bond left it when he died, to Science, at the University. Yet Arthur Bond hisself never even got to high school, idn't that funny? Went to work in the swampland when he was fourteen. If he hadn't gone to work in the swampland, wonder what his life would have been? Without the curse of the worm, I mean.

Anyway, what I'm thinking is that we can't all see in a bottle the face of our buried torment. Arthur Bond was lucky? Worm made him drink until he was sodden on the ground or a lunatic in a brothel. Was Arthur Bond lucky? Worm made him vicious, wild amok in bars, beat up women. Worm took over his life, commanded his life, he had a devil in him, a rank, vile headless devil in him, directing his life. Arthur Bond, older he grew, was at the mercy of the worm, slave of the slightest wish of the worm. Let me tell you two examples. Worm seemed to take it out on women worst of all. Heat of a woman sent that thing into a crazed-out fit. Got to where women wouldn't get close to poor Arthur Bond, they certainly didn't want to be mashed and rolled on like a steamroller, not to mention choked to death, or twisted like an insane chiropractor was ahandlin 'em, worm'd get aholt of that leg of Arthur Bond and jerk it like a crazy dancer. Course somebody that ud awanted that kind of a thing, that kind of a fightin thing, ud a called the leg of Arthur Bond a leg of gold and sought it out; but wasn't nobody like that come to him and guess Arthur Bond ought to have thanked God for it, he'd a died a horrible death of convulsions and probly a broken neck; people stayed away from Arthur Bond. This made Arthur Bond even more lonely and naturally led him to drink more whiskey. Whiskey was puredee wildfire to the worm. Then Arthur Bond would knock down people and break up chairs and bash a man's head in with a bottle. When he killed a man in an alley, where he said the man accosted him to rob him and in self-defense cut half his face off with the butt of a beer bottle, he begged the doctor again to do anything, to even cut off his leg, for when he sobered up he was horrified at what the worm had done, killed a man, and he didn't know what the thing would do next. But the doctor wouldn't amputate. He said he wasn't sure where the worm had his hind part, his vile tail, whether maybe twas in the very groin of Arthur Bond, maybe even in his sack and curled around his balls. Naturally the next thought was was it in his member, my God was his member now a part of the worm, it was too much to suffer and seeing that the worm could possibly take over his body, his whole flesh and body and Lord God with Arthur Bond's head, Arthur Bond's own head of yellow hair and green eyes, that he could finally be just the walkin worm itself with head of yellow hair and green eyes, Arthur Bond went crazy and tried to kill hisself and the worm by drinking a glass of rat poison. He was not successful and lay choking in his own bile, though it was hoped for a while that the worm was poisoned dead until it began to rustle and twinge and tingle in his thigh again, as if to say hello Arthur Bond you fool; so both lived on.

Now the worm struck in vengeance at him. Crazed by the poison it whipped him to the ground. And he died rank green and foaming. People said that in the casket the body of Arthur Bond was in such a sudden trembling from time to time under the continued whippings of the worm that the casket holding Arthur Bond rocked and jumped so much funeral home had to fasten it down to the floor with strong ropes, man'd come in from the woods with his wife to pay his two dollars a month on his Funeral Layaway Plan that the Funeral Home gives, said now what's Arthur Bond trying to do now, crazy drunk, trying to ascend up like the Savior so they have to tie him down? Man'd had a few drinks himself and said if Savior takes up Arthur Bond what'll he do with the rest of us in Sands County tried to live like Christians? Must surely be end of the world, 's wife said, if violent men are taken. Worm had triumphed so and had shrunken the body of Arthur Bond so much to skin and bones looked like it'd sucked his flesh away. Twas like they was aburying the worm that was dressed up to look like a nightmare Arthur Bond, like they was aburyin a worm awearin Arthur Bond's body like a costume for a man.

One more thing more and I'm done talkin about it. Often wondered if the worm lives on in the man's grave or died with him; but didn't matter did it? somebody said. If it's not one worm in the grave it's another, isn't it? somebody said. And a thought's been in my mind that won't vanish, and tis the following, that worms in the grave are worms of death in the dark, and the worm in Arthur Bond was a wild live thing among us all, in the light, we all seen its workings in the daylight, now that I see more about it, oh a very special fearsome thing of our life, very unusual, can't get the word for what it seems to me it twas, can't get it out of my mind some days, and especially nights; in my mind come to me that maybe twas put in Arthur Bond by the very hand of God, it will seem to me in my thinking then when I can't get it out of my mind almost like, my God, almost like the worm of Arthur Bond's got into my mind, God help me a worm in your *mind*, worse ten times than one in your thigh, and I was one that lessened him the most and yet seems like am now the most taken over by thoughts of him, perplexed and restless and confounded; living power of Arthur Bond living on in my mind has begun to make me wonder something about him, something sweet about him, like he is a kind of a Saint in my mind, kind of an angel; maybe twas hand of God put a struggle in Arthur Bond to pull him and throw him and lay him down, to show His mighty works like the Scriptures say, and finally let him go on, free, finally, to a new life hereafter and a better one; had to be better, couldn't be worse'n what he had, pore Arthur Bond, was kind of a Saint; was worm God's worm? Did God put a worm in a man's thigh to show me something, used a worm to show me something and to win eternal life for a man in the hereafter, to be a Saint, to be an Angel, my God the workings of Jehovah's ways, a worm to make an Angel, oh Lord why is there so much darkness in this life before we see the light of things your ways are strange your ways are dark before we see the light.

WHERE'S ESTHER?

◻▬◻

How could we know *that* was what it was? That we were losing
a whole person? We were having a ball. While before our eyes
Esther Haverton was having a downward plunge to—I don't
know what to call it. It began in the Fall, lasted most of the
season, Easter saw it over and Esther at Greenfarm.

Well, she always bent the old elbow a *lot*—who doesn't? But
I mean *lots* when the onset of this started—whatever it is—coming last Fall (now, looking back, we know). Starting at 11 A.M.,
onze heures, that bejeweled hand went right for the Vodka Martini with a deadly grip, oh my dear!

Why didn't somebody stop her? But how could they *know?*
That she was on her way to—*this?* Anyway, what would things
have been like if we'd stopped Esther? Dreary. Morbid. Too
glum to think about. But once Esther Haverton started, you just
couldn't stop her. A whole party stopped for *her.* She was a real
entertainer, you know; a natural performer. Oh she danced and
she switched her bottom and just made everyone roar with laughter. She was here, there and everywhere, like a bird in a room. If
she fell, she was up on her feet before you could help her up; and
not one scratch! She was at all the parties, no one could wait
until she got there and when she got there they wished she hadn't
come, within ten minutes. There were some who cursed her and
accused her of insulting them, including the very host and host-

ess, who were finally upon *each other* like dog and cat. Because of Esther! *She* caused it, turned the closest friends and most devoted lovers upon each other. And how had she done it? No one could guess, could even notice signs of rupture—until suddenly there were these two intimates at each other's throat.

Nevertheless, when Esther left, all followed. The night was young! Into a restaurant, which Esther at once commanded. She was at the waiters as if they had done something personal to her, and they had only asked for her order; called them names of rankest insult, which somehow prompted all her friends to beat on the table, stomp the floor with delight, screaming "Esther!"; and even the waiters liked it.

What *made* Esther? Well, she had the laugh of all times, to begin with. It was so *verbal*. The things that laugh said! Then she just plain had the face for it: a huggable face, sweet-featured, like somebody feeding a baby—so sentimental but with the chic-est hairdo over it my dear, to let you know she meant business. What wrong could a face like that do? Until those lips started curling. They were preparing to emit foul cries, oh my dear! She had a body that rivaled the best, curving tight in various simple but exclusive creations—by somebody she had on West 55th Street, a personal designer—and topped off by a real pair of breasts. *That* I envied, considering my personal limitations. Still, as I told her, I come from a line of humble-breasted women of the Midwest. Never tell Esther Haverton anything. She'll use it back on you literally as if she'd memorized it, at the most unscrupulous time. *Why* did she have to be so unscrupulous? But she was gay-hearted and didn't mean it, I guess. Besides, as we know now, she was losing her poor—marbles? More coffee, please. I love this coffee shop. Never heard of Irish coffee in *here,* thank God! Black's best, anyway.

Thirdly, Esther had the carelessness for it! Why she didn't give a hoot. Why should she? She had all the money in the world. She just sawed her wood, and let it fall where it would, to use an old Midwestern expression. Still, nobody could care *that* little. I think the pills did it—made her tell the world to go peddle its apples. Sawed a lot of timber those pills—whatever they were—some were of colors not even in the rainbow. I got flashes of them when she opened her bag, glowing like a Tiffany lamp, my dear. Yet I never saw her take one as long as I went around with her. End with a dimpled shoulder, and a behind that went with her and not against her—you know, not fighting her—and there you have Esther!

How could anybody know that Esther was—well, I still can't believe it. She was so gay—such a character, and just the best person in the world, would give you her right arm if you asked for it and with her diamond bracelet on it—that's Esther! Yet, here she was, going rockers. We thought it was her natural wit. Anyway, her demeanor in public grew to such infamous proportions and resounded to such acclaim that she was the most vaunted guest. Her profanity increased to dazzling proportions. Esther would slap out a nasty word that would splatter all over a place like she'd thrown a messy pie. It was generally against somebody in our bunch—somebody she had apparently been good friends with, and then this—"You——!" That person would storm out. A phone call the next day got the whole thing aright. People were so forgiving of Esther. Thank goodness, now that I think about it, sober, and see that she was going bonkers. But I don't know how she got by with it, I swear. Anybody else would have had their heads knocked off, but not Esther. Of course they were all drunk, but even then! But thank goodness, we were all forgiving of her, knowing what we do now.

The next day on the phone: "Sugar, I don't remember a word of it. If I said it, forget it. Come for a hair at six." You'd be there at six. By eight you'd had your head knocked off again. Why was that? Why did we sanction that?

Oh, Esther! Racing at night through the streets of gold and laughter, drink here, run on there, drink yonder; and suddenly they were telling you it was 4 A.M. Who cared? Heaven could wait! On to somebody's place. Dawn! and Esther absolutely in-candescent. At those times she was like a blazing serpent, flashing and striking. She caused people to surpass themselves beyond their wildest dreams. It was the *responses* to Esther that held people to her. What you heard yourself say to her was magnificent. What would we have been without her? She made us—*marvelous!* Why she could have led us to the terrace and told us to jump out and fly, and we'd have flown—*somehow*. Esther put wings on you! Once I did a whole soft-shoe routine—complete with rideout—it was at somebody's penthouse—on an open terrace nineteen flights up—and I'd never soft-shoed in my life, couldn't again. Because of Esther! She made wonders out of us. Isn't that weird? Like she had some kind of—you know—*power* over us.

Esther, lying there drab in that room at Greenfarm and not herself at all. If I didn't know her so well, I'd say she was a changeling—that somebody kidnapped Esther and replaced her with a blah stranger. Who wants that nothing person lying there? Another person, that's all, could be anybody, why that's an ordinary person lying there, not Esther. Where's Esther? This calm person lying there is not Esther. As though she existed out of booze. Vodka made Esther! Pour several drinks into this person and out develops who we call Esther! Don't pour the booze, you get *this*. I'm beginning to see. A sober view of Esther, you might say. The most boring conversations—Unity pamphlets strewn around. Why Esther doesn't know Unity from Simplicity—the patterns, I mean. Sweetie, she's an *agnostic*. Only two things she cares about are Dior and Majorska, and she'd cut that in half if she could wear a Vodka bottle designed by Dior; just *dress* in it, my dear. Well, they can have whoever *that* is. That's not Esther! "Where's Esther?" I kept wanting to say. "Who are *you?*" I kept wanting to say. "I don't believe we've met." You zombie! Oh, I need a laugh. Some drinks and a laugh. But with *Esther*.

Well, the whole thing has rather sobered me up. A week on the wagon, without Esther, during which time I've done me some thinking over coffee, as I am right now, and a change is coming over my mind. I'm going to say it. I don't even feel like going back to Greenfarm to visit Esther. She's beginning to shape up in my mind's eye as something I can do without. Why, I've been thinking of some of the things she said about me in public. They're beginning to come back to me, over coffee. I'm beginning to take them seriously (I mean *I* can be serious, too). God damn it. I mean, I'm not a fat-ass, like she called me several times, and once at a seated dinner. And perhaps I am a little flat —you know, like I said—but why did Esther bring *that* to the public eye by shouting it out at lunch at *Maude Chez Elle*? I feel like disliking Esther now. I feel like she *wanted* to hurt me. *In vino veritas,* my dear. All the terrible things she did to us and said to us are dawning back over me after a week of black coffee, and now I'm going to say it: Who needs Esther Haverton? Screw her! Isn't that right? I mean, to hell with Esther! I mean, good riddance.

Well, I guess I'm taking too sober a view. Thinking too much. A stiff drink *does*—may I add—keep you from taking *too* sober a view towards things, keeps you from thinking too much. Maybe I should just go on with the bunch. Heaven can wait. You only come around this way once. I mean, life is hard enough. This isn't *church!* Why should I go on worrying about Esther Haverton! Maybe I should just go on with the bunch. But why go on with that bunch without Esther. Those creeps. I'm mixed up! Let's face it: we need her. In the absence of Esther we are nothing—just about like what *she* is now, without booze. Jesus, it's like we drank Esther. Oh I'm going crazy. When I go into a place where we used to go, with everybody calling, "Where's Esther? Where's Esther?" I feel like a damned ghost. As if nobody saw *me.* And I hear myself asking the same question. "Where's Esther?"

I must admit that the other night, before I went on an alcohol-free diet, on one of our sans-Esther sprees, I found myself, in the absence of Esther, imitating her. Well, I was knocked on my backside within one minute! Do you know what? Only Esther can do it. I feel so drab, so dull, so dead, so plain. And I'm feeling crazy. Nerves jumping out of my skin; rattling the coffee cup. And who sleeps? Just can't find that spot in the bed —and when I think I have, guess who's in it? Old Sleeping Beauty, dozing sweet as a choirboy—which he definitely is *not.* I flee from *that.* Esther knows.

Last night I dreamt I went into the most beautiful bar, dark and cool, deep cushions, soft music: and who do you think was there, elbow on bar, Martini hoisted? Yep, Miss You-know-who: divine Esther! Tongue like a serpent's, poised to strike. Life began! All afternoon we laughed and drank. We drank and we drank. And I was my old self again. Because of Esther. The bar was ours. We never fought, not once. We drank the world away, laughing and laughing. "I want Esther!" I cried when I woke up in the dark. "Esther, Esther! Come back!"

Who wants this life, without the old days? But I tell you they are surely gone. I can see that a mile a minute, now. All those good times, all that laughing—gone. Oh I think I need some help. I don't know what to do. If I drink I'm like a bad Esther—and anyway, what's a drink without her? If I don't drink, I'm like Esther now, drab, dull, dead, plain. Will somebody please tell me what to do? Now that you've heard a little of it? To get over what's happened to Esther?

PRECIOUS DOOR

◻▬◻

For Reginald Gibbons

Somebody's laying out in the field," my little brother came to tell us. It was eight o'clock in the morning and already so hot that the weeds were steaming and the locusts calling. For a few days there had been word of a hurricane coming. Since yesterday we had felt signs of it—a stillness of air followed by an abrupt billowing of wind; and the sky seemed higher, and it was washed-looking.

"Must be a drunken mill man sleeping in the weeds, or a hobo. Could even be your Uncle Bud, God knows," my father told me; "go see what it is."

"Come with me," I asked my father. "I'm scared."

What we found was a poor beaten creature who did not answer my father's calls. My father and I carried the unconscious person onto the back porch and laid him on the daybed.

"I wish you wouldn't let the children see that," my mother said, and drew back into the darkness of the house like her own shell.

"He may be dying," my father said, "can't rouse him. Call the doctor, son, then get me some warm water. Hey," my father called loudly at first and then lowered his voice to a soft summons, "Hey, friend, hello; hello . . ."

The battered friend did not budge, but he was breathing, now quite heavily, almost gasping. The warm water cleaned away some of the blood that was like paste on his lips and cheeks, and then some cool water stroked back his dark hair from his brow; and we saw in that moment when his face and his look came clear to us what would have been called a beautiful young girl if it had been a girl; but it was a man. Something shining came through the damaged face and we knew we had brought a special person into our house out of the weeds of the field. When my father pulled back the stained shirt of the stranger and saw something, he told the children (I was twelve and the oldest) to go outside in the yard. I did not go far but hid under the yellow jasmine against the screen and listened.

"Pardner, you might not make it," I heard my father say, "if the doctor don't hurry up and get here. Because somebody's cut you with a knife." And in another moment I heard my father say, "Who did this to you? Cut you like this?" There was no sound from the wounded stranger. "Hanh?" my father murmured tenderly, "who hurt you like this? Hanh? He can't hear me or he can't talk. Well, you try to rest until the doctor comes," I heard my father say softly. At that moment I felt so sorry for this stranger lying silent in our house that I suddenly cried, there under the yellow jasmine.

The hurricane that was said to be coming toward us from down off the deep southern Gulf kept reaching at us. Now we could smell it; and quick wind, then rain, had turned over us, whipped away, turned back on us. Now it really was close on us and my father guessed we were going to get it. Storms scared my father where little else did. He felt afraid in our old house and always took us to the high school basement. "Mary, you and the children go on to the high school and hurry up," my father called. At this I rushed into the house.

"I'll stay with my father and the hurt man," I announced. There was going to be a discussion of this, but little time was left for it; and I could see that my father was glad to have me stay.

The storm came nearer. It threw down a limb of a hickory tree across the road and a driving rain hit against the side of our house for a few minutes, then stopped.

"It's coming," my father said. "We can't stay out here on this screen porch. Latch the screen door and move things away from the open. We'll move the hurt man into the parlor. What's your name, friend?" I saw my father put his ear to the young man's mouth.

My father lifted up the stranger and carried him like a child inside the house to the parlor, where few people went. It was a cool shadowy room used only for special occasions. It looked like my father wanted to give the wounded man the best we had to give.

I covered things on the porch and pushed things back and brought some firewood to the parlor. "I thought we could build a fire in the fireplace," I announced. "That'd be fine," my father said. "You know how to do it, like I taught you." I saw that he had made a pallet on the floor with the mattress from the daybed.

"Help me put our friend on the pallet," father asked.

When we lifted our friend I was at first afraid to touch him so close, to hold him, but in my trembling grasp his body felt friendly and like something of mine—and more: he felt beloved to me. He must have felt something of the same to my father, for I saw my father's face filled with softness in the light of the fire. Now the fire was going and brightness and warmth were coming from it, suddenly bringing to life on the wall the faces of my grandmother and grandfather who had built fires in this fireplace; they looked down from their dusty frames upon us. Suddenly the man murmured, "Thank you."

"God bless you, pardner," my father said, and I patted the man's head. My breath was caught in my throat, that he was with us.

The storm was here, upon us. Our little house began to shudder and creak under it. Though we didn't say anything, my father and I were afraid that Doctor Browder would never be able to get out to us now; for when we could see what would be the dirt road in front of our house we saw a flowing stream; and when we saw in the lightning some trees fall over the road along the field we knew the doctor could not get to us.

We began to nurse the wounded stranger, my father and I. We washed his wounds. And my father prayed, there in the yellow firelight in the swaying little house my grandfather had built for his family and whose roof and walls and floor had been their safe haven and now ours, a shelter for generations in a world none of us had known beyond this place and a few nearby little towns. My father prayed over the young man, laying his carpenter's hand on the brow of the suffering man and clasping his hand in love and hope. And then I heard my father's words, "He's dead."

We said the Lord's prayer together on our knees by the dead stranger's pallet. The rhythmic clanging of the wind against something of metal, our washtub maybe, tolled over our prayer. And when we opened our eyes at the end of the prayer, my father said, "He looks like somebody." I knew he did, in that moment, for I saw in my sorrow his somehow blessed brow and his pale full lips, his dark bitter hair, familiar as kin. The wind tolled the washtub. My heart was heavy and aching and my face felt flooded but no tears came for a long time. And when they came, I sobbed aloud. My father held me and rocked me as though I were three, the way he used to when I was three; and I heard him cry, too.

I felt for the first time the love that one person might have for another he did not know, for a stranger come suddenly close. The great new swelling love I had for the stranger visitor to our house now filled our parlor. And I hoped then, with a longing that first touched me there on that wild and tender night in our faraway parlor in that hidden little town, that one day I would know the love of another, no matter how bitter the loss of them would be.

In the toiling hurricane that whipped at our house, our trees and fields, lightning showed us what the storm had already done to the world outside. "This must be the worst ever to hit this country," my father said. "God hold down our roof over our heads and receive the spirit of this poor man."

"And protect Mama and Sister and Joe in the school basement," I added.

The flood rose to our front porch. My father and I sat lone
with the stranger. My father had washed him and taken away his
clothes that had been stained again by his wounds and dressed
him in a fresh shirt and workpants. The dead being was a presence in the parlor. We waited.

The sun flared out and streamed down on the waters that
covered the town in the unsettled midafternoon. We looked out
and saw a whole world of things floating by. We ourselves felt
afloat, among them. And then the rain began again, right out of
the sunshine, and put it out. It turned very dark.

"We're lost," my father told me. "We'll all be washed away."

"God please stop the rain," I prayed. The fire had burnt our
supply of wood and it was sinking fast.

"Go get a candle from the bedroom, son," my father asked.
"We'll put it by the body so that it won't lie in the darkness."

When my father called the stranger "the body" I felt, for the
first time, a sense of death and loss. Our friend whom I loved
and grieved for, as though I had long known him, was gone.
Only "the body" remained. Now I understood the hardest part
of death, the grief at gravesides, and what was given up there so
bitterly. It was the body.

What interrupted our mourning was a figure at the window.
A figure of flying hair and tearing clothes with wild eyes and a
face of terror stared through veils of water.

"Somebody," I gasped to my father. "Somebody wants in
from the storm."

"Hot damn Lord help us!" my father cried out, as afraid as
I had ever seen him.

We struggled with the front door. When we unlocked it,
it blasted against us and knocked us down to the floor, and it
seemed to hurl the blowing figure into the house. We saw that
it was a young man in tattered clothes and a thick beard. The
three of us were able to close the front door and to barricade it
with the heavy hat tree, oaken and immemorial, standing in the
same place in the hallway since first my eyes found it. Suddenly
it had life.

"Worst storm I've ever seen," my father said to the man. The man nodded and we could see that he was young.

When he walked into the parlor, drawn there by the candle-light and the fire, he saw the man on the pallet and lunged to it and fell to his knees and cried out and wept over the dead man. My father and I waited with our heads bowed, holding together in bewilderment under the fire's guttering sound and the soft sobbing of the young man. Finally my father said, "He was lying in the field. We tried to help him." But the man stayed on his knees beside the figure on the pallet, sobbing and murmuring. "Boy, boy, boy, boy . . ."

Then my father went to the kneeling man and put a blanket around his shoulders and said softly,

"I'll get some hot coffee, pardner."

I was alone with the two men, dead and alive, and I felt scared but full of pity. I heard the man speak softly, now, in a gasping language I could not understand—or I was too choked with astonishment. And then I heard him say clearly, "Put your head on my breast, boy! Here. Now, now boy, now; you're all right, now. Head's on my breast; now, now."

When my father came into the parlor with coffee, he put it down at the side of the grieving man. "Sit back, now," he said, "and warm yourself."

When the man sat back and pulled the blanket around his shoulders, my father asked him for his name.

"Ben," he said. "He and I are brothers. I brought him up." He would not drink his coffee but looked down at the figure of his brother and said, "We were in the boxcar comin from Memphis. Goin to Port of Houston. We had a plan." And then he cried out softly, "I didn't go to hurt him. I swear to God I didn't mean to hurt him." And then he held his brother's head to his breast and rocked him.

My father and I were sitting on the cold springs of the daybed whose mattress was the dead man's pallet, and I could feel the big, strong wrap of my father's arm around me, pulling my head to his breast. I felt my everlasting love for him, my father, but in my head rang Ben's words, *we had a plan*. My blood rushed in exciting hope. And that hope was that one day I would have enough courage to be this tender as this man was now at this moment, if ever I was lucky enough to find someone who would take my tenderness. And to have, together with someone, a plan. I knew, at this moment, that that was the thing I would look for in my life. And who could hold that from me or tell me I could not have it, that unspeakable tenderness that already I felt to grow in my breast as my blood rushed through me and which was the gift of Ben and his brother to me.

And out of this passion, as though I had been blinded by it and now could see again, I saw Ben lifting up the body of his dead brother from the pallet.

"Thank you for tending to my brother," he said to us, solemnly, and turned to go. "My brother and me will go, now."

"But you'll drown," my father told him. "Wait until the flood is over, for God's sake."

My father stood in front of Ben as if to stop him; but in a growling voice and with a look of darkness, Ben said,

"Get out of our way, my friend."

Ben was going, holding the nestled body against his breast. My father and I stood still as our visitors out of the flood went back into it, through the barricaded front door and into the storm.

"Goodbye, goodbye," I whispered.

"God be with you and God forgive me for letting a man who killed his brother go," my father said, almost to himself.

Through the window we saw, in the fading daylight, the brothers move through the water. Ben was nestling the body of his dead brother in his arms and pressing his head upon his breast. "They'll never make it," my father said.

"But where are they going?"

"They're in God's hands," answered my father. "Although Ben was a murderer, I feel he is forgiven because he came back and asked forgiveness," father said. "The love of God works through reconciliation."

"Father," I asked. "What is reconciliation?"

"It means coming back together in peace," my father answered. "Although there was torment between the two brothers, they have been brought back together in peace."

Through the gray rain, moving through the rising waters, they disappeared, the two men of "reconciliation" who had come back together in peace. My eyes clung to them as long as they could see, trying to hold the loving enemy brothers back from the mist they were slowly melting into.

The days after the rain were worse than the rain. The river swelled and covered farms and roads and many people sat on top of their houses. Though the water around us fell to the lower land, since we were on a rise, my father and I were marooned. The sun had a new hotness, the world was sodden and the smell was of soaked things and rotting things. There were snakes and sobbing bullfrogs and there were crying peafowls in the trees and red crawfish flipped in the mud. In the remoteness and seclusion of our place, through the strangeness of our days, I wept for Ben and his brother so many times I can't remember. A new feeling had been born in me, obscure then but clearer through time. A man in a boat stopped to tell us of the wonders of the storm: gin cotton lay over an acre of water like white flowers; a thousand sawmill logs were aloose, a church steeple had been carried away with its bell, miraculously afloat, and stood gonging like a buoy near Trinity bridge.

And for a while it was reported that a floating door bearing the bodies of two men was seen moving on the wide river through several towns. At one town people had said that when it came through there, the raft was whirling in the currents as though a demon had hold of it; but the men stayed put, though it was considered that they were dead. And another time, near the river's mouth where it flows into the Gulf, they said it rode the crests of dangerous rapids so serenely that it was easy to see the two men, one, alive and fierce, holding the other, dead. I waited to hear more, but after this, there were no further reports of the precious door.

IN THE ICEBOUND HOTHOUSE

◻▬◻

It is true that I have not been able to utter more than a madman's sound since my eyes beheld the sight. I've lost speech. And so they have asked me to write. Since you are a poet, write, they told me. Little do they know what they might get. Little, even, do I.

So I'm writing this in the Detention House, where they're holding me until I can give word. Little do they know what I might give. Little, even, do I. A "suspicious witness" they name me. I am, certainly, a witness—or was. But was there no "suspicious witness" for *me*? To help me explain? Maybe the dead naked girl was my witness. Had she watched from the high window of the Biology Lab? As I loitered near the icebound hothouse? As I knocked on the ice-armored door? As I peered through the ice-ribboned windows; as I waved to the sullen Nurseryman inside? No use wasting time on that, her lips are forever sealed, cold, kissless and silent. But the dead naked girl certainly was my key to the hothouse; it was she who, at last, gave me entrance, opened the icebound door barred to me heretofore. Through her death. Before my eyes, at the sound of crashing glass, sprang open the door, shattering ice over me. I got in! Oh I got into the hothouse all right. Her sacrifice! The diving girl's sacrifice! I notice as I write how my mind throws rapid thoughts. Not like my mind. Which usually operates in languor; at slow bubble; and darkening and thickening, like a custard at simmer. Symptom of my bad head.

But would not working among green things make for a certain bliss? Harmony, peacefulness? What had disturbed the Nurseryman that he was drunken among his growing things? A crocked Nurseryman in the hothouse! Drunk among his plants, drunk in the greenhouse. Drunk in the shooting galaxy of Fuchsias, knocking his head into the Comet blossoms. His drunken breath scalding the Maidenhair Fern; alcohol fumes over the Babybreath. Pissed among the tuberous Begonias.

Seedsman in a warm nursery of sprouts and tendrils, so close to the making of leaf and bud, to the workings of bulb and seed, wouldn't you think the nursing man might be tranquil? What ate at you, green man, that you drowned your sorrows? What blighted your joy, nurse, that you sought relief in the deadening of it? What is the canker worm that ate at your roots? If you, among healing flowers and leaf, got a kind of madness, what about us lost in the bloomless? If the green be mad, then what of the dry? What does it mean that the garden is greening and the gardener withering? For if the gardener walk dumb, be two sheets in the wind, what of us, who speak and are sober and have no garden? "In a world of grief and pain, flowers bloom, even so," to quote an old saying. Even so.

Even so, I was haunted by the drunken Nurseryman. Plotzed, smashed, a bag on. The Phlox grows so straight and is so festered with blossoms: what of the afflicted hand that shakes as it tends, and scatters the blossoms? How can a quivering hand tie a leaning stem? Without a clear head—hung over in the greenhouse—can bulbs be sorted? In a plague of Whitebug was both nurse and patient afflicted? Then who nurses the nurse?

There for most of the month of January, everything was frozen cracking silver. We'd had a "silver freeze": rain all night, a sudden drop in temperature, everything brittle, silvery, ice-encased, breakable trees cracking, streets and sidewalks paved with ice, houses like iced cakes. Fierce, burning world, untraversable, a harsh world of thorns, daggers, blades. Passing every frozen morning in this silver winter, the elegant greenhouse, tropical oasis on that desert campus, in the month of January when everything was frozen silver, I saw him weaving inside the ice-gripped glass. Under a frozen sky I moved like a cripple over the frozen land. The greenhouse was a cake of ice decorated with blooms and silver windows. I could hardly see through the panes with their white icing. Yet inside I saw glimmering colors, salmon and rose and purple and red, glimmering in the roselight lampglow. I was drawn to the glow and laureate warmth of the icebound hothouse. The vision in the frozen hothouse! Glimmering and locked in the icestorm. And through the window I saw the figure of the Nurseryman. Drunk! Worming his way under hanging baskets of showering blooms, staggering around fountains of lace-leaves, lurching through fountainous palms. An evil figure? Would he harm the growing, the blooming? This lone figure, moving among the glowing blooms—he haunted me, haunts me yet. Even now.

Why does the Nurseryman drink? I questioned. Has a giant Begonia, that he nursed almost upon his bosom for weeks when it was sick, died? Has a Maidenhair Fern, fragile as a mist sprayed from an atomizer, evaporated? Did the death of delicate things drive the gardener to bottle? But does he not know, has he not heard that all flowering things fade and die? That the grass withereth when the wind blows over? All things die? Does he not know? I asked the dark of night. Living among green (the most perishable color), was he not accustomed to daily yellowing (leaf) and graying (frond); all things die . . . ? Did insidious insects arrive? That unstoppable march through the ages, millions of legs, millions of antennae moving through the centuries. Did bugs come? And do quick damage, effect sleight-of-hand change on a tray of Pansies so perfect-looking that a gardener would believe they were changeless, like china flowers? Did a dragon worm get to the Ficus tree and draw its infernal saw across the root; did a viper-like insect, thick as a snake, hatch in the very soil that caressed and gently clasped the Tree of Eden plant and in a time when it had gained its power, strengthening itself as the buds fattened, strike with one strike at the bulb of the Tree and bring an end to it? What losses a gardener suffers! But was the gardener not accustomed to devastation by insect? What was the canker eating at the roots of the Nurseryman? Did he reach for the bottle instead of the bug killer? I cannot yet understand this gardener. In his greenhouse all was order. Cleanliness; not one leaf on the floor. The rows of green were neat. But he was disordered. And lurching a little. Yet he never fell over a little cradle of nursing seedlings or crashed against a hanging *Habernaria grandiflora*. He moved cautiously through the rainy tropical leaves and the sunny blooms far away from the blue sea whose light had nourished them and given them color, far away from the hot noons, from the rain wilderness and mossy coves and humid crevices, from soft shadows of hidden glens. Like a ghost he was here, gone, then there. Sometimes I'd see his shadow falling over the green; sometimes he seemed like a statue standing in the shadow of huge leaves, head bowed, fixed like stone.

But why was I banned? Why did the Nurseryman say *no* to me; why did he turn me away when I waved to him, knocking at the bound door that was garlanded with flowers of ice? Why did he turn me away? At the first rejection, when he held up his rough Nurseryman's hand, big as a spade yet gentle enough to touch a bluet without bruising it—when he raised his big hand before me saying *no!* no admittance to the hothouse, I stepped back surprised by the inhospitality—if not cruelty—of being turned away and with that old feeling of expulsion that stabbed me. But I tried again. And again. Each time that the Nurseryman repulsed me he grew more passionate, darker, more threatening —more desperate each day. Why? Each time he reeled more, swooned more. Sometimes his rubeate face would be close to the icy glass of the door and it wavered and glowered through the frozen water. His features were then distorted and a little monstrous. His eyes were dark shadows, his face fiery and forlorn; he seemed a man of sorrows. Sometimes he seemed almost ready to admit me, to open the frozen crystal door to the faery bower of the hothouse. O tender nurse of this forbidden garden, what have you to say?

But what were my feelings as this strange denying relationship grew? At the beginning it was clear to me that I rankled because a figure of power had denied me. Defiance heated me. Rebellion dizzied me. I'd throw a stone through a window, climb to the top of the Biology Lab, which was on the top floor of a building that rose up beside the greenhouse, and drop something —hurl a chair—through the glass roof, and let in the freezing air and so burn the warm flowers, vandalizing the beautiful thing I was denied. Once because the first-grade class didn't elect a boy to be the one to take home for the weekend the class goldfish— a dreaming delicate creature wafting on golden wings through a green waving paradise—but chose a girl, the boy reached into the bowl and squished the golden fish through his fingers like pudding. I felt like that—again—after all these years. Also— beauty denied. I defied those who had held back from me, who had given me the pain of feeling not-taken. Whatever their reason, I had fallen into states of rage and accusation. Not chosen, kept outside—these feelings gave me such heartbreak at first that I wanted to vanish and hide. So abandoned, I thought I'd die, and wished to. But I rose up in defiance.

My next visit to the greenhouse was around midnight (the first had been at twilight). I had to get in. The cold was so bitter. Yet the icebound hothouse was glowing like a radiant stove. I felt that I was dying. My room in the Guest House was bleak with chill; the awful pictures of founders and donors were glaring with comfort and satisfaction. I had felt quite mad in that room of transients' odors and early American pewter, those white curtains scalloped at the bay window, that chintz. If only the Nurseryman would let me in. From the freezing cold outside I saw him in the distance in a drunken trance, there by the sunny orange tree. Seeing me, his old enemy, he held fast for a moment and I thought he was about to come to me to give me, at last, welcome—in a split second a look of yielding, of need, of almost reaching out, had crossed his body. But in another moment up slowly came the awful interdicting hand. I only showed him, in my answer, my own face of need; and then I went away.

The third time was in the early morning at daybreak. As I

stood at the ice-veiled glass door, it happened. I saw it chute. Something like the rushing sound of wings drew my glance upwards. Whatever was falling from the top of the Biology Building in another second crashed through the glass roof of the hothouse. A plume of silver steam rose and floated over the broken greenhouse. Some pressure sprang open the frozen door like a miracle, and I entered, at last, the ripe heat of the Nursery. I was admitted. I was in. The smell of humid mulch and sticky seed was close to the smell of sex, genital and just used. I was for a moment almost overcome with the eroticness of it.

And then the fog rose from the ground and from the very leaves and through the fog I saw the body. The body lay face up, flat on its back. It lay out like an anatomy lesson figure. Arms outstretched, legs spread. Who had leaped from the Biology Building into the frozen lake of the glass roof of the greenhouse? To crash and die among the ferns and blooming Oleander in the frozen month of January? And naked? My God this white body of marble skin and coal-black finest hair lying splashed among the curling ferns. Just as the diver must have envisioned it—if she had planned the leap and had not simply insanely hurled herself down. My door-opener, my admitter. She died for me, I thought.

The drunken gardener edged out of the steaming gloom of a far corner. He shook all over and now could not move, frozen with fear in the hothouse, fixed to the ground near the Camellias. Did he think the body had dropped out of the sky? Fallen like a lavish blossom, some human-like blossom that had been torn loose by the Nurseryman's jerking hand? When I came through the fog to him and we were face to face, the look between us showed how deep had been our knowledge of each other, and then he staggered free and began fidgeting mechanically about the greenhouse like a toy man. He simply bobbled and jacked round and round the greenhouse, in and out of corners and along green byways, a berserk fox-trotter. I saw the body of the young woman whole and unbroken except for a wisp of purplish blood in the corner of her pale-lipped mouth. Flesh among greengrowing things. Leaf and skin. It was the sound that I was still hearing in my ears. Flesh against glass. Stone, rock breaking through glass is different. Flesh and bone crashing through glass, as though against water—you know, without looking, that it is a body hitting the water.

Gazing down upon the greenhouse in winter might have been a bewitching experience for somebody. Rosy in the black nighttime, it would glow below through the frosty glass like a sherbet, like a giant bouquet, like some centerpiece on the white snow table of the field it rested in. Such a delectable vision, such a faery confection of glass, ice, roseglow and bloom, might finally have drawn the gazer into it. Or did Nature? Was Nature arranging a still life (*nature mort!*) in the greenhouse? Adding flesh, skin, bone, hair. But there it lay, dazzling piece of mortality, delivered to the Nurseryman and me, *ex machina*.

Now I saw the Nurseryman begin to shuffle slowly towards me and the fallen body. There he stood gazing down upon the figure for the longest time. He gazed and gazed, as the fog floated up from the freezing once-warm earth of the Nursery. Was it somebody come back? Returned to collect an old debt? Somebody leaving themselves on the Nurseryman's doorstep . . . a self-delivered foundling? How to read the answer in the gardener's eyes. Those eyes! The look of Cain was in those green orbs. I watched them change as they gazed on: now hazel, now blue, now palest green. Chameleon eyes hath the Nurseryman. Or at least half that murderer brother's look—a look of horror and a look of madness—the brute look of the ages: killer's brother. But I saw the other half of the Nurseryman's look—the lover brother's, the keeper's, Abel's look of brotherly tenderness. I, brother to each brother, one-time looker through the iced glass of the forbidden greenhouse, bundled in wool, booted feet grinding on ice, hooded with animal fur to my brow, outsider refused entry, had now arrived within.

A "Visiting Poet" is what I am. Walking around an ancient university with a hole in my breast. And not even on the faculty of this venerable institution. Visiting. Being an "invited" poet keeps me from belonging to any staff. I am a wanderer-visitor to various seats of learning, sitting in a temporary Chair. A One-Year Chair, a One-Term Chair. An academic year here, a semester there. Worst of all—surprise!—I'm not even a functioning poet. I have not produced a poem for some years. The flow has —temporarily, one hopes—frozen, shall we say. I just can't for the time being—give. Yet I go on, in the company of beginner poets in classrooms, speaking of what I can't do. Impotence instructing love. What has frozen the juices, stopped the flow in the Poet-in-Residence with the hole in his breast? You ask? Should I have an answer? If I had an answer I might go to work on it. Maybe a loss of faith? I don't know. Something's stopped. The battery fell out somewhere along the way. Where's the power? Also I became grubby. The shine gone. I felt molty. The flower off me. I felt dry. Love! Love unreturned. Do you know, *est-ce que vous savez,* you who took me from the icebound hothouse and now "detain" me, are you acquainted with fouled love? You will answer that that is a sentimental question, even unscrupulous under the circumstances. "Unscrupulous" indeed! Well, that's *your* word, not mine. I'm not trying to work up pity; nor am I trying to build up a case of self-pity, God forbid. But a poet is a person of love, whether he's producing, at the moment, or not; a person with love to give. He's also somebody who needs to get love back—for Christ's sake. You back there who the hell did you think I was, somebody giving all that passion and not getting anything back? How long did you think I could go on like that? I must admit it was my choice to go on like that. I kept hoping you'd change. That you'd come to me. Give me *something back.* And so I went on; giving, giving; went on too far, went into a territory where I couldn't turn back, where I was lost; a territory that was dark and where I felt dark feelings toward you, resentment and hate. My God, I who could love you so much. I, torn lover, who wanted to put you together with tender hands and wanted to tear you apart with the hands of a savage. Love not got back! You somewhere! Perverter! Spoiler! Perverting what was beautiful, fouling what was beautiful. Fouler! Fouler! Fouler! I don't know what kept me from striking you in those days. Because of your fear, your little lack of courage, your selfish little fear. And I keep walking around with a hole in my breast. I could have talked to the Nurseryman about this. We could have had conversations in the deepest nights and in the veiled and humid morning twilights in the healing flower-hung bloom-graced grottos and little primrose bowers, Wisteria arbors of the Nursery. He might have taken my sorrow, smoothed a little my anger, given me some of the wisdom of a gardener, helped me understand the fouling of passion, the spoiling of love. I might have shown him the photographs, the letters, even some of my early poems written in the gone days of my passion and tender love, while they were still pure feeling in me, poetry, before I found a fouling object. Love indeed! Poem-crusher! Poetry-robber! I could have spoken of betrayal, of the knife-cut of tepid love, the stabbing dagger of half-baked feeling. The Nurseryman might have begun to drink less whiskey. He might have felt needed, of service beyond the watering of mute blooms, the feeding of dumb stalks. Does nobody give a penny in Hell for another's woes? If he did not, if the gardener-Nurseryman did not, and put concern and caring for his brothers into the bottle, at least he could have allowed me the company of flowers, passing blooms for a passing visitor. Well he didn't. Even so. He'd probably have annoyed me with drunken slobber-ings, baby speech. And he couldn't have heard me or would've half-heard me ringing with booze like doorbells in his ears. But I don't know anything and this is all only conjecture. And it doesn't matter now.

But what was between those two, Nurseryman and dead girl, beautiful figure laid out almost obscenely in the leaves and blooms? And why was this sight chosen for me to see, why was I selected as a witness to it? I, no more than a passerby, enchanted by a glowing hothouse in the frozen winter, somehow possessed by a drunken Nurseryman who denied me hospitality when I most needed welcome. Or was there nothing between the two, were they strangers? And therefore was it a murder? Murder in the Biology Lab and at daybreak and the body hurled below, into the greenhouse. There was no stab wound on the perfect body; no prints of a squeezing hand on the fair throat. The classic mound that swelled gently from the bottom of the belly seemed chaste. The fair beautiful body seemed whole and perfect, had fallen, even through glass, whole and perfect, like fruit unbruised —plucked rather than fallen fruit. Was there a sign of struggle in the Laboratory? Paraphernalia overturned? Did Somebody in the heat of quarrel push her through the window? Was there a face of horror at the window when the body fell? Now I saw what passion burned in the Nurseryman's heart. Like a heaving bull. Panting and groaning, he fell upon the naked girl and clutching her to his body rolled and wallowed on the hothouse floor. If she had not already been dead, he might have killed her with his very body. Until the figure of the man and girl, combined into one strange being, half-clothed, with one head of wild and furious hair, lay still under the palms. I managed to take steps, but it was as though each step would draw up the very ground with it, as though my feet were magnets. I dragged closer and knelt to look upon this figure of violence. I saw surely that the Nurseryman was dead. I could not bring myself to touch him to see if he was breathing, but I saw no signs of breathing, heard no breath. The Nurseryman of the cold *No!*, the gardener of the icebound hothouse, had died of passion. I opened my mouth but I could not say any word. Could I have spoken, would I have greeted, at last, the Nurseryman now joined to the body of my admitter to the hothouse? The odd still figure, lasciviously spent, beautiful with white buttocks and tressed with flowing hair, and terrible, too, like a slain beast upon the floor come from the wilds into this fragile garden of poetry and blooming summer, this figure was mine. As though I had created it.

I do not know why I picked up a little spade and slid it as if I were scooping something from the softest part of the flesh of the Nurseryman where his heart hung in the dark of his breast. The spade no doubt dug his heartless heart half out. Had I withdrawn the little scoop it might have spooned out the enigmatic heart to me, like a boiled egg. I wanted the No-man's heart, now not so much in vengeance as in calm curiosity. Almost scientifically. The heart images! I imagined his heart might look like a bell. A bell aloft in the tower of his lungs. A bulb, buried in the depth of his root-veined breast. Testicles, that hung under the shaft of his neck. My God the images. Violence has brought me images. I craved the heart of the dead Nurseryman. They dug out Shelley's heart. They fought on the shore for Shelley's heart. O gardener of this garden, O lost nurse of this Nursery, unhappy and inhospitable host of the icebound greenhouse, what would your heart be like?

And there, shrouded in the warm gathering fog, I sat down with this figure, settled, now, in some kind of understanding far beyond anything I could utter, of the fallen naked girl and the passion-stilled, heart-spaded Nurseryman, and in some kind of joining of them; for strangely I felt the third, we were, somehow, beyond anything I could explain if even I had words, a trio, our experience together and one with the other would never be known but had brought us together in this union, dark brother, wild sister. And there I remained until someone would come. I felt the killing cold creeping in upon the hothouse, and the fog was wrapping us around.

But what could I have to say to those who, hearing the dawn crash, arrived to behold this vision under the palms? And, sleep-thickened, wondered of me what had happened? I was as dumb and as frozen as the gardener had been, I could have been a statue there among the steaming palms. Some did, however, when they got their senses back, recognize the young woman—a sophomore biology student from a neighboring state. The two bodies were so clenched together that they removed them as one, covered with a blanket and carried out into the cold. The little spade made a tent of the blanket as they carried the figure of violence out into the morning cold.

As they took me out of the greenhouse, a chilling vapor rose from the sodden ground. Outside I turned and saw the ruined hothouse. The blooming colors were darkened and already the leaves were blackening in poisonous blotches as if some acid had burned them, and it had only been the winter cold that had touched them. The Nursery was fouled.

My throat felt of iron; my tongue was like a club. I gargled to the questions asked of me. But my case in my head was that the girl stabbed with the spade the violating Nurseryman as I passed by and I'd broken in to be of help. This is a lie I now confess, albeit a lie never told. How can I explain what happened? You expect me to, you, my Captors. But I am afraid and speechless and have no knowledge of anything; I need a friend, someone to help me. I knew I was done for and, without words, I crowed and crooned like a baby and rocked my head No! No! when you came to tell me of my fingerprints on the spade that must have left a moon-shaped scar in the heart of the Nurseryman. The old moon in the new moon's arms. I had never thought of the heart as a moon. Moon in my breast! O moon of my heart! Maybe my old wild poetry will come again to me.

I want to go home! That house rises before me, built once more. Again on the pit floor of my life, it blows into shape before me. That house. It seemed perfect in its simplicity. Its quietness within itself. The humility of it, resting there shady under the trees; the dirt yard, the noble footworn steps. It seemed my last innocence and one of the few beautiful things of openness and plainness that I knew—the woodfire's throbbing glow rosying the room where I slept with my mother while the wind crackled the frozen branches at the window; the peaceful woodfirelight-blessed room, the warmth of the simple room in that strong sure house. Surely it led me to poetry, for it had given me early deep feeling, mornings of unnameable feelings in the silver air, nights of visions after stories told by the lamplight. But oh I see that it held a shadowed life. Even at the best of times the light in that life was contending with a shadow that came back and back and back. "I can never quite get this little handmirror clear," my mother said, "that was my mother's—and her mother's. Out of a lot of lost stuff, or broken, this little mirror has come through. But there's always been a faint little cast on it that I can never get off, can clean and clean; can hardly see it but it's there; you can wipe it off and look back at it later and there it is, come back, that cast, just right there, there in the left-hand corner, see it? Wonder what it is, guess it's in the very glass."

On the frosted frontdoor pane was the figure of a mysterious rider with a plumed hat astride a phantom horse the color of a cloud, silver-gray, with plumed cloud-colored mane and plumed silver tail—a Prince? a Knight? But why, I wonder now, was he rearing back as if startled by the knocker at the door, challenging the arriver at the door, "Who are you and why have you come here?" Who put the rider there? Who of my ancestors put the rider there? Why, there were warm stories told at night, loving as often as fearful, as often gay as melancholy. Who among the old dwellers of these rooms was dark? Who put the dark host at the door, rearing suspicious horse and suspicious plumed dark rider shying back from the homeless traveler, from the guest half-welcome? Even for me when sometimes I returned and came, once more, to that door, tired and wanting home. Even there. Even then. O rider I am done for, the brothers in me have for the last time fought, the dark one won, darkness prevailed, O rider why did I ever come to this university, O why did I not resign when I saw the emptiness of this school, the failed professors, these classes in poetry, these students, this town, the depth of my loneliness and hunger?

Tongues of Men
and of Angels

◻▬◻

I started out to tell about what became of two cousins and their uncle who loved them, according to what the older cousin told me. But some of their kinfolks' lives would have to be told if you're going to talk at all about the cousins and their uncle. So what I have to tell about first is all one family, what I heard told to me and what I watched happen. I have been here in this family's town longer than any of the family, and have in my long time noted—and wonder if you have, ever—the turning around of some people's lives, as if some force moved in them against their will: runaways suddenly arrived back, to the place they fled; berserk possessed people come serene; apparently Godblessed people overnight fall under malediction.

Joe Parrish

Blanch, Louetta's mother, ran away from everybody— mama, papa, husband, child—with a good young Mexican that had worked on the East Texas place, named Juan Melendrez from the Rio Grande Valley. Blanch's husband, Louetta's father, named Joe Parrish, went *loco* at this. He was found lying in the mud of the pigpen, sockeyed and slobbering from what was thought to be a stroke, staring up at the mudcaked pigs grunting over him. And again, some fishermen came upon him prostrate

in the steaming weeds of the river. Cottonmouth water mocca-
sins glided all around him yet no snake bothered him. He's gone
crazy, said the town, and tried to persuade Blanch's folks to put
him in the insane asylum, but they would not. A black woman
was brought by Kansas Tate to pull out the devils that had taken
hold of Joe Parrish, but she said that they were deeper into him
than any she had ever witnessed. She told how devils put roots
into a person that thread around his liver and his lights and rope
his heart and grow thorns into his lungs. This is why he foams
and screams and pants for breath. But then Joe Parrish quieted
for a while and sat on the porch, calm. Until one night he was
missing. He was gone, leaving Louetta a tragic orphan in her
grandparents' house at fourteen.

Now a lot of years later, Joe Parrish came back one night,
and he wanted to see his daughter and to get her to help him,
but found no one left on the place but the uncle. Joe Parrish told
that he was escaped from the Penitentiary, a murderer-convict
that had killed six Mexicans in the Rio Grande Valley. A winged
man with black wings had come near him and unfurled and
curled back again a thin black tongue like a horned toad's and
said, "Get even. Pay back the Mexicans." Now he had broken out
and had come back barefooted and in rags, wanting to hide on
the place.

When told that Louetta had drowned in the well, his old
bedevilment took him again, and again the black-winged figure
came and licked out his black tongue and suggested that at the
bottom of the well Joe Parrish would possibly find better times
for himself. Before the uncle's eyes Joe Parrish lept into the very
well, which had long been without water and was only a cistern
of deep thick mud. Flashlights revealed only the yellow soles of
Joe Parrishes naked feet lying on a floor of black mud, like a pair
of turned-over houseshoes. When the rescuers, about fifty of
them gathered from all over the county, threaded through the
well-wheel a rope with an iron claw at the end of it and hooked
it to Joe Parrishes feet (some said the claw looked like the Devil's
pitchfork but it was used to grab along the riverbottoms for
bodies of the drowned) they strained together as if they were

lifting an enormous bucket of wellwater. Suddenly there was a socking sound deep in the well and its echoing was a sound of horror, and then the tuggers, who had fallen back upon one another upon the ground, saw swaying at the crest of the wellwheel, dripping of mud and blood and clawed by the iron claw, two naked feet. Joe Parrishes feet had been pulled from their ankle sockets. The whole town was sickened for a time by the feet of Joe Parrish. They poured bag after bag of lye into the accurst well on the back porch of the old house and then strong men laid a cement hood over the top of what was now Joe Parrishes tomb. Except for his feet, which of course many thought ought to have been thrown into the well. Instead, they were stolen from the Funeral Home where they had been taken —where else could you take them?—and it was not known whether they were embalmed or whether they were just rank feet in the hands of the thief.

And then began the rumors of the feet of Joe Parrish, one foot or both, cropping up here and there. Some reported seeing a footless man crawling through the woods, howling for his lost feet. But the two feet of Joe Parrish began to haunt people. One person said she saw one of the feet walking on the railroad track one moonlight night and that it chased her; another screamed that a foot was in her bed when she got in, but nobody in her household could find it; and sure enough a woman at a dinner table, wanting the butter, asked somebody to please pass the foot —the town was so foot-haunted; and another, way down in the Rio Grande Valley in a Mexican town, reported being followed home from the midnight shift by two steadily tromping feet. Finally this all stopped. Joe Parrishes feet were never found, or haven't been yet. God knows where they came to rest. You will say that every town old enough to have its stories has some hand or a head or has something walking without peace to haunt people. This town was not any different. But since I am interested in the old places that are lost and the stories in them and how they were almost lost until they were saved by some who had ears and tongues and mouths, I thought I'd mention the story of Joe Parrish.

But one question: what had Joe Parrish done to deserve all this? Is there no meaning to some lives? Doesn't it sometimes seem that a life has reeled through its time without making any sense to the rest of us? Or is it that Joe Parrish was just a toy of a bad angel, a poor soul crazed by jealousy-madness and vengeance, that lept headfirst into a well of mud at the bidding of a bad angel. Are there such angels?

But I have some more to tell.

INEZ MELENDREZ MCNAMARA

Two women arrived in town one day. One was an older but beautiful woman, and the other a beautiful brown young girl of some fifteen years with flowing coarse black hair. It was Blanch and her Mexican daughter, Inez Melendrez. Juan Melendrez had been killed beside Blanch and Inez in the truck as they drove along a road back of Refugio, Texas. They said that three gunshots shot out of the fruit groves. Blanch saw Juan burst into blood as though he were a punctured wine sac, and had enough composure to grab the wheel and put on the brake. Inez was thrown through the door and into the air and came down like somebody under a parachute of black hair into a watermelon field and landed astraddle a large watermelon. Blanch couldn't stop screaming. A car stopped and helped. Juan Melendrez was dead, faceless, in Blanch's lap of blood. Inez was badly hurt—her womb was crushed—and she was told that she could never bear a child.

Blanch thought to come back home. Did she think they would all be waiting with open arms? There was no one there to tell her the story of all that happened, of Joe Parrishes fate and of Louetta's, her daughter's. Her sister and brother in Houston had long ago disowned her and had left their home place to rot and fall in upon their drunken brother, the uncle I will tell you more about (and his two nephews—maybe you will remember) in a while.

When mother and daughter came to the family house, they found doors and windows all boarded up. Blanch came face to face with the forbidding riding figure on the glass pane. She fell back for a moment and felt a cold shudder over her, but then, being a strong woman of Texas prairie and valley, she tore open the front door. The odor of the house was of death and rot, and when she found the well cemented over and read the words drawn with a nail in the cement, THIS WELL ACCURST, and the figure of a skeleton head in the embrace of crossbones, she felt a chill of horror. When she was later told of the content of the well, she pulled her daughter Inez Melendrez to her and told her the tale of Joe Parrish and of Louetta, her daughter, and of Juan Melendrez and of the uncle, her brother and of the red nigger. She was told that the uncle had gone off to Houston to seek his sister and brother and just as she was making plans to go there and find him and to bring him back home, the uncle arrived, but as a wasted corpse in the hands of his nephew. You have already heard of the funeral.

Blanch and Inez Melendrez went on living in the house with the accurst well. She had an altar built over the well and kept a candle burning on it night and day, but you can sure enough believe and will want to know that evil spirits were not in the least held away by the burning light of any candle.

Blanch began to be worried by the sound of somebody walking on the roof. She placed a ladder to the roof so that she was often climbing the ladder day and night, staring at the roof. She had climbed the ladder so many times that she had blisters bleeding in the palms of her hands and the soles of her feet. No sooner had she come down the ladder than up she had to go again. Up and down the ladder she went, night and day. Inez Melendrez feared for her mother's sanity because she herself had not heard anything. One night Inez heard a crash and when she ran outside she found that it had come from her mother Blanch who had fallen off the ladder in the dark and was dead in the Canna Lilies from a broken neck. At last Blanch had peace. But who knows who has peace? It is told that when Inez found her mother dead in the lilies, a black-winged person stood near and with a long black tongue going in and out of its mouth said, "Joe Parrish won." Inez cried out and the figure vanished. She lifted up her mother and carried her into the house, where she laid her in her bed and lit candles around her. That night when Inez dozed, the house burned to the ground, burning Blanch to ashes in it as Inez fled for her life. Nothing but the well was left.

I later came to the place to see what was left of the door. I found in rubble on a jagged piece of glass the perfect head of the horse rearing passionate and proud in his curling delicate mane, and took it. I looked for the rider but never found him. He must have lain on the burnt ground in a thousand pieces of blackened glass. I would give anything to have found the rider of that precious horse, horseman lost forever.

Inez the Chicana was now seventeen. She saw suffering, persecution and unfair treatment of the Mexican people in her county. She deplored the exploitation of her people by rich Anglo Texans. "I am a *Tejana,*" she said. "I am a Texan as well as a *Mejicana.*" She was widely sought after since she was so haughty and beautiful with her fountainous coarse black hair. A rich independent oil man name Ralston McNamara pursued Inez Melendrez and he happened to be one of those who confiscated land wherever he wanted it to drill for oil from it. He took away land from Mexican people, then hired them as cheap labor to work on it with his drilling company, promising a share of profits, which they never got, since they did not know numbers or how to speak English. How could they figure anything out? They seemed to be naturally in disgrace everywhere. Why was this? Many towns would not allow Mexican people to eat in their cafés or to come into their stores. "I'll tell you, give me a nigra anytime over a greasy Mescan" is what you heard.

Ralston McNamara continued to pursue Inez Melendrez and in some time Inez Melendrez married Ralston McNamara. His big wells which he gave to his young bride (she was nineteen) as a wedding present, *Inez No. 1* and *Inez No. 2,* had come in like earthquakes and explosions bursting open the earth and splattering with thick oil mud a countryside of grazing cows and blooming cotton fields and tomato and pea farms, and bringing overnight power and riches to Inez Melendrez McNamara. She at once moved to invest and to buy and to accumulate. She bought a hotel in the Panhandle, acreage in the small town of Houston adjacent to what would one day be a great international airport, and some several miles of the early Houston Ship Channel, along which she built docks and warehouses for cotton and grain. She bought automobile agencies in some small towns like Tomball and Conroe, Texas, and a radio station in the state capital of Austin. Ralston McNamara was amazed at her avarice and her clutching sense of money and was already experiencing spells of impotence with his young wife. Within two years of their marriage he was dead from a split skull brought about by the blade of a machete that fell from a rigging. His head had been sliced in two to the end of his nose. For a time there had been suspicion of foul play among the Mexicans since it was known that the Mexicans were not fond of Ralston McNamara even though he had a Mexican wife. Now all the McNamara fortune fell into Inez' hands and at twenty—and miraculously pregnant—she was perhaps the most powerful person in all Texas and no doubt in the whole Southwest, probably in half the country. Soon after McNamara's death Inez Melendrez McNamara gave birth to an Irish-Mexican boy, who was named Juan McNamara. This boy was the idol of Inez McNamara's eyes. He was not out of her sight. She held him against her breast wherever she went, whatever she did. He slept beneath the cool cover of her coarse black hair. But the shining glory of an immense fortune was darkened by the sickness of a child. Juan McNamara was attacked by a mysterious illness when he was two years old and he lay in a pale languor night and day. The beautiful ivory-colored child could not be healed. Famous doctors came and were of no help. Inez' investments fell; she did not care. She closed shops and offices and warehouses, canceled contracts. People embezzled from her and stole her property. She was in a trance of dread, clutching her dying child to her. She pawned and sold for a nuisance her silver and furs to pay for exorbitant miracle medicines and to bring healers and holy men to her child. But Juan McNamara died. He was three years old and had withered to look sixty.

Inez Melendrez McNamara turned her back on her former life. She brought a bag of cash money and jewels to a Carmelite nunnery in the fields near San Antonio, Texas, and entered it, taking a vow of renunciation and total silence.

No one from the outside world has ever seen her or spoken to her again. Not once has she opened the little door to her cell. The nuns who feed her and take care of her have been pursued by people from all over the world for information about the hidden beautiful woman of sorrows. And some have come with business papers, leases, titles and contracts. The Sisters would not speak to them, although some needed immediate life-saving answers that only Inez could give. Some begged to slip a piece of paper under the door for Inez' signature. There was even one incensed man on the roof of Inez' cell crying down to her to help him salvage some few dollars of his lost fortune, but there was no answer. The Sisters would not speak to anyone of Inez Melendrez McNamara, as though she did not exist. Only one little Novitiate, who was missing and was found in the Shamrock Hotel in Houston wearing a huge emerald and ordering elaborate room service for a bunch of conference salesmen in a penthouse orgy, told some news of Inez before she passed out, champagne-sodden. She told how Inez Melendrez McNamara weighed 350 pounds and that her huge body was cloaked by her coarse black hair, which dragged on the floor, like a shaggy black cape. When the Novitiate sobered up she found herself back in the nunnery, raped so many times that it took some weeks to heal her.

But time has almost carried off forever the story of Inez Melendrez McNamara. I've saved a little of it here.

ORMSBY

What is this wild thing that will cut like a shark-toothed blade through a person until it has hacked him to pieces? Or more, what I am interested in is the change that will come over a wild person, as though a devil had suddenly departed him. Where did the devil go? The Bible says into some swine—that, filled of two men's devils, ran crazy over a cliff and fell into the sea, leaving the two men peaceful after long torment. But I am not interested—right now—in the receivers of the demons that flee insane people, in the swine: it is the wild person that takes my thought right now: a man named Ormsby.

Now Ormsby was a wild red young nigger come down from a poverty-killed back swamp town near Mobile, Alabama, to get work at a sawmill in Moscow, Texas. He was in trouble from the first because he drank whiskey with the Cushata Indians and fucked them and cut them across their throats and faces with a nasty knife. He was wild with his red dick and mean with his knife and was locked up a lot and bound to posts and trees to keep him from tearing up half a town—or his own self.

Look how he changed to a pink-headed loving old nigger:

After the violence in the woods with the raped white girl Louetta, Blanch's daughter you will recall, he ran back toward the Alabama swamp that he grew up in. He hid in weeds and crawled by rivers and walked highways in rags until he stole some clean clothes off a clothesline and put them on. He finally got on a truck that took him as far as Mobile and from there he got to the hidden swampland that he knew and sank into it, hidden from the world. His wretchedness and his self-loathing made him grovel in the alligator excrement and filth of the shallows of the swamp water. He lay naked among the alligators, hoping they would bite him to pieces and eat him up. They did not touch him. Sometimes, blinking, they lumbered over him as he lay in the steaming swamp mud; their claws left deep bleeding gashes on his body whose white scars he carried to his death. The heat was infernal and fierce swamp insects sang in his ears and stung his naked body until he threw himself into the hot swamp water, howling. He could not die.

And then one afternoon in his dementia he heard an urging to go back to Moscow, Texas, to the sawmill and stand up and work honestly and earn his pay. When he determined to go, to turn away out of the hell swampland, he stood up and felt the madness in him leave. And he saw the alligators go crazy, as if they were mad as he had been. They thrashed and lept and beat their horned heads against the cedar stumps in the water and all of them that he had lived with battered themselves to death. The water was blood. When the silence that followed filled the swampland, Ormsby the changed man stood up in a peace that he could not understand; but he got himself ready to go back to the sawmill. He found his filthy clothes and washed them in a spring and they dried in an hour while he scoured his filthy body in the clean springwater until he was fresh again. Ormsby then walked out of the dark hidden place of his madness.

At the sawmill they saw that he was a different man and in trust they gave him a job. Ormsby worked hard and was quiet among the men who could hardly believe that he was the same man who had been chained, hollering and gnashing his teeth, to trees so that others could be safe from him. Because of his long suffering, Ormsby's hair, which had been red, had turned pink.

He came one day into the nearby town where Kansas Tate had lived, asking for her in Niggertown. He was told that she was dead and that he could find out more from the man, the uncle, who still lived on the place where Kansas Tate had worked for so many years.

At the place Ormsby found the uncle, who took right to him, and the uncle told the long story to Ormsby and how Kansas Tate was dead from shock and grief. Ormsby wept and seemed gentle and saintly, yet he was the cause of all the woe and doom that had fallen upon the place. The uncle then told Ormsby his own story of his love for Louetta, of his fathering and nursing and healing Leander, child of rape, when he was dying in a cave from the violence of the KKK, of Leander's lust for Louetta and of Louetta's terrible suicide in the well. Ormsby then told of his long suffering and hiding and how he had been urged back to ask forgiveness. He told the uncle of his terrible deed and begged on his knees for mercy and forgiveness. His pink head shook with the sobs that poured silver tears down his black glistening face and the white signs of the claws of the alligators shone on his black body. The uncle might have straightaway killed Ormsby there in the house. But an extraordinary thing occurred. I forgive you, said the uncle. Who can cast the first stone? They had loved the same woman, and the white man had brought up the black man's son and loved him like his own. The uncle told all this to Ormsby, the pink-headed nigger. Let's try to live together in this place, the uncle said, or the Klu Klux Klan will kill you if they catch you, and me, too. You can live in this house with me. And together, the uncle said, being the only ones left of the whole story, we can wait for the possible return of our son Leander. The town rumbled at a white man and a black man living in the same house, for of course they found out about them. But who among them knew all that had happened? Yet they judged and denounced the two men as derelicts and the KKK rode for many nights around and around the house with burning torches until the dust from their horses' hooves set a cloud over the old family house. But the two men laid low inside. Sometimes they saw the glow of fire at their windows and they looked out to see burning crosses staked in the road and in the fields. It is a miracle that the KKK arm of justice and morality did not set the house on fire, and their threats of this and of tar-and-feathering the two men as a means of punishment and of setting things aright came often in shouts and chants, but the old house stood untouched and the men inside unharmed. This is because, it is said, that some said they saw in a white glowing above the roof of the house the bright figure of a winged man flashing a sword and calling with a powerful voice, "This house is blest by forgiveness. Go away." And all the fires of the burning crossed died out. This is what they say, this is what some saw.

Leander never returned. Some dark nights and on some dark stormy days, one or other of the two men was sure that he saw a figure of Leander, the lost son, coming across the pasture, rising and falling in the high grass; or leaping and darting toward the house like a jackrabbit, at dusk in the twilight; or sometimes on the road in the summer heat, a glowing veil-like shape seemed to be arriving. But Leander never arrived.

Finally Ormsby was found dead in his bed by the uncle one sleety morning in November. The uncle buried him in a grave on the place and put at its head a slab of wood with the words on it, "Leander's father forgiven."

From then on, alone in the house of sorrow and forgiveness, the uncle drank, full of his silent story—except what he would tell of it to me when he would let me through the horseman-cursed door—graced, too by the horseman and the horse—until he closed that door to the old house and walked out on the highway to wait for somebody to pick him up that was going to Houston. There he was going to look for his brother and sister; but we know that he never found them.

Two Cousins

Now the old family land, accursed, had been disinherited by the uncle's brother and sister in Houston—I will tell more about this later—and inherited by two cousins whose whereabouts was not readily known. When one, the older, was found and came to the town he heard all this story. Of course by the time he found out the story nobody knew how much had been added to it but he saved what he heard and what he knew.

His one mission was to find his cousin. The city of Houston was reaching out seventy, eighty miles into towns that were no longer considered towns but additions to the city of Houston. What had been a quiet, ramshackled little town was now called a suburb, and Houston people were building fine homes in it. The chemical age was flourishing, its toxic waste dumps lay festering in hidden ravines or vacant lots, and choking smogs and acid rains seeped into the gigantic shopping malls. The fouled water of rivers choked its own fish. The family land was suddenly worth a good price. It lay, in its modest acreage, in bitterweed and mallow and thistle under half a dozen live oak trees as old as the county. Only some burnt timbers of the house and the cemented well gave signs of the former dark life on the land.

The cousin sought his cousin. There was very little hearsay of him since he had been such a silent figure in the town. None of the Klu Klux would tell anything about him. It seemed to be a case of a person quite thoroughly disappeared from the face of the earth. The older cousin could not sell the land without his cousin's signature. Yet if the cousin were never to come forth to claim his property would it become the possession of the next in line? It was said that fifty years would have to pass before this forfeiture could occur. This would make the older cousin over a hundred years old. The older cousin made a surprising decision and it was to stay home in the old town where he began his life. Why couldn't he build a dwelling for himself on the land which was half his? He planted a grove of white and rose Oleander around the old well, and under two ancient live oaks he built a simple house. As soon as the house was finished—it hadn't been a month—there appeared three blond women with news which the cousin had not been able to find out anywhere, and they brought it with odd good humor. These announced themselves as ex-wives, sisters, of the younger cousin. Each one had married him and divorced him in turn. They explained their ex-husband's one annoying flaw—a defect of speech which turned him unpleasantly silent most of the time, except when he was excited. This impediment was caused by a freak accident. The man had a habit of clenching his doubled tongue between his teeth when he strained at anything, and while sliding on his back under a sawed-off locked door he had slit his tongue down the middle on a protruding nail. It was ridiculous what some said, the women announced darkly. That the KKK had cut off their ex's tongue for talking too much—could you imagine that! they exclaimed. Yet the KKK said that the man had divulged some of their secrets. But it had always been the man's silence that soured marriage, the sisters declared, even before he'd slit his tongue under the door; although they well knew about it when they entered into wedlock. You never knew what he was feeling, the sisters complained. Was the dinner good? No answer. Do you love me? Silence. How could a person live with somebody who couldn't comment on things, have an opinion? the women questioned. Each marriage had lasted only a few weeks. In turn each sister simply couldn't make a go of it, yet each had been so challenged to accomplish what the other could not that she took on the silent one. "He ran through the whole crop of us," the sisters told the older cousin, "and then he left the area." One sister said it was to Port Arthur that he went, to enlist in the Merchant Marine, but of course they wouldn't take him, with a split tongue. Another said that when he married her he had begun to make ungodly sounds, particularly when excited. And the other, the third, said that when her time came the cousin disclosed on their wedding night a brand on his thigh, a letter and a number, which was the mark of a well-known penitentiary. "I had married an escaped convict!" she cried. The three women were so good-natured, overall, that it was hard not to believe their stories. They all vowed that the speechless groom was the hottest lover and that he had the body of a statue. He knew how! they giggled. So they stayed on with him for a while. And for a little while each sister had had the same thought, saying to herself, listen, does he *have* to talk? But life's not all sex, they concluded, in their well-earned wisdom. And they departed, leaving their disturbing news behind them.

The older cousin pondered what to do about his lost kin. He put ads in the newspapers of Texas towns urging his cousin to come back and claim his due. Somebody sent a letter to the older cousin informing him that his cousin was working among the Mexicans in the pea fields of the Rio Grande Valley, where he was known as "El Mudo." He had long ago learned not to speak at all, since he had begun to make such sinister sounds when he tried. But when he drank whiskey he seemed to fall into the possession of demons, for he broke into rages and flailed and kicked in the dust, whirring his tongue in a sound like a rattlesnake. He would finally have to be held down in the dust until he weakened and his horrible sound died out. The poor man, wrote the informant, had no friends. After his ferocity had passed, he was gentle again, a harmless *Mudo* hoeing the peavines in the fields. I have shown him the newspaper ad but he seems not to understand it or to care, ended the letter.

One night in the early dark hours after midnight the older cousin was wakened by a distant sound, and it came closer. With a chill he recognized the horrible sound of his cousin as it had been described to him, the whirring that afflicted him when he was excited. He lay in his bed and heard the sound come closer and then it was at his window, like a snake in the bushes. His cousin had at last arrived. He called his cousin's name. Come in, he said, I've been waiting for you. This is your home.

He heard the window open and saw in the deepest dark the form of a man and heard the terrible sound. His cousin was desperate to speak, to tell something. The older cousin turned on the light and he saw a horrifying gasping figure. He embraced his cousin and said, welcome; please come and let me help you. He knew that his cousin could not speak and so he sat him at a table with paper and pencil and asked him to write to him all that he could not say. But the young cousin fainted and his cousin lifted him into the bed, where the two slept for some hours side by side. In the early dawn the older cousin awoke and saw his cousin writing at the table. He wrote of the horror of his life. How KKK men had accused him of telling their secrets. They had cut off his tongue and put a fish hook in it and hung it on the branch of the tree they tied him to, and all night he saw the organ licking and lapping its drooling saliva. He had been tormented by the image of the lapping tongue and of the genitals of black men he had helped castrate; they seemed to be the same human members. He raved in the nights, sleepless, and then he poured whiskey down his flaming throat to bring deliverance. But the whirring sound began and he became a monster that men would sometimes club with sticks, like a snake, to stop the horrible sound. When men discovered his erotic throat and its tantalizing arrangement of parts, they used him. For the KKK had cut off his tongue where it is fattest and lies beneath the moist and quivering membrane called the uvula. When breath played through these soft meats they quivered and clasped the lingual stub, a chunk of thick meat throbbing at the vestibule of the throat, causing the dry whirring sound men feared. It was a deformity caused by the evil of men. Yet a warm and hospitable sucking and clasping organ had been remade by nature in its healing. This creation was so sexually maddening that once the men discovered it they fought each other over it out of self-loathing and unending whipping prurience, and, still in rabid sexual arousal, an infernal priapism, they slashed open each other's throats and stabbed one another in the bowels and tried to castrate each other. In his trance, the cousin saw that the men seemed to be caught hold of by devils, and it occurred to him that they might have created in him a trap of their own destruction in his lascivious throat. When he lay almost dead from strangling and suffocation and had thrown up some of his insides, in the vision of exhaustion he thought that a winged person who looked like an angel appeared in front of him. "Through man's savagery and nature's remodeling of it," said the winged person, "you have been made the very device of your enemy's undoing: the withering of malevolent energy coming from insatiable lust." Then the person unbound the cousin from the tree where the men had tied him and showed him to the cool river and refreshed him and urged him to go to his cousin, which he did.

The older cousin longed to put his cousin to rest and to pacify the tormenting images before him; heal him. He held his young cousin to his breast and for the first time since their own uncle long ago had held them each under an arm against his breast, the young cousin felt love and tenderness and forgiveness, without a word being spoken; and he felt that his cousin was saying to him, in this way, that you do not have to speak to tell somebody something that is gentle and loving. By showing him the fullness of silence, the older cousin was able to bring his young cousin to some peace and the tormenting images, and even the horrible whirring sound, began to pass away.

It was then that the young cousin was visited again by what he thought was an angel. A big winged male came before him and the cousin asked him, "Are you an angel?" "Yes," said the angel and said that he had come to offer the cousin his tongue and straightway installed it in his mouth and told him to speak with it. The cousin was so afraid for a little while, to have an angel's tongue in his mouth, but it was not for long before he spoke to the angel and told him of his joy and thanks. The angel then told him that he could keep his tongue if he would use it to show the poor Mexican people in the peafields of the Rio Grande Valley among whom he had worked how to spell words and how to add numbers. The cousin said he would try. Some mysterious money came to his hands from a Carmelite Nun who arrived one day. She drove up in a cleanly washed Ford in which another Nun sat. The money was to be used for the teaching of words and numbers to the Mexicans so that they would not be speechless even as he had been and know when they were cheated and how to protect themselves and get better pay.

The cousin returned to the peafields and established a kind of school at night, speaking with the angel's tongue. People of the Valley who had known him before as *El Mudo* didn't recognize him to be the same person until a man cried out "El Mudo!" and then he was recognized by all and beloved. He was now speaking so freely that he did not know whose tongue he was using, his or the angel's. A lot of the time he found that he had not even thought about it—he simply opened his mouth and said the words he had to say.

In some time the angel returned and announced to the cousin that he would take back his tongue and that he might very well see how well he could speak with what he had of his own. "Do what you can with what you've got," advised the angel. "You may now be able to speak better than you think." The cousin was afraid for a while, but when he saw that he could do pretty well with what he had of his own, he lost fear. And he lived on for quite a while, there in the Rio Grande Valley among the Mexicans he loved and helped and who loved him. When he and his brothers and sisters of the fields began to organize the first Union, the KKK blew right in like a fresh washing of white sheets in the red wind of the Valley. *El Mudo* called out to the angel, "Give me your tongue to denounce these men!" And he felt the angel's tongue in his mouth; and with full tongue he drove back with eloquence the men who had once humiliated him, to their astonishment and fear.

It was then that the angel appeared for the last time and told the cousin that it was his own tongue that had spoken the truth before the enemy, for somewhere during his speaking the angel had taken back his own tongue and the cousin without knowing it had gone on fully with his own. In joy, the cousin saw that he had been restored through the help of love and trust.

This is the end of the story of the two cousins whose uncle loved them. Unless some more comes to mind later about the older cousin. The younger one lived on among the Mexican people of the Rio Grande Valley. He never saw his father again, never went over to Shreveport, Louisiana, to find him as he had in his boyhood planned. His mother had died of the TB that cropped up in the family from time to time over two generations, but this was when he was in the torment of another world. He later found that she had been buried in Houston with a burial insurance policy for which she had paid a few dollars a month for years.

The older cousin had finally come home—it looked like. He sank peacefully into the land of his ancestors and lived there in his house built over the foundations of the old, dark house and the ruins of the door that haunted him. I am not sure what he does. I go out to the place and talk with him from time to time. His father, who turned his back on his own brother because of his drunkenness and would not come home to his funeral, died not long ago in an Old Folks' Home paid for by his pension from the oil company he had worked for for over thirty years, brought to his death by a liver cancer caused by "the excessive use of alcohol." Those were the words used. His mother had turned into a recluse and kept planning to come to live with him, but she never came. Interesting how this Houston brother and sister disavowed the old place of their grandparents and their childhood. The truth is that they were just plainly scared to death and in their fear and unhappiness were counseled by the leader of their religious group to wash their hands of the cursed place of so much bloodshed. There's some more in this to be told, about this afflicted man and woman who labored and went down under their own accursedness.

But I'll wait until later to tell it. I've wanted to stick to the two cousins and the outcome of their loving reunion that brought to their family's troubled lives redemption. Or so it has seemed to me.

GHOST AND FLESH

1947–1952

THE WHITE ROOSTER

◻▬▬◻

Walter's Story

There were two disturbances in Mrs. Marcy Samuels' life that were worrying her nearly insane. First, it was, and had been for two years now, Grandpa Samuels, who should have long ago been dead but kept wheeling around her house in his wheel chair, alive as ever. The first year he came to live with them it was plain that he was in good health and would probably live long. But during the middle of the second year he fell thin and coughing and after that there were some weeks when Mrs. Samuels and her husband, Watson, were sure on Monday that he would die and relieve them of him before Saturday. Yet he wheeled on and on, not ever dying at all.

The second thing that was about to drive Marcy Samuels crazy was a recent disturbance which grew and grew until it became a terror. It was a stray white rooster that crowed at her window all day long and, worst of all, in the early mornings. No one knew where he came from, but there he was, crowing to all the other roosters far and near—and they answering back in a whole choir of crowings. His shrieking was bad enough, but then he had to outrage her further by digging in her pansy bed. Since he first appeared to harass her, Mrs. Samuels had spent most of her day chasing him out of the flowers or throwing objects at him where he was, under her window, his neck stretched and strained in a perfectly blatant crow. After a week of this, she was almost frantic, as she told her many friends on the telephone or in town or from her back yard.

It seemed that Mrs. Samuels had been cursed with problems all her life and everyone said she had the unluckiest time of it. That a woman sociable and busy as Marcy Samuels should have her father-in-law, helpless in a wheel chair, in her house to keep and take care of was just a shame. And Watson, her husband, was no help at all, even though it was his very father who was so much trouble. He was a slow, patient little man, not easily ruffled. Marcy Samuels was certain that he was not aware that her life was so hard and full of trouble.

She could not stand at her stove, for instance, but what Grandpa Samuels was there, asking what was in the pot and smelling of it. She could not even have several of the women over without him riding in and out among them, weak as he was, as they chatted in confidence about this or that town happening, and making bright or ugly remarks about women and what they said, their own affairs. Marcy, as she often told Watson, simply could not stop Grandpa's mouth, could not stop his wheels, could not get him out of her way. And she was busy. If she was hurrying across a room to get some washing in the sink or to get the broom, Grandpa Samuels would make a surprise run out at her from the hall or some door and streak across in front of her, laughing fiendishly or shouting boo! and then she would leap as high as her bulbous ankles would lift her and scream, for she was a nervous woman and had so many things on her mind. Grandpa had a way of sneaking into things Marcy did, as a weevil slips into a bin of meal and bores around in it. He had a way of objecting to Marcy, which she sensed everywhere. He haunted her, pestered her. If she would be bending down to find a thing in her cupboard, she would suddenly sense some shadow over her and then it would be Grandpa Samuels, he would be there, touch her like a ghost in the ribs and frighten her so that she would bounce up and let out a scream. Then he would just sit and grin at her with an owlish face. All these things he did added to the trouble it was for her to keep him, made Marcy Samuels sometimes want to kill Grandpa Samuels. He was everywhere upon her, like an evil spirit following her; and indeed there was a thing in him which scared her often, as if he was losing his mind or trying to kill her.

As for Grandpa, it was hard to tell whether he really had a wicked face or was deliberately trying to look mean, to keep Marcy troubled and to pay her back for the way she treated him. It may have been that his days were dull and he wanted something to happen, or that he remembered how he heard her fight with his son, her husband, at night in their room because Watson would not put him in a Home and get the house and Marcy free of him. "You work all day and you're not here with him like I am," she would whine. "And you're not man enough to put him where he belongs." He had been wicked in his day, as men are wicked, had drunk always and in all drinking places, had gambled and had got mixed up in some scrapes. But that was because he had been young and ready. He had never had a household, and the wife he finally got had long since faded away so that she might have been only a shadow from which this son, Watson, emerged, parentless. Then Grandpa had become an old wanderer, lo here lo there, until it all ended in this chair in which he was still a wanderer through the rooms of this house. He had a face which, although mischievous lines were scratched upon it and gave it a kind of devilish look, showed that somewhere there was abundant untouched kindness in him, a life which his life had never been able to use.

Marcy could not make her husband see that this house was cursed and tormented; and then to have a scarecrow rooster annoying her the length of the day and half the early morning was too much for Marcy Samuels. She had nuisances in her house and nuisances in her yard.

It was on a certain morning that Mrs. Samuels first looked out her kitchen window to see this gaunt rooster strutting white on the ground. It took her only a second to know that this was the rooster that crowed and scratched in her flowers and so the whole thing started. The first thing she did was to poke her blowsy head out her window and puff her lips into a ring and wheeze shooooooo! through it, fiercely. The white rooster simply did a pert leap, erected his flamboyantly combed head sharp into the air, chopped it about for a moment, and then started scratching vigorously in the lush bed of pansies, his comb slapping like a girl's pigtails.

Since her hands were wet in the morning sink full of dishes, Mrs. Samuels stopped to dry them imperfectly and then hurried out the back door, still drying her hands in her apron. Now she would get him, she would utterly destroy him if she could get her hands on him. She flounced out the door and down the steps and threw her great self wildly in the direction of the pansy bed, screaming shoo! shoo! go 'way! go 'way! and then cursed the rooster. Marcy Samuels must have been a terrible sight to any barnyard creature, her hair like a big bush and her terrible bosom heaving and falling, her hands thrashing the air. But the white rooster was not dismayed at all. Again he did a small quick hop, stuck his beak into the air, and stood firmly on his ground, his yellow claw spread over the face of a purple pansy and holding it to the ground imprisoned as a cat holds down a mouse. And then a sound, a clear melodious measure, which Mrs. Samuels thought was the most awful noise in the world, burst from his straggly throat.

He was plainly a poorly rooster, thin as some sparrow, his white feathers drooping and without luster, his comb of extravagant growth but pale and flaccid, hanging like a wrinkled glove over his eye. It was clear that he had been run from many a yard and that in fleeing he had torn his feathers and so tired himself that whatever he found to eat in random places was not enough to keep any flesh on his carcass. He would not be a good eating chicken, Mrs. Samuels thought, running at him, for he has no meat on him at all. Anyway, he was not like a chicken but like some nightmare rooster from Hades sent to trouble her. Yet he was most vividly alive in some courageous way.

She threw a stone at him and at this he leaped and screamed in fright and hurdled the shrubbery into a vacant lot. Mrs. Samuels dashed to her violated pansy bed and began throwing up loose dirt about the stems, making reparations. This was no ordinary rooster in her mind. Since she had a very good imagination and was, actually, a little afraid of roosters anyway, the white rooster took on a shape of terror in her mind. This was because he was so indestructible. Something seemed to protect him. He seemed to dare her to capture him, and if she threw a shoe out her window at him, he was not challenged, but just let out another startling crow at her. And in the early morning in a snug bed, such a crowing is like the cry of fire! or an explosion in the brain.

It was around noon of that day that Mrs. Samuels, at her clothesline, sighted Mrs. Doran across the hedge, at her line, her long fingers fluttering over the clothespins like butterflies trying to light there.

"That your rooster that's been in my pansy bed and crows all the time, Mrs. Doran?"

"Marcy, it must be. You know we had two of them, intending to eat them for Christmas, but they both broke out of the coop and went running away into the neighborhood. My husband Carl just gave them up because he says he's not going to be chasing any chickens like some farmer."

"Well then I tell you we can't have him here disturbing us. If I catch him do you want him back?"

"Heavens no, honey. If you catch him, do what you want to with him, we don't want him anymore. Lord knows where the other one is." And then she unfolded from her tub a long limp outing gown and pinned it to the line by its shoulders to let it hang down like an effigy of herself.

Mrs. Samuels noticed that Mrs. Doran was as casual about the whole affair as she was the day she brought back her water pitcher in several pieces, borrowed for a party and broken by the cat. It made her even madder with the white rooster. This simply means killing that white rooster, she told herself as she went from her line. It means wringing his neck until it is twisted clean from his breastbone—if we can catch him; and I'll try—catch him and throw him in the chickenyard and hold him there until Watson comes home from work and then Watson will do the wringing, not me. When she came in the back door she was already preparing herself in her mind for the killing of the white rooster, how she would catch him and then wait for Watson to wring his neck —if Watson actually could get up enough courage to do anything at all for her.

In the afternoon around two, just as she was resting, she heard a cawing and it was the rooster back again. Marcy bounded from her bed and raced to the window. "Now I will get him," she said severely.

She moved herself quietly to a bush and concealed herself behind it, her full-blown buttocks protruding like a monstrous flower in bud. Around the bush in a smiling innocent circle were the pansies, all purple and yellow faces, bright in the wind. When he comes scratching here, she told herself, and when he gets all interested in the dirt, I'll leap upon him and catch him sure.

Behind the bush she waited; her eyes watched the white rooster moving towards the pansy bed, pecking here and there in the grass at whatever was there and might be eaten. As she prepared herself to leap, Mrs. Samuels noticed the white hated face of Grandpa at the window. He had rolled his wheel chair there to watch the maneuvers in the yard. She knew at a glance that he was against her catching the white rooster. But because she hated him, she did not care what he thought. In fact she secretly suspected Grandpa and the rooster to be partners in a plot to worry her out of her mind, one in the house, the other in the yard, tantalizing her outside and inside; she wouldn't put it past them. And if she could destroy the rooster that was a terror in the yard she had a feeling that she would be in a way destroying a part of Grandpa that was a trouble in her house. She wished she were hiding behind a bush to leap out upon *him* to wring *his* neck. He would not die, only wheel through her house day after day, asking for this and that, meddling in everything she did.

The rooster came to the pansy bed so serene, even in rags of feathers, like a beggar-saint, sure in his head of something, something unalterable, although food was unsure, even life. He came as if he knew suffering and terror, as if he were all alone in the world of fowls, far away from his flock, alien and far away from any golden grain thrown by caring hands, stealing a wretched worm or cricket from a foreign yard. What made him so alive, what did he know? Perhaps as he thrust the horned nails of his toes in the easy earth of the flower bed he dreamed of the fields on a May morning, the jeweled dew upon their grasses and the sun coming up like the yolk of an egg swimming in an albuminous sky. And the roseate freshness of his month when he was a tight-fleshed slender-thighed cockerel, alert on his hill and the pristine morning breaking all around him. To greet it with cascading trills of crowings, tremulous in his throat, was to quiver his thin red tongue in trebles. What a joy he felt to be of the world of wordless creatures, where crowing or whirring of wings or the brush of legs together said everything, said praise, we live. To be of the grassy world where things blow and bend and rustle; of the insect world so close to it that it was known when the most insignificant mite would turn in its minute course or an ant haul an imperceptible grain of sand from its tiny cave.

And to wonder at the world and to be able to articulate the fowl-wonder in the sweetest song. He knew time as the seasons know it, being of time. He was tuned to the mechanism of dusk and dawn, it may have been in his mind as simple as the dropping of a curtain to close out the light or the lifting of it to let light in upon a place. All he knew, perhaps, was that there is a going round, and first light comes ever so tinily and speck-like, as through the opening of a stalk, when it is time. Yet the thing that is light breaking on the world is morning breaking open, unfolding within him and he feels it and it makes him chime, like a clock, at his hour. And this is daybreak for him and he feels the daybreak in his throat, and tells of it, rhapsodically, not knowing a single word to say.

And once he knew the delight of wearing red-blooded wattles hanging folded from his throat and a comb climbing up his forehead all in crimson horns to rise from him as a star, pointed.

To be rooster was to have a beak hard and brittle as shell, formed just as he would have chosen a thing for fowls to pick grain or insect from their place. To be bird was to be of feathers and shuffle and preen them and to carry wings and arch and fold them, or float them on the wind, to be wafted, to be moved a space by them.

But Marcy Samuels was behind the bush, waiting, and while she waited her mind said over and over, "If he would die!" If he would die, by himself. How I could leap upon him, choke the life out of him. The rooster moved toward the pansies, tail feathers drooped and frayed. If he would die, she thought, clenching her fists. If I could leap upon him and twist his old wrinkled throat and keep out the breath.

At the window, Grandpa Samuels knew something terrible was about to happen. He watched silently. He saw the formidable figure of Mrs. Samuels crouching behind the bush, waiting to pounce upon the rooster.

In a great bounce-like movement, Mrs. Samuels suddenly fell upon the rooster, screaming, "If he would die!" And caught him. The rooster did not struggle, although he cawed out for a second and then meekly gave himself up to Mrs. Samuels. She ran with him to the chickenyard and stopped at the fence. But before throwing him over, she first tightened her strong hands around his neck and gritted her teeth, just to stop the breathing for a moment, to crush the crowing part of him, as if it were a little waxen whistle she could smash. Then she threw him over the fence. The white rooster lay over on his back, very tired and dazed, his yellow legs straight in the air, his claws clenched like fists and not moving, only trembling a little. The Samuels' own splendid golden cock approached the shape of feathers to see what this was, what had come over into his domain, and thought surely it was dead. He leaped upon the limp fuss of feathers and drove his fine spurs into the white rooster just to be sure he was dead. And all the fat pampered hens stood around gazing and casual in a kind of fowlish elegance, not really disturbed, only a bit curious, while the golden cock bristled his fine feathers and, feeling in himself what a thing of price and intrepidity he was, posed for a second like a statue imitating some splendid ancestor cock in his memory, to comment upon this intrusion and to show himself unquestionable master, his beady eyes all crimson as glass hat pins. It was apparent that his hens were proud of him and that in their eyes he had lost none of his prowess by not having himself captured the rooster, instead of Mrs. Samuels. And Marcy Samuels, so relieved, stood by the fence a minute showing something of the same thing in her that the hens showed, very viciously proud. Then she brushed her hands clean of the white rooster and marched victoriously to the house.

Grandpa Samuels was waiting for her at the door, a dare in his face, and said, "Did you get him?"

"He's in the yard waiting until Watson comes home to kill him. I mashed the breath out of the scoundrel and he may be dead the way he's lying on his back in the chickenyard. No more crowing at my window, no more scratching in my pansy bed, I'll tell you. I've got one thing off my mind."

"Marcy," Grandpa said calmly and with power, "that rooster's not dead that easily. Don't you know there's something in a rooster that won't be downed? Don't you know there's some creatures won't be dead easily?" And wheeled into the living room.

But Mrs. Samuels yelled back from the kitchen,

"All you have to do is wring their necks."

All afternoon the big wire wheels of Grandpa Samuels' chair whirled through room and room. Sometimes Mrs. Samuels thought she would pull out her mass of wiry hair, she got so nervous with the cracking of the floor under the wheels. The wheels whirled around in her head just as the crow of the rooster had burst in her brain all week. And then Grandpa's coughing: he would, in a siege of cough, dig away down in his throat for something troubling him there, and, finally, seizing it as if the cough were a little hand reaching for it, catch it and bring it up, the old man's phlegm, and spit it quivering into a can which rode around with him on the chair's footrest.

"This is as bad as the crowing of the white rooster," Mrs. Samuels said to herself as she tried to rest. "This is driving me crazy." And just when she was dozing off, she heard a horrid gurgling sound from the front bedroom where Grandpa was. She ran there and found him blue in his face and gasping.

"I'm choking to death with a cough, get me some water, quick!" he murmured hoarsely. As she ran to the kitchen faucet, Marcy had the picture of the white rooster in her mind, lying breathless on his back in the chickenyard, his thin yellow legs in the air and his claws closed and drooped like a wilted flower. "If he would die," she thought. "If he would strangle to death."

When she poured the water down his throat, Marcy Samuels put her fat hand there and pressed it quite desperately as if the breath were a little bellows and she could perhaps stop it still just for a moment. Grandpa was unconscious and breathing laboriously. She heaved him out of his chair and to his bed, where he lay crumpled and exhausted. Then was when she went to the telephone and called Watson, her husband.

"Grandpa is very sick and unconscious and the stray rooster is caught and in the chickenyard to be killed by you," she told him. "Hurry home, for everything is just terrible."

When Marcy went back to Grandpa's room with her hopeful heart already giving him extreme unction, she had the shock of her life to find him not dying at all but sitting up in his bed with a face like a caught rabbit, pitiful yet daredevilish.

"I'm all right now, Marcy, you don't have to worry about *me*. You couldn't *kill* an old crippled man like me," he said firmly.

Marcy was absolutely spellbound and speechless, but when she looked out Grandpa's window to see the white rooster walking in the leaves, like a resurrection, she thought she would faint with astonishment. Everything was suddenly like a haunted house; there was death and then a bringing to life again all around her and she felt so superstitious that she couldn't trust anything or anybody. Just when she was sure she was going to lose her breath in a fainting spell, Watson arrived home. Marcy looked wild. Instead of asking about Grandpa, whether he was dead, he said, "There's no stray rooster in my chickenyard like you said, because I just looked." And when he looked to see

Grandpa all right and perfectly conscious he was in a quandary and said they were playing a trick on a worried man.

"This place is haunted, I tell you," Marcy said, terrorized, "and you've got to do something for once in your life." She took him in the back room, where she laid out the horror and the strangeness of the day before him. Watson, who was always calm and a little underspoken, said, "All right, pet, all right. There's only one thing to do. That's lay a trap. Then kill him. Leave it to me, and calm your nerves." And then he went to Grandpa's room and sat and talked to him to find out if he was all right.

For an hour, at dusk, Watson Samuels was scrambling in a lumber pile in the garage like a possum trying to dig out. Several times Mrs. Samuels inquired through the window by signs what he was about. She also warned him, by signs, of her fruit-jars stored on a shelf behind the lumber pile and to be careful. But at a certain time during the hour of building, as she was hectically frying supper, she heard a crash of glass and knew it was her Mason jars all over the ground, and cursed Watson.

When finally Mr. Samuels came in, with the air of having done something grand in the yard, they ate supper. There was the sense of having something special waiting afterwards, like a fancy dessert.

"I'll take you out in a while and show you the good trap I built," Watson said. "That'll catch anything."

Grandpa, who had been silent and eating sadly as an old man eats (always as if remembering something heartbreaking), felt sure how glad they would be if they could catch *him* in the trap.

"Going to kill that white rooster, son?" he asked.

"It's the only thing to do to keep from making a crazy woman out of Marcy."

"Can't you put him in the yard with the rest of the chickens when you catch him?" He asked this mercifully. "That white rooster won't hurt anybody."

"You've seen we can't keep him in there, Papa. Anyway, he's probably sick or got some disease."

"His legs are scaly. I saw that," Mrs. Samuels put in.

"And then he'd give it to my good chickens," said Mr. Samuels. "Only thing for an old tramp like that is to wring his neck and throw him away for something useless and troublesome."

When supper was eaten, Watson and Marcy Samuels hurried out to look at the trap. Grandpa rolled to the window and watched through the curtain. He watched how the trap lay in the moonlight, a small dark object like a box with one end open for something to run in, something seeking a thing needed, like food or a cup of gold beyond a rainbow, and hoping to find it here within this cornered space. "It's just a box with one side kicked out," he said to himself. "But it is a trap and built to snare and to hold." It looked lethal under the moon; it cast a shadow longer than itself and the open end was like a big mouth, open to swallow down. He saw his son and his son's wife—how they moved about the trap, his son making terrifying gestures to show how it would work, how the guillotine end would slide down fast when the cord was released from inside the house, and close in the white rooster, close him in and lock him there, to wait to have his neck wrung off. He was afraid, for Mrs. Samuels looked strong as a lion in the night, and how cunning his son seemed! He could not hear what they spoke, only see their gestures. But he heard when Mrs. Samuels pulled the string once, trying out the trap, and the top came sliding down with a swift clap when she let go. And then he knew how adroitly they could kill a thing and with what craftiness. He was sure he was no longer safe in this house, for after the rooster then certainly he would be trapped.

The next morning early the white rooster was there, crowing in a glittering scale. Grandpa heard Marcy screaming at him, threatening, throwing little objects through the window at him. His son Watson did not seem disturbed at all; always it was Marcy. But still the rooster crowed. Grandpa went cold and trembling in his bed. He had not slept.

It was a rainy day, ashen and cold. By eight o'clock it had settled down to a steady gray pour. Mrs. Samuels did not bother with the morning dishes. She told Grandpa to answer all phone calls and tell them she was out in town. She took her place at the window and held the cord in her hand.

Grandpa was so quiet. He rolled himself about ever so gently and tried not to cough, frozen in his throat with fear and a feeling of havoc. All through the house, in every room, there was darkness and doom, the air of horror, slaughter and utter finish. He was so full of terror he could not breathe, only gasp, and he sat leaden in his terror. He thought he heard footsteps creeping upon him to choke his life out, or a hand to release some cord that would close down a heavy door before him and lock him out of his life forever. But he would not keep his eyes off Marcy. He sat in the doorway, half obscured, and peeked at her; he watched her like a hawk.

Mrs. Samuels sat by the window in a kind of ecstatic readiness. Everywhere in her was the urge to release the cord—even before the time to let it go, she was so passionately anxious. Sometimes she thought she could not trust her wrist, her fingers, they were so ready to let go, and then she changed the cord to the other hand. But her hands were so charged with their mission that they could have easily thrust a blade into a heart to kill it, or brought down mightily a hammer upon a head to shatter the skull in. Her hands had well and wantonly learned slaughter from her heart, had been thoroughly taught by it, as the heart whispers to its agents—hands, tongue, eyes—to do their action in their turn.

Once Grandpa saw her body start and tighten. She was poised like a huge cat, watching. He looked, mortified, through the window. It was a bird on the ground in the slate rain. Another time, because a dog ran across the yard, Mrs. Samuels jerked herself straight and thought, something comes, it is time.

And then it seemed there was a soft ringing in Grandpa's ears, almost like a delicate little jingle of bells or of thin glasses struck, and some secret thing told him in his heart that it was time. He saw Mrs. Samuels sure and powerful as a great beast, making certain, making ready without flinching. The white rooster was coming upon the grass.

He strode upon the watered grass all dripping with the rain, a tinkling sound all about him, the rain twinkling upon his feathers, forlorn and tortured. Yet even now there was a blaze of courage about him. He was meager and bedraggled. But he had a splendor in him. For now his glory came by being alone and lusterless in a beggar's world, and there is a time for every species to know lackluster and loneliness where there was brightness and a flocking together, since there is a change in the way creatures must go to find their ultimate station, whether they fall old and lose blitheness, ragged and lose elegance, lonely and lose love; and since there is a shifting in the levels of understanding. But there is something in each level for all creatures, pain or wisdom or despair, and never nothing. The white rooster was coming upon the grass.

Grandpa wheeled so slowly and so smoothly towards Mrs. Samuels that she could not tell he was moving, that not one board cracked in the floor. And the white rooster moved toward the trap, closer and closer he moved. When he saw the open door leading to a dry place strewn with grain, he went straight for it, a haven suddenly thrown up before his eye, a warm dry place with grain. When he got to the threshold of the trap and lifted his yellow claw to make the final step, Grandpa Samuels was so close to Mrs. Samuels that he could hear her passionate breath drawn in a kind of lust-panting. And when her heart must have said, "Let go!" to her fingers, and they tightened spasmodically so that the veins stood turgid blue in her arm, Grandpa Samuels struck at the top of her spine where the head flares down into the neck and there is a little stalk of bone, with a hunting knife he had kept for many years. There was no sound, only the sudden sliding of the cord as it made a dip and hung loose in Marcy Samuel's limp hand. Then Grandpa heard the quick clap of the door hitting the wooden floor of the trap outside, and a faint crumpling sound as of a dress dropped to the floor when Mrs. Samuels' blowsy head fell limp on her breast. Through the window Grandpa Samuels saw the white rooster leap pertly back from the trap when the door came down, a little frightened. And then he let out a peal of crowings in the rain and went away.

Grandpa sat silent for a moment and then said to Mrs. Samuels, "You will never die any other way, Marcy Samuels, my son's wife, you are meant to be done away with like this. With a hunting knife."

And then he wheeled wildly away through the rooms of Marcy Samuels' house, feeling a madness all within him, being liberated, running free. He howled with laughter and rumbled like a runaway carriage through room and room, sometimes coughing in paroxysms. He rolled here and there in every room, destroying everything he could reach, he threw up pots and pans in the kitchen, was in the flour and sugar like a whirlwind, over-turned chairs and ripped the upholstery in the living room until the stuffing flew in the air; and covered with straw and flour, white like a demented ghost, he flayed the bedroom wallpaper into hanging shreds; coughing and howling, he lashed and wrecked and razed until he thought he was bringing the very house down upon himself.

When Watson came home some minutes later to check on the success of his engine to trap the rooster and fully expecting to have to wring his neck, he saw at one look his house in such devastation that he thought a tornado had struck and demolished it inside, or that robbers had broken in. "Marcy! Marcy!" he called.

He found out why she did not call back when he discovered her by the window, cord in hand as though she had fallen asleep fishing.

"Papa! Papa!" he called.

But there was no calling back. In Grandpa's room Watson found the wheel chair with his father's wild dead body in it, his life stopped by some desperate struggle. There had obviously been a fierce spasm of coughing, for the big artery in his neck had burst and was still bubbling blood like a little red spring.

Then the neighbors all started coming in, having heard the uproar and gathered in the yard; and there was a dumbfounded-ness in all their faces when they saw the ruins in Watson Samuels' house, and Watson Samuels standing there in the ruins unable to say a word to any of them to explain what had happened.

THE LETTER IN
THE CEDARCHEST

◻▬◻

Now this is about the lives of Old Mrs. Woman, Sister Sam-mye, and Little Pigeon, and how they formed a household; but first, about Old Mrs. Woman.

Her early name, and rightful one, was Lucille Purdy; and she had had a pretty good life until she started getting fat. Lucille's husband, a tall, good-looking man, with no stomach, a good chest and a deep voice, but he had evil lips—and whose mother had lived with him and Lucille from the day they married until the day she died in Lucille's arms—had begun to hurrah her some two or three years back, especially when he saw her in her nightgown. He had said, "Lucille, one thing I cannot stand and that is a fat woman; I'll leave you, swear to God, if ever you get fat. . . . " At first Lucille had laughed and said, "Don't worry, Mr. Purdy (no one ever heard her call him anything but Mr. Purdy—when his name was Duke), I won't; I have already given up bread and potatoes."

Yet Lucille kept putting on weight, there seemed nothing she could do to stop the fat acoming; and with the constant increase in stoutness came a more and more nervousness. Naturally. Mr. Purdy's threat seemed to produce as much fat on Lucille as bread and potatoes. She noticed Mr. Purdy had begun to wear a moustache, which made him look younger and devilish, what with those lips, now with fringe on top.

When Mr. Purdy moved into a room to himself, Lucille cried alone in the master bedroom at night. Finally, one night she went into hysterics and accused Mr. Purdy of no longer caring about her. Mr. Purdy lost his temper and said, "You ought to kill yourself, Lucille, because you're slobby and no longer any good to anybody, and you're nervous and going crazy"; and he laid a revolver on the table by the side of Lucille's bed. She lay all night crying and thinking seriously of taking Mr. Purdy up on his suggestion to blow out her brains. But she prayed and remembered the sweet Christian memory of old Mother Purdy who had suffered out her life to the end and then died in her arms; and did not use the gun.

Then Lucille found out Mr. Purdy was carrying on with his stenographer. A voice advised her this on the telephone, and then Lucille called on the phone, made certain investigations, and found it all out to be true. She had hysterics and ordered Mr. Purdy out of the house. He gladly went, admitting everything, said he wanted a divorce, Lucille said she would not give him one to her dying day, he said that he was going to be married to the woman in question (who was twenty-one). And he reminded Lucille of the revolver, to take her out of her misery.

Lucille had a very hard time. She read books from the Normal for the dreams she was having, about white and black horses pulling her up mountains, and about her pulling the same horses up mountains. She was also riding the horses sometimes. The books helped her some (yet they didn't stop the dreams); but it was the minister of her church that really helped her—for a while. Helped her so much that she begun to have giggling and crying spells when she was in his office counseling with him. The minister was stumped as to what to do. The minister suggested that Lucille go into Sunday School work with children, and Lucille added that she loved working with children; so she did this. But other Sunday School teachers complained that Lucille was too fussy with the children, that she would humor them, then pinch them and even slap them, then cry over them. They asked her to take a rest.

It was while she was taking a rest, and crying most of the time, that she decided to go on with the divorce which she had so stubbornly opposed up to now. She took it to court, got the divorce, Mr. Purdy (still not married) left her the big house but took all the furniture out which was his by rights, he said, since it had been his mother's. This left Lucille's house completely bare except for the cedarchest which she had married Duke with, from her girlhood—she had been raised by two old women cousins, and an orphan since she was twelve.

Now Lucille was alone in her big empty house, and still putting on poundage. Her minister advised her to put her house up for sale and move into just a little board cottage somewhere, but the house was all Lucille had and she wanted to cling to it. She made her a cat pallet in the master bedroom and cooked on a gas burner she bought. She barely lived on the monthly allowance Mr. Purdy was compelled by law to send—and when he pleased, sometimes on time, most of the time not. She cried nearly all the time; and the neighbors who had known her all these years naturally began to turn from her and to suspicion her because she acted so funny. If they asked her questions about herself or her husband, she was quick to snap at them, "Ask me no questions I'll tell you no lies," and walk away. Therefore, one by one they let her alone; politely but firmly.

When she went back to her church they would not have her in the Sunday School and so she cried and said she knew it was because she was too fat, the minister couldn't do much with her, she went into a red rage with the woman in the Sunday School, and this is when she asked to have her church Letter out. She got it, read it carefully to see that there were no mistakes in it: "This is to certify that Lucille Marie Purdy is a member of the Lord's Household in good standing and full fellowship and to recommend her as a faithful servant to all those present. . . . " She put it in her cedarchest.

It was then that Lucille decided to take on boarders. She furnished two bedrooms when she found out three young men from the Normal would rent the rooms. The three young men moved in, two in the big room—these were the gentle one and the outspoken one—where Mr. Purdy had gone off to sleep and live when Lucille had got so stout, and one in the corner bedroom next to Lucille's—this one was the young wild one who had worked his way to Spain on a freighter and had gone crazy over bullfights, bringing back from Spain a long black whip which he practiced cracking, even late at night you could hear the stinging hot crackling of it in his room. Lucille's room continued to be the master bedroom, just furnished with a pallet and a cedarchest.

These three young men are a story in themselves, and it is peculiar how life arranged to bring them into Lucille's house, and at such a time in Lucille's life. Often Lucille said, "I know the Lord sent you all here; it is His Divine Hand; there is more love in this household than in any church, I am glad I have moved my Letter into this house." But anyway, these three young men were a nice thing for Lucille to have in her house and Lucille became very nice with them in her house. They wondered about the state of the house, why it was not furnished, and so on, but they did not ask questions. Mostly they were at the Normal all day, and at nights they studied in their rooms or met in one another's room to have their talk and laughter, which Lucille would overhear if she stood against the wall and listened; until one night Lucille knocked on their door at late night and said, "Listen here, since you are still up and talking would you like to move your conversation on down to the kitchen and have you some hot cocoa with it?" and in a little while they had formed the pleasant habit of meeting in the kitchen for hot cocoa every night about eleven. Naturally some talk ensued. The young men told of their work at the Normal and told of their lives and interests, the gentle one told how he wanted to be a poet (Lucille said she often wrote poems and would show him hers); the outspoken one disagreed with most of Lucille's philosophy about life, but in a friendly way that made Lucille feel intellectually stimulated; and the wild one said he only wanted to wander and to travel, free on the road. Lucille responded that her father himself had been a sea captain and roamed and that that was why she was part gypsy, her two cousins raised her but never understood her, she had always had a gypsy heart. Then Lucille had something in common with each of the roomers, she declared; and it wasn't long before Lucille had told the roomers all about her husband leaving her, explaining that he had taken the furniture; and as she told her story she broke out crying. The roomers were very sympathetic and tried to comfort Lucille.

After awhile you had this nice household of Lucille and the three comforting young men. They began to wait on her hand and foot, and Lucille wore fresh dresses and kept the house clean. They refused to allow her to sleep on a pallet and all bought her a daybed. They went through the winter this way. When it snowed so heavily that one time, some of the neighbors were surprised to hear Lucille's voice squealing outdoors and looked out to see her shooting down the slope of her snow-covered lawn on a sled pushed by the three roomers. Life had changed for Lucille, she had a regular household, the roomers had built furniture of tables and bookcases and things and they had chipped in and helped buy other things to make the big living room nice, there was fire in the fireplace, often singing (the wild roomer played a guitar), and Lucille fixed supper every night for the household; they were all around the table like a family.

When spring came, the young wild roomer quit the Normal, he was too restless; and Lucille let him stay on free of charge until he could determine what to do, whether to get a job and study castanets, or what; and they all worked together in the yard and planted flowers in the beds. This is where Little Pigeon comes in.

Being for the most of the time alone over in her house across Lucille's back yard, she lots of the time just stood at her window and watched across to see the life and lights of Lucille's big changed house; all the shades were raised, now. She heard singing and she heard laughing and she saw figures busy in the lighted rooms of the house that had been dark so long. She heard guitars and she heard castanets and she heard the snapping of the bullwhip. Finally, one time when she could not find her purse and had called long distance to Rodunda to ask her widow sister Sammye where she had hidden it but Sister Sammye had just hung up in her face, Little Pigeon thought of the bright and living house of Lucille's across the yard. She decided to knock on the door of this house. She did, and when Lucille came to the door, Little Pigeon said, "Mrs. Woman (for she did not know her name), I have lost my purse."

Now Lucille had had a few experiences with Little Pigeon before, and with Little Pigeon's sister Sammye, too; and she knew about the trouble and disorder of that household over across the yard and wanted nothing to do with it. Earlier, and just after Mr. Purdy had left Lucille, Sammye had come over and asked her please to keep an eye out after Little Pigeon while she was away, and Lucille had tried but it didn't work out—mainly because of Sammye. Lucille wanted nothing to do with the two sisters, and she very quickly said to Little Pigeon, "You better go on back home and look for your purse again, or call your sister Sammye, because I am sure it is not here," and was going to close the door, when one of the roomers, the gentle one, came up and began to make friends with Little Pigeon. He had seen her at her window and he had heard Lucille speak of the crazy woman next door. He invited Little Pigeon in before the fire. Little Pigeon came in timidly, looked all around, and said, "You all have a nice household here. Is it a party?" And they all said no and to sit down. They gave her some cocoa, Little Pigeon told a story about a place she and Selmus, her husband, had gone to when they used to travel around; and then the gentle roomer saw her home (having to stay in Little Pigeon's house for her to show him all her things and tell him the story of them). Little Pigeon kept her new discovery of the party across the yard a secret from her sister Sammye, among other secrets she kept.

This started all the trouble. Constantly Little Pigeon's voice at her back door would call out, "Mrs. Woman! Mrs. Woman!" And when Lucille would answer at her back door, Little Pigeon would have nothing to say but "Can you come over?" quietly. Lucille would give some excuse and not go; but finally she weakened and went over. Usually it was for nothing and Little Pigeon would have nothing to say, except to show her things and ask about the party in Lucille's house. When Lucille would turn around and leave, Little Pigeon would weep very quietly and this would hurt Lucille, for she knew enough about tears. Finally, Lucille found herself over at Little Pigeon's most every day, at one time or another, looking at Little Pigeon's things, which Little Pigeon would count and tell about. Lucille would complain that she had her work to do in her house, to look after her roomers, they were such a handful, and Little Pigeon then began to appear every night at Lucille's house, her face would be at the window or her knock on the door, and they would have to let her in to join them.

When Little Pigeon's sister Sammye would come in from the next town of Rodunda and find that Little Pigeon had been neighborly with Lucille and over visiting in her house, she would be angry and order Little Pigeon to stop ever calling Lucille again. For Sammye had heard the stories in the neighborhood about Lucille; she, in fact, knew the *whole* story, and would have nothing to do with her. In turn, the neighbors would have nothing to do with Little Pigeon *or* Sammye because of Little Pigeon's antics in the neighborhood, her wandering about and her calling the fire department and the police for the slightest thing, and then just to talk with them. Some of the neighbors tried to get Little Pigeon ordered to a Home, but Sammye stopped that and told them to mind their own business; and fell out with the neighbors.

So you had this complicated neighborhood, all enemies to Lucille and to Little Pigeon, having nothing whatsoever to do with either of them; and Lucille and Little Pigeon divided against each other by Sammye, but coming together when she was away.

Then things began to wear in Lucille's household. Lucille began to pick on and pester the roomers, or humor and coddle them, much in the same way as she had treated the Sunday

School children. She would fuss at them when they wouldn't eat, she would order them around, she would criticize their hab- its, she would have spells of temper or poutishness; and some- times she would suddenly change into such wildness, like doing a gypsy dance—even as fat as she still was (she seemed to have forgotten that)—while the wild roomer played his guitar or cracked his long black bullwhip. The outspoken roomer did not like what he saw, and the gentle roomer suffered most of all, for he had to return the clothes of Mr. Purdy which Mr. Purdy had left behind and which Lucille had given to him, and they fit perfectly, when she suddenly asked for them back. The roomers were more and more unsettled in Lucille's house. They could not predict what she would break out and do, without any warning. The household was like a troubled mind, with tormenting ideas, desires and suspicions. The outspoken roomer got fed up with Lucille's talk and tantrums and just stayed out of her way. The gentle one tried to reason with her but he could get no farther with her than the minister had been able to. So he withdrew. The young wild roomer tried to make light of her misery, to liven her up, of course, by cracking his whip suddenly behind her; but this only made Lucille scream into hysterics. Even Little Pigeon deviled Lucille by playing a kind of hide-and-seek with her: face at the window, voice at the back door, vanishing and appearing.

The first thing to go was the hot cocoa at night; no one would come down—just to go through all Lucille's story and spells again. The next was supper; the roomers wouldn't come down to that, either. So Lucille stopped cooking. Her bad crying spells started again.

Well, this situation grew and grew, the roomers were all in their rooms with doors shut; Lucille was shut out and left alone again. Lucille took it out on Little Pigeon and was mean to her, abusing her and teasing her and confusing her. Little Pigeon could not understand and did not know what to do, but she fought back gamely and seemed to have a good time doing it. Finally, when the roomers notified Lucille that they were leaving,

Little Pigeon invited them to move over into her house, where the party, as she called it, could go on; but the roomers packed up and left, taking their furniture with them. Lucille remembered the revolver Mr. Purdy had given her, and his words with it, except that now it seemed to her that the roomers had left the revolver, and in the same way. She was on the point of using it upon herself. Why did everything spoil in her household? It was because she was so fat. She would stand for minutes before the mirror and look at herself, turning round and round. She would do this nude, too; and beat herself in the fattest places, she hated them so. She ran up and down the stairs nude, either to reduce herself or because she was going crazy, who knows. It was this way, running naked up and down the stairs in her empty house, that Little Pigeon found her once, and laughed until she cried. Whereupon Lucille covered herself and began to cry with Little Pigeon, there on the stairs. There was this sympathy between the two poor women. Then is when they became very close; and then is when Sammye enters the picture.

When Sammye came in from Rodunda and found Little Pigeon turned over in the hedge like a toy bird with its spindly legs kicking as if they were unwinding, she picked Little Pigeon out and what do you think Little Pigeon did for thanks? Sassed Sammye and said *she'd* pushed her in the hedge, all to run and get her purse. But Sammye didn't care, she didn't get mad or anything, she just picked Little Pigeon out and took her in the house and washed her off. And said, "You are my sweet sister that I love and adore."

Then Little Pigeon said, "I can't figure it all out. Old Mrs. Woman pushed me in the bush and went back to her house across the yard and the ghost of Sister Sammye come and pulled me out."

Sammye said, "Forget the ghost of Sister Sammye and leave Old Mrs. Woman to her own house. It is all over, your playparty, and I am back here to look after you and to tend to you and I am no ghost either, I am your fleshandblood Sister Sammye. Sweet Little Pigeon." And everything seemed all right.

Now that Little Pigeon and Sammye were old, both their husbands dead, Sammye came up from Rodunda as often as she could to stay with her as long as she could suffer it. Because Little Pigeon was no longer accountable to herself; and, besides, she had to have someone to give her her insulin every morning, no practical nurse would do it, no practical nurse would stay in the same house with Little Pigeon, Sammye had tried it, don't worry, because Little Pigeon thought a nurse was trying to take her money, which was in a bank, and safe there, but that didn't make no difference to Little Pigeon; she worried about it anyway. "Besides, Little Pigeon loves me and I love and adore her," Sammye would say. "She is my sweet sister that I love and adore. She fights me a lot (*I* don't want her Irish linens and her bone china), but that's all right, that don't make me no difference. She's my sweet sister that I love and adore, truly do."

Once Sammye missed her and called through all the house, through all the yard, went up and down the sidewalk calling through the neighborhood, but no Little Pigeon. Then she came back in the house and wondered whether to call the police again. Then Sammye heard a ruckus upstairs. Up she went and there was the kicking legs of Little Pigeon with the rest of her under the bed. Sammye said, "What on earth are you doing under there, Little Pigeon? Come out"; and Little Pigeon said, "Hush up, I'm looking for my lost black purse."

"Oh have you lost that again?" Sammye said.

And Little Pigeon said, "You hush it because you have stolen it anyway"; and out she came fast as lightning. They had it all to go over again, the black purse. They spent half the day looking for it, and of course they found it, Little Pigeon had thrown it in the trashcan. Then said Sammye had done it. And was as mad as all outdoors.

Little Pigeon's life was never hard, she was spoilt from the beginning. She was very beautiful, you could still tell it if you looked at her complexion; she still was, hair real fine and naturally curly, a set of flashing lashy eyes like Miss Maybelline, and a little sweetheart mouth. She was always prettier than Sammye, she was the flighty one, cute as a thimble, had all the boy friends, Sunday beau, Candy beau, every one; Sammye was the practical one, and had nothing. "And what does it matter if she was ugly to me then?" Sammye would declare. "I am sweet to her now and I will be till she dies, I don't care if they say it's for her money, that is a Satanish lie, I am here to look after her when I can be, for she is my sweet sister that I love and adore."

Little Pigeon's husband wedded her when he was twenty and she was eighteen, and they had lots of trips all their life, to Cuba and every place. He knew a lot about horses, bred his own, and Little Pigeon swore he brought his finest horse in the kitchen one morning to have breakfast with them. "But don't pay any 'tention to her when she says that, it's the effect of the insulin," Sammye would say. "Makes her tell the wildest tales. But oh she is so sweet, that sweet sister."

They never had chick nor child, Little Pigeon and her husband Selmus, just all they wanted, big cars and chinaware, Persian rugs and fine furniture. Sammye said she remembers coming to visit them when they were flourishing, and wanting to touch the pretty things, but Little Pigeon would say, "Take your hands off my crystal candy jar," or, "Don't smut up my Dresden compote made of Dresden." Selmus would be down in the basement listening to the radio. He died there, of a sudden, in the basement listening to the horse races. But Little Pigeon was already weakening by then, in her notions of things. She needed insulin then but they didn't know it. She was a sweet thing and cried at Selmus's funeral. When Sammye and Little Pigeon came home from the funeral, Little Pigeon counted her silver that Selmus had given to her, and cried again; but not a tear fell on the silver to smutten it up, you understand; she was careful of that. "Oh now she's sweet and I love and adore her, but I know her bad points, and I know her good points, too, of which they are bountiful," Sammye would say.

"Pity Little Pigeon," Sammye would say. "She's got nothing in this wide world but me and a house full of fine things. (*I* don't want any of them.) Her days run away in a dream. She dusts her porcelain, cleans her pretty Persian rugs, counts her linens and counts her silver. If an ant had crawled over one little spoon of that sterling in the night, Little Pigeon would know it the next morning. Yet she can't see to find her purse."

Well, Sammye stayed as long as she could with Little Pigeon, until she had to go back up to Rodunda to see after her own house. "After all," she said, "I have my own house. Pigeon thinks I can just close that house up and run to her whenever she needs me, but she don't reckon that *I* have a house, too, with my life in it and all my things, not so fine as hers, but my house; and all my responsibilities." Once when Sammye had to leave Little Pigeon, she asked that old Mrs. Whatchamacallit next door please to look after Little Pigeon and not let her catch the house afire or leave the garage lights burning all night and then wake up and call the fire department because she thinks the garage is burning down and it the middle of the night. Now Old Mrs. Whatser-name was in a bad fix, too; but she agreed to watch out after Little Pigeon after hemming and hawing that she had her hands full already. "How come?" Sammye said. "She has nothing to do —her husband's just left her and she's all alone in a big two-storied house in which she cries all day and half the night, I've seen her. Once I said, 'What's the trouble, Mrs.—Thing?' And she said, 'Because I'm the fattest woman in church.' Then said she had taken her Letter out because the church showed favoritism. Said she had her Letter in her cedarchest and was going to keep it there, said that even that cedarchest was a better church than most; and cried and cried. I didn't know what to say to humor her, but I finally said, 'Well I'm sure there are fatter women than you in church,' but guess this was the wrong thing to say." Anyway, she sure was the wrong thing for Little Pigeon, the same devilment in both of them and they fought like dog and cat when they came upon each other outdoors. Sammye said she knew for a fact that Old Mrs. Woman hit Little Pigeon because Little Pigeon showed her where and showed her the blue place it left. Oh well, they was a-pulling stunts right and left, they spit and they spat, and then Sammye had *two* of them on her hands.

Then Old Mrs. Woman and Sammye had it good and proper, and Old Mrs. Woman ended up by saying, "Mrs. Johnson, your sister ought to be in an institution." And Sammye said, "This strikes me as real funny, why don't you let it strike you thataway. If anybody's going to be sent to an institution it ought to be *you*." For a long time after, Old Mrs. Woman did not speak to Sammye and Little Pigeon once, kept all her shades pulled down on the side of the house facing Little Pigeon's, what she did in that big house no one knew, but it was guessed she went on crying and crying. Sammye told Little Pigeon time and time again not to call her anymore, but when Sammye was not watching, Little Pigeon would go to the back steps and call out before Sammye could catch her, "Mrs. Woman! Mrs. Woman!"—until Sammye would go out and shut her up and bring her in. There was this devilish attraction between Little Pigeon and Old Mrs. Woman.

Well, one time Little Pigeon and Sammye had a real frickus, all over the lost purse again, nobody could find it anywhere; and Sammye just couldn't stand it any longer so just walked out the front door and went back to Rodunda, tired of it all. She stayed a few weeks, and no long distance calls came from Little Pigeon, no sound or sign of her; and Sammye said just let her stew and learn her lesson. Finally, though, Sammye got worried and was in a stew herself—that's the way Little Pigeon did her: always turned things back onto *her,* and double—so took the bus and came on to Little Pigeon's. She went in the house, unlocked as usual, and couldn't find her anywhere. She called and she called, but no Little Pigeon. Then she looked out the window and what did she spy but the two of them, Little Pigeon, her sweet sister, and Old Mrs. Woman, prissing arm in arm down the sidewalk like two Queen of Shebas. Old Mrs. Woman and Little Pigeon had made friends! Sammye saw Little Pigeon all dressed up and all fixed up like she had never seen her before, her hair waved and set, lipstick on and rouge on, her ruby earbobs on, her good shoes on, and the right shoe on the right foot, and in her lovely fur coat. Glued onto her and just as prissy was Old Mrs. Woman, fat as ever but primped up, too, and they were going along like this. Sammye raised the window and called "Little Pigeon! Little Pigeon! This is Sister Sammye come to visit her sweet sister, come on in and let me kiss you hello!" But know what Little Pigeon did? Prissed at Sammye and raised her nose, turned her head away and walked on, Old Mrs. Woman clamped onto her and walking straight along without moving her eyes from ahead. This hurt Sammye to the core. But she pulled down the window and sat down in Little Pigeon's living room to think about it. She thought, well I'll leave; and then she thought, no, I'll just stay, that's what I'll do.

Then they came home, after they had had their beauty walk and seen a show, they came in the house and began ignoring Sammye. Sammye could have been a ghost for all she knew. They went into the kitchen, whispering and cooing, and Sammye came in and said, "It's time for your insulin, Little Pigeon," just to see. Little Pigeon turned and declared that only Mrs. Woman gave her her insulin anymore. Then they fixed supper and invited Sammye to sit down and eat, oh they offered her some supper, but they never talked to her at all, they talked about the picture show they had seen, Old Mrs. Woman saying in her baby-talk, "What did the man in the picture show do, Sweetest Thing in This World?" and Sweetest Thing in This World answering, "Killed the woman!" And Old Mrs. Woman spoke back so smart, "Tha-a-a-s right!" It was plain to Sammye that Old Mrs. Woman had taken over Little Pigeon and had made a kindergarten out of Little Pigeon's house, for she saw those tissue paper snow crystals pasted on the sun porch windows. Old Mrs. Woman would coo, "Now drink your milk, Sweet Thing"; and Little Pigeon would drink it right down. Then she said, "Now Sweet Thing it's time for bed, let's go on upstairs." And up they went without a whimper from Little Pigeon. What is this new Little Pigeon, my sweet sister? Sammye thought. She just stood up and said, mad as the mischief at the bottom of the staircase, "Well how do you do!" Then she got her things and went straight back to Rodunda, where she wrote a letter to Old Mrs. Woman at Little

Pigeon's address. "I demand to know," her letter stated, "what have you caused to come over my sister, what have you done to turn her against me?" Said, "If you think you will get her to give you some of her pretty things you are just sadly mistaken, because you won't." Said, "I want you to stop taking her around, and I want you to stop prissing her up and I want you to stop humoring her, right this very minute. She's not *your* sister." Sammye sent the letter.

In a few days a call came for Sammye and it was Old Mrs. Woman on the telephone, long distance, in her creamiest voice, as if she was a receptionist or something—and had never received the letter. "Your sister has lost her purse and says to call you because you have hidden it." Sammye said, "I certainly have not and you will do me the favor of stopping ever calling me about my sister's purse or about any other thing that goes on in my sister's house, I am through. You have done something or said something to lowrate me in the eyes of my sister. You old crazy, you have lost your marbles. You have turned my sweet sister against me and if you are not careful I will take out action against you." She told her upside down, crossways and crooked; then she hung up in Old Mrs. Woman's face and began to think: now use your head, Sammye Johnson, and take aholt of the situation, now that you have told Old Mrs. Woman off. You have fussed and nearly pulled your hair out because of the worry of Little Pigeon, now here is somebody to look after her if you handle it right. Make out a list of what she must do for Little Pigeon, tell her you will pay her by the week, and you have got the practical nurse for Little Pigeon and one she apparently will let stay in the house.

A few days passed and Sammye could find nothing to do with herself. Rodunda was small and there were only a handful of people she would have anything to do with, and they were all busy with their husbands and housekeeping. Sammye begun to realize that she had nothing in her life to do or take her mind and interest because she had centered everything around worrying over Little Pigeon. She suddenly felt how alone she would be not to have to worry or look after Little Pigeon. What did she have? She looked around her house one night and got scared. She put on her things next morning and went to go see Little Pigeon.

But when she got there it was too late. They wouldn't let her in because they shouted out the window that she had hidden Little Pigeon's purse. That settles it, Sammye said; and went back to Rodunda. She kept saying to herself, But Sammye why are you so upset? You ought to be relieved. Take this good thing while you can. You are free of all that worry that was driving you to your grave.

Some nights in her house Sammye got unnerved because she was so all alone. She tried to fix up her house, to have some company, to visit around; but she was so all alone. Often she dreamt of Little Pigeon. Why didn't she think of her sister, why didn't she have the telephone operator call her sister? Finally she said to herself, This is too much of a good thing; and she got on the bus and went to go see Little Pigeon.

But when she got there they wouldn't let her in again, even after three weeks. In fact, Little Pigeon's face at the window looked like she thought Sammye was a stranger or a ghost. She didn't care about her at all. And Old Mrs. Woman wouldn't come to the window at all or unlock the door. Well, Sammye felt like some dream was going on inside that house, that she was left outside some dream. She cried, "I have to get in to see you Little Pigeon, I have to talk to you, I am your Sister Sammye, have you lost your mind?" What could she do? Night was falling and she left and went down to the drug store and ate her a sandwich, to let things settle. She walked on back to Little Pigeon's in the dark, wondering whether she would have her in, this time; and thinking, well, maybe I am a ghost, I've been by myself so long I don't know whether I'm live or dead.

But the drapes were drawn almost to, and when she peeked in between them she saw the two of them by the fire, Little Pigeon just dreaming and purring, Old Mrs. Woman lumped and rolled up into herself whispering some story to herself. But what kind of a room was this? The room was so full of decorations and stuff that there wasn't enough space left in it to cuss a cat in. There were hanging paper lanterns, paper streamers streaming from the ceiling, paper balls and paper stars. They had made a fairyland playhouse out of Little Pigeon's spotless living room. Then Sammye saw Old Mrs. Woman moving around through all the waving shapes and strands of colored paper. She saw her go to the mirror and look in it at herself and say, "I'm not so fat, am I, Sweet Thing?" And heard Little Pigeon answer back, "No, Mrs. Woman."

Sammye said to herself outside the window, "I know one thing and that is that Old Mrs. Woman is crazy. I'll break up *this* playparty." She began to beat on the sides of the house calling, "Little Pigeon! Little Pigeon! Let me in. I am your sweet sister who loves and adores you!" But she could not disturb the dream of this playhouse. She walked round and round the house, trying to understand it and decide what to do. She saw across the yard Old Mrs. Woman's big dark empty house, wrapped in a dream, too. She felt so left out. Then she thought of what to do. She tried the basement door and it was unlocked. She went down there quietly and sat under them to see what else she could hear. Suddenly she heard the music begin, it was "Whispering," and she heard their feet adancing, just like ghost feet. They danced and they danced, then the music stopped and Sammye heard their feet going up the staircase to bed. Then it was all quiet. Sammye went to sleep on the basement divan, cold and peeved, down among the pipes and storage like a mouse or a lonesome cricket.

The next morning they were up there, in the kitchen, over Sammye. She heard them fix their breakfast and eat it, she heard Little Pigeon getting her insulin. Then they went into the dining room and they were in the china and the silverware. Sammye heard Little Pigeon say where each piece came from, how her husband had given her this and that, not to smutten up the Dresden compote made of Dresden, Sammye heard her ghostly voice counting the table service of pure silver, one two three four five—and heard Old Mrs. Woman say softly, "Tha-a-a-s right!"

After awhile Little Pigeon suddenly came into the basement without a word of warning. She saw Sammye sitting there and did not pay her any mind. Finally Sammye spoke out and said, "Hello Little Pigeon!" and Little Pigeon said, "Hush up, ghost of Sister Sammye." She was looking for her purse, very seriously, going through everything in the baesment. Then she said, "Well, I guess it's not down here, guess Sister Sammye's stolen it," and went on up and out in her dream that Old Mrs. Woman had put her into.

This gave Sammye an idea. For then she knew that Old Mrs. Woman had told Little Pigeon that she had passed on, or something, and that her face at the window and around the house had been her ghost and not to worry about it. Sammye made her a plan. "If that's the way they want it, I'll just *be* a ghost, and a good one at that!" she declared. She decided to make her home in the basement for awhile, and started making it nice down there where poor Selmus had come to live when Little Pigeon abused him so, by making him go down there to listen to the horse races, which he adored.

Then when Sammye heard Old Mrs. Woman go out the back door, she watched her through the basement window and saw her going over to her big empty house across the yard. When Old Mrs. Woman was inside her big house, Sammye rapped on the basement ceiling and called out very mournfully, "Little Pigeon! Little Pigeon!" Sammye heard Little Pigeon's feet acoming down the basement stairs. Little Pigeon came in the basement. The two stood looking at each other. Then Little Pigeon said, "You are Sister Sammye's ghost, and go away." Sammye said, "Now looka here, I am *not* my ghost, I am your real Sister Sammye and you are looking straight at me. I am live as a coal of fire, and want to know what's going on in this house that I have to bang on the sides of it and at the windows to try to get in to see my own sister. What has Old Mrs. Woman done to you to change you? Now tell your sweet sister."

Little Pigeon just swanked and said, "Go 'way, ghost of Sister Sammye."

Sammye waited a minute and then said, in a ghost's voice,

"Put out something you treasure for a ghost and he will go away."

"But what?" Little Pigeon asked. "You are trying to get my things, just like Old Mrs. Woman said."

Sammye said, "I don't care about your things, put out the ghost some supper. And never tell a soul."

Well, this is the way Sammye got her supper, for a while.

Then Sammye started working her plan. Sammye thought, I'll wart them to death, I'll be a regular Jonah to those two, I'll give them what they asked for and deserve. When Little Pigeon and Old Mrs. Woman would be out walking, Sammye would steal up into the house and touch her fingers on the silver or on the crystal. When they would come back Little Pigeon would find the prints and smuts of fingers on her things and say, "Somebody's fingers been on my things. The ghost has been here." And Old Mrs. Woman would look with big eyes and not know what to think. Or, again, Sammye would sneak Little Pigeon's purse from where she had it and put it in another place. Sammye would hear the two of them tearing the house down looking for it.

Well, you don't have to hear any more, you can see how it all ended up: Old Mrs. Woman began to get the blame from Little Pigeon for all the stunts Sammye pulled. She tried then to say there was no ghost and to blame Little Pigeon for trying to devil *her,* Little Pigeon was all mixed up but said there most assuredly *was* one, for she had seen it, etc. etc.; and it was the end of their happy honeymoon when Little Pigeon and Old Mrs. Woman had a knock-down-drag-out in the driveway and Old Mrs. Woman pushed Little Pigeon over into the hedge. Then is when Sammye appeared from the basement and picked Little Pigeon out.

Old Mrs. Woman went back over to her big empty house, back to crying; and everything was like it started out, except that Little Pigeon couldn't get *ghost* out of her mind and still thought Sammye was Sammye's ghost and Sammye could not change her mind. So Sammye stayed a ghost; anything to humor Little Pigeon. But otherwise everything was just the same, Sammye had

Little Pigeon back, worrying her to death, calling her long distance at Rodunda when she was not with her, mistreating her and fussing at her when she was with her, and accusing her of stealing her purse or touching her things—Sammye got the blame for everything that was wrong—Sammye was about to pull her hair out with Little Pigeon, said she had no life of her own, said she had nothing, was just a ghost of herself. "But she is my sweet sister that I love and adore," Sammye would still say.

Yet it was peculiar how there seemed to be a real ghost in Little Pigeon's house, just as Little Pigeon had said; for very often they would hear commotions in the basement, and on many mornings they would come down to find the prints of fingers that had touched all over Little Pigeon's things. Sammye would go down to the basement to look around for signs, but there seemed nothing. Once in a while she caught Little Pigeon still going faithfully down the basement stairs with some hot supper for the basement ghost and would have to stop her and try to reason with her that the ghost that used to be down there had gone away and would never come again. But this was difficult, since Little Pigeon was so far gone in her dream of things by that time; so often Sammye would just let her go and play with the ghost she thought was living in the basement. Sweet Little Pigeon.

But when Sammye went down to the basement one day, and just to get something this time, not to investigate or spy, what should she find but Old Mrs. Woman! Sammye smelled a rat and said, looking at her out of the corner of her eye, "Go 'way ghost of Old Mrs. Woman!" Old Mrs. Woman prissed and flaunted and said, "Put out something you treasure for a ghost and she will go away. Ha!"

Then Sammye, who had always been the practical one, decided to use her head. She sat down on the divan that used to be her bed when she was a ghost in the basement herself, and said, "Well, Mrs. Woman, this is foolishness, a ghost pestering a ghost, we'll drive each other into insanity and all end up in the

Home. I'm not going to give up and you're not either. We mind
as well be ghosts together. I've got no household anymore and
you've got none, nor Little Pigeon either, except for what we
make for her, by hook or crook; we mind as well make one whole
household out of three pieces of households. Why don't you
move on in the basement, move your cedarchest with the Letter
in it on over here and I'll move my things in from Rodunda—
and we'll all three have us a household, us two old ghosts and
the sweet Little Pigeon. She can't get us out of her head anyway,
thinks we're here when we aren't and we aren't when we are.
Everybody's everywhere, so far as I can make out, and I'm beginning to not be sure where I am, myself—and I don't believe you
know. This shuttling from house to house is killing us both and
will make ghosts of us before we know it. Come on over, Mrs.
Woman." And then Sammye said something which if she had
said it much earlier in the game would have changed the whole
story from the beginning; and saved a lot of traffic. She said it in
a quiet tone that she used in talking to herself, "All we want, I
guess, is a household that will let us be the way we are."

The two women shook hands, here were the two ghosts
down in the basement making covenant, bargaining to make the
ghost story come true for Little Pigeon upstairs—who already
believed in it anyway and had more or less made it come true,
will or nill.

But Sammye and Old Mrs. Woman had a few things to
settle first. Old Mrs. Woman said, "This basement is as much
your house as it is mine, you seemed to like it well enough to live
down here once. Why don't *you* move in the basement, Sammye
Johnson?" Sammye did not argue and suggested that they take
turns living in the basement, adding that the divan was uncomfortable, though, even for a ghost to sleep on. Old Mrs. Woman
said she would move in her daybed that the roomers had bought
for her; and it was agreed upon. "One last thing," Mrs. Woman
said, "and that is please to note that my name is Lucille Purdy
and you will do me the favor of please calling me the same."

So Lucille moved her cedarchest with the Letter in it into

the basement, and the daybed, too; and the household flourished. In a few years the life of the town all shifted in another direction and moved there, towards the new development of what had been just a no-good thicket, something was suddenly there—oil or mineral or better land or something—that the town craved or thought it did, the way towns do, sometimes; change their shape and size and way, trying to form something —what?—and trying to find something to gather round. It was a time when everything shifted and changed, swarmed and clustered around an idea or a craving, used it up or wearied of it, then scattered to pieces again, it was a time of clashes of cravings, it was like a bunch of sheep moving and wandering, shepherd or no—he only followed when he was supposed to lead and could not summon them all together, or there was no shepherd (maybe that was the trouble), he was lost under the hill.

People of this section followed the town into the thicket where the town became so changed; politicians fought, money came from another part of the country; the town thrived. The old houses in the left-behind section were torn down or simply just abandoned, almost as if in a hurry because of a plague or a flood, this left-behind section became a kind of ghost town— almost as if the whole living town had turned away from Little Pigeon and Sammye and Lucille and would have nothing to do with them. But they stayed behind, and did not even know they stayed behind, they did not even know there was another place to want to go to, their shuttling was through. For the shape of the household in Little Pigeon's house was fixed forever, and it never changed again, it went on aflourishing—it had found something to hold it together, and that was a covenant of ghosts.

In a few years Little Pigeon died, still believing her house had two ghosts living in it, one above and one below, one stealing her purse and the other dancing with her in the paper room; and both of them giving her her insulin, listening to her count her things and tell about them.

After Little Pigeon was buried, the two women Sammye and Lucille had several good years together in Little Pigeon's house; you could see them swanking down the sidewalk on many a sunshiny afternoon, arm in arm, hair all set and good clothes on, strolling through the neighborhood of empty houses and down deserted streets, Sammye in Little Pigeon's ruby earbobs and in her good fur coat, Lucille fat as ever; and few people will ever know what had brought them together to be such friends, who had been such enemies.

Those who know the story to the end say the ghost of Little Pigeon came regularly and counted and touched all her things, but no more to devil the household or to cause it trouble, only just to join it and keep it whole, and that the basement room was always kept nice for her—it was her turn down there, now—until Sammye finally died and left Lucille with too many ghosts for flesh to bear; and so she opened her cedarchest and took out the Letter and put it in her bosom and then took out the revolver Mr. Purdy had given her years ago and ended the last life of the household—joining ghost to ghost, the best household and the longest lasting.

People of the town, the kind who always know mysterious stories about this old house ot that dead person, say the ghosts of two old women walk arm in arm through this ruined section when the sun shines in winter. That you can occasionally still see the three ghosts moving through the house. That one of the women was crazy and another committed suicide, and that the house was a household of violence and hatred and jealousy.

It is true that the house of Little Pigeon still stands, closed up and passed by, as it had always been even when the town was living close around it; so go and look at it if you don't believe it. Go and look through the side windows at the faded paper streamers in the paper room, go around and find the withered tissue snow crystals peeling from the sunporch windows in the back. It has not been sold or rented or tampered with until this day, that anybody knows of, but has grown along in some dream of its own. The trees have grown up high around it and locked branches over it as if to roof it away from the world, and the hedges are uncropped and rank, high and thick as a wall. This makes it seem ghosthouse enough, and it is true that the house is known only as the house where three old evil women lived, a crazy woman and her sister and a woman who shot herself. But that's one story. And if you know the whole story, as now you do, you can come stand at the window and hear a ghostly voice counting out the silverware and linens, or the riffle of ghost feet to the music of "Whispering"; and then you can have it all straight and can understand the household that was covenanted for there. And can understand the town, too; and can have your own story, ghost story or flesh story, out of the whole thing.

Anyway, that is the story about the lives of Old Mrs. Woman, Sister Sammye and Little Pigeon, and how they formed a household in a town that passed them by.

PORE PERRIE

◻▬◻

For James McAllen

"Tell me the story of pore Perrie. Tell how she lived all her life till she died."

"Hush asking me 'cause I don't want to tell it. 'Twas buried with pore Perrie in her grave. . . ."

"The flesh of it is buried, but we have the ghost of it again. Pore Perrie's grave holds only half the story—the other's yet to come."

"Then let me bring the half to the half myself. When Perrie and I join in the Polk plot in the cemetery, laid side by side, we'll settle it all, ghost and flesh, under the dirt. Dirt takes everything back again, in the end. Now let us alone. Leave us to dirt."

"But this is a good time to tell, while I'm here and you're here—and we may never be again. For soon (tonight) I moan be on my way; I cain't stay. So tell it to me because I want to get it all straight. Let me have it from your mouth now, and for the last time, and then I can have it again from my memory as I go on, on the road."

"Some one of you always passing through and stopping by, asking my stories, asking my time, asking my grief, won't let a life be. Worse than a bed of red ants. Be glad when my life's story settles down into the ground, a fallen message to be told out no more, locked in the box of my bones: message and bone go back into dirt. (Blood kin buried together settle their *own* stories, a family graveyard plot is a mailbox of messages all reading each other—who ever thought they lie quiet together and in peace at last, gladly beyond?)

"But go get me something to fan with, my cardboard fan from the church is done fanned out; the newspaper will do. . . ."

2

"Well if you see yonder at those bunch of houses by the boxy churchhouse and see the little squatty one huddling next to it like a chick to a hen, then that's the house where we all lived during the story of pore Perrie. And if I tell you about it one more time, about Aunt Perrie and Uncle Ace (when he was home) and Son, man and boy, then I want you to hush ever asking me about it again. Because you know good and well that I've told it to you, chapter and book, time and time over, and this will be the last, until I go to my grave. Pore Perrie."

3

The thing of it is, Son was over in Benburnett County working for a while with a rigging outfit when suddenly Aunt Linsie began to have his letters. Son wrote and said Aunt Linsie can you tell me about Aunt Perrie, all how she was when I wasn't there to see, all how she lived and how she died. This gave Aunt Linsie a chance to write one of her long good letters that was like a story she was telling (when you can get her to tell one); and she wrote back, "Son to begin with why don't you stop keeping me in a tumult, I should think you'd have seen for yourself, your pore Aunt Perrie's ghost is haunting you and I'm glad, this is because you ought to have been here with her when she needed you (and not just skimming and skirting round the place here the way you did, like a ghost of yourself), not everywhere you were during those days, there's plenty of ghosts will tell you that, won't let you rest pretty soon, it's your conscience, thas all, Son," etc. etc. . . .

Son wrote back and said, "All right Aunt Linsie, I know I've led you and Aunt Perrie a life, but none of that ghost stuff, this is no ghost, I just want to know about Aunt Perrie and am asking you."

Aunt Linsie wrote back and said, "Well, Son, if this is some other stunt of yours I'll cherish it against you the rest of my life, for pore Perrie was my own sister and your only mother in this world and gave a goodly part of her life to raising and tending to you when you was a boy; but anyways you remember how she was such a stout woman when you left? She fell off so you wouldn't have recognized her as the same pore Perrie after you and Ace left, and when she died (that death's part yours and you know it) we buried her as small as a Cheedee. If you're hurrawing about pore Perrie I can't stand it, that pore suffering thang Perrie."

Son wrote a letter back that said, "No, Aunt Linsie, I'm not making light of Aunt Perrie, how could I? So write me back and tell me what I ask, then I'll tell you why I'm asking."

Aunt Linsie's answer said, "Son don't you know by now there's no room anywheres in the world, no quarters in any house or billin, that can hide you from your own folks, they live in your memory and blood, you bring them in a room when you move in. You can build a house against weather, but you can't build it against your own conscience. Get right, face your life, all what's in it, and that includes pore Perrie, was like your own mother, called you her own, and then you treated her like you did, *when are you going to settle down?* That's all right, you're coming outa the little end of the horn now, and I know it and you know it; but I'll help you outa your trouble, will do it till I'm dead and gone (and then who'll do it then, oh who, I wonder?)"

Son's answer said, "Aunt Linsie, hush lecturing me. I'm not perfect and I know it; and Uncle Ace was not perfect. But there was only one man in this wide world who was perfect and He was crucified. Just don't devil me. I expect you're right on most of what you say. The thing of it is, I all of a sudden see Aunt

Perrie's life so plain, plainer than I could ever see when I was looking, and I can see her rooms in our house, the one with the machine she pumped and sewed at, with the wooden drawers full of spools and bias tape. *I want to get something straight.*"

(Aunt Linsie did not answer, and the next thing she knew, Son was on the place.)

4

"Now listen to me while I tell you the story of pore Perrie, because it'll be the last and enough. Then hush ever asking me about it.

"Well, as you know, because I've told you, they called us the Polk Sisters in this town of Crecy Texas. We were the seamstresses of the town. Our mother and father died young and Perrie took me and brought me up. Our house was a good house —'cept for the 'shackley steps in back—built next to the Campbellite church (now a Presbyterian one); cool in summer and then with a vine on every string that strung the porch like a harp, and cold in winter; but good lives found a home in it. Pore Perrie sat on the porch in summer and sang the hymns along with the congregation next door despite they was Campbellites, for hymns are the same in all Houses of God, she said. She had her own church there behind the vines. In the front flowerbeds was a duke's mixture of Rainlillies after it rained, Touchmenots, Old Flags and Calico, with always a grasshopper on the Calico. There was a frail Huisache tree on the side of the house, brought there from a West Texas place by a cousin long ago who said it might live, she couldn't say, in this damper climate; but it did, grew up pretty as a tree on a calendar, spraying out its yellow insect blooms and so limber that even a bird would bend it to light there, and scatter the blossoms. On one side was the churchhouse and in the afternoons the shadow of the churchhouse lay on the grass and Son played in the shadow; and on the other side was the patch. In back was the clothesyard where there lived several White Leghorn hens that left enough eggs for us to eat and bake with, and there was a few Golden Seabright Bantams just for ornament and for Son to have. Back of that was the grove of little pinetrees.

"Perrie and me were both cut out by the Lord, who had his designs for all of us, to be missionaries; but I gave my life to Perrie and Perrie had a lame foot, to begin with, and then she spoiled the Lord's design by marrying—against all wishes—and so late. . . . And there my story commences. Or ends . . . 'cause I don't want to tell it anymore. Hush making me."

"Tell it out, this is the time to tell."

5

"When Perrie Polk married—so late (she was thirty-eight and I was twenty-eight)—Ace Wanger, a traveling lumber sales-man living in hotels and all that kind of boarding-house life, she adopted a child, little Son, through the Methodist Church Or-phanage, because she could have none of her own. The Church was this orphan child's parentage, and that's the way Perrie wanted it.

"Now Uncle Ace had been an orphan too, a foundling of some kind, nobody knows or ever knew who his folks were; and he would never talk about it. He took our home when he came into it as Perrie's husband and he took little Son as his son, as you will see; but this so late and after so much misery.

"Son grew along, in the house and in the yard, me and Perrie doing our sewing, Ace away on the road three weeks out of four all over Texas and Arkansas with his lumber, and little Son playing around the sewing machine that Perrie was pump-ing. When he could call a name he said Aunt Perrie and Aunt Linsie and Uncle Ace. So there was this household. All in the little house you can see right chonder, that nobody lives in since I moved, just a shell of a house.

"Son was the best child in this world, then; never put his fingers in the sewing-machine pedal, never took the bobbins or the needles, sat very quiet—whose child? As he grew along he never gave any trouble, not even to switch his legs, and when he was old enough in the summertimes—we never even had to send him to Bible School in the summertime—but he went of his own choosing—nor give him a real blistering. Pore Perrie and I would watch him through the window where he played in the woodpile and wonder where Son came from.

"By the time he was twelve he had turned real dark complected and very very nervous. His nerviousness so worried Perrie that she took him to Doctor Browder for it. Perrie said Doctor Browder said this is the most nervious child ever I saw in my practice, but think he'll outgrow it—Perrie said Doctor Browder said—*if* he has his tonsils and adenoids out. Son had these out, and then we got him glasses. But we had to take him out of school.

"Then we trained him ourselves, with the Bible, Stories of the Bible, Children of Faraway Lands—put out by the Missionary Society; and had him count eggs and tomatoes. He planted and pruned and toted round the place; and grew along.

"By the time he was seventeen his distress began, finding him dark and lean and beginning to be very different. He was so nervous that if he'd be sitting by the washhouse studying something on his mind—oh I wonder what?—and the Leghorn rooster would crow in his face, Son would startle up and chunk a rock at him. Once he did this; and hit the Leghorn rooster in the head and killed it—to give you a notion of how Son was in those days. We didn't know what to do with Son, and pore Perrie worried and worried. I worried too. Uncle Ace was no help, as he should have been, for he was always off traveling. So what could we do, so what could pore Perrie do? We tried to quieten Son down. We read him out of the Bible—*My mother and my brethren are these* . . . Saint Luke eight twenty-one.

"The thing of it is he had never had it told to him that he was an orphan. People who knew it kept it quiet; but they tried to tell him about it in ways that people have about a stranger— as you will later see. Some came to Perrie and said Son probably had some foreign blood in him, did he have nigra blood in him maybe? Did he have any papers? These things hurt pore Perrie, and hurt me; but Perrie said Son was Child of the Church and any parentage beyond that was unbeknownst to her. Once I said, 'Perrie regg'n it is the time to tell, do you think Son is of the age to have it told him'; but Perrie said, 'Not yet.'

"Something had happened between Perrie and Ace, as it was bound to. One day in July he wrote a letter from Memphis and said he had a new job that would keep him there and he was going to take it and stay. Perrie would not quarrel with him and sent him all his things. There had never been a whole minute's talk between Son and Ace, but suddenly when it was known that Ace was gone, and to stay, Son's change happened. He was gone from his room one July morning soon after and there was a message left saying, 'I have gone to Memphis to see Uncle Ace.'

"A long terrible time and no word. Perrie was ailing most of the time now, her lame foot had caused her hip to ache so that she could scarcely pump the sewing machine. I said a mite, not much; but I was grieving. We ate supper together quietly. There was a medicine show come through, but we didn't go. A Preacher Healer from the 'Postolics came to town and the town filled his tent and several were healed by the Miracle; but Perrie said that if the Lord had taken her one side it was for His uses and that he had strengthened the other for her own; it was His Design; she pumped left-footed and would not go to the Healer. Now that's enough; quit asking me. My mouth is shut."

"But tell how the letters started. Tell about the letters."

6

"Well, then the letters started. First Son wrote and said, 'Aunt Perrie why did you have to let me find it out for myself that I am somebody's son we never knew, probably a bastard'— he wrote that word. 'Uncle Ace has told me again what was first told to me on the Church Hike the Fourtha July.'

"Perrie wrote back and said, 'Son I never wanted to hurt you and you were too young to know, besides. If you hadn't run off I'd have told you, or had Brother Riley at the church to tell you. But I have been your mother as good as any mother could have been; and your Aunt Linsie, too. If you had no mother then think how you had *two* mothers showering all their love and care on you, count your blessings Son, and don't make light of me. For I done the best I could.'

"Son wrote a letter back that said, 'Aunt Perrie I am working in a lumbermill out of Memphis and like it; and if I had two mothers in Crecy Texas then I have three in all, but one to begin with and that one to end with, will you please do me the favor of telling me who my mother was, and where; and I'll be much oblige.'

"Perrie wrote back an answer that Son was to please not change his nature and his ways, that he was please not to hurraw about three mothers, that she would tell him now that who or where his mother and father were never would be known, and to send his things on home and come on with them. To just count her, Aunt Perrie, as his mother and go on with his life. 'For I have raised you,' Perrie's letter said, 'In this house and yard in Crecy Texas to the best of my gumption, under the shadow of the Church and in the name of God. You was a good child and now can be a good young man. I ask you to abide in the Lord who is our only Father.'

"No answer.

7

"On the Fourtha July on account of the celebration at the Picnic Grounds all the heavens was aglow for two hours, just one solid blast, shook us all up, you'd have thought the world was coming to an end; and about nine o'clock I looked out and here was Son coming from the to-do and we could see something was wrong, that he had been hurt. He looked so hurt. Perrie said, 'Son commere to me and tell me who or what it is that's hurt you; I can tell when something has hurt you, and come and tell me.' But Son wouldn't say. And I thought, because he was so peculiar and so changed, *what child is this?* And I thought child o child what is ever going to happen to you in this world I wonder, oh what will your life be, if we could just put it into the right hands, see that it goes right and good and doesn't get hurt or astray—who will ever look after you, you little thing. But I know we can't help, no one can do that for nobody, have to go this way and that, find our ground and try to stand our ground, learn our wisdom and then try to be strong enough to bear our wisdom, O hep this little boy, child a mine, is what I thought.

"Well, Son wouldn't tell and so Perrie didn't press him, he went to bed and I said, 'Perrie regg'n what's the matter with him?' and Perrie said, 'Let him alone, Linsie, he'll tell dreckly.'

"The next day he was so peculiar, we was so far apart, wouldn't say much, face right peaked, until that afternoon Perrie said he come to her with the wildest face and said, 'Aunt Perrie I've hurt myself and I'm scared, maybe we ought to call Doctor Browder.' Perrie said, 'Son what have you done to yourself, come talk to me, come let me see.' Son said, 'Aunt Perrie I can't tell you or show you, 'cause you see I was climbing over a bobwire fence at the Fourtha July fireworks and I slipped and fell upon the bobwire. I didn't look until we got in the light of the fireworks and then I saw blood on myself.'

"Oh, I said, this is when he needs his Uncle Ace, but let Ace stay on away on the road, let him stay until Doomsday, we can get along without him (this boy was always trying to run away from where he was or from people he was with to be by himself, as if to still something rankling in him, as if to put something to rest within him or for some reason we could never know. But everytime he broke and ran away, and mind you this, he harmed or wounded himself in some way: it was the harm and the wound that brought him back, then, time and time again, so as to heal harm and hurt, it seemed). 'Come let *me* see,' I said, 'Son.'

" 'Nome,' he said, 'you can't see, either, just call Doctor Browder.'

"Doctor Browder come and he and Son went in the back

room and closed the door, and we heard Doctor Browder say, 'Son let me see you, let me see what have you done to yourself.'

"After that we scarcely knew Son anymore, he was a stranger in the house. It was just a little after this that the letter came from Ace saying he was staying in Memphis and then Son left his message and left. [*Child a mine, child a mine, something touched you and changed you all over. I know some hand touched that good boy Son and left him never the same again. Some hand led him away from pore Perrie (Lord hep me forget his face, his head of hair, let me forget him all over, the way he was all over, bless his hide, he was the only thing I ever had. I remember him in the garden counting the tomatoes for arithmetic, I remember him in the clothesyard bumping like a ghost through the wet sheets, I remember him in the pinegrove; child a mine.)*]

"And that's the end of this story. Don't ask me no more. Because I'm old, poor Perrie's buried in her grave, and Ace, too —you know this—and Son is out somewhere in the world on the road like his Uncle Ace before him. There is no more to tell."

"But tell it all, Aunt Linsie, tell about the two Sons, the ghost and the flesh of Son. This is the time. Go on to the end, and then we'll let it alone, the sad story, forever. By telling it true we'll keep it straight and never tell it again. We'll let it go.

"Pore Perrie."

8

"One summertime something made a ghost out of the Huisache tree—spun a web around the top of it—some treedevil that lime wouldn't drive away; it seemed the touch of Satan. It was so hot and no Gulf hurricane would come, to bring a norther, the whole world stood still, trees hot and tired with their limp leaves hanging like a panting animal's tongue, flowers in a trance; and us all fanning ourselves. At dark in the evenings a ghost would come. He would linger at the edge of the yard just when Perrie would be feeding the chickens or bringing in the clothes, and Perrie would come in the house white yet her calm prayerful self, but not to mention a ghost. Finally she told me one evening at the suppertable. 'He is at the window,' she said. 'The ghost of Son. And next he will be in the house. He comes closer and closer.' I sat still and told no lie by opening my mouth.

"(Oh don't ask me no more, 'cause I'm uneasy to tell it; don't ask me no more. You've heard it—don't beg me no more.)"

"Tell how it wasn't the ghost of Son, Aunt Linsie, tell how it was the flesh and blood Son. Go on, go ahead, make haste and tell it . . ."

"It was no ghost atall but the genuine flesh of Son. I had known it for some time, had met him in the grove. He was dressed like a tramp and he said, 'Aunt Linsie commere and don't be afraid of me, I'm Son and I'm all right. I've come back to see you all, to see the house, to see the place, if everything and everybody is all right.'

" 'Well come on home, come on in the house,' I said, 'Son, pore Perrie's waiting for you, in her sickness, in her quiet Christian sorrow.'

" 'Nome Aunt Linsie,' Son said. 'Never tell her I've been here. I'm going away again, after a little while. Just come to see everything for myself, and not in dreams or imagination, but everything the way it really is and was. Look by the Huisache tree and find some money I've left for you and Aunt Perrie. And cross your heart you'll never tell her I was here.'

" 'All right, Son,' I said, 'if that's the way you want it, that's the way it has to be. Except I wish you'd come on through the yard and into the house and have yew some supper with us.'

"Then Son went away. I watched him go. He had that same walk.

"But he'd be back again, I'd see him here and there on the place, got to looking for him, would see him behind the barn, in the field, and at the Huisache tree on a moonlight night—he was leaving his money again—and sometime by the chimney window, eyes between the green fringe of the velveteen curtains in the living room. Pore Son, Lord hep this boy; *what child is this?* I thought and prayed; he can't stay and he can't go away. Pore

Perrie. Perrie would see him and say in a low voice her prayer, *'Go away, ghost of Son, go 'way and let me be.'*

"Then he'd be gone again for a while, no sign of Son. I'd look and look for him, but he'd have disappeared, and for a long time sometime, no sight of Son. I'd wait for the flesh of Son and Perrie would wait for his ghost.

"Perrie got weaker and weaker, and sweeter, like a lovely angel. She took to her bed. We had this ghost and this flesh between us, but we never mentioned it, never broached the subject, but it was between us, living and real. It bound us together and broke us apart—we'll settle it one day.

"One night at the end of this hottest summer in our memory, the saving storm came. The trees were nervious and jumpy, but all in the house was green and still. Then it hit. I was in my bed in my front room, next to Perrie's middle one; and I said Lord let it come, it has been trying to come for so long, it has been so slow, let it come, our salvation. Son had not been around the place for some time, but I knew he was there, somehow I knew it. Then in a brightness of white lightning I saw him at my window, and I spoke out, 'Hello Son, please to come in out of the storm.' But the blackness of the night flashed on again, like black lightning, and took away his face. I knew pore Perrie would see him, her ghost, at her window, for he would be there next; so I got up and put on my kimona and using the lightning like a lamp, went to her room. I stood in the doorway and saw this in the lightning: Perrie was standing before her window, beautiful and white as a Saint, naked, the white voile curtains waving and falling and rising round her like the garments of an angel. She seemed young, like a vision of herself, frail and fleshly, and this vision was burned upon my sight, and upon the sight of Son, whose face was there at the window like a lantern; and it will be there till we both of us die, Son and me, I know to God.

"That was the last of the life of pore Perrie, for I picked her up when she folded on to the floor and put her in her bed, a little bundle. I sat the rest of the night through by her side, both of us quiet, Perrie quiet forever—so small and so beautiful in her corpse, the storm raving round the house in great boots, sloshing in the muddy yard and road, and the trees wild and hysterical, Son somewhere outdoors in the storm, me saying, *'Son, Son come on in, come on in and join us now'*; and the night passed. When Doctor Browder came the next morning I said Perrie has passed away, into God's Kingdom; and Doctor Browder said rest her weary Christian soul.

"Pore Perrie was buried in her grave, you know it well, where it tis and what grave will hold her eternal neighbor, room for me, when I will come. And that Uncle Ace is not there beside her but over alone in a corner of the Crecy graveyard—how Son brought him back to bury him, how they had wandered all over three States together, two pore homeless thangs, Son writing me the letters to tell him again all about pore Perrie; he never could seem to get it all straight. This Noah's bird that went forth from the ark kept coming back to us, coming back, with no place to rest his foot; until the last time he came with his burden, his pore homeless, childless, wifeless father; and then he went away for good, in peace, and never returned. He must have been put on this earth to rove about and nurse the wandering homeless, to find them graves to rest in, to bring them to *that* home again, yet he was homeless too and I wonder who will go out to find *him* and bring *him* back? He is aloose forever and in what world and on what way I wonder? The world is too big; we lose people in it. This weatherbird flies into all the four corners of the wind, Lord pity pore little suffering children, oh come on home Son and let's cry together like we use to, even when you were little we would cry together . . . even if you were playing in the clothesyard I'd just run out to you under the shadetree and grab you and cry and you would cry with me. You little trembling thing you already knew (how *did* you know?) what breaks a heart; nobody ever had to tell you a thing you just knew. That's your purpose you were placed in the world to cry with people, you were sent for grief, called to the grieving world. But I know you're a gay little thing, too, and that's why I know you're meant for grief because you are so gay and are so good to laugh with, oh we've had our laughs, laughed until we cried . . . *why don't you send your clothes on home you said you would where are your things?*

"Go on now. *That is all I will tell and I will never tell it again.* Now I've told you it and I never will again. Go on now and hush ever thinking about it.

"Pore Perrie."

9

(The thing of it is, they say Son still comes to Crecy once in a while. That Linsie would see him at the edge of the grove and go out to meet him, after Perrie passed away, speak his name, "Son," and say, "Commere Son," only to find him not there at all. She would see him and then she wouldn't. Had he come, or hadn't he? Sometimes she would see a lantern going over the ground or hanging in a tree in the grove; sometimes it was just the light in the brooder. Was he there or wasn't he? They say a Peeping Tom with a flashlight has been seen at windows of Crecy houses. That the 'Postolics say the Devil was seen walking in the pastures at night with a torch. That somebody has been living with the Gypsies up on the hill. That a Negro on the road saw Son and Linsie dancing naked in the pinegrove one night. And that Linsie's seen Son all through the house, behind the beaded curtains between the hall and middle bedroom, his face at the frosted pane on the front door and called, *"Son Son commere to me and tell me what is in your craw."*

The thing of it is (and then I'm through, this story is done), when Linsie is buried in the family plot next to pore Perrie, these two sister-mothers will have this to settle between themselves there under the dirt. Linsie has a message for pore Perrie, and it won't be long, now, before she takes it to her. They have this Son between them, until Doomsday, ghost and flesh.

And now I'm moving on (oh hear my song); this is the story as it was told to me; and as I go on, on the road, with a message to deliver, *I* want to get it all straight. There is this Son's pain to understand and tell about and I look for tongue to tell it with.

Pore Perrie.)

GHOST AND FLESH, WATER AND DIRT

Was somebody here while ago acallin for you. . . .

O don't say that, don't tell me who . . . was he fair and had a wrinkle in his chin? I wonder was he the one . . . describe me his look, whether the eyes were pale light-colored and swimmin and wild and shifty; did he bend a little at the shoulders was his face agrievin what did he say where did he go, whichaway, hush don't tell me; wish I could keep him but I cain't, so go, go (but come back).

Cause you know honey there's a time to go roun and tell and there's a time to set still (and let a ghost grieve ya); so listen to me while I tell, cause I'm in my time a tellin and you better run fast if you don wanna hear what I tell, cause I'm goin ta tell . . .

Dreamt last night again I saw pore Raymon Emmons, all last night seen im plain as day. There uz tears in iz glassy eyes and iz face uz all meltin away. O I was broken of my sleep and of my night disturbed, for I dreamt of pore Raymon Emmons live as ever.

He came on the sleepin porch where I was sleepin (and he's there to stay) ridin a purple horse (like King was), and then he got off and tied im to the bedstead and come and stood over me and commenced iz talkin. All night long he uz talkin and talkin, his speech (whatever he uz sayin) uz like steam streamin outa the mouth of a kettle, streamin and streamin and streamin. At first I said in my dream, "Will you do me the favor of tellin me just who in the world you can be, will you please show the kindness to tell me who you can be, breakin my sleep and disturbin my rest?" "I'm Raymon Emmons," the steamin voice said, "and I'm here to stay; putt out my things that you've putt away, putt out my oatmeal bowl and putt hot oatmeal in it, get out my rubber-boots when it rains, iron my clothes and fix my supper . . . I never died and I'm here to stay."

(Oh go way ole ghost of Raymon Emmons, whisperin in my ear on the pilla at night; go way ole ghost and lemme be! Quit standin over me like that, all night standin there sayin somethin to me . . . behave ghost of Raymon Emmons, behave yoself and lemme be! Lemme get out and go roun, lemme put on those big ole rubberboots and go clompin. . . .)

Now you shoulda known that Raymon Emmons. *There* was *somebody,* I'm tellin you. Oh he uz a bright thang, quick 'n fair, tall, about six feet, real lean and a devlish face full of snappin eyes, he had eyes all over his face, didn't miss a thang, that man, saw everthang; and a clean brow. He was a rayroad man, worked for the Guff Coast Lines all iz life, our house always smelt like a train.

When I first knew of him he was livin at the Boardinhouse acrost from the depot (oh that uz years and years ago), and I uz in town and wearin my first pumps when he stopped me on the corner and ast me to do him the favor of tellin him the size a my foot. I was not afraid atall to look at him and say the size a my foot uz my own affair and would he show the kindness to not be so fresh. But when he said I only want to know because there's somebody livin up in New Waverley about your size and age and I want to send a birthday present of some houseshoes to, I said that's different; and we went into Richardson's store, to the back where the shoes were, and tried on shoes till he found the kind and size to fit me and this person in New Waverley. I didn't tell im that the pumps I'uz wearin were Sistah's and not my size (when I got home and Mama said why'd it take you so long? I said it uz because I had to walk so slow in Sistah's pumps).

Next time I saw im in town (and I made it a point to look for im, was why I come to town), I went up to im and said do you want to measure my foot again Raymon Emmons, ha! And he said any day in the week I'd measure that pretty foot; and we went into Richardson's and he bought *me* a pair of white summer pumps with a pink tie (and I gave Sistah's pumps back to her). Miz Richardson said my lands Margy you buyin lotsa shoes lately, are you goin to take a trip (O I took a trip, and one I come back from, too).

We had other meetins and was plainly in love; and when we married, runnin off to Groveton to do it, everybody in town said things about the marriage because he uz thirty and I uz seven-teen.

We moved to this house owned by the Picketts, with a good big clothesyard and a swing on the porch, and I made it real nice for me and Raymon Emmons, made curtains with fringe, putt jardinears on the front bannisters and painted the fern buckets. We furnished those unfurnished rooms with our brand new lives, and started goin along.

Between those years and this one I'm tellin about them in, there seems a space as wide and vacant and silent as the Neches River, with my life *then* standin on one bank and my life *now* standin on the other, lookin acrost at each other like two diffrent people wonderin who the other can really be.

How did Raymon Emmons die? Walked right through a winda and tore hisself all to smithereens. Walked right through a second-story winda at the depot and fell broken on the tracks— nothin much left a Raymon Emmons after he walked through that winda—broken his crown, hon, broken his crown. But he lingered for three days in Victry Hospital and then passed, sayin just before he passed away, turnin towards me, "I hope you're satisfied. . . ."

Why did he die? From grievin over his daughter and mine, Chitta was her name, that fell off a horse they uz both ridin on the Emmonses' farm. Horse's name was King and we had im shot.

Buried im next to Chitta's grave with iz insurance, two funerals in as many weeks, then set aroun blue in our house, cryin all day and cryin half the night, sleep all broken and disturbed of my rest, thinkin oh if he'd come knockin at that door right now I'd let him in, oh I'd let Raymon Emmons in! After he died, I set aroun sayin "who's gonna meet all the hours in a day with me, whatever is in each one—*all those hours*—who's gonna be with me in the mornin, in the ashy afternoons that we always have here, in the nights of lightnin who's goan be lyin there, seen in the flashes and makin me feel as safe as if he uz a lightnin rod (and honey he *wuz*); who's gonna be like a light turned on in a dark room when I go in, who's gonna be at the door when I open it, who's goin to be there when I wake up or when I go to sleep, who's goin to call my name? I cain't stand a life of just me and our furniture in a room, who's gonna *be* with me?" Honey it's true that you never miss water till the well runs dry, tiz truly true.

Went to talk to the preacher, but he uz no earthly help, regalin me with iz pretty talk, he's got a tongue that will trill out a story pretty as a bird on a bobwire fence—but meanin what?—sayin "the wicked walk on every hand when the vilest men are exalted"—now what uz that mean?—; went to set and talk with Fursta Evans in her Millinary Shop (who's had her share of tumult in her sad life, but never shows it) but she uz no good, sayin "Girl pick up the pieces and go on . . . here try on this real cute hat" (that woman had nothin but hats on her mind—even though she taught me *my* life, grant cha *that*—for brains she's got hats). Went to the graves on Sundays carryin potplants and cryin over the mounds, one long wide one and one little un—how sad are the little graves a childrun, childrun ought not to have to die it's not right to bring death to childrun, they're just little toys grownups play with or neglect (thas how some of em die, too, honey, but won't say no more bout that); but all child-run go to Heaven so guess it's best—the grasshoppers flyin all roun me (they say graveyard grasshoppers spit tobacco juice and if it gets in your eye it'll putt your eye out) and an armadilla diggin in the crepemyrtle bushes—sayin "dirt lay light on Raymon Emmons and iz child," and thinkin "all my life is dirt I've got a famly of dirt." And then I come back to set and scratch aroun like an armadilla myself in these rooms, alone; but honey that uz no good either.

And then one day, I guess it uz a year after my famly died, there uz a knock on my door and it uz Fursta Evans knockin when I opened it to see. And she said "honey now listen I've come to visit with you and to try to tell you somethin: why are you so glued to Raymon Emmonses memry when you never cared a hoot bout him while he was on earth, you despised all the Emmonses, said they was just trash, wouldn't go to the farm on Christmas or Thanksgivin, wouldn't set next to em in church, broke pore Raymon Emmons' heart because you'd never let Chitta stay with her grandparents and when you finely did the Lord purnished you for bein so hateful by takin Chitta. Then you blamed it on Raymon Emmons, hounded im night and day, said he killed Chitta, drove im stark ravin mad. While Raymon Emmons was live you'd never even give him the time a day, wouldn't lift a hand for im, you never would cross the street for im, to you he uz just a dog in the yard, and you know it, and now that he's dead you grieve yo life away and suddenly fall in love with im." Oh she tole me good and proper—said, "you never loved im till you lost im, till it uz too late, said now set up and listen to me and get some brains in yo head, chile." Said, "cause listen honey, I've had four husbands in my time, two of em died and two of em quit me, but each one of em I thought was goin to be the *only* one, and I took each one for that, then let im go when he uz gone, kept goin roun, kept ready, we got to honey, left the gate wide open for anybody to come through, friend or stranger, ran with the hare and hunted with the hound, honey we got to *greet* life not grieve life," is what she said.

"Well," I said, "I guess that's the way life is, you don't know what you have till you don't have it any longer, till you've lost it, till it's too late."

"Anyway," Fursta said, "little cattle little care—you're beginnin again now, fresh and empty handed, it's later and it's shorter, yo life, but go on from *here* not *there*," she said. "You've had one kind of a life, had a husband, putt im in iz grave (now leave im there!), had a child and putt her away, too; start over, hon, the world don't know it, the world's fresh as ever—it's a new day, putt some powder on yo face and start goin round. Get you a job, and try that; or take you a trip. . . ."

"But I got to stay in this house," I said. "Feel like I cain't budge. Raymon Emmons is here, live as ever, and I cain't get away from im. He keeps me fastened to this house."

"Oh poot," Fursta said, lightin a cigarette. "Honey you're losin ya mine. Now listen here, put on those big ole rubberboots and go clompin, go steppin high and wide—cause listen here, if ya don't they'll have ya up in the Asylum at Rusk sure's as shootin, specially if you go on talkin about this ghost of Raymon Emmons the way you do."

"But if I started goin roun, what would people say?"

"You can tell em it's none of their beeswax. Cause listen honey, the years uv passed and are passin and you in ever one of em, passin too, and not gettin any younger—yo hairs gettin bunchy and the lines clawed roun yo mouth and eyes by the glassy claws of cryin sharp tears. We got to paint ourselves up and go on, young *outside,* anyway—cause listen honey the sun comes up and the sun crosses over and *goes down*—and while the sun's up we got to get on that fence and crow. Cause night muss fall—and then thas all. Come on, les go roun; have us a Sataday night weddin ever Sataday night; forget this ole patched-faced ghost I hear you talkin about. . . ."

"In this town?" I said. "I hate this ole town, always rain fallin—'cept this ain't rain it's rainin, Fursta, it's rainin mildew. . . ."

"O deliver me!" Fursta shouted out, and putt out her cigarette, "you won't do. Are you afraid you'll *melt?*"

"I wish I'd melt—and run down the drains. Wish I uz rain,

fallin on the dirt of certain graves I know and seepin down into the dirt, could lie in the dirt with Raymon Emmons on one side and Chitta on the other. Wish I uz dirt. . . ."

"I wish you are just crazy," Fursta said. "Come on, you're gonna take a trip. You're gonna get on a train and take a nonstop trip and get off at the end a the line and start all over again new as a New Year's Baby, baby. I'm gonna see to that."

"Not on no train, all the king's men couldn't get me to ride a train again, no siree. . . ."

"Oh no train my foot," said Fursta.

"But what'll I use for money please tell me," I said.

"With Raymon Emmons' insurance of course—it didn't take all of it to bury im, I know. Put some acreage tween you and yo past life, and maybe some new friends and scenery too, and pull down the shade on all the water that's gone under the bridge; and come back here a new woman. Then if ya want tew you can come into my millinary shop with me."

"Oh," I said, "is the world still there? Since Raymon Emmons walked through that winda seems the whole world's gone, the whole world went out through that winda when he walked through it."

Closed the house, sayin "goodbye ghost of Raymon Emmons," bought my ticket at the depot, deafenin my ears to the sound of the tickin telegraph machine, got on a train and headed west to California. Day and night the trainwheels on the traintracks said *Raymon Emmons Raymon Emmons Raymon Emmons,* and I looked through the winda at dirt and desert, miles and miles of dirt, thinkin I wish I uz dirt I wish I uz dirt. O I uz vile with grief.

In California the sun was out, wide, and everbody and everthing lighted up; and oh honey the world *was* still there. I decided to stay a while. I started my new life with Raymon Emmons' insurance money. It uz in San Diego, by the ocean and with mountains of dirt standin gold in the blue waters. A war had come. I was alone for a while, but not for long. Got me a job in an airplane factory, met a lotta girls, met a lotta men. I worked in fusilodges.

There uz this Nick Natowski, a brown clean Pollock from Chicargo, real wile, real Satanish. What kind of a life did he start me into? I don't know how it started, but it did, and in a flash we uz everwhere together, dancin and swimmin and *everthing*. He uz in the war and in the U.S. Navy, but we didn't think of the war or of water. I just liked him tight as a glove in iz uniform, I just liked him laughin, honey, I just liked him *ever* way he was, and that uz all I knew. And then one night he said, "Margy I'm goin to tell you somethin, goin on a boat, be gone a long long time, goin in a week." Oh I cried and had a nervous fit and said, "Why do you have to go when there's these thousands of others all aroun San Diego that could go?" and he said, "We're goin away to Coronada for that week, you and me, and what happens there will be enough to keep and save for the whole time we're apart." We went, honey, Nick and me, to Coronada, I mean we really *went*. Lived like a king and queen—where uz my life behind me that I thought of onct and a while like a story somebody was whisperin to me?—laughed and loved and I cried; and after that week at Coronada, Nick left for sea on his boat, to the war, sayin I want you to know baby I'm leavin you my allotment.

I was blue, so blue, all over again, but this time it uz diffrent someway, guess cause I uz blue for somethin live this time and not dead under dirt, I don't know; anyway I kept goin roun, kept my job in fusilodges and kept goin roun. There was this friend of Nick Natowski's called George, and we went together some. "But why doesn't Nick Natowski write me, George?" I said. "Because he cain't yet," George said, "but just wait and he'll write." I kept waitin but no letter ever came, and the reason he didn't write when he could of, finely, was because his boat was sunk and Nick Natowski in it.

Oh what have I ever done in this world, I said, to send my soul to torment? Lost one to dirt and one to water, makes my life a life of mud, why was I ever put to such a test as this O Lord, I said. I'm goin back home to where I started, gonna get on that train and backtrack to where I started from, want to look at dirt a while, can't stand to look at water. I rode the train back. Somethin drew me back like I'd been pastured on a rope in California.

Come back to this house, opened it up and aired it all out, and when I got back you know who was there in that house? That ole faithful ghost of Raymon Emmons. He'd been there, waitin, while I went aroun, in my goin roun time, and was there to have me back. While I uz gone he'd covered everythin in our house with the breath a ghosts, fine ghost dust over the tables and chairs and a curtain of ghost lace over my bed on the sleepin-porch.

Took me this job in Richardson's Shoe Shop (this town's big now and got money in it, the war 'n oil made it rich, ud never know it as the same if you hadn't known it before; and Fursta Evans married to a rich widower), set there fittin shoes on measured feet all day—it all started in a shoestore measurin feet and it ended that way—can you feature that? Went home at night to my you-know-what.

Comes ridin onto the sleepinporch ever night regular as clockwork, ties iz horse to the bedstead and I say hello Raymon Emmons and we start our conversation. Don't ask me what he says or what I say, but ever night is a night full of talkin, and it lasts the whole night through. Oh onct in a while I get real blue and want to hide away and just set with Raymon Emmons in my house, cain't budge, don't see daylight nor dark, putt away my wearin clothes, couldn't walk outa that door if my life depended on it. But I set real still and let it all be, claimed by that ghost until he unclaims me—and then I get up and go roun, free, and that's why I'm here, settin with you here in the Pass Time Club, drinkin this beer and tellin you all I've told.

Honey, why am I tellin all this? Oh all our lives! So many things to tell. And I keep em to myself a long long time, tight as a drum, won't open my mouth, just set in my blue house with that ole ghost agrievin me, until there comes a time of tellin, a time to tell, a time to putt on those big ole rubberboots.

Now I believe in *tellin*, while we're live and goin roun; when the tellin time comes I say spew it out, we just got to tell things, things in our lives, things that've happened, things we've fancied and things we dream about or are haunted by. Cause you know honey the time to shut you mouth and set moultin and mildewed in yo room, grieved by a ghost and fastened to a chair, comes back roun again, don't worry honey, it comes roun again. There's a time ta tell and a time ta set still ta let a ghost grieve ya. So listen to me while I tell, cause I'm in my time atellin, and you better run fast if you don wanna hear what I tell, cause I'm goin ta tell. . . .

The world is changed, let's drink ower beer and have us a time, tell and tell and tell, let's get that hot bird in a cole bottle tonight. Cause next time you think you'll see me and hear me tell, you won't: I'll be flat where I cain't budge again, like I wuz all that year, settin and hidin way . . . until the time comes roun again when I can say oh go way ole ghost of Raymon Emmons, go way ole ghost and lemme be!

Cause I've learned this and I'm gonna tell ya: there's a time for live things and a time for dead, for ghosts and for flesh 'n bones: all life is just a sharin of ghosts and flesh. Us humans are part ghost and part flesh—part fire and part ash—but I think maybe the ghost part is the longest lastin, the fire blazes but the ashes last forever. I had fire in California (and water putt it out) and ash in Texis (and it went to dirt); but I say now, while I'm tellin you, there's a world both places, a world where there's ghosts and a world where there's flesh, and I believe the real right way is to take our worlds, of ghosts or of flesh, take each one as they come and take what comes in em: take a ghost and grieve with im, settin still; and take the flesh 'n bones and go roun; and even run out to meet what worlds come in to our lives, strangers (like you), and ghosts (like Raymon Emmons) and lovers (like Nick Natowski) . . . and be what each world wants us to be.

And I think that ghosts, if you set still with em long enough, can give you over to flesh 'n bones; and that flesh 'n bones, if you go roun when it's time, can send you back to a faithful ghost. One provides the other.

Saw pore Raymon Emmons all last night, all last night seen im plain as day.

The Grasshopper's Burden

Here was this school building in the town, holding young and old, this stone building that looked from the front like a great big head with flat skull of asphalt and gravel and face of an insect that might be eating up the young through its opening and closing mouth of doors; and across its forehead were written the words: "Dedicated to all high emprise, the building of good citizens of the world, the establishment of a community of minds and hearts, free men and women."

In this building and in its surrounding yards were many people, children and teachers—it was a world:

This was a rainy afternoon in Social Studies and Quella could not stand hearing the story of Sam Houston read out by different people in the class. She was just waiting for two-thirty, when she would get her pass to go to the auditorium where the May Fete in which she was a Royal Princess (and one of two elected by the whole school) would be practiced.

Miss Morris, who would never at any time in her life have been a Royal Princess, she was so ordinary, was the Social Studies teacher and listening as she sat in good posture at her desk to the story of Sam Houston as if it were a brand-new tale just being told for the first time. She did not like to sign a pass—for anything, May Fetes included. Miss Morris had a puckered mouth just like a purse drawn up. She knew everything about children, whether they told a story about undone homework; and especially about boys, if they had been smoking or had a jawbreaker hidden over their last tooth, or a beanshooter in their blouse—she surmised a beanshooter so dreadfully that it might have been a revolver concealed there. And when she fussed at a boy who was mean by stealing a girl's purse and going through it, showing all a girl's things to other boys in the class, Miss Morris would draw her pursey mouth so tight that she seemed to have no lips at all and stitches would crack the powder around it. Then she would shake this boy hard, often causing bubblegum or jawbreakers to fall from him everywhere and roll hard on the floor under all the seats. She did not like to sign a pass.

But Quella must have an early pass, not only to keep from having to read her turn at Sam Houston but to give her time to go get her hair ready for the May Fete practice. She thought what an early pass might be for—not to go to the Nurse to see if she had mumps because it felt sore by her ear, because yesterday she had said this and caused a lot of attention, but all the M's in her row and the L's and N's on both sides of her row shrank away from her and even Helena McWorthy had not wanted to go around with her between classes, the way they did, seeing what was in the halls together, or let her use her powder puff or blue woman's comb, just to get mumps. And she could not have something in her eye because not long ago she had got an easy pass from Miss Stover in Math for this and the Nurse, a little mean woman that smelled like white, had said, "I find nothing whatsomever in your eye that does not naturally belong there," and wrote this on a note to Miss Stover and then glared at her with the whites of her eyes.

Quella sneaked a good black jawbreaker into her mouth, acting like she was just brushing her hand across her mouth, and Miss Morris never knew. Then she sat, waiting for a reason to get an early pass to dawn upon her. She could hear the voices of this one and that one reading out about Sam Houston—forever Sam Houston! They had had him in the Third Grade and they had had him in the Fifth. And now, even in the Seventh and as far as Junior High School they had to have him again. It was Mabel Sampson, the biggest girl, reading now. If she would say *thee—ee,* Miss Morris would stop her and make her say it *thuh;* and she could not even pronounce the word that clearly spelled *Puritan* but said it *Prutan.* Mabel Sampson was so dumb. Because Mabel Sampson was bigger than the rest in the class, she deviled them and snooted them whenever and wherever she could, to make it plain that she had somewhere (and Quella was going to find out) passed all the rest of them on her way to something and would get there first.

And then it was Billy Mangus reading. He was fat and white and whined a lot, and the worst boy to sit in front of if you were a girl and an M. She and Helena McWorthy just hated him for what he would do with redhots. He would plant these little dots of sticky candy in Helena McWorthy's beautiful hair and she would not even know it or feel them there and go all through the halls between classes having redhots in her hair until someone laughed at her and made fun of her and picked them out to eat them. Or Billy Mangus would bore a sharpened pencil into Helena's back right through an Angora sweater or even her Mexican bolero which her aunt brought her back from Tijuana, Mexico. Helena was a very quiet girl. She would let Quella stroke her, huddled blinking in her seat, keep her always right and everything about her straight, plait and unplait and plait again her hair, arrange her ribbons. Helena would go anywhere holding Quella's hand, submissive to be with her. She had little chinkapin eyes fixed close to the bridge of her nose like a cheap doll's, dull and with scant white eyebrows. Her almost white hair, which was long and divided down her back, was infested with lures like sometimes two red plastic butterflies lighted there, or a green Spanish comb staked over one ear, and always red or blue knitting yarn wound through a spliced hawser of it, which arched over the top of her head from ear to ear. Helena had discovered that a pencil, too, might be stuck there and stolen often by Billy Mangus, who sat behind her alphabetically, and have to be fussed for.

Billy Mangus was reading and Quella wondered if his false

tooth in front was wiggling, and she stretched over to see. No. It must be locked in place now. But if he wanted to, Billy could, by unlocking this false tooth some way with his tongue, cause it to wiggle like a loose picket in a fence. This tooth was his special thing in a class or anywhere if he wanted to unlock it. Suddenly she just had to see it wiggle and she did not know why but she shouted, right in the middle of the reading, "Wiggle us your tooth, Billy!" This made Miss Morris very outdone and Billy Mangus giggled and the whole class tittered. Miss Morris made everything quiet, then stared so hard at Quella and all the class sat very still to watch Miss Morris do one of her stares, hold her rocky eyes, never even breathing or blinking, right on a pupil until he had to look down first. Quella did not know whether to try to outstare Miss Morris by doing just the same to her until *she* put her eyes down, or to look to see if Billy Mangus was wiggling his tooth. But she decided she would rather see the tooth and turned to look; and so Miss Morris won. "Sit up straight, Quella, and do not talk one more time out of turn!" Miss Morris said, very proud because she had won a staring contest.

Quella sat up in her seat and there seemed nothing to do, so she remembered her lips, if they had enough lipstick on them. Very carefully she opened her nice black patent-leather purse and got out her lady's mirror which was of red-skinned leather and had some redhots sticking to it. She cleaned them off into her purse to save them and held out the mirror for her lips to see themselves. She put her lips in a round soft circle. She saw them in her mirror, red enough, sweetheart lips, so beautiful. Then she made different shapes with them, some kissing shapes, some like "OOOOO!"; and one like being prissy, or a word like "really!"; or like the Nurse saying, "I find nothing whatsomever in your eye that does not naturally belong there." But she would not do her lips like Miss Morris at a mean boy, for then it would spoil the lipstick. Last, she gently kissed a piece of composition paper to leave her lips there. Liz her sister kissed letters at the end and all over, she mailed her lips to boys, and she would, too, when she began to write letters to somebody besides her Grandmother in Yreka, who would certainly not be thrilled with kissing lips in a letter.

Then she put her mirror back in her purse and spied her big blue comb in there. She scraped some redhots off it and brought it out and raked her hair with it. It was a good feeling. She thought of Helena's bunch of hair and how she wanted right now to be behind her plaiting it and fixing it as she did in Science, where they did not have to sit alphabetically. She seined her hair again through the net of her comb, right in back this time, being very careful not to comb down the red ribbon which was pinned there like an award for something. If a boy pulled at it, this would make her mad and stamp her foot and have to slap him. She lolled the black jawbreaker around in her mouth and devoured the sweet juice from it.

Then suddenly there was something being unwrapped cunningly in the L's across from her. She looked to see Charlotte Langendorf, the ugliest girl, holding something sticky and blue in her lap. It had been wrapped in wax paper. "What is that stuff?" she whispered across to Charlotte. "A thing we cooked today in Cooking and I am going to eat it when the eating period comes," Charlotte whispered, glad someone had noticed it. "Let me see it," Quella whispered again. "I won't eat it, cross my heart. I have Cooking next period and I need to know what we will cook." Charlotte passed it secretly across and Quella looked at this peculiar thing which they would cook next period. She examined it, smelled of it, and wanted right then to taste some of it. "What is it?" she asked. "It smells funny." "I don't know," Charlotte whispered back, "but it's something we made out of ingredients. Miss Starnes told us how." Quella tasted it. It was not good to eat at all, not even cooked; but she had another taste. "Let me have it!" Charlotte whispered severely. "Give me back my cooking!" Quella gave it back. "It smells tacky," she said. Then she looked ahead of her in the front of the S's and watched Bobby Sandro's broken arm in a cast, how he was writing tattoos on it, in a cast and a sling from breaking it in Gym and he did not have to write because of it. And then at Suzanne Prince's bandaged-up finger, so she couldn't write, too, saying it was bitten by their cat that went insane.

And then she surveyed the whole row of mean boys, every one of them mean, not a one cute, whose names began with B as though all the meanest were named alike, and she thought how they would step on your saddle shoes to dirty them. Then she thought of several things in a row: horses and their good gentle one named Beauty they used to have; of a fight in the rain before school by Joe and Sandy and how all the girls stood purposely to get their hair wet and be so worried about it; of Liz and her boy friend Luke Shimmens who owned a hot-rod and took them riding around town and up and down dragging Main blowing the horn and backfiring and seeing different kids walking along and waving out at them.

Then there seemed nothing else going on to see or do, and Quella wanted to have an early pass again. Wayne Jinks was just finishing his paragraph. When it was over she raised her hand and popped it to jingle the jingles round her wrist. Miss Morris said, "Do you want to read next, Quella?" "Nome," Quella said, and prissed, "it is time to go to May Fete practice."

Miss Morris said a surprise. "All right, take a pass and go ahead." And she took a pad of passes from her drawer and wrote on one. She tore it off and gave it to Quella, looking for a moment as if she were going to stare at her. But Quella went out of the room quickly.

She was in the hall with a pass in her hand, going down the very quiet hall that did not have another single person in it. She passed all the rooms, sometimes seeing through a door pane some teacher writing on a blackboard or standing talking to a class. She noticed as she went along that without any other kids, alone in the hall (and this same thing was true when she was by herself with a teacher) she was no more than somebody quiet and courteous. But when the others were around, she could be all the things they were, shouting and slapping boys and eating at the wrong time, provoked with the way things were or excited about them. She stopped by the closed door to the Teachers' Room where all their mailboxes were, like pigeons' holes. No one was in there. She remembered seeing the teachers gathered in front of their boxes before the first class began, fumbling, dipping and rising like homing pigeons. She came by Mrs. Purlow's room where the Stuttering Class was—in there was George Kurunus and she spied him through the glass pane of the door, sitting like some kind of an animal. She heard Mrs. Purlow's perfect words, like "lit-tle," like "yel-low" floating across the room, how she would say every word right. And next was Mrs. Stanford, who would treat you so very nice when you met her in the grocery store after school or on Saturdays, with her hand on your head, saying, "How's little Quella?" and patting you, but mean in class and acting as though she never had seen you in a grocery store in her life, or anywhere. Then here was the typing class. It was like a heavy rain in there. And old Miss Cross, who had been teaching how to type for thirty years, standing at the front of the class pointing with a long stick at the letters on a chart and saying "A" and then an enormous clack! to make an A, then "B" and another clack to make this letter. Then faster, and it was like a slow gallop of a horse on pavement and Miss Cross with her stick like a circus trainer, "A - S - D - F - G." And next was Miss Winnie's room where this teacher cried a lot and for this was called Weeping Winnie and spoke in a soft cooing voice and seemed so sad. She always lost her voice the Ninth Period and said, "Cheeldrin you will have to write today, my voice is gone."

As she went along she would walk like different kinds of people, or in different ways, very quickly and hopping; or as she had seen Miss McMurray, the English teacher and very pretty, going down the halls—as though she were carrying a bag of eggs, afraid to break them, or a sleeping baby that might be waked; and like the Royal Princess with a train that she had been voted to be in the May Fete. Then she meandered in big S's or in zigzags from one side of the hall to the other; or smeared one finger along the wall, loitering, browsing, lolling at every drinking fountain to sip a long time or spew the water back. She saw some faded redhots and the little stone of a jawbreaker in one fountain.

Once she thought of Helena and wished Helena could be with her. Helena was such a beautiful name. She came to her sister Liz's room and peeked in. The good-looking Mr. Forbes was teaching them some important senior subject and they were all listening as if what he was saying had to be learned to take out in the world when they would soon go. She looked to see what color his tie was today. Liz had counted seventeen different ties in seventeen days on Mr. Forbes and he wore so many different kinds of coats and trousers that they said he changed sometimes between classes. Yes, he had his saddle shoes on, too. Then she saw Mr. Forbes looking towards the door where she was. She ducked down quickly to wait until he turned and she could look again for Liz, to see how she looked sitting up in class.

As she crouched there she suddenly heard someone coming down the hall and looked to see who could it be. It was the awful deformity George Kurunus writhing and slobbering and skulking towards her. She was afraid of him and thought she would scream as all the girls did when he came to them; but she knew if you went up to him not afraid of his twisted face and said George to him and talked to him he would not do anything to you. Together, all the kids played with him, at him, as though he was some crazy and funny thing like a bent toy on a string; but no one ever wanted to be with him alone. Often a class would hear a scratching at the door and would see his hoodlum face at a door pane like Hallowe'en and be frightened until they saw it was just George Kurunus. Then the class would laugh and make faces back at him and the teacher would go to the door and say "Now, George . . ." and shoo him away; and the class would titter. The boys all went around with him as if he was something they owned, something they could use for some stunt or trick on somebody, their arms around his shoulder; and they talked and laughed with him and told him ugly jokes and things about girls and sicked him on certain girls. Why did this deformity George have to be in a school? He couldn't even hold a word still in his mouth when he said it, for it rattled or hopped away—this was why he was in Stuttering Class, but it did him no good, he still broke a word when he said it, as if it were a twig, he still said ruined words.

He could not speak a word right and whole no matter how hard he tried or how carefully. But if you live among breakage, he may have reasoned, you finally see the wisdom in pieces; and no one can keep you from the pasting and joining together of bits to make the mind's own whole. What can break anything set back whole upon a shelf in the mind, like a mended dish? His mind, then, was full of mended words, broken by his own speech but repaired by his silences and put back into his mind. The wisdom in all things, in time, tells a meaning to those things, even to parcels of things that seem to mean disuse and no use, like scraps in a mending basket that are tokens and remnants of many splendid dresses and robes each with a whole to tell about.

Whenever the Twirling Class for girls in the Black and Gold Battalion practiced on the football field, here was this George on the field, too, like some old stray dog that had to be shooed away. And in a marching line of some class to somewhere, the library or a program in the auditorium, he ruined any straight marching line and so was put last to keep the line straight. But at the end of a straight marching line he twisted and wavered like the raveling out of a line and ruined it, even then; he was the capricious conclusion and mocking collapse of something all ordered and precise right up to the tag end. When he walked, it seemed he always ran upon himself like someone in the way—or like a wounded insect. He was a flaw in the school, as if he were a crack in the building.

This day he had sat in his row by the window and the sun was coming in upon him. It warmed his vestigial hand, lay upon a page of his book. It touched some leaves of a begonia on the teacher's desk and showed their white lines and illuminated the blooms to like glass flowers. *Flower* was a word, but he could not say it. The sun came in and lay upon Miss Purlow's face and showed where the round spot of rouge ended and her face's real skin began. The sun made, also, between Miss Purlow and the blackboard, a little transparent ladder leading up and out through the window. Specks of golden dust were popping in it, dancing and whirling on out the window. Then suddenly Miss Purlow walked through it and broke it, but it joined together again, in spite of Miss Purlow, and made him glad. Miss Purlow went to the blackboard and wrote upon it some perfectly shaped words in her pretty curlimacue handwriting that said:

> "Come into the garden, Maud,
> For the black bat, night, has flown . . ."

Then she read them aloud, musically and perfectly, and he so wanted to have these words in his mouth. Miss Purlow asked him to say them after her but he could not, they fell away from him, they were all hers; yet he had it perfect, the little melodious collection of words, in his mind from Miss Purlow's mouth, a small tune of sounds that hung clear and warbling in his ears like birdsong. He turned and shuffled away, to leave the room. Miss Purlow called at him that she would report him to the Principal again as soon as the class was over, but he did not care, he opened the door and went away from this room where he could not speak and where words tormented him.

Then here he was, ruining a quiet hall for Quella. Although with other children she laughed at him and thought him a funny thing, alone she was afraid of him and detested him. Where was this George going? He was shuffling closer. She stood up and pressed against the wall and watched him, hating him. It was said that if he ever fell down he could never get up unless somebody helped him, but just lie there scrambling and waving his arms and legs, like a bug on its back, and muttering. His little withered left arm was folded like a plucked bird's wing and its bleached and shriveled hand, looking as though it had been too long in water, was bent over and it hung limp like a dead fowl's neck and dangling head. But he could use this piece of hand, this scrap of arm quickly and he could snap it like a little quirt and pop girls as they passed him in the hall. Here he came, this crazy George Kurunus, a piece of wreckage in the school. What did *he* want? She looked to see if *he* had a pass in his hand. No. Certainly he was not going to practice for any May Fete. Why should *he* be in the halls and without a pass?

She shrank close to the wall, but did not want to be caught there by him. She decided to run fast past him, not looking at his goblin face and not going close enough to him to be popped by his whip of an arm. She darted and fled past him, wanting to push him down and leave him wriggling there in the hall. He said some sound, all drunken and gargled, to her as she passed him; but he did not try to pop her. She ran looking back at him and when she came to the turn of the hall that led to the lavatory, she ran around it fast, then crept back to peek around and see if he was still going on or coming after her. George Kurunus was staggering along, his knees scraping each other, sounding like a little puffing train in the hall, without ever looking back. This made her furious and she was going to yell, "Stuck u-up!" until she remembered she would be heard and was supposed to be going to the auditorium.

She ran in to the girls' lavatory and was dramatically hiding from him there, panting faster than she really had to. She stopped to listen and heard his *sh-sh-sh-sh* down the hall away from her. This was another narrow escape she would tell Helena Mc-Worthy about.

Then it was time for the May Fete practice and she went to the auditorium that always seemed so cool when the whole school wasn't in it. There were the royalty, already assembled: Joe Wright, the handsome King, also the Chief Yell Leader; Marveen Soames, the beautiful Queen; the other Princess, Hazel May Young, not pretty but with personality, and all the Dukes and Duchesses. Miss McMurray, the perfect-walking English teacher, was there to take charge.

They all marched down the aisle, very proud, and the King and Queen mounted the throne, the Princesses and Princes, Dukes and Duchesses swaggered to their places around the throne. The King had on his silver crown and was holding his tinfoil wand. When it was time to crown the Queen, the biggest moment of all, and everything was real quiet, all the empty seats in the auditorium hushed and watching, she spied in the glass frame of the auditorium door the terrible face of George Kurunus, like a grasshopper's face. He was watching the May Fete and had it all in his eye. This George Kurunus was everywhere, why did he have to be everywhere she was? But she turned her eyes away from him, upon all the beautiful royalty, and they went on with the practice. Then suddenly it was the bell for the next class, which was Homemaking—a dreary place for a Princess to go: to a cookstove after a coronation.

The Homemaking teacher was Miss Starnes and there she was, waiting for the girls at the door, smiling and standing straight. Miss Starnes would stand before her class reading from some book. Each day she had a fresh rose or some other flower from her own garden stuck to her strict dress, and the way she maneuvered her mouth and bowed and leaned her head towards the girls sitting before her made them know that she knew she was saying something good, as though she were smacking her lips and golloping something like a dessert. Yet Miss Starnes was very serious and meant what she would say or read and paused often, sticking out her chin (which had hairs on it) for emphasis.

The girls in Homemaking class who sat before her were not sure at all what these words meant, but they sat there, among the linen dresses and the fancy aprons hanging on hangers, which last year's class had made with its own hands and left the prices pinned on to show that they were good enough to be bought in any store. Then there was a manikin on a stand—in a corner by the American flag, which the manikin seemed to need to drape around itself to hide its nakedness, headless and with a pole running right up through her to be her one leg; and in an adjoining room—the kitchen—there were rows of little stoves where Miss Starnes told the girls things to cook.

The bell had rung and all the girls were in their seats—any chosen seat and not alphabetically—and "responsibility" was a word Miss Starnes was already smacking off her lips to the girls in Homemaking. "Domestic re-spon-si-bi-li-ty." These were words Miss Starnes started right in telling to the class, things they should be or do in the good home they would have or make —and which lay off somewhere in the vague unknown and which they could not quite see as something of theirs but just imagine and did not even particularly want, now. But whatever or wherever or however this place "The Home," they would be there, all these girls, going industriously around in aprons, there would be a lot of busy sewing and a difficult cooking, and . . . "Domestic re-spon-si-bi-li-ty" . . . these words Miss Starnes was saying.

Quella was going to start in plaiting and unplaiting Helena McWorthy's hair when Miss Starnes kneaded and worked her lips and they were getting ready to say another careful word to the class. "E-con-o-my." The manikin was standing there in the corner trying to be that word, which was a good thing to be. The manikin was a pitiful thing, undressed, or something headless like a fowl, or something deformed, but proud and seeming to want to help Miss Starnes with the lecture by standing there as though it, too, were teaching Homemaking. It was about the size of her mother in her short slip in the summertime, Quella observed.

And then Miss Starnes led them in the kitchen and they were going to cook their lesson. "I know what it will be," Quella told the others. "Like some stuff Charlotte Langendorf cooked first period and carried in wax paper to Social Studies—of potatoes or something." But Miss Starnes was saying that in this class today there would be cooked pudding and to light the stoves and listen to some things she would say about the making of pudding, and to put on their white cook aprons. "Ingredients" was a word about pudding which Miss Starnes was saying, and it seemed just the word for what milk and sugar, which they were already mixing, looked like together. There was a gregarious stirring. Then Miss Starnes told about the soft ball that the mixture would make in a cup of cold water to show it was ready.

Here and there already a soft ball was found in a cup and a girl would raise her hand to tell it to Miss Starnes.

Just as Quella and Helena's mixture made a soft ball for them in their cup of cold water, a staccato bell-ringing that was certainly not the regular bell resounded in the school building, and it was fire drill. Although the mixture was ready and showed its undeniable sign, all the Homemaking girls had to leave it and line up in twos and march behind Miss Starnes through the hall smelling of their mixture, which even then, though it was not yet anything but ingredients, made them feel important because they had caused this smell to move all in the corridors just as they were moving now, and even reach around as far as the algebra room, where there were no good smells, and hang under the noses of the class doing unknowns. The girls marched and fretted.

When the Homemaking class got outside under the trees where the school busses were waiting for school to be out, and stood in their right place under the cottonwood trees, Miss Starnes suddenly thought about the windows in Homemaking and remembered she had not closed and locked them according to fire drill instructions. "Quella," she said carefully as though she were saying "do-mes-tic" or "e-con-o-my," "please to run back to Homemaking and close all the windows tight and see that no stoves are burning."

"Don't I need a pass?" Quella asked.

"No, Quella. Run."

She was alone in the hall again. The pudding will be ruined, she thought. If the school burns, they will have to save the pudding and the May Fete pretties. She could smell smoke, and then once she was sure she saw a flame lick out of Boys' Lavatory, but she would never go in *there* to put it out. She went very fast to Homemaking and in the room she went right to her and Helena's cup with the soft ball in it. She felt it. It was still soft. She went around looking at other cups. Margy Reynolds' was not ready but was still just ingredients in a cup of water. But some hand or finger had been in it all, in all the cups and pans, who had been meddling in Homemaking? She thought she heard the crackling of flames above her, so she rushed to close the windows, and as she ran out, she swiped her finger through her and Helena's ready mixture and strung it along the stove and floor and on her dress; but she licked it up quick and slammed the door.

Then she ran through the hall, not liking the halls this way, with no pass, without classes in the rooms, no different teachers standing or sitting there as she passed them. How scarey the school seemed now, full of the echoes of her clapping feet and her panting. She passed Miss Purlow's room and looked in through the door. On the blackboard were written the lines in beautiful penmanship:

> "Come into the garden, Maud,
> For the black bat, night, has flown . . ."

and under the lines was—what? Was it a joke or what? There was a curious disheveled chaos of giant and dwarf runaway shapes, tumbled and humped and crazy . . . like the Devil's writing or like a ghost's. She ran.

Then she was by the auditorium and stopped to make sure there was no flame in there to eat up all the May Fete pretties—the dresses and the paper flowers, the paper wand and all the paper streamers. She could feel something in there! There was some live thing in there! She listened. No sound. She looked through the pane of the auditorium door and what should she spy but George Kurunus sitting on the King's Throne like a crazy king in a burning building. On his head was the silver crown and in his ruined hand the silver wand. He was into everything, who would keep him out of all the things at school; he was a disturbance in this world of school and in her own world, touching and tampering with everything she did. She thought she saw him rise and come down from the throne and down the aisle towards her, after her; and she ran away and down the hall, now full of smoke she was sure, hearing him after her—*sh-sh-sh-sh*—and seeing rags of flame waving out from alcoves and recesses at her.

She ran out the door and into the open, without looking back. If the schoolhouse burned it would burn him like a cricket in it. She would not tell.

She was thrilled to see all the boys and all the girls lined under the trees and gladly joined them. She stood shivering under the trees in her place in line, waiting to see what was going to happen, in the unearthly quiet that lay over all the school people, over all the school building. Suddenly at a window on the second floor she saw his face, as if her fear of fire had a face and it was George Kurunus'. No one else seemed to see it—was she imagining it? for she now had the insect-headed and devil-bodied image of him in her head. No, there it was, his face, looking down at her, she was sure. And then she thought she saw him crying! If he was crying she wanted to save him from the burning building, to call out that he was in there, or to run in and save him herself; hurry! hurry! hurry! But suddenly the all-clear bell that would bring them all back to where he was, separate and waiting, but never back to him whirred out, convulsing through her whole body and through his own tilted body like electric shock . . . it was all a nightmare: if there had been no fire then there had been no George in the empty building, she thought.

Now they all began to move, in their colors like a field of flowers jostling in the wind; and she saw again, for sure, his grasshopper face at the window, watching them coming back to the skulled building of stone that held him like an appetite or a desire that would surely, one day, get them every one: all the beautiful schoolchildren gathered and moving like the chosen through the heavenly amber afternoon light and under the golden leaves—the lean ball-players, the agile jitterbuggers, the leaping perch of yell leaders, the golden-tongued winners of the declamation contests, Princes and Princesses, Duchesses and Kings, and she, Quella, among them, no safer than the rest but knowing, at least, one thing more than the rest.

CHILDREN OF OLD SOMEBODY

◻▬◻

For Katherine Anne

Her nis non hoom, her nis but wildernesse:
Forth, pilgrim, forth! Forth, beste, out of thy stal!
Know thy contree, look up, thank God of al;
Hold the hye wey, and lat thy gost thee lede:
And trouthe shal delivere, hit is no drede.
                              —CHAUCER, *TROUTHE.*

On the road, the dust at his feet, where was he bound, where
was he to go, our Old Ancestry? He seemed to find no rest for
the sole of his foot. For he knew another country that had a
landscape he could not wink or water out of his eye; and he had
another language in his ears.

Where was the leader, whom to follow, shall we follow a
follower? was the thought that hissed like a snake in the brake of
the brain of his times and led to confusion in the flock, for a
thought can destroy. It was a time when everything shifted and
changed, swarmed around and clustered on an idea or a craving,
used idea and craving up, or wearied of them, then scattered to
pieces again; it was a time of confusion of cravings, it was like a
bunch of sheep dispersed and broken, shepherd or no . . . he only
followed when he was supposed to lead, another sheep, one of
the broken flock, and could not summon them all together; or
there was no shepherd (maybe that was the trouble), he was lost

under the hill. Yet the permanent gesture was passing up and down, hovering, vanishing.

Fallen to the grasshopper, the plague year at hand; brother against brother, the community broken into Real Estate, a price on the head; flesh sealed up, men in a male prisonhouse, the women gone mad—where was the road, the wayfarer's flower, the bird in the air, the roadside spring? It was out of this broken flock that he broke, free and loose, to keep the idea of himself uneaten in his brain. Preserve my image of myself, he thought; set my skull over this image like a glass cover. Losing this, befouling this image is whoring all our hope, the fiendish betrayal of Satan, the destruction of our Old Ancestor.

So he was a shape of dust—and if all things return to dust, fall back into it, dust was his great pile, he the dust-grubber, himself formed of the dust of the ground, from which he would find the first things formed out of the ground and bring them to himself and to us all to see what would we call them. Breathed out of dust, he was yet the enemy of all dust-eaters; he would save the dust from the appetite, from the blind voracious driving bite of hunger: the grasshopper and the worm. Then, before it all is eaten, he would have his hands in it, on it, to touch it to smut it with his fingermarks—but even more: to shape it, out of its own dust and with the miraculous light of his own dust, and thus set it away, preserved. Shaped from no more than the small and agitated dust of dancers' feet on the side of the hill, all his aim and all his desire was to return to the dust to prospect in it and to save the grubbings. Consider this old road-runner: he is shuttler, hoverer: face at windows, fingers at panes, stick-knuckles on doors. But the dust is at his heels and his feet are on the road that he thinks to lead him for a little while to the blood beginnings of himself.

So the figure of Old Somebody comes to mind; this is to consider Old Somebody, who had no more of a name than what people gave him when he was not there to hear it.

Once, in another house, in another country, there passed on the road by the side of the house an old stranger who sometimes turned off to come to the back door and knock upon it with a stick he always carried. We of the house would know his knock on the house and though we seldom went to answer him with fear, unless it was after dark and a convict had escaped, we always felt a vague unearthly question in us as we went to answer his knock, as though some great unnameable phenomenon, like weather or like love, knocked on our house to call us away or to tell us something. This old stranger would knock and call out, "Somebody! Somebody! Hello-o-o!"; and for this we came to call him Old Somebody. What fears or visions the children of the house might have had of him no elder would ever know, for children's images sink into nameless depths of themselves—there is this loss to recapture, to salvage up from the fathoms, hovering over the depths to rescue the shape when it rises. We came, then, people of the house he knocked on, to the back door to see this old knocker covered with dust. Given a begging—some momentary mercy; a biscuit or a cold potato or a dipper of well water— he would turn away and we would watch him through the window as he took his road again and went on.

To threaten children in the house against the repetition of any mischief they had it in their minds to commit, the elders warned them that they should be given to Old Somebody to take away next time he came, as any begging, unless they corrected their ugliness in advance or dried up and straightened their face right that very minute. "Old Somebody's goan come get you and carry you off down the road if you don't hush it right up." So they used Old Somebody for a threat: we would be delivered into the hands of a passing figure of dust if we did not behave. And what we had to grow into was the knowledge that, behave or no, his hands would have us, this old haunting threat, this old vagrant intimidation.

And so we learned that the dust trembles at the touch of dust, agitates its own kind, rouses it, bestirs it, recruits its gratuitous army of it, dust, that becomes a choir of dust; and everything is taken, behave or no, by Old Somebody. For in the winter the ghostly fruit that clove to the unleafed branches would crumble at the touch and fall to the ground, fruit of dust. We dug holes in the ground and cupped our hands around our mouth and cried into the dirtholes "Old Somebody! Old Somebody!" and covered up our cry with dirt, while elders thought it was a warning to a doodle-bug that his house was on fire.

Tales told of him tried to create him in the minds of us listeners. It was told how when the boardinghouse where Old Somebody once lived burnt to the ground, how he appeared suddenly as if risen up out of ash and was seen fingering the ash —and how he found something and disappeared with it. Was it some old ashen vanity of his past that he grubbed for and found, some object his flesh had loved, some locket or letter or picture frame with the face once in it vanished?

And it was also told how he lolled and haunted about in the winter orchards touching and gathering the ghosts of summer fruit that hung like balls of dust on the bare branches. Was it to save them? How moss was Old Somebody's beard, how the Devil's Snuffbox, sifting to rusty powder in the hand that picked it from the ground, was Old Somebody's dippingsnuff; how the urchins of dust in corners that the broom could not snare were the restless children of Old Somebody. He belonged to all ghostly, elusive, vanishing things. All vanishing things! We would not give our life, our heart, our soul to the Devil of all vanishing things. Yet how they haunted and begged the heart and how one grieved after them. We knew that it was said to us that we must cleave to the permanent things and let all vanity pass; but think how because a life was given, haunted and called after by all vanishing things from the first, to vanishing things that appear and then slip away so suddenly, passing through the hands and on away, think how a life so given therefore suffered and was cursed and set on evil ground, unstable in unstable things. But what else could be done but to claim unto oneself, *passager* himself, what was his, all passing things. We pass with them and in them . . . they do not leave us behind but pull us on down and away with them. But to leave something of us both behind, a shape of dust in the dust, was the task, so early taken, of Old Somebody's children.

We grew into the kind of men who wished only that our life might be often enough in our own hands—something that arrives, knocks, announces itself, is looked upon in a clear, still moment, goes away, and appears again—to give us a feeling, and a sense of its shape, so that we could describe it and get that joy of recognition from it that comes from handling something one wants to *know,* all over, as a lover, though later lost. For such children made up their mind that in their time all their purpose and all their desire would be to discover and establish, for themselves, at least—and, they hoped, for many men—a sense of self as related to this coming and going that asked to be shaped; and if we could set down a line, a chain, a continuity to keep a touch between men before us and ourselves, all linked together through what happened, burst living again and into new being out of dust, then we might leave figures of dust in our time and out of our time, and go into the dust that was ours, waiting for other hands to shape us, and joined there. We grew into the kind of men who kept, by nature and as if we had made them and named them, a restless, loving watch on things—there was some shape to this roving watch of ours. Beyond this, indeed all around this, lay a huge, roiled and anxious shapelessness, the impulsive and unquiet and suspicious doings of men, hunts to kill, plots to gain, plans to trick to glory or increase. But we knew where the exquisite and delicate morsels of dust were given to us: the sweet glaze on trees called rawsum, the little bled and crystalline droplet of gum on a fallen plum, the tiny single sup of nectar at the end of a shoot of sweetgrass. Exhalations, musks, juices, gums and icings, we knew them as well as any bee or hummingbird or butterfly that fell into insect of dust at the end of any summer. These were there, then, for us to come and see, come and get, for us to admire and touch, our own discovered shape of things.

One time in the afternoon when Old Somebody knocked, the elders went to the door and the children followed. We saw him with eyes like dusturchins in his face, a clayey face white in the cheek hollows, blue ridge along the corona of the lips, blue at the mouth's corners, and hoods of flesh over the dust-shot eyes: a figure clothed in dust: he had been walking a dry country. Who was his mother, who was his father, what was his race? Did he want an answer—what answer could we give him? The beggings were given him, and after he went away, the children threatened, the elders gathered in the kitchen and built their story of him so as to make another accounting of him and so answer away his call. He was the child of the Summer Hill people who had long since passed away. The elders as children had known his old folks. Bright Andrews had finally married his little housekeeper, Cora, and at an old age this accident of a child was born. The child grew up on the place, so far behind all the rest of the people of Summer Hill, the only small one, the rest all old and past him, a kind of unpossessed foundling. When he became a young man he had suddenly disappeared, gone to where, nobody knew . . . but to get his world. Years passed; he passed out of the minds of his people and might, to their minds, never have been born, only a passing fiction. One day he returned, so changed by whatever had happened to him that he was not even recognized. He was turned away from the door of his own people's house— his half-sisters and brothers and their married children. He began to wander up and down, appearing, vanishing, hovering. It was said that he wanted the graves of his mother and father, Cora and Bright Andrews. It was said that he lived in a cave in the hills beyond the cotton gin; it was said he lived under a broken bridge. But his was a life never told; there was no tongue that could tell it. That was his life, that was his accounting.

Yet surely Cora Andrews remembered how she kept him quiet in her shell of flesh, like my own image of him in my mind, Bright Andrews stiff abed with his stroke and knocking on the wall with his stick when he wanted something. And surely she could not forget how when she felt the pain of her child she went quietly into the woods and brought him into this world with her own hands and hid him in a hollow log. One day he, this secret child, would have his own truth as one day I would have his truth, and mine in his. Our search and our waiting were, then, the same. It all went into the mind of a child, listener, this accounting of the elders who shaped Old Somebody's life with their guessing tongues; and something closed up around it there in my mind, a soft shell to hold it. This mind would shape it all again one day, all its own, when something would touch the shell that kept it and it would open and the life within it would come out.

A knock opened it. Long later on the midnight watch at sea, I heard suddenly from the deck, after unconsolable loss, the knocking of the masts in the quiet midnight, and his image came back to me. "Somebody! Somebody! Hello-o-o!" the soft voice called with the knocking. He was back, Old Somebody. Walking the road of the waters, knocking on this riding house of men, this sleeping and watching family with whom I watched or among whose mysterious breathing beings I walked at night, shining my flashlight on their nameless faces; he had come back. Something of mine so precious, another vanishing beautiful thing, had been lost to sea; but something, too, was restored. This old man of dust had settled the dust with the waters, knocking on the waters of the grave of my loss, "Hello! Hello-o-o!" his stick on the waters. Dust of my loss was a pilgrim gone in peace to the waters, O waters hold him, settled forever, while I and you, Old Somebody, dust-bound, shore-bound, walk the shore and the waters, knocking and calling "Hello! Hello-o-o!" where no door opened. Far away from the borrowed house and the road that once brought him past it, but he still upon it, I upon that road now, borrowed child, I with his help saw my truth of him: the buried shell opened at his knock, he had called up his own buried image left years ago with me, and the figure of dust rose to its life and meaning out of the deeps and took its everlasting shape.

For they had lately put me down from the ship into the waters in a little leaf of a boat and sent me to wait upon the spot where a plane had fallen into the sea, to hover at the rim of the broken waters to watch when a body would rise from the depths, and capture it. I waited on the leaf, at the spot of this destruction, and behold he came rising up like a weed, the drowned sailor. I, whose hands had named and shaped and blessed this sunken shape, dipped my hands into the water and lifted it from it and brought back the salvaged shape lying across my knees, sea-boy lie light on my body, to the ship; welcome us back to the ship that enchanted us, so back we rode to the enchantress in our sorrow, welcome with garlands and vows to the temple; sleep in soft bosoms forever and dream of the surge and the sea-maids. Back we rode back to the ship in our grief, see how I found him I who shaped him, see how I returned him—tumbleweed of dust on the desert sea, the sea's dust which I, rover upon water, must settle, unquiet dust that blows in the deserts of the mind; dust can settle dust—back to the ship of our beginning. In the days and nights that followed, one a burial day, and with the help of Old Somebody who had returned, knocking, to take this begging away, I made my accounting.

When she had him she had him in the woods, alone, and then she put him in a hollow log and never told a soul. She came back several times a day to nourish him, and at night she kept a watch on him through her window. He was, then, a little woods animal nested in the hollow tube of this old log on Summer Hill; and he lived like this for quite a while. When he first got his sight he watched at the nether end of the log the little speck of light that was his daytime and in his unmothered nights he saw there sometimes the spangle of a star or the horn of a moon. This little druid never complained of his log life, it was only another hollow for him to curl in; and his first sounds, not counting the gurgles to his mother's milk as he took it from her when she came to give it, sitting on the log, were the tap and scrape of creatures' feet over his wooden dome and heaven. What was this little knocking?

This little tree spirit, could you believe it, lay unmolested by the life of the ground or by gypsies, never an ant stung it or snake bit it, there was no hostility between its world and the creatures' world, that hostility is learnt; he slept, little camper, right among the leaves and grass, a little seed dropped and left in the soil; can you believe it; waking to find a beak of horn over it or the adoring fierce eye of something of the woods hung over it. Its sky was the roof of a log and its moon the eye of a creature.

Now in old histories we can read of such, like of Childe Percival and like of little princes, secret folk, kept in secret woods places by charmers or enchanters. But would you believe it that this child could be put there in our sensible time, so far along later after old fables have faded away into just stories to be told for want of fable, after all the fancies had perished, and that it flourished, this child, and thrived; and that its mother, an old woman startled by a child out of her, could keep it all so quiet and in her heart and never tell a soul. This little pipping never doubted its beginning just as it never doubted the womb it came from while it was in it, but accepted it as right and took the nourishment that was piped into it from the veins and ducts it never thought to question. So with this new life of this little sprout within this hollow log.

Can you wonder, then, that when Cora, its mother, finally fetched it from its hollow and brought it out into the light of day, for good, it might have thought it was being born again, and that its eyes, with so much light after so much gloom, squinted into long bushy caterpillar shapes with a green fleck shining in the middle; and wouldn't you wonder, then, that there was before its eyes eternally a speck of light; it could not blink it out, the speck of light was singed into its vision as the blast of the sun itself is when you look long enough at it: you will see this ball of light wherever you look, as though your eyeballs were the burning globe of a sun in your head. Another thing about this child was that its hide was speckled with moles and spots, and that its hide was downy with hair, even on its back. So when its mother Cora Andrews took it out for good she had a kind of little animal that she had robbed from the summer woods; and the day she took it away it is said that the woods began to faint away and die into an autumn.

There is a lot of traffic in our life because we are unhoused. This rough, uncosseted, uncircumcised, spotted and downy being, put into the world beyond his beginnings, never knew, of course, of its deliverance from the log in the woods, nor why it had the speck of light in its eyes or the knocking in its ears; but its life was one long and incessant searching for the meaning of its own household and to name its blood.

That day Bright Andrews rose from his bed and came on good legs through the woods and saw ahead of him the young man's vision and the meaning of manhood, the whole tormented striving: his woman suckling his child, sitting on the log, was all the beginning. His little creature was curled upon her breast and joined to her in a connection that he had known with her, a suckling coupling. He watched, behind a tree, his child at his woman's breast, here was this woods family; but he would not join them, yet. He lingered on the edge of this woods household and filled his eye with it, then he crept away.

He came, later at night and by the light of a lantern, to be by himself with it, to take his own child to his arms and look at it all over, yearning to suckle it but knowing he could reach the child only through the woman, no other way, rocking it in his cradled arms, crying with an unutterable new pride at it, loving it more than anything he had ever known in this world, his lantern hanging in a tree, bringing the little being to the light like a moth to see its marks and features, to find its eyes' color, to see the look on its face. Is it a boy, he whispered, and found its tiny unharming and untormenting boy's sex and fingered its precious hide.

Cora found him standing under the light with his armful bundle like her vision of womanhood. She thought, now I have given it to him, this child, for him to come and see, to come and get, to come and adore. She stood longer, quiet, watching the creator adoring its begotten. It was made in the grass of the woods, she thought, it is a little animal. She could bear it no longer and she called out "Bright!" and when he saw her he could not speak but only looked darkly at her. She came to them under the light, the family was complete; and without a word they placed the child in its nest. Then they stood for a moment look-ing upon each other until they met against each other and fell down into the grass together, he lowering her gently and descending over her like a falling tree, terrible; and then he was upon her, sweet and soft, and his wide wing-like folding in of her clapped her in to him up against his loins. He smelled the grass around her nested head and smelled her juices that oozed from her to greet him. Flesh onto flesh by the light of the lantern in the trees, they threshed and harrowed the grass, their bed of earth, grinding gently and clapping swelling against swelling, worming in the grass; he beating her with his body and the one body of them flipping in the leaves like a dying fowl until they lay still in the leaves. Thus they adored their child that lay, ghost of their passion, in the log, chastening themselves.

"But what will we name it?" he asked softly, lying upon his narrow pallet of her. She could not think; it seemed so nameless.

"Just Little Somebody," she finally said, "until it names itself."

He fell back to his bed, an old stiff man again, and he did not judge his dream. Cora kept the dream and never told it, even to the dreamer.

Where it went when it left, this vision of their flesh, this dream of an old man stiff abed and a woman who hid it in a log, where it went in the years that followed was to all places that would join it to its own flesh's vision and bring it its own time; and in the end it joined itself to dust and loved it more than the world or any creature, and got its name—who will tell or whisper or knock it out?—and saw its own flesh fall away from it into dust and cast unsettled upon the water and the road.

Where its parents, Cora and Bright Andrews, went was into dust, into all elusive, ghostly and vanishing things, a handful of dust and a clasp of bones in a country graveyard, marked by tilted gravestones, the end of all wandering, peace we are home, pilgrims come in peace, we wait for a pilgrim.

So we learned that there is no house he does not knock on, no room in which to hide away from him. And the rapping on the side of any house we are ever housed in builds for a second that old sudden vision of Old Somebody. What is it he knocked the dust with his stick for, what was it he rapped out on the dust?

Say it, say it, whisper it out, stick-message, knock it out in the dust, a bird's foot knocking on the ground, say it, say it, do not be afraid. If we build the bridge of flesh we must cross over, over it, into the land of dust, and burn the bridge of burning flesh behind us: *cross over flesh to reach ghost*. The dust yearns for dust, but dust will have its flesh and, having it, deliver it over with its own hands, into dust.

Where is he, Old Somebody, where has he gone? Into the heart, into the spirit, where we must settle him; and out of the heart, out of the spirit, he rises, the dust that blows, his ghost, our Old Ancestry. He is the ghost of fruit on winter fruit trees, he is the snuffbox that crumbles in the hand, he is the ash of houses, he is the dusty hound on the road, a ladder of dust in the light of a lantern in the trees.

And on he goes, on the road, the dust at his heels; there is no rest for the soles of his feet. Think how in the towns he passes through they are electing mayors, raising funds for churches where there will be christenings and marriages, funerals and soul-savings; where there are halls for town meetings, jails for correction, fines for punishment and awards for deeds. Or how in the cities he rings around with his circle of dust there is all this ten times over—causes, codes, contests, beliefs. He is passing on the road, he is the gesture, the connection of dust, the old simplicity, the old common particle, our old ingredient, carrying our truth on the nap of his back.

I give him my accounting and his, and hope he will take it to his disturbed dust and that it will settle his dust as he has settled mine. See how an old Shape hidden in the depths and folds of the mind can appear, knocked for, when it is time, and show its meaning, salvage the dust of the truth, give a biscuit of courage and a dipper of faith and put us on the road again to who knows where?

For our feet have been broken by the ways we have gone, we have walked the waters and cinders; and the blood of our feet stains the wave and the dust. There is no balm for the soles of our feet.

BLOOD KINDRED

1952–1975

THE FACES OF
BLOOD KINDRED

□■□

James came to stay in his cousin's house when his mother was taken to the hospital with arthritis. The boys were both fourteen. James was blond and faintly harelipped, and he stuttered. His cousin was brown and shy. They had not much in common beyond their mysterious cousinhood, a bond of nature which they instinctively respected; though James mocked his cousin's habits, complained that he worried too much about things and was afraid of adventure. James owned and loved a flock of bantams, fought the cocks secretly, and his pockets jingled with tin cockspurs. His hands even had pecked places on them from fighting cocks in Mexican town.

James' father had run away to St. Louis some years ago, and his mother Macel had gone to work as a seamstress in a dress factory in the city of Houston. Macel was blond and gay and good-natured, though the cousin's mother told his father that she had the Ganchion spitfire in her and had run her husband away and now was suffering for it with arthritis. When they went to the hospital to see Aunt Macel, the cousin looked at her hands drawn like pale claws against her breast and her stiffened legs braced down in splints. The cousin, white with commiseration, stood against the wall and gazed at her and saw her being tortured for abusing his uncle and driving him away from home and from his cousin James. James, when taken along by force, would stand at his mother's bedside and stare at her with a look of careless resignation. When she asked him questions he stammered incoherent answers.

James was this mysterious, wandering boy. He loved the woods at the edge of his cousin's neighborhood and would spend whole days there while his aunt called and searched for him by telephone. She would call the grandmother's house, talk to a number of little grandchildren who passed the phone from one to another and finally to the deaf old grandmother, who could scarcely understand a word. But James was not there and no one had seen him. Once Fay, one of the young aunts living in the grandmother's house, called at midnight to say they had just discovered James sleeping under the fig trees in the back yard. Jock her husband had almost shot him before he had called out his name. Years later, when the cousin was in high school, he heard talk between his mother and father about Fay's hiding in the very same place while the police looked for her in the house —why, he did not know. At any rate, they had not found her.

He was a wild country boy brought to live in the city of Houston when his parents moved there from a little town down the road south. He said he wanted to be a cowboy, but it was too late for that; still, he wore boots and spurs. He hated the city, the schools, played away almost daily. The cousin admired James, thought him a daring hero. When he listened to his mother and father quarrel over James at night after they had gone to bed, his tenderness for him grew and grew. "He's like all the rest of them," his mother accused his father.

"They are my folks," the cousin's father said with dignity. "Macel is my sister."

"Then let some of the other folks take care of James. Let Fay. I simply cannot handle him."

Poor James, the cousin thought, poor homeless James. He has no friend but me.

One afternoon James suggested they go to see some Cornish fighting cocks on a farm at the edge of the city. The cousin did not tell his mother and they stole away against his conscience.

They hitchhiked to the farm out on the highway to Conroe, and there was a rooster-like man sitting barefooted in a little shotgun house. He had rooster feet, thin and with spread-out toes, and feathery hair. His wife was fat and loose and was barefooted, too. She objected to the cousin being there and said, "Chuck, you'll get yourself in trouble." But Chuck asked the cousins to come out to his chicken yard to see his Cornish cocks.

In a pen were the brilliant birds, each in its own coop, some with white scars about their jewel eyes. Stretching out beyond the chicken pen was the flat, rainy marshland of South Texas, over which a web of gray mist hung. The sad feeling of after-rain engulfed the cousin and, mixed with the sense of evil because of the fighting cocks and his guilt at having left home secretly, made him feel speechless and afraid. He would not go in the pen but stood outside and watched James and Chuck spar with the cocks and heard Chuck speak of their prowess. Then the cousin heard James ask the price of a big blue cock with stars on its breast. "Fifteen dollars," Chuck said, "and worth a lots more. He fights like a fiend." To the cousin's astonishment he heard James say he would take the blue one, and he saw him take some bills from his pocket and separate fifteen single ones. When they left they heard Chuck and his wife quarreling in the little house.

They went on away to the highway to thumb a ride, and James tucked the blue cock inside his lumberjacket and spoke very quietly to him with his stuttering lips against the cock's blinking and magnificent ruby eye.

"But where will we keep him?" the cousin asked. "We can't at my house."

"I know a place," James said. "This Cornish will make a lot of money."

"But I'm afraid," the cousin said.

"You're always 'f-f-fraid," James said with a tender, mocking smile. And then he whispered something else to the black tip that stuck out from his jacket like a spur of ebony.

A pickup truck stopped for them shortly and took them straight to the Houston Heights, where James said they would get out. James said they were going to their grandmother's house.

Their grandmother and grandfather had moved to the city, into a big rotten house, from the railroad town of Palestine, Texas. They had brought a family of seven grown children and the married children's children. In time, the grandfather had vanished and no one seemed to care where. The house was like a big boarding house, people in every room, the grandmother rocking, deaf and humped and shriveled, in the dining room. There was the smell of mustiness all through the house, exactly the way the grandmother smelled. In the back yard were some fig trees dripping with purple figs, and under the trees was a secret place, a damp and musky cove. It was a hideaway known to the children of the house, to the blackbirds after the figs, and to the cats stalking the birds. James told his cousin that this was the place to hide with the Cornish cock. He told the cock that he would have to be quiet for one night and made a chucking sound to him.

The cousins arrived at the grandmother's house with its sagging wooden front porch and its curtainless windows where some of the shades were pulled down. The front door was always open and the screen door sagged half-open. In the dirt front yard, which was damp and where cans and papers were strewn, two of the grandchildren sat quietly together: they were Jack and Little Sister, whose mother was divorced and living there with her mother. They seemed special to the cousin because they were Catholics and had that strangeness about them. Their father had insisted that they be brought up in his church, though he had run away and left them in it long ago; and now they seemed to the cousin to have been abandoned in it and could never change back. No one would take them to Mass, and if a priest appeared on the sidewalk, someone in the house would rush out and snatch at the children or gather them away and shout at the priest to mind his own business and go away, as if he were a kidnapper.

"Our mother is sick in bed," Jack said to James and the cousin as they passed him and Little Sister in the yard. Their mother, Beatrice, was a delicate and wild woman who could not find her way with men, and later, when the cousin was in college, she took her life. Not long after, Little Sister was killed in an automobile crash—it was said she was running away to Baton Rouge, Louisiana, to get married to a Catholic gambler. But Jack went on his way somewhere in the world, and the cousin never saw him again. Years later he heard that Jack had gone to a Trappist Monastery away in the North, but no one knew for sure. James grumbled at Jack and Little Sister and whispered, "If-f-f you tell anybody we were here, then a bear will come tonight and e-e-*eat* you up in bed." The two little alien Catholics, alone in a churchless house, looked sadly and silently at James and the cousin. They were constantly together and the cousin thought how they protected each other, asked for nothing in their orphan's world; they were not afraid. "My pore little Cathlicks," the grandmother would sometimes say over them when she saw them sleeping together on the sleeping-porch, as if they were cursed.

James and the cousin went around the house and into the back yard. Now it was almost dark. They crept stealthily, James with the Cornish cock nestled under his lumberjack. Once it cawed. Then James hushed it by stroking its neck and whispering to it.

Under the fig trees, in the cloying sweetness of the ripe fruit, James uncovered the Cornish cock. He pulled a fig and ate a bite of it, then gave a taste of it to the cock, who snapped it fiercely. Before the cousins knew it he had leaped to the ground and, as if he were on springs, bounced up into a fig tree. The Cornish cock began at once to eat the figs. Jim murmured an oath and shook the tree. Figs fat and wet fell upon him and the cousin.

"Stop!" the cousin whispered. "You'll ruin Granny's figs."

"Shut up." James scowled. "You're always 'f-f-fraid."

The cousin picked up a rock from the ground and threw it into the tree. He must have hurled it with great force, greater than he knew he possessed, for in a flash there shuddered at his feet the dark leafy bunch of the Cornish cock. In a moment the feathers were still.

"I didn't mean to, I didn't mean to!" the cousin gasped in horror, and he backed farther and farther away, beyond the deep shadows of the fig trees. Standing away, he saw in the dark luscious grove the figure of James fall to the ground and kneel over his Cornish cock and clasp the tousled mass like a lover's head. He heard him sob softly; and the cousin backed away in anguish.

As he passed the curtainless windows of the dining room, where the light was now on, he saw his old grandmother hunched in her chair, one leg folded under her, rocking gently and staring at nothing; and she seemed to him at that moment to be bearing the sorrow of everything—in her house, under the fig trees, in all the world. And then he heard the soft cries of Beatrice from her mysterious room, "Somebody help me, somebody go bring me a drink of water." He went on, past the chaos of the sleeping-porch that had so many beds and cots in it—for Beatrice's two children the little Catholics, for Fay's two, for his grandmother, for his grandfather who would not stay home, for Fay and for Jock the young seaman, her third husband, with tattoos and still wearing his sailor pants. He thought of Jock, who cursed before everybody, was restless, would come and go or sprawl on the bed he and Fay slept in on the sleeping-porch with all the rest; and he remembered when he had stayed overnight in this house once how he had heard what he thought was Jock beating Fay in the night, crying out to her and panting, "you f . . ."; how Jock the sailor would lie on the bed in the daytime smoking and reading from a storage of battered *Western Stories* and *Romance Stories* magazines that were strewn under the bed, while Fay worked at the Palais Royale in town selling ladies' ready-to-wear, and the voice of Beatrice suddenly calling overall, "Somebody! Please help me, I am so sick." Once the cousin had gone into her sad room when no one else would and she had pled, startled to see him there, and with a stark gray face scarred by the delicate white cleft of her lip, "Please help your Aunt Bea get a little ease from this headache; reach under the mattress— don't tell anybody—your Aunt Bea has to have some rest from this pain—reach right yonder under the mattress and give her that little bottle. That's it. This is our secret, and you musn't ever tell a soul." Within five years she was to die, and why should this beautiful Beatrice have to lie in a rest home, alone and none of her family ever coming to see her, until the home sent a message that she was dead? But he thought, hearing of her death, that if he had secretly helped ease her suffering, he had that to know, without ever telling—until he heard them say that she had died from taking too many pills from a hidden bottle.

The cousin walked away from the grandmother's house and went the long way home under the fresh evening sky, his fingers sticky with fig musk, leaving James and the dead cock under the fig trees. If he could one day save all his kindred from pain or help them to some hope! "I will, I will!" he promised. But what were they paying penance for? What was their wrong? Later he knew it bore the ancient name of lust. And as he walked on he saw, like a sparkling stone hurling toward him over the Natural Gas Reservoir, the first star break the heavens—who cast it?— and he wished he might die by it. When he approached the back door of his house, there was the benevolent figure of his mother in the kitchen fixing supper and he wondered how he would be able to tell her and his father where he had been and what had happened to James. "We went to the woods," he cried, "and James ran away." Later that night when James did not come back, his father telephoned the grandmother's house. But no one there had seen him.

The cousin cried himself to sleep that night, lonely and guilty, grieving for much more than he knew, but believing, in that faithful way of children, that in time he might know what it all meant, and that it was a matter of waiting, confused and watchful, until it came clear, as so much of everything promised to, in long time; and he dreamt of a blue rooster with stars on its breast sitting in a tree of bitter figs, crowing a doom of suffering over the house of his kinfolks.

James stayed away for three days and nights; and on the third night they had a long-distance call from James' father in St.

Louis, saying that James had come there dirty and tired and stuttering. They had not seen each other for seven years.

Long later the cousin was in a large Midwestern city where some honor was being shown him. Suddenly in the crowded hall a face emerged from the gathering of strangers and moved toward him. It seemed the image of all his blood kin: was it that shadow-face that tracked and haunted him? It was James' face, and at that glance there glimmered over it some dreamlike umbrageous distortion of those long-ago boy's features, as if the cousin saw that face through a pane of colored glass or through currents of time that had deepened over it as it had sunk into its inheritance.

There was something James had to say, it was on his face; but what it was the cousin never knew, for someone pulled him round, his back to James, to shake his hand and congratulate him —someone of distinction. When he finally turned, heavy as stone, as if he were turning to look back into the face of his own secret sorrow, James was gone; and the cousins never met again.

But the look upon James' face that moment that night in a strange city where the cousin had come to passing recognition and had found a transient homage bore the haunting question of ancestry; and though he thought he had at last found and cleared for himself something of identity, a particle of answer in the face of the world, had he set anything at peace, answered any speechless question, atoned for the blind failing, the outrage and the pain on the face of his blood kindred? That glance, struck like a blow against ancestral countenance, had left a scar of resemblance, ancient and unchanging through the generations, on the faces of the grandmother, of the aunts, the cousins, his own father and his father's father; and would mark his own face longer than the stamp of any stranger's honor that would change nothing.

OLD WILDWOOD

On a soft morning in May, at the American Express in Rome, the grandson was handed a letter; and high up on the Spanish Steps he sat alone and opened the letter and read its news. It was in his mother's hand:

"Well, your grandaddy died two days ago and we had his funeral in the house in Charity. There were so many flowers, roses and gladiolas and every other kind, that the front porch was filled with them, twas a sight to see. Then we took him to the graveyard where all the rest are buried and added his grave, one more, to the rest.

"At the graveyard your father suddenly walked out and stood and said the Lord's Prayer over his daddy's grave, as none of the Methodists in the family would hear a Catholic priest say a Catholic prayer, nor the Catholics in the family allow a Methodist one; and your grandaddy was going to be left in his grave without one holy word of any kind. But both were there, priest and preacher, and I said what a shame that your poor old daddy has to go to earth without even 'Abide with Me' sung by a soloist. His own begotten children marrying without conscience into this church and that, confounding their children as to the nature of God, caused it all, and there it was to see, clear and shameful, at the graveyard. Then all of a sudden your two great aunts, my mother's and your grandmother's sweet old sisters,

Ruby and Saxon Thompson, one blind and the other of such strutted ankles from Bright's Disease as could barely toddle, started singing 'Just As I Am Without One Plea,' and many joined in, it was so sweet and so sad and so peaceful to hear. Then we all walked away and left your grandaddy in his grave."

The grandson lifted his eyes from the letter and they saw an ancient foreign city of stone. So an old lost grandfather, an old man of timber, had left the world. He folded the letter and put it in his pocket. Then he leaned back and settled upon the pocked stone of the worn steps, supporting himself upon the opened palm of his hand. He rested a little, holding the letter, thinking how clear pictures of what had troubled his mind always came to him in some sudden, quiet ease of resting. He considered, as a man resting on stone, his grandfather.

Yes, he thought, the little old grandfather had the animal grace and solitary air of an old mariner about him, though he was a lumberman and purely of earth. His left leg was shorter than his right, and the left foot had some flaw in it that caused the shoe on it to curl upwards. The last time the grandson had seen his grandfather was the summer day when, home on leave from the Navy, and twenty-one, he had come out into the back yard in his shining officer's uniform to find his grandfather sitting there snowy-headed and holding his cap in his hand. Grandfather and grandson had embraced and the grandfather had wept. How so few years had changed him, the grandson had thought that afternoon: so little time had whitened his head and brought him to quick tears: and the grandson heard in his head the words of a long time back, spoken to him by his grandfather that night in Galveston, "Go over into Missi'ppi one day and see can you find your kinfolks . . ."

Where had the grandfather come from, that summer afternoon? Where had he been all these years? The grandson had scarcely thought of him. And now, suddenly, on that summer day of leave, he had heard his mother call to his father, "Your *daddy's* here," with an intonation of shame; and then his mother had come into his room and said, "Son, your grandaddy's here. Go out in the back yard and see your grandaddy."

When he had put on his uniform and stepped into the yard, there he saw the white-headed little man sitting on the bench. And there, resting on the grass and lying a little on its side as though it were a separate being, curled and dwarfed, was his grandfather's crooked foot, old disastrous companion.

The grandfather was an idler and had been run away from home, it was said, by his wife and children time and time again, and the last time for good; and where did he live and what did he do? Later, on the day of his visit and after he had gone away, the grandson's mother had confessed that she knew her husband went secretly to see his father somewhere in the city and to give him money the family had to do without. It was in a shabby little hotel on a street of houses of women and saloons that his father and his grandfather met and talked, father and son.

As he sat with his grandfather in the yard on the white bench under the camphor tree that summer, and now on this alien stone, the grandson remembered that the first time he had known his grandfather was on the trip to Galveston where they went to fish—the grandson was fourteen—and how lonesome he was there with this little old graying limping stranger who was his grandfather and who was wild somewhere that the grandson could not surmise, only fear. Who was this man tied to him by blood through his father and who, though he strongly resembled his father, seemed an alien, not even a friend. The grandfather had sat on the rocks and drunk whiskey while the grandson fished; and though he did not talk much, the grandson felt that there was a constant toil of figuring going on in the old man as he looked out over the brown Gulf water, his feet bare and his shoes on the rock, one crooked one by one good one. On the rock the boy gazed at the bad foot for a long, long time, more often than he watched the fishing line, as though the foot on the rock might be some odd creature he had brought up from the water and left on the rock to perish in the sun. At night he watched it too, curled on the cot in the moonlight as his grandfather slept, so that he came to know it well on both rock and cot and to think of it as a special kind of being in itself. There on the rock, as on the cot, the bad foot was the very naked shape of the shoe that concealed it. It seemed lifeless there on the rock, it was turned inwards toward the good foot as though to ask for pity from it or to caricature it. The good foot seemed proud and aloof and disdainful, virile and perfectly shaped.

On the rock, the grandfather was like a man of the sea, the grandson thought, like a fisherman or a boat captain. His large Roman head with its bulging forehead characteristic of his children shone in the sun; and his wide face was too large for his small and rather delicate body, lending him a strangely noble bearing, classic and Bacchian. There was something deeply kind and tender in this old gentleman grandfather barefooted on the rock, drinking whiskey from the bottle. The grandson felt the man was often at the point of speaking to him of some serious thing but drank it all away again out of timidity or respect.

Each night they straggled back to their room in a cheap Gulf-front cabin full of flies and sand, and the grandson would help his grandfather into his cot, where he would immediately fall to sleep. Then the grandson would lie for a long time watching his grandfather breathe, his graying curly hair tousled over his strutted forehead, and watching the sad foot that sometimes flinched on the sheet with fatigue, for it was a weak foot, he thought. Considering this man before him, the grandson thought how he might be a man of wood, grown in a wilderness of trees, as rude and native and unblazed as a wildwood tree. He held some wilderness in him, the very sap and seed of it. Then, half fearing the man, the grandson would fall asleep, with the thought and the image of the blighted foot worrying him. He was always afraid of his grandfather, no doubt because of the whiskey, but certainly for deeper, more mysterious reasons which he could not find out in this man who was yet so respectful to him.

One night after the grandfather had been drinking on the rock all day, he had drunk some more in the cabin and finally, sitting on the side of his cot, he had found the words he had to say to the grandson. He had spoken to him clearly and quietly and in such a kind of flowing song that the words might have been given him by another voice whispering him what to say.

"We all lived in Missi'ppi," was the way he began, quietly, to speak. "And in those days wasn't much there, only sawmills and wildwoods of good rich timber, uncut and unmarked, and lots of good Nigras to help with everything, wide airy houses and broad fields. It all seems now such a good day and time, though we didn't count it for much then. Your granny and I moved over out of Missi'ppi and into Texas, from one little mill town to another, me blazing timber and then cutting it, counting it in the railroad cars, your granny taking a new baby each time, seems like, but the same baby buggy for each—if we'd have named our children after the counties they were borned in, all twelve of them, counting the one that died in Conroe, you'd have a muster roll of half the counties of Texas—all borned in Texas; but not a one ever went back to Missi'ppi, nor cared. Twas all wildwood then, son, but so soon gone.

"I had such man's strength then, the kind that first my grandfather broke wilderness with into trail and clearing, hewed houses and towns out of timber with, the kind his grandsons used to break the rest. Why I fathered twelve children in the state of Texas and fed them on sweet milk and kidney beans and light bread and working twelve hours a day—mill and railroad—working Nigras and working myself and raising a family of barefooted towheads chasing the chickens and climbing the trees and carrying water, playing tree tag in the dirt yard stained with mulberries. Your granny wasn't deaf then, had better hearing than most, could hear the boll weevils in the cotton, could listen that well. We all slept all over the house, beds never made, always a baby squalling in the kitchen while your granny cooked, or eating dirt where it sat in the shade as your granny did the washing in the washpot on the fire with Nigras helping and singing, or riding the hip of one of the big girls or boys . . . my children grew up on each other's hips and you could never tell it now the way they live and treat each other.

"I didn't have any schooling, but my grandfather was a schoolteacher and broke clearing and built a log schoolhouse and taught in it—it still stands, I hear tell, in Tupelo—and lived to start a university in Stockton, Missi'ppi; was a Peabody and the

Peabodys still live all over Missi'ppi, go in there and you'll find Peabodys all over Missi'ppi. You know there's a big bridge of steel over the Missi'ppi River at Meridian; that's a Peabody, kin to me and kin to you. Another one, John Bell, built a highway clean to the Louisiana line and starting at Jackson; that's some of your kinfolks, old John Bell, such a fine singing man, a good voice and pure black-headed Irishman with his temper in his eyes. Called him Cousin Jack, he was adopted, and just here in Galveston, to tell you the truth, I've been wondering again who from; I've wondered often about John Bell all these years, studied him time and again. When I came he was already in our family, running with the other children in the yard, seems like, when I first saw him, and we all called him Cousin Jack, and of all my family, brother and sister and even my own children, John Bell was the best friend ever in this world to me. Aw, John Bell's been heavy on my mind—John Bell! He was one to go to. Cousin Jack was not ascared of anything, brave everywhere he went and not ascared of hard work, spit on his hands and went right in. Went to work at fourteen and helped the family. Was a jolly man and full of some of the devil, too, and we raised a ruckus on Saturday nights when we was young men together, we'd dance till midnight, court the girls on the way home and come on home ourselves singing and in great spirits. John Bell! Fishing and singing on the river with a pint of bourbon in our hip pocket and a breath of it on the bait for good luck. But something always a little sad about John Bell, have never known what it could be. Maybe it was his being adopted. He knew that; they told him. But it was more than that. Then he married Nellie Clayton, your granny's niece, and I have never seen him again. He built a highway clean through the state of Missi'ppi and I always knew he would amount to something. Died in 1921, and now his children are all up and grown in Missi'ppi. They are some of the ones to look for. Find the Bells.

"Time came when all the tree country of East Texas was cut, seemed like no timber left, and new ways and new mills. I brought all my family to Houston, to work for the Southern

Pacific. Some was married and even had babies of their own, but we stayed together, the whole kit and kaboodle of us, all around your granny. In the city of Houston we found one big old house and all lived in it. Then the family began to sunder apart, seemed like, with some going away to marry and then coming home again bringing husband or wife. I stayed away from home as much as I could, to have some peace from all the clamoring among my children. I never understood my children, son, could never make them out, my own children; children coming in and going out, half their children living there with this new husband and that, and the old husbands coming back to make a fuss, and one, Grace's, just staying on there, moved in and wouldn't ever leave, is still there to this day; and children from all husbands and wives playing all together in that house, with your granny deaf as a doornail and calling out to the children to mind, and wanting care, but would never leave and never will, she'll die in that house with all of them around her, abusing her, too, neither child nor grandchild minding her. I just left, son, and went to live in a boarding house. I'd go home on Sundays and on Easters and on Christmas, but not to stay. There's a time when a person can't help anything anymore, anything. Still, they would come to me, one or another of my sons and daughters, but not to see how I was or to bring me anything, twas to borrow money from me. They never knew that I had lost my job with the S.P. because I drank a little whiskey.

"And I never went to any church, son, but I'm fifty years of age and I believe in the living God and practice the Golden Rule and I hope the Lord'll save me from my sins. But I never had anybody to go to, for help or comfort, and I want you to know your father didn't either, never had anybody to go to. But I want you to know you do, and I will tell you who and where so you will always know. I don't want you ever to know what it is not to have anybody to go to.

"So when you get to be a young man I hope you'll go over into Missi'ppi and see can you find your blood kinfolks. Tell them your grandaddy sent you there. Haven't been over there

myself for thirty years, kept meaning to but just never did. Now
I guess I never will. But you go, and when you go, tell them you
are a Peabody's grandson. They're all there, all over there, all
over Missi'ppi; look for the Peabodys and for the Claytons and
look for the Bells . . ."

After the grandfather had finished his story, he sat still on
his cot, looking down as if he might be regarding his bare
crooked foot. The grandson did not speak or ask a question but
he lay quietly thinking about it all, how melancholy and grand
the history of relations was. Then, in a while, he heard his grandfather get up softly, put on his crooked shoe and the good one,
and go out, thinking he was asleep. He has gone to find him
John Bell, the grandson thought. The creaking of his bad shoe
and the rhythm of his limp seemed to the grandson to repeat his
grandfather's words: Peabodys and the Claytons and the Bells.

The grandson did not sleep while his grandfather was gone.
He was afraid, for the tides of the Gulf were swelling against the
sea wall below the cabin; yet he thought how he no longer feared
his grandfather, for now that he had spoken to him so quietly
and with such love he felt he was something of his own. He
loved his grandfather. Yet now that he had been brought to love
what he had feared, he was cruelly left alone in the whole world
with this love, it seemed, and was that the way love worked?—
with the unknown waters swelling and falling close to the bed
where he lay with the loving story haunting him? There was so
much more to it all, to the life of men and women, than he had
known before he came to Galveston just to fish with his grandfather, so much in just a man barefooted on a rock and drinking
whiskey in the sun, silent and dangerous and kin to him. And
then the man had spoken and made a bond between them and
brought a kind of nobility of forest, something like a shelter of
grandness of trees over it all. The tree country! The grandson
belonged to an old, illustrious bunch of people of timber with
names he could now name, all a busy, honorable and worthy
company of wilderness breakers and forest blazers, bridge build-
ers and road makers, and teachers, Claytons and Peabodys and

Bells, and the grandfather belonged to them, too, and it was he who had brought all the others home to him, his grandson. Yet the grandfather seemed an orphan. And now for the first time, the grandson felt the deep, free sadness of orphanage; and he knew he was orphaned, too. That was the cruel gift of his grandfather, he thought. The crooked foot! John Bell!

In this loneliness he knew, at some border where land turned into endless water, he felt himself to be the only one alive in this moment—where were all the rest?—in a land called Mississippi, called Texas, where? He was alone to do what he could do with it all and oh what to do would be some daring thing, told or performed on some shore where two ancient elements met, land and water, and touched each other and caused some violence of kinship between two orphans, and with heartbreak in it. What to do would have the quiet, promising dangerousness of his grandfather on the rock in it, it would have the grave and epic tone of his grandfather's ultimate telling on the side of the cot under one light globe in a mist of shoreflies in a sandy transient roof of revelation while the tide washed at the very feet of teller and listener. And what to do would have the feeling of myth and mystery that he felt as he had listened, as though when he listened he were a rock and the story he heard was water swelling and washing over generations and falling again, like the waters over the rock when the tide came in.

Suddenly he heard footsteps, and when the door opened quietly he saw his grandfather and a woman behind him. They came in the room and the woman whispered, "You didn't tell me that a kid was here."

"He's asleep, John Bell," the grandfather whispered.

Something began between the two, between the grandfather and the woman, and the grandson feigned sleep. But he watched through the lashes of his half-closed eyes as through an ambush of grass the odd grace of his grandfather struggling with the woman, with whom he seemed to be swimming through water, and he heard his grandfather's low growl like a fierce dog on the cot, and he saw his grandfather's devil's foot treading and gently kicking, bare in the air, so close to him that he could have reached out to touch it. And then he knew that the foot had a very special beauty and grace of moment, a lovely secret performance hidden in it that had seemed a shame on his person and a flaw upon the rock. It had something, even, of a bird's movements in it. It was the crooked foot that was the source and the meaning of the strange and lovely and somehow delicate disaster on the bed; and it was that shape and movement that the grandson took for his own to remember.

John Bell!

The two people drank out of a bottle without saying a word, but they were celebrating something they had come through, as if they had succeeded in swimming, with each other's help, a laborious dangerous distance; and then they rose to leave the room together. But at the door, the grandfather called softly as he lifted the bottle once more to his mouth, "For John Bell . . . ," and the name rang deeply over the dark room like the tone of a bell upon the sea.

When they were gone, the grandson rose and looked out the window and saw the water with a horned moon over it and smelled the limey odors of shrimp, saw the delicate swaying starry lights of fishing boats; and there in the clear light of the moon he saw the rock he and his grandfather fished on. The tide was climbing over it and slipping back off it as if to cover it with a sighing embrace, like a body, as if to pull the rock, for a swelling moment, to its soft and caressing bosom of water; and there was a secret bathing of tenderness over the very world like a dark rock washed over with moonlit sea water and whiskey and tenderness and the mysteriousness of a grandfather, of an old story, an old ancestor of whom the grandson was afraid again. Now the grandfather seemed to the grandson to have been some old sea-being risen out of the waters to sit on a rock and to tell a tale in a stranger's room, and disappear. Would he ever come again to fish on the rock in the Gulf and to snore on the cot in the cabin? But as he looked at the world of rock and tide and moon, in the grandson's head the words of a pioneer sounded, quiet and plaintive and urgent: Go over into Missi'ppi when you get to be a young man and see can you find your kinfolks, son. Look for the Claytons and look for the Peabodys and look for the Bells, all in there, all over Missi'ppi . . . And the bell-rung deepness of a name called sounded in the dark room.

John Bell!

There in the room, even then, alone and with the wild lovely world he knew, tidewater and moonlight tenderly tormenting the rock outside, and inside the astonishing delicate performance tormenting the room, and the shape of the foot on both room and rock, the grandson thought how he would do, in his time, some work to bring about through an enduring rock-silence a secret performance with something, some rock-force, some tide-force, some lovely, hearty, fine wildwood wildwater thing always living in him through his ancestry and now brought to sense in him, that old gamy wilderness bequeathed him; how shaggy-headed, crooked-footed perfection would be what he would work for, some marvelous, reckless and imperfect loveliness, proclaiming about the ways of men in the world and all that befell them, all that glorified, all that damned them, clearing and covering over and clearing again, on and on and on.

He went back to his cot and lay upon his young back. Not to go to sleep! but to stay awake with it all, whatever, whatever it was, keeping the wilderness awake in this and many more rooms, breathing sea-wind and pinesap. Because—now he felt sure—the thing to do about it all and with it all would be in some performance of the senses after long silence and waiting— of the hair that would grow upon his chest like grass and of the nipples of his breast, of the wildwood in his seed and the sappy sweat of the crease of his loins, of the saltwater of his tears, the spit on his palms, the blistering of the blazer's ax-handle, all mortal stuff. To keep wilderness awake and wild and never sleeping, in many rooms in many places was his plan in Galveston, and the torment that lay ahead for him would come, and it would hold him wakeful through nights of bitter desire for more than he could ever name, but for some gentle, lovely and disastrous heartbreak of men and women in this world. And in that room that held the history of his grandfather, the little poem of his forebears and the gesture of the now beautiful swimming and soaring crooked foot, he knew for himself that there would be, or he would make them, secret rooms in his life holding, like a gymnasium, the odors of mortal exertion, of desperate tournament, a violent contest, a hardy, laborious chopping, manual and physical and involving the strength in his blistering hands and the muscles of his heaving back, all the blazer's work, the pioneer's blazing hand! Or places upon rocks of silence where an enigma lay in the sun, dry and orphaned and moribund until some blessed tide eventually rose and caressed it and took it to its breast as if to whisper, "Belong to me before I slide away," and what was silent and half-dead roused and showed its secret performance: that seemed to be the whole history of everything, the secret, possible performance in everything that was sliding, sliding away.

Finally, his breast aching and its secret that lived there unperformed, but with the trembling of some enormous coming thrill, the distant disclosure of some vision, even, of some glimmering company of humanity of his yearning with whom to perform some daring, lovely, heartbroken and disastrous history; and with terror of listener and sadness of teller, the grandson fell alone to sleep and never heard his grandfather come back to his cot, that night in Galveston.

Now they had buried the grandfather. Bury the good man of wilderness, he thought; bury in Texas dirt the crooked foot that never walked again on the ground of Missi'ppi where mine has never been set. And find him John Bell in the next world.

His hand upon which he had rested was aching and he relieved it of his weight and sat upon the solid slab of ancient travertine stone. There, engraved in the palm of the hand he had leaned on, was the very mark and grain of the stone, as though his hand were stone. He would not have a hand of stone! He would carry a hand that could labor wood and build a house, trouble dirt and lay a highway, and blaze a trail through leaf and bramble; and a hand that could rot like wood and fall into dust.

And then the grandson thought how all the style and works of stone had so deeply troubled him in this ancient city, and how he had not clearly known until now that he loved wood best and belonged by his very secret woodsman's nature to old wildwood.

RHODY'S PATH

Sometimes several sudden events will happen together so as to make you believe they have a single meaning if twould only come clear. Surely happenings are lowered down upon us after a pattern of the Lord above.

Twas in the summer of one year; the time the Second Coming was prophesied over the land and the Revivalist came to Bailey's pasture to prove it; and the year of two memorable events. First was the plague of grasshoppers (twas the driest year in many an old memory, in East Texas); second was the Revival in the pasture across from the house.

Just even to mention the pestilence of hoppers makes you want to scratch all over. They came from over toward Grapeland like a promise of Revelations—all counted to the last as even the hairs of our head are numbered, so says the Bible and so said the Revivalist—making the driest noise in the world, if you have ever heard them. There were so many that they were all clustered together, just one working mass of living insects, wild with appetite and cutting down so fast you could not believe your eyes a whole field of crops. They hid the sun like a curtain and twas half-daylight all that day, the trees were alive with them and shredded of their leaves. We humans were locked in our houses, but the earth was the grasshopper's, he took over the world. It did truly seem a punishment, like the end of the world was upon us, as was prophesied.

Who should choose to come home to us that end of summer but Rhody, to visit, after a long time gone. She had been in New Orleans as well as in Dallas and up in Shreveport too, first married to her third husband in New Orleans, then in Dallas to run away from him in spite, and lastly in Shreveport to write him to go to the Devil and never lay eye on her again. We all think he was real ready to follow the law of that note. Then she come on home to tell us all this, and to rest.

Rhody arrived in a fuss and a fit, the way she is eternally, a born fidget, on the heels of the plague of hoppers. They had not been gone a day when she swept in like the scourge of pestilence. She came into our wasteland, scarce a leaf on a tree and crops just stalks, dust in the air. So had the Revivalist—as if they had arranged it together in Louisiana and the preacher had gone so far as to prophesy the Second Coming in Texas for Rhody's sake. She could make a man do such.

Already in the pasture across the railroad tracks and in front of the house, the Revivalist was raising his tent. We were all sitting on the front porch to watch, when we saw what we couldn't believe our eyes were telling us at first, but knew soon after by her same old walk, Rhody crossing the pasture with her grip in her hand. We watched her stop and set on her suitcase to pass conversation with the Revivalist—she never met a stranger in her life—and his helpers, and we waited for her to come on home across the tracks and through the gate. Mama and Papa and Idalou and some of the children stood at the gate and waited for her; but the bird dog Sam sat on the porch and waited there, barking. He was too old—Idalou said he was eighteen—to waste breath running to the gate to meet Rhody.

The hooded flagpole sitter was a part of it all. He had come in advance as an agent for the Revival and sat on the Mercantile Building as an advertisement for the Revival. He had been up there for three days when the grasshoppers come. Twas harder for him than for anyone, we all imagined. The old-timers said he had brought in the plague of hoppers as part of prophecy. They raised up to him a little tent and he sat under that; but it must have been terrible for him. Most thought he would volunteer to come on down, in the face of such adversity, but no sir, he stayed, and was admired for it. He couldn't sail down his leaflets that advertised the Revival, for the grasshoppers would have eaten those as fast as if they had been green leaves from a tree. But the town had already had leaflets enough that read, "The Day of Judgment Is at Hand, Repent of Your Sins for the Lord Cometh . . ."

The first night he was up twas a hot starry night. We all sat on the porch till late at night rocking and fanning and watching him. There he was over the town, a black statue that hardly seemed real.

When the Revivalist first appeared at the house to ask us for cool water, we invited him in on the back porch. He was a young man to be so stern a preacher, lean and nervous and full of his sermon. His bushy eyebrows met together—for jealousy, Idalou told us after he was gone, and uttered a warning against eyebrows that run together. He started right out to speak of our salvation as if it might earn him a drink of water, and of his own past sinful life in cities before he was redeemed. He wanted our redemption, the way he went on sermonizing, more than a cool drink of water; but water was easiest to provide him with and best at hand, as Aunt Idalou said after he had gone. He was a man ready to speak of his own frailties and Mama praised him for this. He wanted to make us all free and purged of man's wickedness, he said, and his black eyes burned under his joined eyebrows when he spoke of this. When he had left, one of the children—Son—helped him carry the pail of well water to the pasture, and then we all broke into sides about who would go to the Revival the next night and who would watch it from the front porch.

When Son came back he was trembling and told that the Revivalist had two diamond rattlesnakes in a cage, right in Bailey's pasture, and that he had shown him the snakes. Then he told us that the preacher was going to show how the Lord would cure him of snakebite as a demonstration of faith. He had converted and saved thousands through this example of the healing power of the Lord, saying his famous prayer as he was struck by this rattling spear, "Hand of God, reach down and help antidote the poison of the diamond rattler of Sin."

Rhody added that she had already found out all this when she came through the pasture and stopped to converse with Bro. Peters—she already knew his name where we hadn't. Then she added that the Revivalist and his company—a lady pianist and three men who were his stewards and helpers—were going to camp in Bailey's pasture during their three-day stay in town and that at the last meeting, the flagpole sitter himself was going to come down and give a testimonial. She further informed us that she had taken upon herself the courtesy to invite Bro. Peters and his lady pianist to eat supper with us that night. We were all both excited and scared. But Mama and Idalou began at once to plan the supper and went in to make the fire in the stove to cook it with.

Rhody was not much changed—a person like Rhody could never change, just add on—as she was burdened by something we could not name. We all noticed a limp in her right leg, and then she confessed she had arthritis in it, from the dampness of New Orleans, she said. Her face was the same beautiful one; she had always been the prettiest in the family, taking after Granny, who had been, it was a legend that had photographic proof right on the wall, a very beautiful young woman. But Rhody's face was as if seen through a glass darkly, as the Bible says. More had happened to Rhody during the years away than she would ever tell us. "Some of the fandango is danced out in her," Aunt Idalou said, and now we would all see the change in Rhody that we all hoped and prayed for.

Rhody was thrilled by the sight of the flagpole sitter. She said she was just dying to meet him. She told us that this town had more excitement in it than any city she had been in—and that included several—and she was glad she had come on home. She unpacked her grip and took out some expensive things of pure silk her husbands had bought for her, and there were presents for us all. Then she put her grip in the pantry as though she was going to stay for a long time but no one asked her for how long. In the early days, Rhody had come and left so often that her feet had trod out her own little path through Bailey's pasture and we had named it Rhody's Path. It ran alongside the main path that cut straight through to town. We never used it, left it for her; but if she was gone a long time, Mama would say to one of us who was going to town, "Use Rhody's Path, the bitter-weeds are taking it over, maybe that'll bring her home," the way mothers keep up their hopes for their children's return, though the weeds grow over and their beds are unused. Mama kept Rhody's room the way Rhody had it before she left for the first time, and the same counterpane was always on the bed, fresh and clean, the big painted chalk figure of a collie was on the dresser, the fringed pillow a beau had given her with "Sweetheart" on it, and the framed picture of Mary Pickford autographed by her, "America's Sweetheart." "She's got sweetheart on the brain," Mama used to say. She carried sweetheart too far.

Anyway, the Revivalist took Rhody's Path to come to supper on. Around suppertime here came Bro. Peters and the lady pianist across Bailey's pasture on Rhody's Path, he tall and fast-walking, the little pianist trotting behind him like a little spitz to keep up with him. They came through the gate and onto the front porch, where we all greeted them, and Rhody was putting on a few airs of city ways that made Idalou look at her as if she could stomp her toe. We were introduced to the pianist, whose name was Elsie Wade, a little spinster type with freckled hands and birdlike movements of head. Miss Wade asked the Lord to bless this house and said that good Christians always gathered easily as if they were blood kin, which they were, Bro. Peters added; and we all went in the house, through the hall and onto the back porch. It was a late summer evening and the vines strung across the screen of the porch were nothing but strings after the grasshoppers had devoured them, but through the latticework of string we could see the distant figure of the flagpole sitter that the setting sun set aglow. Rhody kept wanting to talk about him. She said she thought he looked keen up there. Bro. Peters told that the flagpole sitter had been a drinking man, wild and in trouble in every county of Texas and Louisiana, until he was saved by a chance Revival Meeting in Diboll where he was sitting on the County Seat flagpole as a stunt for something or other. The night he came down to give himself to the Lord at the meeting brought wagonloads of people from far and wide, across creeks and gulleys to hear and see him, and many were saved. From that time on he gave his services to the Lord by way of the difficult and lonely task of sitting on a flagpole for three days and nights as a herald of the coming Revival. The flagpole sitter and the diamond rattlers were the most powerful agents of the Gospel and redemption from sin and literally brought thousands of converts into the fold, Bro. Peters told. Rhody said she was dying to meet him and Bro. Peters assured her he would make the introduction personally on the last night of the Revival.

We sat down to a big supper for summertime: cold baking-powder biscuits, cold kidney beans, onions and beets in vinegar, sweet milk and buttermilk, fried chicken—there was nothing green in the garden left after the grasshoppers had taken their fill. Idalou told Bro. Peters and Miss Elsie Wade that she had fed the Devil with some good squash that she had rescued from the grasshoppers but burnt to a mash on the stove; and Bro. Peters said that the Devil liked good summer squash and if he couldn't acquire it through his agents of pestilence he would come by it on a too-hot stove—but that he was glad the Devil left the chicken; and all laughed, Rhody loudest of all.

Afterwards we went to the porch and while Idalou played the piano Son sang some solos, "Drink to Me Only," etc. But Rhody spoiled the singing by talking incessantly to the Revivalist. Then Elsie Wade applied her rolling Revival technique to the old piano that no one could talk over, not even Rhody, and made it sound like a different instrument, playing some rousing hymns which we all sang faintly because of our astonishment at the way such a slight little thing as she manhandled the piano as if it was a bull plow.

In the middle of one of the songs there was somebody at the

front door, and when Idalou went she found it to be a man from Bro. Peters' outfit over in the pasture. He was anxious to speak to Bro. Peters. Idalou asked him in, but Bro. Peters, hearing the man's voice, was already in the hallway by the time the man entered. "Brother Peters!" he called. "One of the diamond rattlers is aloose from the cage." Bro. Peters ran out and Elsie Wade seemed very nervous, inventing a few furbelows on the treble keys as she looked back over her shoulder with a stiff pencil-like neck at the conversation at the front door. Her eyes were so small and glittering at that moment that she seemed like a fierce little bird that might peck a loose snake to death. Idalou invited her to wait in the house, though. "The diamond rattler is our most valuable property," Elsie Wade said, "next to the flagpole sitter."

All night long they were searching for the diamond rattler with their flashlights. We locked all the doors and stayed indoors and watched the lights from the windows. We started a bonfire in the front yard. There were fires in many places in the pasture. The bird dog Sam was astonished that we brought him in the house, but he would not stop barking; and Idalou said he would die of a heart attack before daylight if they didn't catch the valuable property of the viper, he was so old. It was a sinister night. At a certain hour we heard that the flagpole sitter had come down to help find the scourge of Sin. And then suddenly like a shot out of the blue Rhody jumped up and said she couldn't stand it any longer, that she was going out to help the poor Revivalist in his search for the diamond rattler. Everybody objected and Aunt Idalou said over her dead body, that Rhody's arthritis would hinder her if she had to run; but Rhody, being Rhody, went anyway. So there was that anxiousness added.

We all watched from the parlor window. In the light of the bonfire's flame we could see the eerie posse, darting here, kicking there, and we saw that the Revivalist carried a shotgun. The flagpole sitter had arrived in such a hurry and was so excited that he had not had time to take off his long black robe and hood that he wore on the flagpole, and his priestlike shape in the light of the fires was the most nightmarish of all. On went the search through the dark hours after midnight, and it seemed the Revivalist was looking for his Sin, like some penance, a dark hunter in the night searching for evil. And now Rhody was by his side to help him, as if it could be her sin, her evil, too. They seemed to search together.

We never knew, nor will, exactly what happened. When we heard the shot and saw flashlights centered on one spot, we knew they had found the snake; and when we saw them coming on Rhody's Path toward the house, the Revivalist carrying in his arms something like a drowned person, we knew it was Rhody. They came up on the porch, the Revivalist saying sternly, "Call the doctor, she was bitten on the hip by the diamond rattler and has fainted." He bit her bad leg.

They laid Rhody on the bed and Bro. Peters began saying his famous prayer asking the Lord to reach down and pluck the poison from his child. "The snake is killed—the flagpole sitter shot him," one of the men said.

It was Aunt Idalou who scarified the snakebite with a paring knife and saved the life of Rhody until the doctor got there. Though she did it without open prayer, she prayed to herself as she worked on Rhody and used solid practical ways of salvation —including leaves of Spanish dagger plant in the front yard, which Son ran and got, and hog lard. When the doctor got there he marveled at the cure and said there was little more to do except for Rhody to rest and lie prone for a few days. Idalou said she could count Rhody's prone days on one hand and Rhody commented that at least the snake had the common sense to strike her bad leg.

When the commotion was over and danger was passed, someone asked where the Revivalist was. He was nowhere to be found. In the early morning light, just breaking, we saw the pasture empty. There was no sign of anybody or anything except the guttering black remains of the bonfires. The flagpole on the Mercantile Building had nothing sitting on it. The whole Revival company had vanished like a dream . . . and had it all been one, the kind Rhody could bring down upon a place?

We hoped that would teach Rhody a lesson, but Aunt Idalou doubted it seriously. Anyway, Rhody stayed on with us till the very end of summer. Then one day there was that familiar scrambling in the pantry and it was Rhody getting her grip out. There was a mouse's nest in it. She packed it, saying she was going to Austin, to get her a job or take a beauty course she had seen advertised. When she had finished it, she told us, she might come back to Charity and open her a beauty parlor. We all doubted that, knowing she couldn't stay put for long in any one place, beauty or none.

We all kissed her good-bye and Aunt Idalou cried and asked the plain air what had branded her youngest child with some sign of restless wandering and when would she settle down to make a household as woman should; and we watched Rhody go on off, on the path across the pasture with the grip in her hand, going off to what, we all wondered.

"Well," Mama said, "she'll pull a fandango wherever she goes. But through some miracle or just plain common sense of somebody always around to protect her, with hog lard, or just good plain prayer, she'll survive and outlast us all who'll worry ourselves into our graves that Rhody will come to put flowers on, alive as ever." Rhody went out and took the world's risks and chances, but simple remedies of home and homefolks rescued and cured her, time and time again. She always had to touch home, set her wild foot on the path across the pasture that led back to the doorstep of the house, bringing to it across the pasture, from the great confused and mysterious world on the farther side, some sign of what had lately happened to her to lay it on the doorstep of home.

But with the world changing so fast and all old-time word and way paying so quickly away, she will have to correct *herself* in the world she errs in and by its means; or, in some way, by her own, on her own path, in the midst of her traveling. Surely we knew she needed all of us and had to touch us there, living on endurable and permanent, she thought, in that indestructible house where everything was always the way it had forever been and would never change, she imagined; where all, for her, was redeemed and put aright. Then, when she got something straight —what it was no one but Rhody ever knew—she'd gather her things and go off again.

"The sad thing is," Idalou said, rocking on the front porch looking at the empty pasture and the sad-looking path that Rhody took, "that years pass and all grow old and pass away, and this house will be slowly emptied of its tenants." Had Rhody ever considered this? And what would she do when all had gone and none to come home to?

But surely all of us who were listening to Idalou were thinking together that the path would remain, grown over and hidden by, but drawn on the earth, the pasture was engraved with it like an indelible line; and Rhody's feet would be on it, time immemorial, coming and going, coming and going, child of the path in the pasture between home and homelessness, redemption and error. That was the way she had to go.

ZAMOUR, OR
A TALE OF
INHERITANCE

For Dorothy Brett

It is said—and true—that Wylie Prescott became the richest man in one part of Texas because of the accident of inheritance. But few people know the circumstances of his coming to power and wealth. That is the tale to be told.

One time were two sisters in a faraway county of Texas called Red River County, and they had little black beards. Their names were Cheyney and Maroney Lester—they were not twins but close to being that—and even when they were just young girls of about fourteen they had begun to grow a sprouting of black beard.

The way it began was that Cheyney's beard started to show first and then Maroney's. Cheyney was very distraught and par- ticularly as she felt she might fall into bad light with her sister Maroney, whom she worshiped. But Maroney came to her and said quietly, "Don't worry, dear sister Cheyney, this will make no difference between us—and besides, now I will tell you that for a long time I have noticed the same thing slowly happening to me." The two sisters embraced and vowed they would stay together for the rest of their lives. This bond was stronger than death, although death kept it, too, and a very beautiful one to see, endearing the Lester sisters to all Red River County.

Red River County was a wildwood in those days, neighbors far pieces apart, scattered along the wide red river and upon the red land. Rain would leave red puddles in the gullies, and red dust stained the water in stock tubs. It had a wildness to it, too, this county, and where it rose to hilly places there were rocks and trees of hard wood, there where the water of the red river could not soften it. It was a beautiful wilderness and plain simple folks lived in it, and until the time of this tale, very few ever left the county and practically none that would never come back to it. This was all in about nineteen-fifteen.

Now there was a younger sister in the Lester family, ten years younger than Maroney and Cheyney; and her name was Princis Lester. Princis Lester grew along with her sisters and never spoke one word about the difference between her own aspect and theirs, though she took notice of it at an early age. She came to regard it as just the way they were, and there was no talk about it. But when she reached the self-regarding age of eighteen, and as she was slender and beautiful and chestnut-haired where her sisters' hair was of the coldest black, and they plump as two biscuits, Princis considered point-blank for the first time the plight that had befallen her sisters and thought death more desirable.

She said to herself, if this were to happen to me, I would just kill myself, looking at her face very carefully in the mirror. She drew farther apart from her sisters, though she had never been close to them, for Cheyney and Maroney seemed to hang apart in space from her, two little hemispheres joined by this isthmus of hair. Anyway, times were changing and Princis was taking her start in a new time. There was a new commissary up a few miles on the riverbank, and there were gatherings of young and old here, giving the chance to farm people to dress up and look at each other and adding one more to the opportunities of Sunday church and family meetings up and down the valley.

Princis asked no questions of her sisters about what she

considered a fatal infirmity—they might have been dwarfs or albinos from the way she regarded them. Still, they were sweet and gentle, laughing little creatures, her sisters; and in the autumn she listened to them laughing in the apple orchard in their nunlike felicity, and she watched out her window at them sitting in the apple trees like charming coons throwing down the fruit. What did they have that she didn't? she asked herself at the dresser. A beard, she answered herself directly. The beard seemed to make all the difference, even that of blessed happiness. But she liked them, they were so loving with her, their own young sister Princis, they never once looked closely at her face to see if there was the slightest trace of beard, they never once mentioned it; and if she had not been their sister and that close kin to them, Princis might never have noticed their peculiarity after being with them for a little while, the way other more distant kinfolks seemed not to notice, coming once and a while on Sundays to visit in the afternoons. Eccentricities that take on price and preciosity in cities become humble matter of fact in country places among country folk.

She yearned to go away to a city, to get her a job or learn to be a beauty operator, or take a course in something, as so many others were doing. But she waited. She finished high school and then her mother and father died within a year. She stayed on at home until she was twenty-five, yearning to run away. There was such a distance between her and her sisters, one she felt she could never bridge, never as long as she lived—she could not cross that bridge of hair. The neighbors and cousins were miles down the road and there were few callers besides them. She waited on. At night as she sat by the light of the glass lamp while her sisters played the xylophone in the parlor, she would scout her face very carefully in her hand mirror. Sometimes she fell into a kind of trance before the face in the mirror as though it put her into a sleep. Then the whole world lay only in the oval pool of her mirror.

One time at the supper table, Princis suddenly cried out to her sisters, "Stop staring at me!" and left the table. Maroney said to her, "Why, Princis, our own beautiful little sister, we were not staring at you." But Princis put on her coat and went out the back door. It was drizzling and December. She walked in the orchard under the dripping fruitless trees. "This means I must run away," she told herself, "or I will end up by harming my two sisters, who mean no harm to anyone."

What was that little cry she heard in the dark orchard, some animal or what? She walked softly toward the cry and saw two lovely burning lights. Those were its eyes. She went closer toward the lights, and it was a cat that leaped away from her. She pursued it. Up it went, scratching into a tree, where its eyes burned like some luminous fruit growing on the bare branches.

"Kitty!" she called. "If you are wet and cold, come to me. I am Princis Lester and I will do you no harm. We can be friends with each other, if you will come on down."

She waited and watched the lights swinging through the tree. Then the cat came slowly down to where she stood and brushed a greeting against her. She picked him up, and he let her, and she felt how friendly his wet fur was to her hand, as though she had known it always. But its coat felt torn—it had been hounded by some animal.

Walking back toward the house with the cat, she said to it, "You have been lost in the cold rain and darkness. You had lost your way because you were nobody's cat and now you are mine; and what will I call you?"

In the house, Princis saw that the cat was a big black congenial male with cotton-eyes. She took off her new orange velveteen coat and wrapped him in it and took him into the parlor to show to her two sisters, and this would be an offering, too, to make up to them for what she had said at the supper table.

"Look here!" she said. "I have found a friend in the orchard."

Cheyney and Maroney ran delighted to Princis and the cat, whose head shone wet and black where it nestled in the orange velveteen. But the cat grumbled and spat at them and wanted to claw out to keep them away. Cheyney and Maroney drew back together, and Princis said, "He is just nervous," and took him into her room.

She sat down on her bed with the cat, dried him and brushed him with her hairbrush and said to him, "But what will I name you, because you are mine to keep." Some beautiful name, she thought. What beautiful names did she know? She could not think of any; but then suddenly a name breathed into her head, almost as though someone else were whispering her a name: Zamour! It was a lovely name she had seen on a poster nailed to a tree on the road and advertising a magician who would come to the commissary with a carnival that she never saw.

And so Zamour became Princis' own. He either stayed in her room behind closed doors or walked with Princis in the orchard where they had met. He stayed away from Cheyney and Maroney, never taking to them, and they, in their kind way, did not press themselves upon him but let him go his way under his own affections.

When Princis was thirty, she met at the commissary a young railroad man named Mr. Simpson. She spied upon him regularly at the commissary from then on. As each got to know when the other would come to buy supplies, each made a secret plan. She knew by his eyes that he would one day come to call on her, and she told Zamour about it, and that they would have to watch and wait for him to come. She and Zamour played a secret game together—"When Mr. Simpson Comes"—and they often sat together on the front-porch swing to watch for him or in her bedroom at night, with only the little blue glass lamp burning, playing the game of waiting for him maybe to come while Princis looked at her face in the hand mirror.

Though she never invited Mr. Simpson, she knew he would come. The night he came sure enough to call, her sisters were playing the xylophone in the parlor, "Beautiful Ohio," their favorite, over and over, such a music of gliding in a dream. Princis and Mr. Simpson sat in the hall on the hat-tree seat until the concert would be over and they could go into the parlor. But

Cheyney and Maroney went on playing "Beautiful Ohio," their favorite, over and over, a music to rock a canoe or swing a seat in a Ferris wheel.

Mr. Simpson told Princis that he was an orphan from St. Louis, had no folks, and that he was being transferred to the city of Houston to work in the railroad yards there—he was a switchman—and Princis told him without catching a breath a word that might be used to sing "Beautiful Ohio" with: *elope:* that she would like to elope with him, a beautiful word that loped into her mouth out of the music and lovely enough, too, to name a cat by if she had not first found the gift of the lovely word Zamour nailed to a tree.

Mr. Simpson was so thrilled by Princis' generous offer that he took it, right there in the hall sitting on the seat of the hat tree that could have been the seat of a gondola they rocked in to the music whose glassy purlings sounded like a dripping and rippling of water to throb together upon and move a boat—toward all their future ahead. And so they eloped that very night, before the xylophone concert was ever over.

"Now we will have a chance to know each other," Mr. Simpson told her, "and we will make our future of a long time together until we are very old, when we will have my pension. That is why it is good to be a railroad man."

"And Zamour's future, too," Princis added. "For he will go with us."

Princis pinned a note on the hat tree saying, "I have eloped to Houston to get married and to make my future. Love, Princis."

Princis sent her sisters one postcard, showing a view of Houston looking north toward Red River County; and for many, many years there was no other word exchanged between them.

This was the time when people from small towns and farms were migrating to bigger towns and small cities, the time of change in Texas. Princis and Mr. Simpson moved into a small frame house in a neighborhood on Hines Street in Houston. The block of houses, called the Neighborhood by those living there, was inhabited by migrants from little towns, and a few were even from Red River County. These people had changed their style of living and slid into the pattern of the city. But oddly enough— for one would have thought she would be the first to change— Princis Lester did not alter, but from the day she settled there went on living as if she were still in Red River County. Something in Red River County kept her.

She did not dress up and catch the bus to spend all day in town, picking through Kress's or having a Coke and sandwich in a department store luncheonette, gazing at women to see if their purse and shoes matched; nor did she spend her afternoons in vaudeville matinées at the Prince Theatre that bubbled dazzling lights even in the daytime; nor shop in Serve-Yourself Piggly Wigglys: she had a charge account at a little grocery store nearby where the man whom she knew personally reached up to the top shelf with a clamping stick to get her a box of Quaker Oats. "Whenever I get homesick for Red River County," one of the neighbors said, "which is less and less—it's all so changed, not like it used to be there—I just go look in Mrs. Simpson's house and feel I've been home to Red River County right on Hines Street in Houston. Why does she harbor home and past?"

When Princis raised the windows in her little house, she put sticks there to hold them up until Mr. Simpson explained to her that windows held up by themselves in the city of Houston. She had her Singer sewing machine and she pumped the pedal to make her print dresses with country flowers on them; she made her own sunbonnets and wore them in the Neighborhood and even in the house or when she swung on the front porch, like her sisters. She put her crocheted counterpane on the bed and her doilies, turned under her own hand, on the dresser and on the arms of the upholstered chairs to protect them.

Princis Lester's Houston behavior was an uncalculated change, among other changes, which at first surprised Mr. Simpson and then pained him literally to death. Princis kept herself from Mr. Simpson, and this took him by such surprise that he could not understand. She had shown him such a yielding eye at the commissary and in the hall under the hat tree. Still, for a while it was an excitement and a challenge to such a man as he, and he pacified himself by thinking about all Princis could give him, all the newly broken wilderness of future awaiting them both, when she was through her waiting. She turned, within the very first year, back toward her ancestry, and this in a world turning toward the other direction, so that such a new world could not support the change—it gave no ground to build upon, she might as well have made a house of mosquito netting; and against what weather could such a flimsy dwelling protect her? Princis became, in the Neighborhood, a curio left behind by a diminishing race, the last of the little country women, as if that race were finishing in her in a little house on a street in a city.

She seemed the last carrier of the bred-up aspects of a played-out species of large ears, small neat heads, faces no bigger than a coffee cup, dainty claws of hands with which to shell pea and bean, to cup a chick, to gather eggs one at a time and not to break any, to hang out small washings, dip one dipper of well water but not to draw a bucketful. When old Mrs. Graves first spied Princis Lester from her two-story boarding house across the street that once, when she and Mr. Graves first came to it from Benburnett County, was their home full of their seven children, she said to old Mr. Graves, sitting in his cane-back rocker in the one room they now lived in, "That new little woman in the Neighborhood will come to change and we will see her do it. Where are all the fine country women that once came to the Neighborhood, where have they all gone in the world? Something has changed them all away." The Graves house had been the grand house of the whole street which ran fifteen blocks between grammar school at one end and junior high at the other. On a corner, it claimed two lots, one a wide space of trees and with a small greenhouse, a chicken yard in the back. It had even had awnings. Now the cars of the boarders were parked under the trees and there was no grass there, only a sort of soiled dirt from drippings of cars; some blown-out tires were lying around, and on Sundays some boarders washed their cars there. The greenhouse was a wreck of glass, roof caved in and the stalks of perished flowers still in it. In summer, though, trumpet vines covered the ruin. But in winter it was ugly to see. The servants' quarters were now rented to a woman from California who, at her age, was studying piano. Some nights it seemed she was trying to show off by playing the "March Slav" so loud for all the Neighborhood to hear.

Though Princis Lester stayed Red River County, Mr. Simpson took to ways of the Neighborhood and drew away from the house and from Princis. He was not a waiting man and he had waited beyond his capacity. Now it seemed to him that he had made a bad bargain at the commissary in Red River County, and he used these words one night to tell Princis Lester so. He started bowling two nights a week with the Hines Street Team while the wives sat in the boxes at the bowling alley and had their beer and cigarettes, yelling when the team made good strikes; or he went to baseball games and wrestling matches, or played dominoes in town somewhere; and he wanted Venetian blinds. More and more Princis was alone, except for one other thing she brought from Red River County and that was her friend Zamour.

In the evenings Princis Lester, in her straight-down country dress falling like a sack down her body, would stand on the front porch or walk up and down the sidewalk on Hines Street in the twilight and call to Zamour to come in. "Zamour! Zamour!" she would call, in a sweet song, until Zamour, plain country cat, would come dallying in on his delicate high hind legs and too-short front ones, so that he seemed to be coming down a ladder to his destination. Sometimes Mr. Framer, one of the neighbors and a policeman, when he was off duty sitting on his front porch cooling off with his bare feet cocked up on the banister, would mimic her and whistle back an insinuating whistle, until his wife, Mercel, came out of the house smoking her cigarette to tell him he ought to be ashamed. They were Rockport County people who drank their homebrew and fished on the jetties at Galveston on Sundays. They painted all the flowerpots red on their front porch and made a garden in their back yard with painted Roman-art bullfrogs standing on the rim of a fish pool, a goose, and a little elf sitting on a toadstool. Their garden was of city mode, azaleas and camellias; but there was always one row of onions and one of bell peppers and a little greens.

Time passed and Princis withdrew more and more from the city and from the Neighborhood. She would not answer the knock of visiting ladies from the houses in the block, and one in particular, a Christian woman from the Neighborhood church who said she brought greetings from the Married Couples' Class, and had a bob with a permanent wave in it. No one saw Princis Lester any more, walking in her sunbonnet to the grocery store in the late afternoons with Zamour following her and the two of them having their conversation. She and Zamour kept indoors. Neighbors watched her forlorn-looking house through their windows, ferns on the porch burnt up from lack of water, newspapers and circulars in yellow drifts on the porch. They wondered if she was sick or not. The men on the bowling team knew that Mr. Simpson had moved to the Railroadmen's boarding house in town and told their wives.

Then one afternoon there was suddenly the announcement of Zamour on the sidewalk, and sure enough at twilight the Neighborhood heard the call "Zamour! Zamour!"; and something was broken, like a long drought. They saw Princis walking up and down the sidewalk again. Her some sort of confinement was over, it was probably out of embarrassment or mourning at the flight of Mr. Simpson. Month after month, they followed this single daily appearance of Princis Lester at twilight, with only the calling of Zamour to let the Neighborhood know she was there, and her total silence and absence the rest of the time. "I think that's why she calls the cat so long and so sadly," one of the neighbor women said, "to let us know she is still there. For how else would we ever know, if it were not for the sign of the cat?" "And when she does come out, to call the cat," another said, "she looks white as a ghost. But that's because of the heavy powder she wears on her face, as if she'd fallen into the flour bin. Still, that's the old Red River County way: all caked powder, an inch thick, and no rouge."

One day Mr. Simpson fell very ill and was taken to the Southern Pacific Hospital. He lay there month after month, still a young man and sinking ever so slowly toward his death because of drinking. Princis Lester talked once to the doctors who came and made her let them in by crying out that it was a death message—and she said at the door, "About who, my sisters?" The doctors told her that her husband must have been drinking all his life, for he had a cancer of the spleen from it. Did she know? they asked her. "No," she said to them. "I never knew Mr. Simpson that well."

Princis would not go to see Mr. Simpson at the hospital. She wrote a postcard to Red River County—but not to her sisters—and asked her cousin, a twenty-year-old boy named Wylie Prescott, to come and try to get him some kind of job in the city and stay in her house until Mr. Simpson could die. He came—he was from the Prescott branch of the family, kin some way to her, her mother's younger brother's son, she remembered; and he had very little to say, or Princis heard little of what he said. She did not even ask him about Red River County. He took the back bedroom to have for his, though he never seemed to be in it.

The young cousin began a secretive life, the city provided him this opportunity, and he got a job driving a large dusty truck which he parked on Hines Street in front of the house at night. He made his own secret life right away, or found it; and some-times in the humid evenings, now, the Neighborhood would see Princis and Zamour sitting in the swing on the front porch and the cousin on the front steps playing his guitar. The Neighbor-hood, living their ways, would all be in their houses: the Catho-lics on the corner in theirs, the one who had the big tomboy named Sis, in theirs; those in the rotting two-story Graves house in theirs—all the roomers in their hot lighted rooms, their cars parked in front of the house and their radios on at different stations—while the decrepit owners, Mr. and Mrs. Graves, sat pushed back into one room they lived in, with pictures of their seven children and their wives and children on the walls. The yards had been watered and the mosquitos had come, suppers were over, the oleanders were fragrant, and there was the sound of accelerating night traffic on the close boulevards. Tree frogs were in the trees, for there usually had been no rain for three months, and their song was as if the dry leaves were sighing. Then Princis Lester would stroll up and down the sidewalk, ghostly in her thick face powder, arms folded as if it were chilly, her felt houseshoes on, with bonbons of fuzz on the toe, calling, "Zamour! Zamour!" and there was the faint strumming of her cousin's guitar accompanying her little cat call.

It was her cousin Wylie Prescott who came in late one night and saw something, after sitting in his truck in front of the house with Mercel Framer, with whom he had become good friends, playing poker and drinking beer with her to keep her company because Mr. Framer the policeman had night duty. What the cousin saw was Princis Lester sitting in her bedroom by the low light of a little lamp, gazing like a statue into a mirror she held in her hand. Zamour was sitting on her shoulder watching and poised as if to catch a bird in the mirror. They did not even hear him come in. He watched Princis and Zamour, then shut the door very quietly and went on peeping through the crack. There she and Zamour sat, frozen in a spell of gazing. He went on to bed, thinking, "As long as they don't mess with my playparties I won't bother theirs."

When Mr. Simpson finally died, Wylie Prescott disappeared, so far as the Neighborhood could make out, for the truck was gone and no sign of him. Princis Lester took Zamour in out of the Neighborhood for good and they kept together in the little house very quietly, to wait for Mr. Simpson's pension. Every morning at five-thirty the faint click of the alarm clock, turned off now but still set at the hour when Mr. Simpson used to get up to go to the railroad yards, was like a little ghost living on in the clock. "Mr. Simpson is still living in that big ticking clock," she told Zamour. "But when his pension comes, we're going back to Red River County." She played a game with Zamour, to wait for the pension. "When we go back to Red River County, what shall we take with us?" Princis named things first—she would take this, and she would take that; what would Zamour take? Zamour did not seem to want to take anything, only looked up at her through his cotton-eyes, arched his back for her to put her fingers in his fur, and rubbed against her legs, shimmering up his tail. They had grown so close.

Most of the time Zamour had been so much like a person, a beautiful, loyal, and loving person, that Princis had forgotten that he was just a mortal cat, and she talked to him, did nice things for him, making plans for him in Red River County. "We'll plant a little garden and have some okra in it, have our cow, and there'll be a shade tree for us, when Mr. Simpson's pension comes and we go back to Red River County"; and she would run her fingers through his fur until Zamour would stretch himself long and electric under her caress. But when she would come upon him sprawled on the bed, involved in his frank bestial sleep, mouth gaping and wild teeth bared in his cat snore, she realized, passing to another room, that Zamour was just a dumb beast and could play no game with her, speak no conversation. "Why go back to Red River County at all?" she asked herself despondently. "He is no one to be with." Then was when she was so very lonely that she wished to see her sisters. She wrote a little letter to them and said, "Do not be surprised but I am coming back to the house in Red River County when Mr. Simpson's pension comes."

Her sisters were still there in the old house. There had been a few postcards exchanged during Mr. Simpson's illness and upon his death. What would they think when they saw her coming through the gate to the house, carrying Zamour and her suitcase? Or would she surprise them, come at night without their expecting her, walk up the road hearing their xylophone music which they had played together for years, hymns and sacred songs and some songs out of their girlhood, but most of all "Beautiful Ohio," their best one. People passing the old house on the hill at night would hear the sounds of the xylophone and used to say, "Those are the sweet bearded Lester Sisters." She would open the door, the music would stop, and Cheyney and Maroney would run to her in their delicate bracelets of beard that seemed to hang from the tips of their ears and loop round their chins, and take her back; and the three of them would live the rest of their lives together there in Red River County.

But no . . . she could not. They were of another tribe, it seemed to her, almost as if they were of another color and language; they had their own ways, their own world—she was an alien there. There would always be the question in her mind, did they love her or did they mock her. It would only mean another waiting with the face mirror, to see if it would come to her, and with them waiting and watching, too—she was sure they would wait and watch, for how could they help it? I am not like them, I am not like them, she told herself; they make me feel so lonely and unusual . . . and she could not go back to them. She and Zamour would find a little cottage of their own near her sisters and they would live happily there on the pension. She would go to see her sisters once in a while, as the other kinfolks did, be nice with them, listen to their music, accepting their difference, as she had when she was young. The pension was what to wait for.

It was so long, her waiting. Now she and Zamour mostly sat in the upholstered chair in the living room facing the front door, waiting for the deliverer of the pension. She made a nice place of waiting there. She and Zamour would not go out for anything, for fear of missing the person who would come. Every morning as soon as the click of the shut-off alarm sounded in Mr. Simpson's clock, she would rise in a nervous haste and rush to her waiting place and begin to wait. Sometimes she fell asleep in the chair, waiting, forgetting everything but the waiting, and wake in the morning still in the chair; and go on waiting there.

The chair took her shape, as if it were her body, and Zamour, who sat in his place on the back of the chair as if on her shoulder, had grown so nervous that in his waiting he had clawed it to its stuffing of straw and clotted cotton. But Princis had not heard or seen this. In the Neighborhood there was a wedding once, and Mercel Framer was shot at by her husband early one morning when he came home off night duty to find her in a parked truck with a stranger in front of his house, causing some scandal and commotion on Hines Street; and a baby of the Catholic family in the corner house had died—the funeral was held in the house and the cars were parked as far as the front of Princis' house. But she went on waiting, bridelike, in her chair, and never had a single notion of birth or death or scandal beyond this sensual embrace of the chair and the longing for the knock on the door as if a bridegroom would be there to come in and take her so full of anxiety and saved rapture. If she had to get up from the chair for a moment, the chair seemed to carry on the waiting for her, though it clung to her and was loath to let her go, they were so locked together. But she would instruct Zamour to keep his place and take over until she got back—and she came back to the chair panting, as if in desire, to plug herself savagely into it and be fitted tightly, shuffling henlike in it until she settled in a satisfaction on this nest of waiting.

If there was a knock on the door she would grow rigid and whisper to Zamour, "That's Mr. Simpson's pension, there they are"; and go to the door with a welcome ready—just to find a salesman of Real Silk Hosiery or Avon Products who, looking at her, stepped back as if frightened and went away. When the delivery boy had brought the groceries the last time—how long past?—and told her she could not charge them any more because they did not believe at the store that the pension would ever come, he stood away from her and stared at her. "They all must think I am crazy," she said to Zamour, and considered herself for a moment, then added, "because my face must show the secret waiting"; and went back to the chair.

Still the pension would not come, and she waited and she

waited. What it was or how much, she could not guess; but the pension was what all railroad people talked about and waited for, and when it came, one beautiful morning, everything would be all right. How it would come or who would bring it she was not sure, though she imagined some man from the Government looking like Mr. Simpson in the commissary, when he was so fresh and full, arriving on her porch calling her name and as she opened her front door handing to her, as tenderly as though it were some of Mr. Simpson's clothes, a package with the pension in it.

One afternoon of the long time a rain storm began, and a neighbor knocked on her door to try to tell her there would be a Gulf hurricane in the night. When Princis spied the neighbor through the curtains she did not break her connection with the chair but sat firmly clasped by it and would not answer nor listen, seeing that it was no one bringing the pension. But the neighbor knocked and knocked until Princis went to pull back the curtain and glare at the woman to say "Give me my pension!" and Princis saw the woman draw back in some kind of astonishment and run away into the Neighborhood. "The Neighborhood is trying to keep the pension from us," Princis told Zamour.

The rain fell harder, and in a time the rain began to fall here and there in the room. She did not care. But the rain began to fall upon her waiting place, upon her and upon Zamour and upon the good chair. "They are trying to flood us out, before the pension comes," she said. She went to get the mosquito bar she had brought from Red River County and stretched it, between two chairs, over the upholstered chair, the way children make a play-tent; and over the mosquito bar she put a faded cherry-colored chenille bedspread she had made many years ago, just to make the tent-top safe. "This will preserve us from the Neighborhood," she told Zamour.

But where was Zamour? He had suddenly escaped the back of the chair in a wet panic. She managed to catch him, brought him back and wrapped him in her old orange velveteen coat with only his wet head showing; and huddled in the Chair under the tent, nursing Zamour, she went on waiting. The water was falling, everywhere now there was the dripping and streaming of water. She began to sing "Beautiful Ohio," but in the middle of the song she spied her favorite ice-blue glass lamp that she had had all these years, and she crawled out of the tent, leaving Zamour in his swathing and rescued the lamp. It was so dark. Would the lamp yet burn? She plugged it in the socket near the tent, and yes, it still glimmered pale snowy light that made her warm and glad. She brought it into the little tent. She took up "Beautiful Ohio" again, right where she had left off. The tent began to leak wine-colored water and she remembered that old sweet red water in the gullies of home when the summer rains came. There is my home, she remembered.

The wind rose and the rain poured down; and after dark, her blue lamp miraculously burning, a portion of the roof over the living room where she and Zamour sat, lifted and was gone. "What is the Neighborhood doing to destroy us?" she cried to Zamour. "They are tearing our house down and turning the Gulf of Mexico upon our heads." And she remembered the leering face at her window of the woman who had come with some threat and warning to her. "Still," she spoke firmly, "they cannot keep our pension from us. We will wait here." Through her mind went the question, "What else is there of mine to save in under this tent from the destruction of the Neighborhood?" She thought of the cherished things she had possessed so long, to take back to Red River County in the game she had played with Zamour: the golden thimble—no, let it go; Maroney, her eldest sister, had mailed it to her parcel-post as a wedding present. The alarm clock with Mr. Simpson getting up in the morning in it: no. The little setting hen of milk glass who sat on her savings of dimes and nickels and pennies—she would get her, for she had been one of the things in this house to wait with her, waiting so brightly on her milk-glass nest full of savings. She found the glass setting hen and brought her back into the tent. The savings were dry, thanks to the way the little hen sat tight over the nest part.

Now the water was deep on the floor and the tent was

sagging and dripping. Still the lamp burned. One other thing she suddenly thought of and that was her face mirror that was willed to her by her grandmother, it was bronze and had green mold in the crevices, but on the back were the figures of two shy lovers under a tree. She had forgotten the mirror for so long during all this waiting for the pension. She waded through Red River and found it, feeling it out in the darkness, where it had always been, in the dresser drawer, and waded back to the tent with it, her hand sliding at once into the intimacy on the handle which she had worn by clasping it so long. It felt as familiar as a part of her body. "If the pension would come," she begged.

As she got to the tent with the mirror, Zamour turned suddenly fierce and leapt at her like a tiger. She could not catch him, screaming, "Zamour! Zamour!" and Zamour bounded through the water into the darkness. She flounced through the waters of the darkness after him and she could hear him wailing and tearing at the wallpaper and knocking over the furniture. Had Zamour lost his mind, after all she had done to try to keep them both patient? No, cats hate water, she thought. I must pacify Zamour. She cornered him where he had run and leaped, on top of their tent, and in the pale light of the lamp beneath she saw Zamour's face wild and daring her to reach out to him. She reached out, murmuring, "Zamour, Zamour, it is just water"; and as she put out her wet hands, the mirror clasped in one of them, Zamour attacked her and clawed her face, and fled. She cried out and began to weep, fell back onto the floor of water, holding up the mirror to keep from breaking it, and she lay there crying, "O Lord," and buried her bruised face in her hands.

But what did she feel there on her wounded face, was it blood, was it water, and was it fur like the very coat of Zamour? She crawled on her hands and knees, the face mirror still in her hand, into the tent, muttering, "Lord, don't let the light of the little glass lamp go out"; and by the light of the lamp she held up the bronze mirror and saw in it her bearded face, and it bleeding, and the mirror cracked. Accompanying the watery sounds in her house she heard the low gurgling of Zamour somewhere in the dark drenched wilderness, like the sounds of a whimpering baby. She called out, "Zamour! Zamour! do not cry; come back to our tent, I am Princis, remember me; I will do you no harm." But Zamour would not come, he only wailed and sobbed his forlorn watery sounds of fear and alienation in the darkness. She humped under the ruined tent, in the sodden chair, and quietened. Then she whispered, "It is here, it has come, what is mine. Cheyney and Maroney, my two sisters of Red River County, I can come home to you now." And then the light of the lamp went out.

She sat in her chair under the tent in the wilderness. In her lost darkness, she tried to make up her life again like a bed disturbed by a restless sleep. What had led her to where she was, waiting for a pension that would never come? She could not name herself any answers—she would salvage Zamour.

She crawled out of her tent on hands and knees and the tent of gauze and chenille fell upon her like a net. She crawled on, dragging the tent, and hunted through the swamp for Zamour, ever so quietly. She might have been the quietest beaver. She saw two gleams—those were his eyes. She oared herself closer, closer, ever so softly. What was this lost and trackless territory she crawled through, it was like a jungle slough, it was not any place she had ever known, neither sea nor land, but a border-shore of neither water nor earth, a shallows where two continents divided. Zamour, Zamour, her heart begged as she waggled closer to his burning eyes, but her lips could not utter his name. Zamour, Zamour, something deep in her whimpered and bleated, as if it were cold, as though retrieving Zamour he might warm her like a collar of fur.

On her knees, she reached out to the two low gleamings and were they coals of fire that burnt her to the quick, or were they the eyes of a rattlesnake whose fangs struck her at her face? and she bouldered back, then reared up, bearlike, scrawling and paw-ing with her hands and arms to claw this fiend away. She heard the crashing of objects Zamour collided with as he escaped her. Was this wildcat clawing the world down upon her? She heard him making a sound that was familiar to her, somewhere, it was a ripping to pieces; and then she heard the burst of glass and the sound of spilling coins, and she remembered her lost waiting place with the chair and the lamp and the setting hen. Which way was this place, to go back to? Where was the light, where was the face mirror? Over there, she thought, still on her haunches. No . . . over here. And then she knew they were forever lost. She had no way, no sign to go by.

She lifted up, feeling now so light, like a buoy, and rising from her knees she sank again, at rest, like stone into the shallows where she was, another waiting place, as if she might from that moment on be a permanent mossy rock in these reefs and tides —of what geography? She breathed. It was all over. She gave it all up then. The tent was hanging from her as though she would carry it forever like a coat of hair. "I give up the lamp and the mirror and Zamour, and even the pension. I give up even the last thing," she said to herself; and, giving it all up to the last thing, she rested and settled, being this rock of nobody, no one she had ever known, renouncing all the definitions, the landmarks, the signs she had gone by to get to this nowhere in this dark bog of debris, on this lightless floor of the mud of her accepted eternity.

But what was that little cry? She found out two lights burning in the faraway distance. Some mercy ship is coming on some channel, she thought; what are those two mercy lights? It was an indestructible sign, lighting her memory back to an orchard on a frosty night and the sound of a cry and the glimmer of two eyes in a tree, and the meeting of two friends. *Zamour!* What was that watery music played out by the rain's hammering drops on broken glass but the tinkling little hammerstrikes of the xylophone . . . and oh her two sisters! She would survive in this dark world she sat in, she would start from there. For it was hers to begin with, to make her own. Something of her own had come to her and there was this to begin with: she was the sister of her two sisters, Cheyney and Maroney Lester, and their own blood. If this darkness ever lifted and the waters ran away, if there was enough light to go by, she would try to find her sisters; and if there was no light she would go by darkness, rising out of these waters, and find her sisters wherever they were in this night waterworld and arrive there, steering herself home, to join them, crying, "See, I am your sister, Princis Lester." They would take her in, be so glad, there would be no more watching, no more waiting, *for they were sisters*. And they would live together in a home of warm felicity.

But Zamour uttered a kind of witch's cry again, from somewhere, somewhere, as if to call her to his claws again; and Princis Lester cried out in the darkness, "Zamour! I give up even you." What time of night was it, because there was suddenly a bright light shining upon her and could there be a voice she heard saying, "Arise, shine; for thy light has come." Who, what had come for her? There were voices and knockings at the front door. They called her name. Why could she not answer? Then they beat upon her door and called her name, "Mrs. Simpson! Mrs. Simpson! Let us in!"

"My name is Princis Lester," she murmured, "sister to my two sisters in Red River County."

Then, how many of them there were, she could not tell— she had not dreamt there were so many survivors in the world— but enough to pound and kick against her door, calling her name louder and louder. She would not answer a thing, she could not move, until a loud strong voice called:

"Mrs. Simpson! Let us in! *Your husband's pension has come!*"

And at that call that echoed through the darkness, she began a lumbering crawl. Shaggy and dripping she buffaloed through the water, slowly slowly, dragging the immense weight of herself and the ragged tent over what seemed sharp rocks and broken shell of a sea floor, across the gravel and shale of the widest shore, slowly slowly toward the light; and found the door. Rising to her knees with her last gasp of strength, she pawed open the door and ogled into the dimming light and the blurring faces of what shining company of bright humanity that looked first like the young face of Mr. Simpson in the commissary, then like the faces, ringleted with hair, of her two sisters; and then there were no faces but it could be the guttering light of Zamour's eyes.

"Hanh?" she murmured, with a look of mercy and salvation in her terrible tilted face; and this was how the Neighborhood caught her. Hanging from her as though it were the frazzled coat of a hounded animal was the rag of the chenille and mosquito-bar tent. A black shape shot through the door and into the Neighborhood, and it was Zamour.

That was quite some years ago; and for some years, quite a few, Princis Lester was in the Home, in the county seat of Red River County, resting. She could not tell anyone there what happened, or had no mind to—who knew which? She prinked her beard that wreathed her face like a ruff of titian down and took deep pride in it, it was her one interest. She seemed to be dozing at peace in it, something safe in a nest. There was a purity about her that everyone admired. She was the cherished one of the Home, quietly gleeful, considerate of others, craving no favors but getting them in abundance. She had a peculiarly enviable quality that made the others there long to be like her, even down to the beard. Some said, "What does Princis Lester have that the rest of us don't, to make her so . . ." and they could not find a word to put to her to describe how she was; and another would answer, "A beard." One or two came to her at first, before they knew her, and said, "Listen here, Princis Lester . . ." and mentioned barbering or miracle creams that would burn a beard away; but in time they could not imagine Princis Lester any other way: take her beard away and she would no more have been Princis Lester of Red River County than any of them if they had hung a false beard about their face and said, "I am Princis Lester." It has, they said, to be in your heredity.

Princis' sisters came to see her regularly during their lifetime —it was a precious sight to see them chuckling and softly crooning together—and they would pat each other through long, smiling conversations. Then the time came for the two sisters to die, they were chosen almost at the same time, which seemed right— Cheyney first, then Maroney right after; and they lay buried side by side in Red River County. Oil was discovered on the land where the Lester house once stood, called, now, the Prescott Lease and a very rich strike. Princis Lester still sat like a memorial hedge in the Home, up at Winona, very very old and still, but living her life on.

The pension? It came, finally, after all the red tape of officials and signatures. Amounting to about twenty-eight dollars a month for a switchman with not too many years' service, it waited for years in a file marked "unclaimed" until Princis Lester might one day have her mind to claim it with, until it was clear that she would never find mind for the pension; and so it waited to go to her nearest of kin, her cousin, Wylie Prescott, when she passed on, along with her few personal possessions.

Zamour lived out of doors in the Neighborhood for a long time, a renegade, like the black ghost of Princis Lester. He would not take up with anyone, but he would eat out of anybody's saucer or come up to be petted in a kind of suspicious, faithless way. He showed no trust in anyone, that was plain to see, considering all day long, as he seemed to, what we humans do to poor animal kind. Some of the neighbors, whenever they could lure him, tried to ask him what happened in that little house where he lived so long with Princis Lester, he seemed so close to speaking sometimes. But of course he had no tongue to speak with, he was dumb beast and so there was no story to be had from him. His poor cat brain held the secret. One day the Neighborhood saw him walking away, tail in the air as if a balloon were tied to it—Princis Lester might have been beside him and speaking to him as they walked to the grocery store, for Zamour had that old dalliance in his gait. They saw him go on away, to somewhere; and he was never seen again in the Neighborhood.

Time passed, and with it Princis Lester, laid by her sisters to make three graves in Red River County. "Those are the graves of the bearded Lester Sisters," visitors to the cemetery remarked to each other. It was time for the next generation, and out of it rose the figure of Wylie Prescott to take his inheritance.

Wylie Prescott became a big figure of his generation in Texas, oil king and cotton king, cattle king and lumber king, and something important in the Legislature. He married a girl from a prominent old lumber family of Trinity County and added her inheritance to his. They had a daughter named Cleo and when she was sixteen took her to France and bought up a boatload of old, expensive antiques. While in France, Mr. Prescott went so hog-wild over French châteaux that he bought a whole one and had it moved, piece by piece, from Normandy to Houston, where it was put right back together again exactly as it had looked in some early century. It occupied a huge estate of many wooded acres, and Houston people drove by on Sundays and pointed at its towers topping the trees, telling each other that it was a French château from France. In it were all the French tapestries and coppers and cloisonnés, and among these were a once broken but now mended milk-glass setting hen, a golden thimble, and a cracked hand mirror, left behind to Wylie Prescott, heir to all Zamour and Princis' waiting, with this tale hidden in them for no one ever to know, and Wylie Prescott's secret.

Though Cleo Prescott never asked questions about these old-time Texas relics that were now quite sought after as antiques, she showed more of a fondness for them than for any of the valuable French antiques; and when she fondled them, Wylie Prescott would warn her never to look in a cracked mirror because, according to the superstition, it would bring a curse of bad luck to women.

And that is the tale of Princis Lester and Zamour and the inheritance that followed them.

BRIDGE OF MUSIC, RIVER OF SAND

Do you remember the bridge that we crossed over the river to get to Riverside? And if you looked over yonder you saw the railroad trestle? High and narrow? Well that's what he jumped off of. Into a nothing river. "River"! I could laugh. I can spit more than runs in that dry bed. In some places is just a little damp, but that's it. That's your grand and rolling river: a damp spot. That's your remains of the grand old Trinity. Where can so much water go? I at least wish they'd do something about it. But what can they do? What can anybody do? You can't replace a *river*.

Anyway, if there'd been water, maybe he'd have made it, the naked diver. As it was, diving into the river as though there were water in it, he went head first into moist sand and drove into it like an arrow into flesh and was found in a position of somebody on their knees, headless, bent over looking for something. Looking for where the river vanished to? I was driving across the old river bridge when I said to myself, wait a minute I believe I see something. I almost ran into the bridge railing. I felt a chill come over me.

What I did was when I got off the bridge to draw my car off to the side of the road and get out and run down the river bank around a rattlesnake that seemed to be placed there as a deterrent (the banks are crawling with them in July), and down; and what I came upon was a kind of avenue that the river had made and paved with gleaming white sand, wide and grand and empty. I crossed this ghostly thoroughfare of the river half-way, and when I got closer, my Lord Jesus God Almighty damn if I didn't see that it was half a naked human body in what would have been midstream were there water. I was scared to death. What ought I to do? Try to pull it out? I was scared to touch it. It was a heat-stunned afternoon. The July heat throbbed. The blue, steaming air waved like a veil. The feeling of something missing haunted me: it was the lost life of the river—something so powerful that it had haunted the countryside for miles around; you could feel it a long time before you came to it. In a landscape that was unnatural—flowing water was missing—everything else seemed unnatural. The river's vegetation was thin and starved-looking; it lived on the edge of sand instead of water; it seemed out of place.

If only I hadn't taken the old bridge. I was already open to a fine of five thousand dollars for driving across it, according to the sign, and I understood why. (Over yonder arched the shining new bridge. There was no traffic on it.) The flapping of loose boards and the quaking of the iron beams was terrifying. I almost panicked in the middle when the whole construction swayed and made such a sound of crackling and clanking. I was surprised the feeble structure hadn't more than a sign to prohibit passage over it—it should have been barricaded. At any rate, it was when I was in the middle of this rocking vehicle that seemed like some mad carnival ride that I saw the naked figure diving from the old railroad trestle. It was as though the diver were making a flamboyant leap into the deep river below—until to my horror I realized that the river was dry. I dared not stop my car and so I maneuvered my way on, mechanical with terror, enchanted by the melodies that rose from the instruments of the melodious bridge that played like some orchestra of xylophones and drums and cellos as I moved over it. Who would have known that the dead bridge, condemned and closed away from human touch, had such music in it? I was on the other side now. Behind me the music was quieter now, lowering into something like chime sounds and harness sounds and wagons; it shook like bells and tolled like soft, deep gongs.

His hands must have cut through the wet sand, carving a path for his head and shoulders. He was sunk up to his mid-waist and had fallen to a kneeling position: a figure on its knees with its head buried in the sand, as if it had decided not to look at the world any more. And then the figure began to sink as if someone underground were pulling it under. Slowly the stomach, lean and hairy, vanished; then the loins, thighs. The river, which had swallowed half his body, now seemed to be eating the rest of it. For a while the feet lay, soles up, on the sand. And then they went down, arched like a dancer's.

Who was the man drowned in a dry river? eaten by a dry river? devoured by sand? How would I explain, describe what had happened? I'd be judged to be out of my senses. And why would I tell somebody—the police or—anybody? There was nothing to be done, the diver was gone, the naked leaper was swallowed up. Unless somebody had pushed him over the bridge and he'd assumed a diving position to try to save himself. But what evidence was there? Well, I *had* to report what I'd seen, what I'd witnessed. Witness? To what? Would anybody believe me? There was no evidence anywhere. Well, I'd look, I'd search for evidence. I'd go up on the railroad trestle.

I climbed up. The trestle was perilously narrow and high. I could see a long ways out over Texas, green and steaming in July. I could see the scar of the river, I could see the healed-looking patches that were the orphaned bottomlands. I could see the tornado-shaped funnel of bilious smoke that twisted out of the mill in Riverside, enriching the owner and poisoning him, his family and his neighbors. And I could see the old bridge which I'd just passed over and still trembling under my touch, arching perfect and precious, golden in the sunlight. The music I had wrought out of it was now stilled except, it seemed, for a low, deep hum that rose from it. It seemed impossible that a train could move on these narrow tracks now grown over with weeds. As I walked, grasshoppers flared up in the dry heat.

I saw no footprints in the weeds, no sign of anybody having walked on the trestle—unless they walked on the rails or the ties. Where were the man's clothes? Unless he'd left them on the bank and run out naked onto the trestle. This meant searching on both sides of the trestle—Christ, what was I caught up in? It could also mean that he was a suicide, my mind went on dogging me; or insane; it could also mean that nobody else was involved. Or it could mean that I was suffering a kind of bridge madness, or the vision that sometimes comes from going home again, of going back to places haunted by deep feeling?

Had anyone ever told me the story of a man jumping into the river from the trestle? Could this be some tormented spirit doomed forever to re-enact his suicide? And if so, must he continue it, now that the river was gone? This thought struck me as rather pitiful.

How high the trestle was! It made me giddy to look down at the riverbed. I tried to find the spot where the diver had hit the dry river. There was absolutely no sign. The mouth of sand that had sucked him down before my very eyes had closed and sealed itself. The story was over, so far as I was concerned. Whatever had happened would be my secret. I had to give it up, let it go. You can understand that I had no choice, that that was the only thing I could do.

That was the summer I was making a sentimental trip through home regions, after fifteen years away. The bridge over the beloved old river had been one of my most touching memories—an object that hung in my memory of childhood like a precious ornament. It was a fragile creation, of iron and wood, and so poetically arched, so slender, half a bracelet (the other half underground) through which the green river ran. The superstructure was made more for a minaret than a bridge. From a distance it looked like an ornate pier, in Brighton or early Santa Monica; or, in the summer heat haze, a palace tower, a creation of gold. Closer, of course, it was an iron and wooden bridge of unusual beauty, shape and design. It had always been an imperfect bridge, awry from the start. It had been built wrong—an engineering mistake: the ascent was too steep and the descent too sharp. But its beauty endured. And despite its irregularity, traffic had used the bridge at Riverside, without serious mishap, for many years. It was just an uncomfortable trip, and always somewhat disturbing, this awkward, surprising and somehow mysterious crossing.

Some real things happened on this practical, if magical, device for crossing water. For one thing, since it swayed, my mother, in our childhood days, would refuse to ride across it. She would remove herself from the auto and walk across, holding on to the railing, while my father, cursing, drove the rest of us across. My sister and I peered back at the small figure of our mother laboring darkly and utterly alone on the infernal contraption which was her torment. I remember my father getting out of the car, on the other side, waiting at the side of the road, looking toward the bridge, watching my mother's creeping progress. When she arrived, pale, she declared, as she did each time, "I vow to the Lord if my sister Sarah didn't live in Riverside I'd never to my soul come near this place." "Well you could lie down in the back seat, put the cotton in your ears that you always bring, and never know it, as I keep telling you," said my father. "I'd still know it," my mother came back. "I'd still know we was on this infernal bridge." "Well then take the goddam train from Palestine. Train trestle's flat." And, getting in the car and slamming the door, "Or stay home and just *write* to your damned sister Sarah. Married to a horse's ass, anyway."

"Mama," said my sister, trying to pacify the situation. "Tell us about the time you almost drowned in the river and Daddy had to jump in and pull you out."

"Well, it was just right over yonder. We'd been fishing all morning, and . . ."

"Aw for Christ's sake," my father said.

On the other side of the bridge, after a crossing of hazards and challenges, there was nothing more than a plain little town of mud streets and weather-faded shacks. The town of poor people lived around an ugly mill that puffed out like talcum some-thing called Fuller's Earth over it. This substance lay on rooftops, on the ground and in lungs. It smelled sour and bit the eyes.

As I drove away toward that town, haunted by the vision of the leaping man and now so shaken in my very spirit, lost to fact but brought to some odd truth which I could not yet clear for myself, I saw in the mirror the still image of the river bridge that had such hidden music in it, girdling the ghost of what it had been created for, that lost river that held in its bosom of sand the diving figure of the trestle that I was sure I had seen. I was coming in to Riverside and already the stinging fumes of the mill brought tears to my eyes.

FIGURE OVER THE TOWN

◻▬◻

In the town of my beginning I saw this masked figure sitting aloft. It was never explained to me by my elders, who were thrilled and disturbed by the figure too, who it was, except that he was called Flagpole Moody. The days and nights he sat aloft were counted on calendars in the kitchens of small houses and in troubled minds, for Flagpole Moody fed the fancy of an isolated small town of practical folk whose day's work was hard and real.

Since the night he was pointed out to me from the roof of the little shed where my father sheltered grain and plowing and planting implements, his shape has never left me; in many critical experiences of my life it has suddenly appeared before me, so that I have come to see that it is a dominating emblem of my life, as often a lost lover is, or the figure of a parent, or the symbol of a faith, as the scallop shell was for so many at one time, or the Cross.

It was in the time of a war I could not understand, being so very young, that my father came to me at darkening, in the beginning wintertime, and said, "Come with me to the Patch, Son, for I want to show you something."

The Patch, which I often dream about, was a mysterious fenced-in plot of ground, about half an acre, where I never intruded. I often stood at the gate or fence and looked in through the hexagonal lenses of the chicken wire and saw how strange this little territory was, and wondered what it was for. There was the shed in it where implements and grain were stored, but nothing was ever planted nor any animal pastured here; nothing, not even grass or weed, grew here; it was just plain common ground.

This late afternoon my father took me into the Patch and led me to the shed and hoisted me up to the roof. He waited a moment while I looked around at all the world we lived in and had forgotten was so wide and housed so many in dwellings quite like ours. (Later, when my grandfather, my father's father, took me across the road and railroad tracks into a large pasture —so great I had thought it, from the window of our house, the whole world—where a little circus had been set up as if by magic the night before, and raised me to the broad back of a sleepy elephant, I saw the same sight and recalled not only the night I stood on the roof of the shed, but also what I had seen from there, that haunting image, and thought I saw it again, this time on the lightning rod of our house . . . but no, it was, as always, the crowing cock that stood there, eternally strutting out his breast and at the break of crowing.)

My father waited, and when he saw that I had steadied myself, he said, "Well, Son, what is it that you see over there, by the Methodist church?"

I was speechless and could only gaze; and then I finally said to him, not moving, "Something is sitting on the flagpole on top of a building."

"It is just a man," my father said, "and his name is Flagpole Moody. He is going to sit up there for as long as he can stand it."

When we came into the house, I heard my father say to my mother, lightly, "I showed Son Flagpole Moody and I think it scared him a little." And I heard my mother say, "It seems a foolish stunt, and I think maybe children shouldn't see it."

All that night Flagpole Moody was on my mind. When it began raining, in the very deepest night, I worried about him in the rain, and I went to my window and looked out to see if I could see him. When it lightninged, I saw that he was safe and dry under a little tent he had raised over himself. Later I had a terrible dream about him, that he was falling, falling, and when I called out in my nightmare, my parents came to me and patted me back to sleep, never knowing that I would dream of him again.

He stayed and stayed up there, the flagpole sitter, hooded (why would he not show his face?), and when we were in town and walked under him, I would not look up as they told me to; but once, when we stood across the street from the building where he was perched, I looked up and saw how high he was in the air, and he waved down at me with his cap in his hand.

Everywhere there was the talk of the war, but where it was or what it was I did not know. It seemed only some huge appetite that craved all our sugar and begged from the town its goods, so that people seemed paled and impoverished by it, and it made life gloomy—that was the word. One night we went into the town to watch them burn Old Man Gloom, a monstrous straw man with a sour, turned-down look on his face and dressed even to the point of having a hat—it was the Ku Klux Klan who lit him afire—and above, in the light of the flames, we saw Flagpole Moody waving his cap to us. He had been up eighteen days.

He kept staying up there. More and more the talk was about him, with the feeling of the war beneath all the talk. People began to get restless about Flagpole Moody and to want him to come on down. "It seems morbid," I remember my mother saying. What at first had been a thrill and an excitement—the whole town was there every other day when the provisions basket was raised up to him, and the contributions were extravagant: fresh pies and cakes, milk, little presents, and so forth—became an everyday sight; there he seemed ignored and forgotten by the town except for me, who kept a constant, secret watch on him; then, finally, the town became disturbed by him, for he seemed to be going on and on; he seemed an intruder now. Who could feel unlooked at or unhovered over in his house with this figure over everything? (It was discovered that Flagpole was spying on the town through binoculars.) There was an agitation to bring him down and the city council met to this end.

There had been some irregularity in the town which had been laid to the general lawlessness and demoralizing effect of the war: robberies; the disappearance of a beautiful young girl, Sarah Nichols (but it was said she ran away to find someone in the war); and one Negro shot in the woods, which could have been the work of the Ku Klux Klan. The question at the city-council meeting was, "Who gave Flagpole Moody permission to go up there?" No one seemed to know; the merchants said it was not for advertising, or at least no one of them had arranged it, though after he was up, many of them tried to use him to advertise their products—Egg Lay or Red Goose shoes or Have a Coke at Robbins Pharmacy—and why not? The Chamber of Commerce had not brought him, nor the Women's Club; maybe the Ku Klux had, to warn and tame the Negroes, who were especially in awe of Flagpole Moody; but the Klan was as innocent as all the others, it said. The pastor was reminded of the time a bird had built a nest on the church steeple, a huge foreign bird that had delighted all the congregation as well as given him subject matter for several sermons; he told how the congregation came out on the grounds to adore the bird, which in time became suddenly savage and swooped to pluck the feathers from women's Sunday hats and was finally brought down by the fire department, which found the nest full of rats and mice, half devoured, and no eggs at all—this last fact the subject of another series of sermons by the pastor, drawing as he did his topics from real life.

As the flagpole sitter had come to be regarded as a defacement of the landscape, an unsightly object, a tramp, it was suggested that the Ku Klux Klan build a fire in the square and ride round it on their horses and in their sheets, firing their guns into the air, as they did in their public demonstrations against immorality, to force Flagpole down. If this failed, it was suggested someone should be sent up on a firemen's ladder to reason with Flagpole. He was regarded now as a *danger* to the town, and more, as a kind of criminal. (At first he had been admired and respected for his courage, and desired, even: many women had been intoxicated by him, sending up, in the provisions basket, love notes and photographs of themselves, which Flagpole had read and then sailed down for anyone to pick up and read, to the embarrassment of this woman and that. There had been a number of local exposures.)

The town was ready for any kind of miracle or sensation, obviously. A fanatical religious group took Flagpole Moody for the Second Coming. The old man called Old Man Nay, who lived on the edge of the town in a boarded-up house and sat at the one open window with his shotgun in his lap, watching for the Devil, unnailed his door and appeared in the square to announce that he had seen a light playing around Flagpole at night and that Flagpole was some phantom representative of the Devil and should be banished by a raising of the Cross; but others explained that what Old Man Nay saw was St. Elmo's fire, a natural phenomenon. Whatever was given a fantastical meaning by some was explained away by others as of natural cause. What was right? Who was to believe what?

An evangelist who called himself "The Christian Jew" had, at the beginning, requested of Flagpole Moody, by a letter in the basket, the dropping of leaflets. A sample was pinned to the letter. The leaflet, printed in red ink, said in huge letters across the top: WARNING! YOU ARE IN GREAT DANGER! Below was a long message to sinners. If Flagpole would drop these messages upon the town, he would be aiding in the salvation of the wicked. "The Judgments of God are soon to be poured upon the Earth! Prepare to meet God before it is too late! Where will you spend Eternity? What can you do to be saved? How shall we escape if we neglect so great salvation! (Heb. 2:3)."

But there was no reply from Flagpole, which was evidence enough for the Christian Jew to know that Flagpole was on the Devil's side. He held meetings at night in the square, with his little group of followers passing out the leaflets.

"Lower Cain!" he bellowed. "You sinners standing on the street corner running a long tongue about your neighbors; you show-going, card-playing, jazz-dancing brothers—God love your soul—you are a tribe of sinners and you know it and God knows it, but He loves you and wants you to come into His tabernacle and give up your hearts that are laden with wickedness. If you look in the Bible, if you will turn to the chapter of Isaiah, you will find there about the fallen angel, Lucifer was his name, and how his clothing was sewn of emeralds and sapphires, for he was very beautiful; but friends, my sin-loving friends, that didn't make any difference. 'How art thou fallen from Heaven, O Lucifer, son of the morning!' the Bible reads. And it says there that the Devil will walk amongst us and that the Devil will sit on the rooftops; and I tell you we must unite together to drive Satan from the top of the world. Listen to me and read my message, for I was the rottenest man in this world until I heard the voice of God. I drank, I ran with women, I sought after the thrills of the flesh . . . and I admonish you that the past scenes of earth *shall be remembered in Hell.*"

The old maid, Miss Hazel Bright, who had had one lover long ago, a cowboy named Rolfe Sanderson who had gone away and never returned, told that Flagpole was Rolfe come back, and she wrote notes of poetic longing to put in the provisions basket. Everybody used Flagpole Moody for his own purpose, and so he, sitting away from it all, apparently serene in his own dream and idea of himself, became the lost lover to the lovelorn, the saint to the seekers of salvation, the scapegoat of the guilty, the damned to those who were lost.

The town went on tormenting him; they could not let him alone. They wished him to be their own dream or hope or lost illusion, or they wished him to be what destroyed hope and illusion. They wanted something they could get their hands on; they wanted someone to ease the dark misgiving in themselves, to take to their deepest bosom, into the farthest cave of themselves where they would take no other if he would come and be for them alone. They plagued him with love letters, and when he would not acknowledge these professions of love, they wrote him messages of hate. They told him their secrets, and when he would not show himself to be overwhelmed, they accused him of keeping secrets of his own. They professed to be willing to follow him, leaving everything behind, but when he would not answer "Come," they told him how they wished he would fall and knock his brains out. They could not make up their minds and they tried to destroy him because he had made up his, whatever it was he had made his mind up to.

Merchants tormented him with proposals and offers— would he wear a Stetson hat all one day, tip and wave it to the people below? Would he hold, just for fifteen minutes every hour, a streamer with words on it proclaiming the goodness of their bread, or allow balloons, spelling out the name of something that ought to be bought, to be floated from the flagpole? Would he throw down Life Savers? Many a man, and most, would have done it, would have supplied an understandable reason for his behavior, pacifying the general observer, and in the general observer's own terms (or the general observer would not have it), and so send him away undisturbed, with the feeling that all the world was really just as he was, cheating a little here, disguising a little there. (Everybody was, after all, alike, so where the pain, and why?)

But Flagpole Moody gave no answer. Apparently he had nothing to sell, wanted to make no fortune, to play no jokes or tricks; apparently he wanted just to be let alone to do his job. But because he was so different, they would not let him alone until they could, by whatever means, make him quite like themselves, or cause him, at least, to recognize them and pay *them* some attention. Was he camping up there for the fun of it? If so, why would he not let them all share in it? Maybe he was there for the pure devilment of it, like a cat calm on a chimney top. Or for some very crazy and not-to-be-tolerated reason of his own (which everyone tried to make out, hating secrets as people do who want everything in the clear, where they can attack it and feel moral dudgeon against it).

Was it Cray McCreery up there? Had somebody made him another bet? One time Cray had walked barefooted to the next town, eighteen miles, because of a lost bet. But no, Cray Mc-Creery was found, as usual, in the Domino Parlor. Had any crazy people escaped from the asylum? They were counted and found to be all in. The mind reader, Madame Fritzie, was importuned: There seemed, she said, to be a dark woman in the picture; that was all she contributed: "I see a dark woman . . ." And as she had admonished so many in the town with her recurring vision of a dark woman, there was either an army of dark women tormenting the minds of men and women in the world, or only one, which was Madame Fritzie herself. She could have made a fortune out of the whole affair if she had had her wits about her. More than one Ouija board was put questions to, but the answers were either indistinguishable or not to the point.

Dogs howled and bayed at night and sometimes in the afternoons; hens crowed; the sudden death of children was laid to the evil power of Flagpole Moody over the town.

A masked buffoon came to a party dressed as Flagpole Moody and caused increasing uneasiness among the guests until three of the men at the party, deciding to take subtle action rather than force the stranger to unmask, reported to the police by telephone. The police told them to unmask him by force and they were coming. When the police arrived they found the stranger was Marcus Peters, a past president of the Lions Club and a practical joker with the biggest belly laugh in town, and everybody would have known all along who the impostor was if he had only laughed.

A new language evolved in the town: "You're crazy as Moody," "cold as a flagpole sitter's ——," "go sit on a flagpole" and other phrases of that sort.

In that day and time there flourished, even in that little town, a group of sensitive and intellectual people, poets and artists and whatnot, who thought themselves quite mad and gay —and quite lost, too, though they would turn their lostness to a good thing. These advanced people needed an object upon which to hinge their loose and floating cause, and they chose Flagpole Moody to draw attention, which they so craved, to themselves. They exalted him with some high, esoteric meaning that they alone understood, and they developed a whole style of poetry, music and painting, the echoes of which are still heard, around the symbol of Flagpole Moody. They wrote, and read aloud to meetings, critical explanations of the Theory of Aloftness.

Only Mrs. T. Trevor Sanderson was bored with it all, shambling restlessly about the hospital in her Japanese kimono, her spotted hands (liver trouble, the doctors said) spread like fat lizards on the knolls of her hips. She was there again for one of her rest cures, because her oil-money worries were wearing her to death, and now the Catholic Church was pursuing her with zeal to convert her—for her money, so she said. Still, there was something to the Catholic Church; you couldn't get around that, she said, turning her spotted hands to show them yellow underneath, like a lizard's belly; and she gave a golden windowpane illustrating *The Temptation of St. Anthony* to St. Mary's Church, but would do no more than that.

There were many little felonies and even big offenses of undetermined origin in the police records of the town, and Flagpole was a stimulus to the fresh inspection of unsolved crimes. He drew suspicions up to him and absorbed them like a filter, as though he might purify the town of wickedness. If only he would send down some response to what had gone up to him. But he would not budge; and now he no longer even waved to the people below as he had during the first good days. Flagpole Moody had utterly withdrawn from everybody. What the town finally decided was to put a searchlight on him at night, to keep watch on him.

With the searchlight on the flagpole sitter, the whole thing took a turn, became an excuse for a ribald attitude. When a little wartime carnival came to the town, it was invited to install itself in the square, and a bazaar was added to it by the town. The spirit of Flagpole had to be admired, it was admitted; for after a day and night of shunning the gaiety and the mockery of it all, he showed his good nature and good sportsmanship—even his daring—by participating! He began to do what looked like acrobatic stunts, as though he were an attraction of the carnival.

And what did the people do, after a while, but turn against

him again and say he was, as they had said at first, a sensational-
ist? Still, I loved it that he had become active; that it was not a
static, fastidious, precious and Olympian show, that Flagpole did
not take on a self-righteous or pompous or persecuted air, although my secret conception of him was still a tragic one. I was
proud that my idea fought back—otherwise he was like Old Man
Gloom, a shape of straw and sawdust in man's clothing, and let
them burn him, if only gloom stood among the executioners,
watching its own effigy and blowing on the flames. I know now
that what I saw was the conflict of an idea with a society; and I
am sure that the idea was bred by the society—raised up there,
even, by the society—in short, society was in the flagpole sitter
and he was in the society of the town.

There was, at the little carnival, one concession called "Ring
Flagpole's Bell." It invited customers to try to strike a bell at the
top of a tall pole resembling his—and with a replica of him on
top—by hitting a little platform with a rubber-headed sledge-
hammer; this would drive a metal disk up toward the bell. There
was another concession where people could throw darts at a
target resembling a figure on a pole. The Ferris wheel was put so
close to Flagpole that when its passengers reached the top they
could almost, for a magical instant, reach over and touch his
body. Going round and round, it was as if one were soaring up
to him only to fall away, down, from him; to have him and to
lose him; and it was all felt in a marvelous whirling sensation in
the stomach that made this experience the most vaunted of the
show.

This must have tantalized Flagpole, and perhaps it seemed
to him that all the beautiful and desirable people in the world
rose and fell around him, offering themselves to him only to
withdraw untaken and ungiven, a flashing wheel of faces, eyes,
lips and sometimes tongues stuck out at him and sometimes a
thigh shown, offering sex, and then burning away. His sky at
night was filled with voluptuous images, and often he must have
imagined the faces of those he had once loved and possessed,
turning round and round his head to torment him. But there

were men on the wheel who made profane signs to him, and women who thumbed their noses.

Soon Flagpole raised his tent again and hid himself from his tormentors. What specifically caused his withdrawal was the attempt of a drunken young man to shoot him. This young man, named Maury, rode a motorcycle around the town at all hours and loved the meaner streets and the women who gave him ease, especially the fat ones, his mania. One night he stood at the hotel window and watched the figure on the pole, who seemed to flash on and off, real and then unreal, with the light of the electric sign beneath the window. He took deep drags of his cigarette and blew the smoke out toward Flagpole; then he blew smoke rings as if to lasso Flagpole with them, or as if his figure were a pin he could hoop with the rings of smoke. "You silly bastard, do you like what you see?" he had muttered, and "Where have I seen you before?" between his half-clenched teeth, and then he had fired the pistol. Flagpole turned away then, once and for all.

But he had not turned away from me. I, the silent observer, watching from my window or from any high place I could secretly climb to, witnessed all this conflict and the tumult of the town. One night in my dreaming of Flagpole Moody—it happened every night, this dream, and in the afternoons when I took my nap, and the dreaming had gone on so long that it seemed, finally, as if he and I were friends, that he came down secretly to a rendezvous with me in the little pasture, and it was only years later that I would know what all our conversations had been about—that night in my dream the people of the town came to me and said, "Son, we have chosen you to go up the flagpole to Flagpole Moody and tell him to come down."

In my dream they led me, with cheers and honors, to the top of the building and stood below while I shinnied up the pole. A great black bird was circling over Flagpole's tent. As I went up the pole I noticed crowded avenues of ants coming and going along the pole. And when I went into the tent, I found Flagpole gone. The tent was as if a tornado had swept through the whole inside of it. There were piles of rotten food; shreds of letters torn and retorn, as small as flakes of snow; photographs pinned to the walls of the tent were marked and scrawled over so that they looked like photographs of fiends and monsters; corpses and drifts of feathers of dead birds that had flown at night into the tent and gone so wild with fright that they had beaten themselves to death against the sides. And over it all was the vicious traffic of insects that had found the remains, in the way insects sense what human beings have left, and come from miles away.

What would I tell them below, those who were now crying up to me, "What does he say, what does Flagpole Moody say?" And there were whistles and an increasingly thunderous chant of "Bring him down! Bring him down! Bring him down!" What would I tell them? I was glad he had gone; but I would not tell them that—yet. In the tent I found one little thing that had not been touched or changed by Flagpole; a piece of paper with printed words, and across the top the huge red words: WARNING! YOU ARE IN GREAT DANGER!

Then, in my dream, I went to the flap of the tent and stuck out my head. There was a searchlight upon me through which fell a delicate curtain of light rain; and through the lighted curtain of rain that made the people seem far, far below, under shimmering and jeweled veils, I shouted down to the multitude, which was dead quiet now, "He is not here! Flagpole Moody is not here!"

There was no sound from the crowd, which had not, at first, heard what I said. They waited; then one voice bellowed up, "Tell him to come down!" And others joined this voice until, again, the crowd was roaring, "Tell him that we will not harm him; only tell him he has to come down!" Then I waved down at them to be quiet, in Flagpole Moody's gesture of salute, as he had waved down at people on the sidewalks and streets. Again they hushed to hear me. Again I said, this time in a voice that was not mine, but large and round and resounding, "Flagpole Moody is not here. His place is empty."

And then, in my magnificent dream, I closed the flap of the tent and settled down to make Flagpole Moody's place my own, to drive out the insects, to erase the marks on the photographs, and to piece together, with infinite and patient care, the fragments of the letters to see what they told. It would take me a very long time, this putting together again what had been torn into pieces, but I would have a very long time to give to it, and I was at the source of the mystery, removed and secure from the chaos of the world below that could not make up its mind and tried to keep me from making up my own.

My dream ended here, or was broken, by the hand of my mother shaking me to morning; and when I went to eat breakfast I heard them saying in the kitchen that Flagpole Moody had signaled early, at dawn, around six o'clock, that he wanted to come down; that he had come down in his own time, and that he had come down very, very tired, after forty days and nights, the length of the Flood. I did not tell my dream, for I had no power of telling then, but I knew that I had a story to one day shape around the marvel and mystery that ended in a dream and began in the world that was to be mine.

INTERVIEW

1982

An Interview with William Goyen

What starts you writing?
It starts with trouble. You don't think it starts with
peace, do you?

Reginald Gibbons: A passage from "Nests in a Stone Image" could serve as epigraph for all your work:

> He had come here out of some loss and bereavement and to sit and have back again, as it wanted to come back to him, with whatever face or feature, shape or name, what he had lost; . . . to control it and keep it from chaos again, to give it its meaning that it waited for . . . This was what claimed him.

William Goyen: I found a kind of statement for myself there, didn't I?—through real deep suffering. It's really meditation. It's kind of a salvation—a lot of those pieces are really my little salvation pieces: they represent my being rescued again from deep suffering.

Q: Rescued by what?

WG: I felt that I was rescuing myself. I got a sense of myself, in a flash. It was a spiritual experience, of course. And with that clarification, I was able to move on out of what might have destroyed me. I don't know that I have ever felt that I have been lifted by a higher power—a god or anything. By divinity. It must have been art, then—a sense of one's self suddenly frees him, at least for that time, and one is able then to go on.

Q: The story is quite free of what readers normally expect from a story—

WG: God bless them!

Q: —it doesn't give them a plot or character development.

WG: But I see that it was a form I found for myself, and used over and over again, in a whole body of work, without knowing that I was using it. I didn't put it up on the wall and say, "This is the form I will now follow." But it was deep pain, a feeling of utter isolation and removal from the community of human beings—that kind of lostness. And then, through an acuteness of feeling and an awareness of things around me, coming back to life, through life around me—in this case—in the story you quoted from, "Nests in a Stone Image"—people in the rooms around the speaker in the story. In his misery and isolation he was surrounded by human beings, all singing and making love and talking, and life was in those rooms around him, and then rising. It was always the rising action, that I felt, over and over again.

Q: That's what you mean by the sense of form?

WG: Coming up, yes, from the bottom, rising to the top and then being freed of that pain and being *identified,* is surely what it was, wasn't it?

The form was new each time. But two things—it's about love, and total giving in love till there was nothing left, total faith in life and love; and then feeling destroyed and abandoned, and then finding again . . . through life going on. Despite my misery, life was just going on! Those were such great revelations, do you know that? Suddenly you heard people next door saying, "Well, do we need eggs? Well, let's see, we need eggs, bread . . ." They're making a list of groceries! And writing checks. That life was restored to me, so often not through great bursts of something, like St. Paul's revelation, but through just the trivial, which I still hold to, the everyday trivial detail. That has always pulled me through.

Q: Is the meaning of a story as much in the act of telling it as it is in its substance?

WG: It has a spiritual significance. Someone wrote that about my work—that the liberating, therefore spiritual, significance of storytelling was in the very telling itself, a kind of a prayer or meditation or apotheosis of feeling, a dynamic spiritual action. So: the need to tell, on the part of a lot of characters I have written about, like Raymon Emmons ["Ghost and Flesh"].

But in some writers what one gets is diction more than voice. That is, it's *thick speech*, rather than voice. There's a great difference between speech and voice. "Correcting" the speech of my characters, as some copy editors wish to do, affects the voice. That's the pitfall of some writers, some of the Southern writers, who get hung up on diction and speech. Synge was in danger of that, too. There is a quality of voice that is, I guess, undefinable. I feel I know what that is, and I have to wait for it, and that determines my work: voice. I can't fake it, and I can't find it if it's not there. I have to hear it. This I know for myself. Sometimes the voice, the same voice, tells me a bunch of stories.

People in my life told me stories, and I sang. They had the speech, and I got the voice. And I place the burden for that difference on angels, good and bad. Some people seem to have a good angel, or a bad one (can there be bad angels?), and yet some have none at all.

Q: Still, you have to work at the art—the angel's not going to do the work for you, is it?

WG: But it can put a tongue in my mouth for a little while ["Tongues of Men and of Angels"]. That's what happened to me.

When I first rode a bicycle, I couldn't ride it without my father pushing me, holding me there, and I said, "But what am I going to do? Don't let loose! Don't let loose!" (We had just a little hill.) He said, "Son, I wouldn't let you aloose, don't you worry." And one day, he *had,* and I was going right along! And I looked back, and he wasn't there, and I was doing it! From then on I rode the bicycle.

Now, when I'm really working, really writing, I have the feeling it's coming from outside of me, through me. An absolute submission, absolute surrender. It's being *had,* being possessed. I'm being used.

Q: Are you very curious to define that "it" that is using you?

WG: No. I recognize it, and know when it's *not* there. It's like being in love, or being mad—all those radical emotions.

Q: Are you reluctant to talk about it?

WG: There's something in me that shuts it off.

Q: Is it like that moment when Dante describes Virgil and Statius walking ahead, speaking of poetry, and Dante won't repeat what they said?

WG: I'm not able to talk about it. St. Paul speaks of the inexpressible, what you *don't* repeat. There are some revelations I have, he said, that there are no words for, and why should I try? There is a reticence.

Q: In an interview with William Peden, you said "the storyteller is a blessed force in telling his story to a listener; a redemptive process occurs, and it's therefore a spiritual situation, and one cannot avoid that." What do you mean, "a spiritual situation"?

WG: It has to do first of all with distinguishing simply between spiritual and material. It's not, "How much am I going to get for it?" And if it doesn't have to do with tangible rewards, then it has to do with intangible ones, with my spirit, with my own yearning toward something higher than I, something by definition divine, some outer higher power working through me, that I have no power over or at least did not create.

I remember Marian Anderson was my first experience with what truly was a spiritual moment. Suddenly when she sang she was purely an instrument for the spirit, pure spirit. Through her mouth, here was this blessed moment, the light and the fire were on *her,* way beyond her training or the song itself. I was sixteen; I identified thoroughly, purely, with her. "That's where I belong, I come from that," I said. "That's why I feel so alone, because I belong to whatever that was."

Q: What's your sense of the occasion of a story? What starts you writing?

WG: It starts with trouble. You don't think it starts with peace, do you? It's an occasion that brings a whole cluster of occasions together.

Q: You don't worry about the connections between them?

WG: No. The bridges start forming. That's the fun sometimes, and the slavery too, in making the bridges. They are always implied, because they come of their own volition, I feel.

Trusting the connection *is* the process of work.

Everything I've written has been generated that way. I once spoke of medallions [Interview, *Paris Review 68*, Winter 1976]: when my mother made a quilt, she made what she called medallions first, a whole bunch of separate pieces. They don't do the whole quilt at once! When these were all together—till then, you don't see the connections, but it makes a whole.

Q: I think of your work as domestic in a similar sense.

WG: I understand. One of those stories I saw as a kite—and we used to make our own kites. The idea of buying a kite! *Who* bought a kite? We made it out of stuff at home. String, newspaper—and it flew, it flew. But it was made domestically. That's what you call domestic invention. The cruder the better, sometimes. I think of writing as that very often. I'm most comfortable with things that happen at home. . . .

> *Without art . . . would I just have been a kind of evangelist?*

Style is, or has been, for me, the spiritual experience of my material.

Q: How do you mean, "spiritual"?

WG: Well, people say craft, and I'm talking on the other side of craft. Of course, I know my craft, I know what I will let go and what I won't, and I know when it's not the best. More and more I know about the control of words. But I'm talking about the spiritual experience of Arthur Bond ["Arthur Bond"]

—to have experienced those characters and the world they have created around them through their own infirmities or . . . life in the world has become a spiritual revelation of the human being that I would not have got by studying the work of other writers.

Q: What's the bridge between that experience and the words that make up a story?

WG: The bridge is the transformation. An artist transforms. He can't just stay where life is as he finds it, not at just the *level of life*. Or so it is for me: the art of it becomes the transformation that must occur of that spiritual experience into the controlled craft so that the vision is tied down, is anchored everywhere, by craft. "Arthur Bond" had to be anchored in all kinds of detail, and mostly painterly detail—there was some yellow (the color came to me), the worm with the head of a doll: it all became very pictorial for me. But the man was caught in a spiritual wrestling. This was what I experienced first, his wrestling. "It is not his fall you see, but this man's wrestling," Shakespeare said about one of the kings.

Q: The word "spiritual" then doesn't mean "religious"?

WG: Not at all. It has to do with a certain program of action. By that I mean I don't come into this experience to get my eyebrows longer, or my muscles stronger, or my belly flatter. So it is therefore *not physical*. O.K.? That's as clear as I can make it. Something else is involved beyond the corporeal. Shall we all start there? I can't define it any more than that. That's what I mean by my spirit. It is not my body. So let's go away from whatever we think of as physical and try to get into an area that is noncorporeal. Something happens to me which changes my attitude toward . . . you. What is that? It's not that you've given me a lot of money, or bought me a house, or given me a reward. What changed my attitude toward you? Something, I say, came from outside me. And I see as I say this that I tend to look up, because we've been told that heaven is above us, though it may not be at all, it may be quite lateral, I don't know. But it has come from beyond me somewhere, it is not anything I have learned, been taught, or even done. So that the *spirit* is involved in this change of feeling between me and you.

Style, then, is directly related to that experience. So that style is a spiritual manifestation of the experience of the story, for me. My stories *are* spiritual.

And yet there are an awful lot of *genitalia* in them.

Q: Why is that?

WG: That's spiritual, too, I guess. "Ghost and Flesh," I wrote—one's expressed right through the other, for me.

Q: Is there some writing that, you feel, doesn't have this spiritual element?

WG: I don't feel it's in most contemporary writers that I try to read. I feel that they really are too busy with repeating themselves, and repeating their own success, not necessarily material.

Q: But despite your artistic intransigence on this point, I know that as a person you have been extremely generous and helpful to many writers who haven't displayed much of the spiritual in this sense, at all, haven't reached that level of art.

WG: I've tried to lead them toward it, I guess. That's all I can give them. An opening out. That's obviously why they have come to *me*. I'm not proselytizing and I'm not looking for disciples. I think that's my freedom as a teacher—I don't think people should write like me. I couldn't, by my nature, stay very long in a classroom, teaching. I've started out thinking, this is a class about craft, and that's what we'll be about. But halfway through it I soared into this other thing, we're off into another realm. I can't talk about writing very long without talking about seeing that *possible* transformation. And this is what I talk about a lot. There has to be a change, some change has to pass over what happens to me, what I experience. It seems to come from a deeper reality than a knowledge of what *literary device* I can use to bring the change.

So I like to talk about style that way, and maybe finally I will write about it a little. In the past few years I've had fresh experience with these things—style, image, and life-writing—in my work. Image brings a spiritual revelation of the very life-material itself. . . .

When I first wrote *The House of Breath,* and it was published in that very form, in *Accent,* it was called "Four American Portraits As Elegy." I wrote four lives: "Aunty," "Christy," "Swimma," and "Folner." *In A Farther Country* is written the same way. And so is *Come, The Restorer*. This too is style.

Q: It seems less style than shape.

WG: It *is* shape. The design is the last thing that comes, for me, yet it is the first thing, as well as the last. But without it I'm lost. I get it early. But then I have to lose it, and the feeling is that I'll never get it back. But finally it's the design that I'm able to see, specifically, the architecture of it. The two parts of "Leander"* were pretty much of a whole, and actually the second part is contained in the first few pages of the first. It is *there*. All these people seem to me to be out of some book of the accurst. They're evil figures. They're demonic figures. They frightened *me* to death, those three sisters! Or they're just spiteful figures, or just nuisance figures. But the horror of the Klan, the blackness of that, the evil of them, just pervaded that whole land. And there always seemed to be henchmen of it, and it seemed to be a nightmare of mutiny and banditry. This is the world I was in.

Q: At the end of "Had I a Hundred Mouths," the narrating nephew sees his cousin in white sheet and hood, with others. Then that Klan nephew is tormented and tortured by the Klan in the second part of the work, for having spoken of their doings.

WG: Because he told their secrets. And what were they? That they had had children by black women, and that they had hanged black men for fucking white women. They had scapegoats. Those are horrors, horrors! A medieval world of terror. You know it *was* like that, to me; as a child I really felt that. I lived around all of that. There was a man preaching the salvation of my soul in a tent across the road from my house, but up on the hill beyond there the Ku Klux were burning their crosses and I saw them run tarred and feathered Negroes through the street. I saw them running like that, twice. Aflame. We stood and watched that.

---

* Goyen's title for the unfinished novella whose two completed parts are "Had I A Hundred Mouths" and "Tongues of Men and of Angels."

Q: What sort of reactions were apparent in those around you?

WG: They were terrified. Just as if you were a Jew and those were Nazis. Most of them simply lived in terror and hid. It was that kind of world, as I saw it. And it could only have to do later with the brutality that I wrote about and also with salvation. It was also full of the erotic and the sensual and all that, for me, too. It was a maelstrom, it was a cauldron.

Q: Does that world seem another universe now, as if you were writing about something you could present only emblematically, that sort of horror?

WG: How is it another universe? It seems very contemporary. If they murdered how many hundreds in those camps in Beirut . . . the terrorism around us . . . Hollywood is a town of absolute terroristic violence. It's a cursed place. It's full of a violence that comes out of a whole lot of things, but out of abuse, and persecution. . . .

But the town, the environment, which for me was the river and the fields, and the wonderful things that bloomed, that are so much in my stories, was still stalked by some horror all around it. And the tales I heard—a whole lot of that is stated in "The Icebound Hothouse." That story comes to be about that. And at the end there is an apotheosis, again, to say, "Why did I ever think that that house, that door, where I'd like to go home, that promised hospitality to the one who was arriving—why did I think that there were all sunny stories of joy and laughter?" The door is a dark door. Whose chose that door? Who is the dark presence in that house? This is a culmination for me of the *House of Breath* metaphor, all these years later—this is what I came upon in finishing this story. So it is precious door again.

And now as I grow older and I go through these experiences —of almost dying, and changes of place, as from the East to the West, here—I keep getting closer to those images of terror and horror, as well as of the sublime pastoral garden.

Q: So there's a way to redeem that experience?

WG: Yes, and it's art and the holy spirit, which are one for me, more and more. Without art, without the process of memory, which is the process of art, and the spiritual experience of it, which for me is style, what else would I do about it? Would I be an addict? Would I be dead from alcoholism and addictions of one kind or another? Would I just have been a kind of evangelist?

Q: Are you saying holy spirit with small h and small s?

WG: Well, you know, I tend to capitalize where other people always strike things down to l.c. That means that I'm elevating it, somewhere, that's what it means in my head, and I insist on keeping that, because it is somehow elevating it beyond the pedestrian lower case.

I think there's no such thing as meaningless suffering, and this is spoken by someone who sees the terror of life. You know, there's a recent book called *The Horror of Life*? Of course, I bought that faster than I'd buy something called *Days in My Garden*. And it's the lives of five people who all view life as horrible. This life-view was one of horror and fear. Baudelaire, De Maupassant, Flaubert, Jules de Goncourt, Daudet. It turned out that they were all syphilitic and had a horrible disease. I'm not talking about that. I'm not talking about the horror of life. But the horrible and the terrible element in life. Why would I endure life if I thought *life* was horrible? What good would I gain by enduring? Enduring is a hopeful action.

Q: Flannery O'Connor said in answer to those who criticized the apparently despairing content or material of modern novels that people without hope don't write novels.

WG: Of course it's an act of hope, and faith. Art is redeeming, and art is an affirmation. There's no other way. The creation, the result, may not be very wonderful in some cases, or even very good, but I'm given joy and faith again through watching people's impulse to make something, and their energy in making it, their willingness to make something.

Q: You also seem to agree with Lowell, however, that poetry is *not* a craft. Do you think that the craft-mentality of the writing schools is all right? Does craft drive out art?

WG: I don't think that's possible. Art won't have it. There's no way possible to substitute anything for art. I believe in the absolute hegemony of art, and craft can't hurt it.

Q: You have said that "elegance in fiction frightens me, and exquisiteness." Even if you were speaking there of style, I suspect that "elegance" applies also to the impulse to wrap things up a little too neatly. *You* certainly leave a lot of things just flapping their wings in the air. That can seem to mean something in itself. Do you worry about being too symbolic?

WG: No. I don't have any worry about being symbolic, I don't think I'm symbolic. Arcadio *has* got two genitals—

Q: But you take a figure like Leander, and you castrate him. He is desexed; he is half white, half black. He was a man and is no longer a man; Arcadio is half man and half woman: these things are emblematic. Not that I can put a ready meaning to them, but you seem to be interested in more than the shape of a man, you're interested in the significance of the shape of a man.

WG: And yet, you know, how emblematic is a woman with one breast? I saw a great photograph yesterday in a bookstore, a huge life-size photograph of a very beautiful woman with a wonderful breast, and on the other side was a tattoo of roses across no breast at all. She had had one removed, and yet the photographer was saying, "This is all right. This is beautiful. Don't be horrified. She *has* one breast!" But it was a *creature*: it seemed almost like Leander. I said, "What a defamation of a beautiful thing!" I heard myself say that. "How *defaming* to take a breast off her! How they slaughter women in the name of cancer." But I was with a woman, and she said, "But look how beautiful, it's all right." So I caught myself. It was kind of a wreath of roses tattooed. So that is very emblematic—that's what I'm talking about: there's a breast, I could *suck* that breast! That's very exciting. On the other hand, there's a kind of monster.

Q: And a kind of symbol? Not a real rose, but the picture of a rose?

WG: No, a woman, who is saying, "I am a woman, and I am beautiful still."

Q: Is it the physically grotesque that interests you?

WG: I really mean more of a spiritual deformity. Of course, dwarves, and humpbacks, and harelips, and so forth. That's only the beginning for me. I can't linger on that very long but it delivers me from the boring reality of realistic reporting. Since I am *not* writing Zola-istic realism, then everyday reality, the detail of it, is obviously not going to sustain itself for me, forever. I'm not Dreiser, I'm not interested in that at all. I'm aware that there is no everyday trivia in itself; that beneath it, or going on within it, there's always some slight deformity of thought or action. It's the hidden life I'm talking about.

I'm not writing within the vogue for the bizarre. My insights are deeper and deeper into what we're talking about, and the revelations that are coming to me make me more and more aware of an overwhelming imagery of the crude and the violent, but I mean more than that. I suppose it's always been with me, and I can see it back in *The House of Breath,* my earliest work. It really has more to do with tenderness, rather than less. It's not hardness of heart that is happening. I see more and more brutality, and the metaphor that exists in brutality. It may be that in my earlier work I gentled that, but I see it more now. It begins in the latter half of *Arcadio,* for me, and continues on through Leander's story ["Had I A Hundred Mouths"] and the last I've written ["Tongues of Men and of Angels"].

Q: Far from the sorrow and the wonder and gratefulness that surround the erotic in "Ghost and Flesh," you're moved to consider it a dark power.

WG: True.

Q: A dark power over men, not a mystery in their lives that is constructive or renewing.

WG: Yes. It *was* a great power, that's true. I'm really astonished by all that, myself, it's still new for me, I have no hypothesis about it yet. Where I am in this work—and it's leading me more and more—there's a tenderness, always, at the core. "Had I A Hundred Mouths" is a tender story—the love of that man, and the love of the black man: those people have a tenderness that is almost old-fashioned. But what I really see is that within that tenderness is a brutality and a striking violence of feeling and action. It has nothing to do with disillusionment—I was never more spiritual in my life. It has nothing to do with losing faith, or any of those clichés. It's that the light is on *that* now, I *see* that: I see lust as demonic. I have never known it to be anything else! Have you? Good Lord! The lust is the very devil working, a demon in me—*my* lust. I don't know about anybody else's. I've had a demon in me.

Q: How can *la Santa Biblia* and that lust inhabit the same creature, as they do in Arcadio?

WG: It's the human arrangement, it's just our very nature, I think. It created people like St. Paul, but oddly enough it didn't create a man like Jesus, did it? We don't think of Jesus as a lustful man, but it's very possible that Paul was—he's so angry against women, against marriage, against sex.

Q: Is that fruitful anger?

WG: Fruitful in his case—he did a lot of good work, and he did walk among real violent, lustful characters—all those Romans! I think lust is a very rare feeling, and one of the grand emotions. Arcadio is a grand figure of lust and tenderness, I think.

Q: With a Bible in his hand?

WG: Sure. Redemption is what he was looking for. And the Bible is the handbook of redemption. It's the song at the end of a life, he's an old man, in his seventies. And he seems a bit deranged, too—I don't know *what* he is! He's gone a bit mad. I'm not sure how much is true and how much is false of what he's telling me at the end. He's now such a fabricator that he's one of the *great* fabricators.

Q: Near the end of an interview, in French, you mentioned St. Francis, and the sense that certain saints had of sexuality, of the erotic and the sensual. I think the popular image of St. Francis is of someone feeding the birds from his open hand, and not of him as a sensual creature.

WG: Have you ever fed a bird? It's very exciting. These holy people were walking around with the same impulses that I have, or else they wouldn't be able to reach me. They had the same equipment that I have, if they were men, the same desire, man or woman. Those desires were not submerged; they exist; the Pope perhaps wakes with a hard-on.

I think there is an inevitable confrontation with the spiritual in every human life at some time or other.

Q: Right in the most sensual experience? Eating?

WG: Coming. Absolutely. Certainly all the nailing, and the Penitente things, are sensuous. No: sensual.

Q: You want the word that seems more animal?

WG: Yes. The French *sensuelle* is the word that applies to all those almost genital actions. St. Francis to my mind was a genital human being. St. Theresa was—she no doubt menstruated. This is what I mean—this helps me to find purity and holiness. It's even there in the act of hiding away: like that woman in my story, Inez Melendrez McNamara, who went into that convent ["Tongues of Men and of Angels"]. Her hair became more and more sexual. Her body itself became more voluptuous.

Q: At the same time, *Arcadio,* like Leander's story, leads to genital horrors.

WG: I see people who have emasculated each other. I see people who have been made Leanders of, by wives and husbands, by lovers. My God, the brutality of love-relationships! A mastectomy would be more benevolent than what men do to women's bodies sometimes, making them loathe their bodies or abusing them or hating them or whatever. That's why that picture of that woman with one breast, and one scar, was such an *affirmation*: She said "I am beautiful." So that in a way Leander means that to *me*—as much as all the other abuses of whites upon blacks, and so on. People render each other sexless, finally; they can castrate each other, and the denial can close up the genitals of a woman and she can grow together. She's been denied that, or it's been abused. . . .

Q: Were there some writers whose influence you felt you had to reject or throw off?

WG: Oh sure. I had to work through them. Because a lot

of them are standing in the way. We have to go through their legs or get around them or really just kind of *have* them, in order to be free of them, or let them have us. Thomas Wolfe. Singing people. Whitman. Early Saroyan. I had to find out whether I could do it or not, and since I didn't have anything to replace it with yet—I tell students this: since you don't have anything to offer yet, then *take* what they have to offer, and spend it. If somebody wants you to make love to them that badly, then go ahead and do it. Just go ahead and do it, get out, get through it! Never James—though he astonished me. The same as Proust: those were abundances, flowerings. They confirmed me.

Q: Why is a minor writer like Saroyan more of a problem than a writer like James or Proust?

WG: Saroyan speaks very much to young people. That great freedom—"I'm leaving, I'm going to do what I have to do, get out of my way, let me fly!" But his spiritual transformation was not mine; his style, finally, was not one that I could graft on to me as my own. It was *his* spirit.

Q: Did you read Sherwood Anderson?

WG: He didn't attract me. I didn't know what Ohio was. I hardly knew what Texas was, but I was determined to find out. I did find stories that knocked the hell out of me, and made me want to write—but write my own stories. Flaubert's "Saint Ju-lien, l'Hospitalier"; Thomas Mann's "Tonio Kröger." I suddenly found literature through classes at college. I had been cutting classes trying to learn how to compose music, and hiding out in vaudeville theaters, and trying to say something through *performing*. I hadn't found the *word* yet. I settled for that, really, when my father told me that I couldn't perform, that I was not *allowed* to, and almost at the same time in my life I came upon writing, and the whole thing burst open for me. I was reading French and Spanish, and German, too, early—languages were easy for me and I was studying them. *Lazarillo de Tormes*! Poetry: Goethe's lyrics. Heine's. Rimbaud. Blake.

The American writing around me seemed to all just hang at that level of life that I spoke about, just at whatever tide there was—there was Hemingway, whom I couldn't abide. Fitzgerald, totally foreign to me. I didn't know about that world, the swell life. Or even Fitzgerald's own transformations. Hemingway seemed to me to be like the brutes that I knew that I wanted to escape from, in Texas. That physical bravado, that leanness of style, that was anathema to me. Why would I not use three adjectives? Why not? I was a rhapsodist, why would I cut down on my adjectives? What was Hemingway trying to tell me, what was he hiding?

So those people were around me, and I chose Whitman, and Saroyan, and Wolfe.

Q: But you chose them as enemies, did you not?

WG: No, I had to go through them. Then I went into people who had a profound influence on me—like Milton, Chaucer, Dante.

Q: It was a long time between 1937, graduating from Rice, and 1950, when you published *The House of Breath*. Were those figures riding with you all that time?

WG: All that time. They rode with me on a godforsaken aircraft carrier, for five years. I got into the ship in 1939 and I got out of it in nineteen fucking forty-five, at the end of the war. *That's* where *I* was. I had to study ballistics, command a battery of antiaircraft guns. But I was carrying these people with me. I was shooting off in my bunk when I should have been in love affairs of all kinds, I should have been in *life*, breaking my heart. That's a forced monastic living—since I'm a late bloomer, that's something to think about. I can see the deprivation of that; but I can see too that it probably added years to my life because I was physically in good shape. I realize as I talk now the extent of a residing anger in me, resentment, bitterness, about that. I've never really assessed that time. It did free me from all the crippling influences in my life, the crippling circumstances—family dependence, Texas, and probably from excessive study and scholarly isolation. I have never really realized the madness of those years. I went quite mad at the end of the fourth year of it, quite crazy, I had to be under morphine on the ship. I became so

enraged at the war that my rage couldn't be contained by my
body or quietened by one thousand men. We were near the coast
of Japan. When would it end? It was all right for a while, but
will this go on!? I was a captive. I felt punished. For what? What
had *I* done? I recall these maniac feelings. I was a wild man on
the ship, a rebel, an outlaw. My poetic and voluptuous youth, I
felt, was dying and passing away a mile a minute in the China
Sea in 1944. . . .

*He thought how he had always wanted to belong to a
landscape, yet it seemed his destiny to be only a figure
riding through many landscapes.*

Q: One could divide your stories into those in which up-
rootedness is central, and those others in which for a moment that
homelessness is conquered and there is a sense of getting back.

WG: I had a sense of myself—which has lessened a bit, but
is still an underlying sense of myself—as a *passager,* as someone
passing through. So many of my stories were almost ballads—
saying that I'm on my way, I'm just passing through, I've sung
my song, now I'm going on, I just stopped by here. That came
out of my feeling that I couldn't live in Texas, that I couldn't live
among my own, that something alienated me, that I was drawn
apart. And that was a heartbreak for me. I accepted it as a kind
of destiny and often as a curse. I couldn't be there, whatever
those reasons were, and that led me to an immense homesickness,
a longing for where I couldn't be. It's an exile. I don't know what
the exiling factors or forces were, may never know.

Q: Were they personal more than artistic?

WG: An artist moves, goes out, comes back and then leaves
again.

Q: You're not speaking about a cultural question, about the
writer who goes to New York because there is no one to read
him in Texas?

WG: No, of course not. When I went back, it was almost—
just a death, one of my deaths. I couldn't get over waking and

hearing Texans. I couldn't believe their speech! At once I thought, "This is where I belong! I'm here, I'm home here!" And then my second feeling, on the heels of that, was that they would never let me become a part of them. I talk like that, that's my speech, and those are all my people, but why is it I can't be a part of them? Why am I here in this room alone, isolated and exiled from them, just outside my door?

I still feel that when I go home.

Q: Is that relationship something you expect to find, or aren't surprised to find, in other people's work, or do you feel it's peculiar to you?

WG: It seemed to be so deep in me that I thought, if I read it somewhere else, I felt confirmed, or affirmed. I didn't associate it with Joyce and with the classic exile of Joyce, because I felt that Joyce's was much more planned, reasonable, he was much less bewildered by the forces upon him, at him, and he was dealing with a whole huge culture, a literary and an ethnic culture, the whole Celtic renaissance. My case seemed a very personal thing, almost demonic—a curse: dark. Therefore the meditational quality, a prayer-like quality, almost "Help me, Save me, Deliver me."

Q: Given the passages rising at the ends of some stories, it seems to me that prayer was addressed to the language itself.

WG: True.

Q: And you have called them songs, those stories, as well.

WG: They always came like anthems, or serenades. And they were sung, finally; it was an anthem-, a joyous hymnal-feeling I had, even in "Arthur Bond," that late. The language is always a principal character in the story for me; I suppose that's why I can't read so many other writers. They feel they're giving me whole characters and they probably are but the characters don't interest me if I can't hear them speak or identify them with *words,* by which they are delivered to me.

Q: Your literary mode, your literary consciousness, your artistic devices, and your gypsy experience, have all been extremely cosmopolitan, but even when you start on West Twenty-third Street with Marietta Chavez McGee [*In A Farther Coun-*

try], you always go back to that rural reality, in your work, more a different place in the mind than a geographical place, a world of fewer emblems and more powerful ones, which we seem to say is rural, mostly. A good example is "Old Wildwood," which begins in Rome, but goes back to the funny little motel cabin on the shore of the Gulf of Mexico.

WG: That saves me each time, though, because it's the detail of the small scope that keeps me from being lost in the Rome of it, or in the New York City of it, because I am not really writing about Rome, or I would have to find the detail of Rome.

Q: *That* sort of fictional texture doesn't interest you, does it?

WG: No. The *house,* therefore. I look for containment. I see this now, and I guess I do at a certain point know when I'm engulfed by too much, and then I really try to get into some little manageable harbor, get anchored somewhere, and it's in simple and homely detail, and often in bizarre detail. An absolutely recognizable detail, that seems trivial. I have to be contained by a house, or a place. I'm then free to do what I want.

Q: And yet, if sometimes you suggest containment, at other times you suggest freedom of a roaming, wandering sort.

WG: Sometimes people just go, and you never hear from them again. Or they come back very different from what they were when they left. What makes them come back? Or changes them—if some force took that demon out of them and put it into swine? Later I'd like to talk about the swine! Somebody was exorcised through me, I took over people's demons and I went on off with those demons, a lot of the time. *They* went off pure and fine. They flew on off, like angels, and I was cursed! I was the pig. The cliff by the sea beckoned me.

The bizarre, and the supernatural, that we were talking about—I thought sometimes I was the receiver of a cursedness. I felt often that I was a carrier: that image. I've written about the carrier, in *The House of Breath*. That image of myself, carrying, benignly walking through and infecting others, or receiving what others put onto me. . . .

Q: You describe Lois Fuchs [*In A Farther Country*] falling in love at thirty-five with a seventeen-year-old boy, who then dies, as if she has cursed or infected him.

WG: That's what I'm talking about. But I can't account for these people—not Leander either. I'm not responsible for *accounting* for Uncle Ben ["Had I A Hundred Mouths"], although it seems I'm his creator. I'm therefore held, it seems, accountable. But I don't believe the artist is held accountable. Is he, maybe? Morally, we feel that he is. Do we just abandon characters to the destiny that life has for them? Do we let them go into life out of the art we have made? Or do we hold them within our art and try to account for them totally through art? I don't think so. Leander was restored to life, I guess—he had to take his chances out there maybe. I was done with him, in a way. I came upon my own redemption in the streets somewhere, as creator-narrator, and looked upon my own flesh and felt my own reality in Leander now at large from my own creation.

Q: In the French interview [*Masques,* Summer 1982] you were asked if all your characters weren't either waiting for something or wounded. Is that waiting a kind of disablement like the physical disablement that afflicts some of them?

WG: I think they're waiting for miracles, for wonderful visitations—they're waiting for the marvelous.

Q: Is the marvelous that important?

WG: I'm not didactic—it's just surprise, waiting for the wonderful surprise. It's probably waiting for the Second Coming, underneath. I'm sure that's all I've ever been writing about. Salvation, redemption, freedom from bondage, complete release. All those people from those little towns, that's what they were brought up to wait for: the end of the world, when the trumpets would sound, and they'd be free of all this daily labor. That's the whole black southern thing. Rebirth, a new life, heaven—freedom from pain, bondage, travail.

Those characters in my stories all *are* waiting. They're really kind of hopeful people, expecting more. They're open to something. They are forerunners. They've lost place—a lot of them are displaced, that's their sorrow.

"But there's a better place I know," don't you know that's what they say? "I accept that I've lost my place, my home, my town, my river—a whole river is gone!" When Jessy comes back to her mother, in *The House of Breath,* she says to her, "Life is loss, Mama." Her mother is just waiting, sitting in a chair. She had closed the blinds, and the wind played memory through them. Jessy says, "Life is loss, don't you know that? I know that, and I'm only ten years old."

Q: How do you feel now that you have adjusted to living in Southern California, after several years?

WG: I feel exhilarated, it's encouraging and hospitable to me, for my work, because I *am* in a foreign country. This is the way I've been able to accept it. The people are foreigners to me and I am in a strange land. I'm at home in a strange land—always my image of home was of someplace where I would put down the deepest roots and build a permanent place and I would never stray from that. But of course that was pure fallacy, pure idiocy, a fake way of thinking about my life, that was never possible, I would never allow that, anyway. It's not anything I really would care about!

Beckett said this for me at a time when I was looking for the statement, that the artist lives *nowhere.* "*L'artiste qui joue son être est de nulle part. Et il n'a pas des frères.*"

Q: Who would have guessed this of a writer like you, as concerned with such specific speech and with the exile's return?

WG: But that place has become a language, now, for me. That's a language of its own; I've created a language, as I did for Arcadio, that was never spoken there. That's become my *style,* for me.

Q: You're not reproducing a speech?

WG: Not at all, not the way those Southerners do. I'm not a "Texas writer" or a "regional" one. I'm not interested in that, I never really was. I was making a *language* out of *speech.* If you harm that language, you're harming the life of that work, and you're harming the character himself. You're re-dressing him. You're saying, "No, he wouldn't have this kind of a hat on, he wouldn't have that color eyes." It's a violation. The language has become paint, as for a painter—the quality of the paint, the texture. A Cézanne local mountain is *paint*. . . .

Q: You revise and revise your work, don't you?

WG: But something is never changed. And that's what I know not to change. I can't say that it's words: it's the vision, and it is never changed. There are no "revisions" for me, in that sense. I'm really in trouble if I try to change that. But it's not as if my first *draft* were holier than any other.

Q: Your attitude is nothing like that of the Beats, then, for whom the spontaneous composition was sacred?

WG: Those states were induced, those visionary states. Now, in the last five years, I've read the Beats, and I've found there's something there. But at that time, the fifties, they were crazy, and I was trying to be sane. My God, I *started* by being crazy, why would I want to induce insanity? And writing kept making me sane, at least tying me down somewhere. So I couldn't hear any of that, then. They scared me, too. *Wild* people . . . I find that when I get a little depressed or morbid I want to stop talking. It's probably that I've just used it up. That's a good sign, to me.

Q: A clear signal, you mean?

WG: Yes, I think it is, to let it alone So that I don't get into other feelings—fear. And the kind of memory that is not creative. There *is* a destructive memory, too, that has nothing to do with recreating life, and I know when it is, more and more. I used to brood on it, and use it, and think it was a part of my creativity— it really was demonic. It came when it came. I was a prey to it. I drank to stop that, obsessed and on the verge of insanity. I'm through that. I was afraid of those things of *mind,* and I just joined the ranks of many others. The destructive memory was all that would come to me then, and you have to learn through the destruction—if you survive—when it is creative, when it is a building thing. I think some poets never knew that. I thought at that time that the idea of insanity in poets was somewhat hallowed. And there was such a false feeling about that. There still is. I have not much patience with it now, I just consider them ill, people who need help. And once they are restored, then their process goes on again. But the madness of the poet, and the poetry that came out of madness and suicide and all that—it impresses me less and less. Too much destructive memory. And I feel that a lot of poets begin to use that as a way of life, a pattern of behavior, even as a creative pattern.

Q: How do you distinguish between the creative and destructive memory?

WG: Through surviving it. And through knowing when to let it alone. This is why I am physical, thank God. I *am* physical. I would use sex. I would go digging—I dug whole *arroyos,* irrigation ditches where there was no water, in New Mexico. I made adobes, and lifted, and built.

This was healing, I thought—to go into the detail of everyday life again. That was my survival, that's why I'm here, I knew that. Because basically I wanted health, I wanted an art that was healthy and healing, that had life-force in it, life-*strength*. When it got into this darkness, I knew more and more to let it alone. If I was in a relationship, a love-relationship, that was dark, and was caught in it, with no way to escape from that, then it was very very dangerous for me. Or if I went *home*—often I would go home thinking that would restore me, but I found that black angel there, though home was a great source of restoration and healing for me, I *thought*. This was when I was not writing. But if there were traps that I couldn't escape—I won't stay where that black angel is—then that's a dangerous time for me. And it looked to me that California might be the final trap for me. And it seemed that that dark angel, that bad angel, that I wrote about, was here.

I came here thinking: sunshine, the flowers, and a new way of life, from New York apartment living—and I never *have* been able to live in New York, really. Ever! I've done it, but only happily in my own place, my own rooms, a nest—a life-giving place.

Q: Not in the *city,* only in your nest there?

WG: That's right. As my present self, I'm not able to handle the place now.

Q: But when you go home, aren't you wiser and stronger than before?

WG: But what I'm shown is that I'm *not,* and that's the last straw! I come there vulnerable. I have come there out of seeking, and to seek is to be vulnerable, I guess. I have come there seeking, saying, "Well, *that* will save me," and already now I'm open to any kind of force that can get me down, destroy me. Also I suppose that wisdom reveals that often there was a dark angel where we thought there was a bright one. I said, "Those people sitting on the porch, and singing together at night, and those stories they told, in the twilight . . . who was the dark figure in that house? Who among them chose that front door pane with that forbidding figure that says 'Don't come in this house—Who are you?—don't enter here—you're not welcome here.' " When I'd come with my suitcase, saying, "I'm here!" I'd see that figure on that horse saying "Come in!" and yet "Don't! It's just pain and darkness."

That house is still there, and so far as I know, that door is still there. A very precious, suspicious, dangerous door.

> *I feel everything of mine is on the ground, now, but not gathered. There are still some things on the tree, that have to get ripe, but the great body of my work is on the ground, but not gathered.*

Q: You have prepared a new selection of your stories, and you seem to want a larger audience for this book in particular— not that any writer doesn't want the largest audience possible.

WG: I've been thinking about the curious kind of recognition that I have experienced, a curious misreading or misjudging of my work, I think. Or misplacing! I suppose I don't need an explanation for it, and the reason I may seem to be asking for one is that I don't understand it when people say my work has been ignored in Texas or the country as a whole, and it has such an audience in Europe. I used to get sick over that, to suffer over it, and something seemed wrong. I was turning out work, and it seemed worthy of being recognized, I mean of being *acknowledged*, at least. Acknowledgment of my existence as an American writer: neither praise, nor dispraise, but, "Here!"—with my hand up. "Present!"

—REGINALD GIBBONS

This interview was transcribed from six hours of taped conversation recorded over three days in November 1982, at William Goyen's house in Los Angeles. He had been mortally ill but had apparently recovered almost completely; matters of art and life were much preoccupying him, and he had found fresh revelations about them, he felt. I had published one of his stories in *TriQuarterly*, and was planning a large section devoted to his work in an upcoming issue. This interview was at his invitation, and his talk was wide-ranging and urgent. There were certain things of which he wanted to *speak*, he said. He had not written about them; perhaps he sensed he would not have strength or time to devote to them. After he had carefully revised the edited transcript the full interview was published, with my brief introduction to his work, in March 1983 in *TriQuarterly*. Besides this interview, he completed only one other work before his death— the lecture on art and illness called "Recovering" [*TriQuarterly*, fall 1983].

—R.G.